PRAISE FOR

THE GATHERING STORM

"[Bridges] delivers an imaginative, complex blend of history and magic." —*Publishers Weekly*

"An atmospheric and complicated vampire tale." —*Kirkus Reviews*

"The plot is rich and intriguing." —*SLJ*

"This alluring fantasy gives fans of the Luxe series a new society to enter, albeit with some fear." —*Booklist*

"Readers will want to grab a blanket and hot cup of cocoa and settle in for this wonderfully atmospheric blend of history and magic." —*The Bulletin*

"Bridges could become a worthy successor to Libba Bray with this historical fantasy. Her lush settings, secret rituals and paranormal creatures make for an atmospheric political adventure. . . . Katiya is a strong female hero whose further adventures are worth following." —*VOYA*

THE KATERINA TRILOGY

Volume I

THE GATHERING STORM

Robin Bridges

EMBER

Text copyright © 2012 by Robin Bridges
Cover photograph copyright © 2012 by Michael Frost

All rights reserved. Published in the United States by Ember, an imprint of Random House Children's Books, a division of Random House, Inc., New York. Originally published in hardcover in the United States by Delacorte Press, an imprint of Random House Children's Books, New York, in 2012.

Ember and the E colophon are registered trademarks of Random House, Inc.

Visit us on the Web! randomhouse.com/teens

Educators and librarians, for a variety of teaching tools, visit us at randomhouse.com/teachers

The Library of Congress has cataloged the hardcover edition
of this work as follows:
Bridges, Robin.
The gathering storm / Robin Bridges. — 1st ed.
p. cm. — (The Katerina trilogy ; v. 1)
Summary: In St. Petersburg, Russia, in 1888, royal debutante Katerina
Alexandrovna, Duchess of Oldenburg, tries to hide a dark secret—that she has the
ability to raise the dead—but when she uses her special skill to protect a member
of the Imperial Family, she finds herself caught in a web of intrigue.
ISBN 978-0-385-74022-7 (hc) — ISBN 978-0-375-89901-0 (ebook)
ISBN 978-0-385-90829-0 (glb)
[1. Supernatural—Fiction. 2. Courts and courtiers—Fiction. 3. Good and evil—
Fiction. 4. Russia—History—1801–1917—Fiction.] I. Title.
PZ7.B76194 Gat 2012
[Fic]—dc23
2011026175

ISBN 978-0-385-74023-4 (tr. pbk.)

RL: 5.6

Printed in the United States of America

10 9 8 7 6 5 4 3 2 1

First Ember Edition 2012

For Parham, who is grander than any duke or prince

A NOTE ABOUT RUSSIAN NAMES AND PATRONYMICS

Russians have two official first names: a given name and a patronymic, or a name that means "the son of" or "the daughter of." Katerina Alexandrovna, for example, is the daughter of a man named Alexander. Her brother is Pyotr Alexandrovich. A female patronymic ends in "-evna" or "-ovna," while a male patronymic ends in "-vich."

It was traditional for the nobility and aristocracy to name their children after Orthodox saints, thus the abundance of Alexanders and Marias and Katerinas. For this reason, nicknames, or diminutives, came in handy to tell the Marias and the Katerinas apart. Katerinas could be called Katiya, Koshka, or Katushka. An Alexander might be known as Sasha or Sandro. A Pyotr might be called Petya or Petrusha. When addressing a person by his or her nickname, one does not add the patronymic. The person would be addressed as Katerina Alexandrovna or simply Katiya.

The Gathering Storm

❦

Summer 1880, St. Petersburg, Russia

O ur family tree has roots and branches reaching all across Europe, from France to Russia, from Denmark to Greece, and in several transient and minute kingdoms and principalities in between. This tree is tangled with all the rest of Europe's royalty, and like many in that forest, my family tree is poisoned with a dark evil.

When I was seven, I sneaked into Maman's red-and-gold parlor and watched one of her séances from behind one of the Louis XVI sofas. She and her friends were forever trying to summon relatives or famous people, as it was a fashionable pastime among the aristocracy. I do not know whose spirit they evoked, but a chill settled in the room that night as all the candles went out. My thin summer nightgown did nothing to keep me warm.

A sad lady in white appeared in the gilded Italian mirror

over the fireplace. She told Maman she would never have grand-children.

I'd never seen my mother turn so pale. Her hands trembled and the teacup she was holding began to shake. One of the other ladies—my aunt, I think—screamed and fainted.

It upset Maman so much I wanted to bring the lady in white back myself so she could tell Maman something happier. I ran out into the garden and under the lilac tree, closed my eyes, and chanted the nonsense words I'd heard Maman say. A cold, clammy feeling washed over me again, and I smelled the most horrible wet-earth smell of decay and rot. The garden began to fill with a gray, damp mist. This had been a foolish mistake.

I looked around in fear, but there were no spirits present in the garden at all. I breathed a sigh of relief and felt silly. The games Maman and her friends played were just that—games. I told myself that Maman had simply gotten carried away.

But then I spotted something on the ground under the lilac tree. I bent down to look more closely. A toad lay on his back, not breathing, his eyes a blank black stare.

I wondered what had killed him. I wished aloud that he had not died.

Still not breathing, now the toad blinked and uttered a long, mournful croak. Slowly, his pale belly began to move as he stirred to life. His stare was still blank, but the toad croaked again as he righted himself and crept closer to me.

I jumped back in terror. My throat closed up and I felt as if I couldn't breathe. Had I brought this creature back to life, merely by wishing it? This was horribly wrong. I ran inside, ignoring the mud on my nightgown, ignoring my dirty bare feet. Too fright-ened to step quietly, I made a terrible racket racing up the main

4

stairs and knocked one of Maman's favorite cloisonné-studded icons from the wall. I did not stop to retrieve the broken frame. I just kept running.

I hurried up to the children's floor, where I climbed into my bed and hid under the quilt. I pretended to be asleep when my nurse came upstairs to check on me.

The scent of death and decay was gone. All I could smell was the comfortable scent of my bed linens, which had been washed in rose water. The nurse left after laying her fat, cold hand against my cheek. I could smell the lemon and vodka on her fingers from her bedtime tea.

I never said a word about the toad to anyone.

And men loved darkness rather than light.
—JOHN 3:19

CHAPTER ONE

Fall 1888, St. Petersburg, Russia

An afternoon spent solving quadratic equations would have been infinitely more pleasant. I smelled like a salad. Cucumber slices for soothing puffy eyes. Blackberry vinegar for brightening dull skin. Goat's milk and honey for softening rough hands. I politely declined when my cousin offered a pinch of her goose-lard-and-pomegranate facial cream.

It was Friday afternoon and our lessons had been canceled at the Smolny Institute so everyone could prepare for the ball. Because dressing up like a doll was much more important than studying literature or learning arithmetic.

Matrimony. That was the true mission of the Smolny Institute for Young Noble Maidens. It was nothing more than a meat market for Russia's nobility, where princes from all across Europe sent their daughters, intending them to marry well. So there I sat, Katerina Alexandra Maria von Holstein-Gottorp, Duchess of Oldenburg. Great-great-granddaughter of Empress Josephine on my mother's side, great-great-great-granddaughter of Katerina the Great on my father's side. Princess of the royal blood. Royal meat for sale. I would rather have been dead.

I once told Maman I wanted to attend medical school and work at one of Papa's hospitals in St. Petersburg or Moscow. I always accompanied her to the Oldenburg Children's Hospital when she made her charity visits at Christmas and Easter. I thought it would be wonderful to take care of sick children and discover cures for diseases. But Maman was horrified by the idea.

"What man would marry a doctor?" she asked, not bothering to wait for an answer. "What a foolish notion!"

But someone needed to find cures for such illnesses as meningitis, which had taken my younger brother before his first birthday. Why couldn't that someone be me? I'd been only three at the time and too little to understand, but his death had devastated our family. I could remember hearing both of my parents sobbing night after night. There had been too much death in my childhood. My brother, my grandparents, my favorite aunt. I looked forward to the future, when science could perform miracles. And when we would not have to live in fear of disease.

One of our maids, Anya Stepanova, had a brother Rudolf, who attended the School of Medicine in Kiev. My father, a great believer in philanthropy, had paid Rudolf's tuition. I begged Anya to tell me about his studies, but they did not interest her. Even she was more absorbed with the petty female plots that went on at Smolny. As she fixed my hair for the ball, she told me and my cousin Dariya Yevgenievna the latest gossip about our fellow student Princess Elena.

"She's a witch, I tell you," Anya whispered as she fussed with my curls. "I saw her earlier in this very room holding a moth by one of its wings over a candle and chanting. She was making some sort of charm, I'm sure of it."

"Don't be ridiculous," I said, shivering all the same. I couldn't help feeling sorry for Elena, even if she was a witch. If she couldn't keep her powers hidden here at Smolny, what hope did I have? Raising the dead was my own secret, a talent I kept hidden, even from myself when I could.

"It's true," my cousin Dariya agreed. "Do you know what the cook said about Elena's dead sister?"

With a frightened whisper, Anya crossed herself. "Holy Mother of God!"

One of Princess Elena's sisters had died two years earlier at Smolny. If she was indeed one of the ghosts rumored to haunt these halls, then why didn't she appear to her sister in our dormitory? Unless the ghost was too frightened of her own sister to haunt her.

"There are no ghosts at Smolny," I said, thinking that if there were, I would certainly know. "Anyway, Elena is dancing with the tsar's son tonight. The tsar and the empress would never allow him to dance with a witch."

Dariya sighed. "And how do you think Elena managed to catch the tsarevitch's eye in the first place? You and I both know she's using magic."

11

Our silver-haired headmistress, Madame Tomilov, swept into our room just then with a basket of white corsages, one for each of us. "Here we are, girls. Time to take a flower for your dress."

Dariya and I helped each other with ours. "Don't give me that one, Katiya," my cousin said as I reached for one. "It's *yellow*," she whispered. "You know it's bad luck to give someone a yellow flower."

"It's just a little brown around the edges," I said.

"Just pick another one, please, Katiya?" she begged.

I sighed heavily and gave her my flower, pinning the faded rose on my own dress.

Dancing at St. Petersburg balls was extremely formal. We spent hours in class every day practicing the steps for the quadrille and the mazurka. We spent even more time dancing than we did studying French, the official language of the Russian court and the language spoken by all polite society. I hated the difficult polonaise, but it was one of the favorites of our empress and was usually the first dance at every ball.

Only the eldest students of Smolny, the White Form, were allowed to attend the annual Smolny Ball, given by the empress in our honor. The younger girls, the Brown and Blue Forms, would have to wait several years for their turn. The Browns moped sadly as we finished getting ready. "I wonder what the empress will wear," one of the Browns said wistfully. She begged us to wake her when we returned so we could tell her every last detail.

Madame Tomilov frowned at everyone, as if she could scare us into being on our best behavior. "Be mindful of your futures, ladies. Everyone will be watching you tonight.

12

Do nothing to stain your reputation or that of Smolny Institute."

I amused myself by thinking up ways I could do just that. Not that I would, of course. But the thought was so tempting!

The sleighs arrived to carry us to the Winter Palace for the ball. Dariya and I, wrapped in our woolen cloaks, our hands tucked into warm fur muffs, climbed into the first one in line. Three more girls piled in, and we were almost full. Then Elena rushed over, giggling as she joined us in the now-crowded sleigh. "This night is going to be unforgettable," she promised, shoving Aurora Demidova into Erzsebet of Bavaria. Ignoring the girls' complaints, Elena smiled. "Can't you feel the magic in the air?"

My cousin rolled her eyes at the Montenegrin princess. She muttered under her breath, "No good can come of this, Katiya. I have a horrible feeling about tonight."

I shivered, feeling nothing but the bitter cold. I was certain that, witch or no witch, Elena would not do anything foolish. But as I looked back across the line of sleighs, full of excited young girls, I had a terrible vision. A brilliant bluish-white light illuminated each girl's face.

This vision was, unfortunately, very familiar.

Death would be dancing with us at the ball that night.

I crossed myself and prayed it would touch no one I loved.

CHAPTER TWO

❧

Princess Elena caused a stir when she opened the ball with the tsarevitch Nicholas Alexandrovich, the heir to the throne of Russia. She looked like an angel gliding across the marble floor in her white dress. We all looked like angels, all in the same virginal white with our hair coiffed perfectly in braided chignons.

"It's heaven on earth!" Dariya said with a sigh.

Boys from the Corps des Pages, the elite military academy, lined up in chairs directly across the cavernous ballroom from the girls of Smolny Institute. They looked very smart and very handsome in their black military uniforms. Dariya had spent the entire sleigh ride to the palace considering which of these cadets were foreign princes and which ones were the most suitable to marry. As Elena and the tsarevitch finished the opening polonaise in the enormous Nicholas Hall, the young men rushed toward us to claim our hands for the next dance. The meat market had opened for business.

Rumors flew from one end of the room to the other, from the youngest Smolny maid to the oldest lady-in-waiting, about a possible engagement between Princess Elena and the tsarevitch. Her father was the King of Montenegro, and a close ally of the tsar, but there were many more princesses of larger and more important countries for Russia to make alliances with. As coldhearted as it may sound, this match seemed improbable to me. But Elena already looked like she was in love.

I kept my eye on Elena throughout the night, even as I danced one tedious set after another. A grim-looking, pale young cadet was my first partner. He barely spoke two words to me when I tried to be polite and ask about his lessons at Vorontsov Palace. But our dance was over soon, and with a quick, halfhearted bow, he slipped back into the crowd.

Another cadet replaced him, and then another. Their faces blurred together in the wild crush. It was not much different from dancing with my fellow students during our lessons. The ballroom was a flurry of white dresses and black uniforms, all of us twirling under the bright lights of the glittering chandeliers. It grew hotter and stuffier with each dance, and the petticoats under my gown became sticky and damp.

The entire ballroom had begun to smell of sweat. The heavy colognes and perfumes everyone wore did nothing to disguise it. I wished I had a fan to keep the stench away from my nose. I settled for a glass of lemonade.

The dance master called for the mazurka and Dariya squealed. "This is my favorite! Oh, Katiya, I don't know why I was worried about tonight. I never dreamed the ball would be so wonderful!" She blushed when a handsome blond cadet took her hand and led her onto the dance floor. I smiled, happy for my cousin.

The tsarevitch did not dance the mazurka but stood beside his mother, the empress. Elena danced with the pale and grim cadet I'd partnered with earlier.

"Duchess, would you do me the honor?" I spun around to see the tsarevitch's younger brother the grand duke George Alexandrovich standing before me.

I placed my gloved hand in his. "The honor is mine, Your Imperial Highness."

He led me onto the dance floor and bowed as the music started. Like all the other girls, I curtsied deeply in response to my partner. Then he put one hand lightly on my waist and we were off.

Dancing with the grand duke was nothing like dancing with fellow students in Madame Metcherskey's class. Very conscious of his hands touching me, I felt a strange light-headedness as we promenaded around the ballroom.

I must confess: like Dariya, I'd always been fond of the mazurka. The boys stamped their feet and the girls kicked their heels and it was so much livelier than the other dances. And the music the orchestra played was by Glinka, one of my favorite composers.

The grand duke did not speak as we completed our circuit of the ballroom. He did not speak when we crossed hands and turned clockwise.

16

There was no need for us to make polite conversation. As he got to one knee with one hand on his hip, the other barely holding my fingertips as I pivoted around him, the grand duke looked up at me, his eyes sparkling under the brilliant lights. The faintest hint of a smile was beginning to form on his lips. He was having fun after all.

I smiled back.

It grew even hotter in the ballroom at that moment. I could feel myself blushing.

I completed my circle around the grand duke, and he stood with a click of his heels. A hundred pairs of boot heels clicked together at once as the mazurka ended.

With one last gracious bow and a polite smile, the grand duke excused himself to join his brother. I needed to catch my breath. Another glass of lemonade would be nice as well, I thought.

Dariya pushed through the crowd and swung me around, squeezing my hands. "*Mon Dieu*, Katiya!" she gushed. "This has been the best night of my life!"

I smiled and squeezed back. The night was not quite as terrible as I'd feared either.

～∾⌒∾～

We sat down to dinner at half past ten, right after the mazurka. Elena's two older sisters met us in the grand dining room. All the Montenegrin princesses favored each other: tall, with raven-black hair, eyes just as dark, and strong noses.

"You look beautiful," Elena's sisters said to her. "Papa and Mama would be so proud of you!"

17

I'd heard sinister tales about Elena's sisters. Even though they were rumored to be witches, they were still the toast of St. Petersburg society, coyly appearing at all the smartest balls and card parties. Princess Militza was engaged to the grand duke Peter Nikolayevich, cousin of the tsar on his father's side and also my cousin on his mother's side. Another sister, Princess Anastasia, known as Stana, had her eye on my uncle the Duke of Leuchtenberg.

As we were shown to our seats, I was shocked to see the tsarevitch and his brother being seated at my table—next to Elena.

I whispered to Princess Militza, "To what do we owe such an honor?"

"It is the tsarevitch who is honored tonight, dining with daughters of King Nikola," she answered. Militza tended to think the universe revolved around her father's tiny kingdom of Montenegro.

"Oh. Then I am honored as well," I said with a reverent bow of my head to her. She nodded regally, oblivious to my sarcasm. On the other side of me, Dariya snickered softly.

The food had been prepared under the direction of the empress's French chef. The soup was excellent, the fish not so much. I discreetly pushed it around on my plate, certain no one would concern themselves with what a silly Smolny student ate or did not eat. The empress was entertaining her Danish relatives at her own table, the tsar having already returned to his private quarters after a brief appearance.

Besides, I knew all uneaten food would be given to the beggars outside at the end of the ball. I believed I was doing my part to help them by leaving more food for the poor. I just hoped they liked fish more than I did.

I glanced around our table, where Elena was laughing and batting her eyelashes at everyone. She caught my eye and winked. The tsarevitch was talking to a young officer to his left. Elena turned to his younger brother the grand duke George Alexandrovich, on her other side, and whispered something.

He looked toward my plate and nodded. "Not fond of the salmon, Duchess?"

All eyes at the table were suddenly on me. The devil. Elena winked at me again as she slipped something out of her locket and sprinkled it over the tsarevitch's plate. Was that the charm my maid had seen her with earlier? With a dead moth? She had deliberately diverted everyone's attention toward me. Was she really trying to cast a spell on the tsar's son? *Mon Dieu!*

I couldn't let the princess harm a member of the imperial family. The tsarevitch was a kind young man. He did not deserve to be bewitched.

I stared at my own dinner plate with a cold, clammy feeling in my stomach. I took a sip of wine, knowing there was one way I could ruin her spell. For as long as I could remember, I'd had a terrible curse. I'd never told my parents about it, even though I sometimes wondered if I'd inherited it from my mother. I was too ashamed to ask her.

I hadn't purposefully used the curse since I was ten. But I suspected that there was something dead on His Imperial Highness's plate, so I knew I could ruin Elena's spell. There was no other way to stop her.

The tsarevitch laughed at something his brother had said, and lifted his fork again. I had to hurry. I focused my attention on his dinner plate, hoping no one would notice.

And that God would forgive me.

As I concentrated, the dead moth crawled out from under the tsarevitch's fish.

"Good Lord!" he said. As he moved to poke the insect with his fork, it flew up at Elena, who shrieked. A mortified servant whisked the tsarevitch's dinner plate away.

Dariya, who discreetly hid her face behind her napkin, looked startled at first, then tried very hard not to laugh.

The grand duke George frowned at me with his mysterious blue eyes before turning to his brother. "Didn't fancy the fish either, Nicky?"

"To be honest," Nicholas said, "it did have a queer taste." He laid his napkin on the table.

"Yes, it certainly did, now that you mention it," Princess Militza said, glancing at her sister.

Elena grew unhappy. She would have to find another way to charm the tsarevitch. He would think me insane if I told him what had happened, if I warned him about the Montenegrins.

The servants finished clearing the rest of our dishes from the table and brought out fruit compotes. Still slightly nauseated, I picked at mine. Elena ate her compote glumly, smiling only when someone spoke to her.

It was not long before the empress had finished dining and risen from her table, signaling a return to the dancing. Militza grabbed my arm and hissed in my ear, "Walk with me, Katerina Alexandrovna. You must see the beautiful fountain in the winter garden. It's just at the other end of this hallway."

An icy chill slid down my spine. I was terrified that someone would discover what I'd done. Especially one of the Montenegrin princesses.

The garden was in a large two-story glass room, full of heavily scented flowers and lush greenery. In the center, an enormous multitiered fountain babbled soothingly.

"Can you keep a secret, my dear?" Militza asked as her cold and perfectly manicured hands clutched mine.

"I've been known to keep them before," I replied, still shaky from what I had done to the moth. Years earlier, I'd promised myself I would never do such a horrible thing again. It was unnatural.

"I believe there is an evil presence here at the ball tonight."

My heart pounded. "Evil?"

"Yes. Evil. Nothing else could have disrupted Elena's spell," Militza said, watching my face very closely.

"A spell!" I gasped at her recklessness, wondering why she would admit to such a thing. "Elena could be exiled for witchcraft!" I added.

"Not if the Romanovs do not find out. And I know you will not tell them, Katerina Alexandrovna."

"Why should I protect her? She was casting a spell on the heir!"

"Because your magic is far more terrible than ours. The tsar holds my father in high esteem. And you would not want the tsar to discover your nasty little secret."

My mouth went dry and my palms began sweating inside

my white kidskin gloves. "You must be making fun of me," I said, trying to be as lighthearted as possible. "I don't know what you are talking about."

"Come now." Militza narrowed her eyes. "Several people in that dining room could sense that something deliciously wicked had just happened. Especially the empress." She paused and seemed almost gleeful at the look of horror on my face. "You are fortunate there are so many witches and other . . . creatures present tonight. It will take weeks for the tsar's men to discover it was you, an innocent-looking viper."

I was speechless. The Montenegrin princess could see the fear in my eyes.

Militza smiled. "Necromancy is the most vile, the blackest of the black arts, Duchess. Certainly you cannot think the tsarina could allow one such as you to remain under her roof? Or indeed, even to continue attending Smolny?"

She had me trapped in her web. "What do you want from me?" I whispered.

She smiled once more and put her arm through mine, leading me back toward the ballroom. "I want you to meet the rest of my family. My mother would put your talents to good use. Come home with us for Christmas holidays."

I tried to pull away from her. "But my parents—"

"Will be very shocked and disgusted if they discover what their clever daughter has been doing. Unless they already know? Do your parents know how to raise the dead as well?"

"Of course not!" I felt the panic rising in my body. "And they know nothing of my problem."

"Problem?" Militza laughed. "In my family, it would be considered the greatest gift. You'll see."

As soon as we returned to the ballroom, Militza joined her fiancé for a waltz. I retreated to the pretty winter garden. I had no desire to dance anymore. I just wanted the night to be over.

I stood in front of the fountain, lost in my own thoughts, and did not know anyone else was in the garden until a voice whispered in my ear, "Whatever spell you are casting now, I promise you it won't work."

I spun around to see Grand Duke George Alexandrovich glaring at me. My heart dropped to my stomach as I curtsied feebly. "Your Imperial Highness, I can assure you—"

"Your aura is tainted with the blackest magic. You have been doing something sinister and I know my brother's dinner was involved."

I squirmed under his intense gaze. I wanted to tell him that I'd just saved his brother from the clutches of the Montenegrins, but I was terrified they would come after my family.

Nor did I want my parents and brother to incur the tsar's wrath. What had I gotten myself into? And how did the grand duke know the color of my aura?

There was a power struggle, subtle but deadly, within the aristocracy of St. Petersburg. There was a Light Court and a Dark Court, each presided over by a powerful faerie. Everyone within the nobility aspired to be claimed by one of these ladies. One could be loyal either to the empress or to the grand duchess Miechen, but everyone was loyal to the tsar. The Romanov dynasty had traditionally been aligned with the Light Court, even though none of the tsars had ever married a faerie until Alexander married Dagmar of Denmark in 1866. His brother shocked the entire Romanov family by marrying the Dark Court faerie Miechen in 1874.

All that was known of the faeries was that they were ethereally beautiful and tended to read minds. No one knew the full extent of their powers. The superstitious lower classes knew only that our tsar was incredibly strong, and that our empress looked as young and beautiful as she had when she'd married the tsar.

And who knew what mysterious gifts the tsar's son standing in front of me had inherited from his mother? "Your Imperial Highness, please forgive me. It . . . it was nothing more than a schoolgirl dare."

"A dare? Meddling with magic? Against my brother?"

"It was extremely foolish. We . . . I mean . . . I meant him no harm." If he did not see the auras of the Montenegrins and recognize Princess Elena for the witch that she was, I would not be the one to enlighten him.

He glared at me as I tried to remember how old the grand duke was. Seventeen, perhaps? A year older than me, but surely not as old as my brother. He certainly made a handsome faerie. His soft brown hair fell down into his eyes, which, although not as kind as his brother's eyes, were quite attractive. *Mon Dieu,* where had that thought come from?

He took my gloved hands in his as I tried in vain to stop trembling. "Black magic is punishable by exile," he said.

"And any attempt to cast a spell on a member of the imperial family is punishable by death." He stared at me, no doubt seeing much more of me than I wished him to. "I am certain this will not happen again."

Punishable by death? I felt weak and nauseated and realized he was holding me up. "Never again, Your Imperial Highness."

"Very good, Duchess." With a click of his boot heels, he made a sharp bow and left me. Of course he did not offer to escort me back to the ballroom. We did not want to start any more rumors that evening.

I wondered about the auras he claimed to see. The popular author Marie Corelli wrote romantic novels in which pulsing bodies of energy surrounded all living beings. The grand duke might have been able to see auras as well as Princess Militza, but I saw something much more ominous surrounding everyone.

The light I saw was not life but death. A cold light that seemed to grow stronger as a person drew nearer to the end. When a person died, sometimes the cold light was all that remained: the ghost of an individual. Perhaps it was the doppelganger I had read about in my cousin Dariya's German romances. Perhaps it was an aura that I saw detaching itself from a dying body. Everyone has a cold light. Little by little, we are all dying every day.

I used to sneak out of my bedroom and watch my mother conduct séances at her parties. Spiritism may have been fashionable, especially among Maman's friends, but reanimation of the dead was another thing entirely. What I had done tonight was unholy. I swore to myself I would never do such an abominable thing again.

I might have saved the tsarevitch from a malicious love spell, but from the moment I had used my terrible power, the cold light of everyone at the Winter Palace had grown brighter. Death was now closer than before.

CHAPTER THREE

꧁꧂

That night, after the ball, I dreamed about hundreds of moths, fluttering through my bedroom window and down the dark hallways with their gray paper wings. One slipped into each room, landing on the mouth of the sleeping girl inside. What they were doing on all those girls' lips, I could not tell.

I woke up to a cold room, my breath visible in the gray light of early morning. The last remnants of the strange dream faded away as freezing air shocked my lungs. Someone had opened our window again in the middle of the night. I tiptoed across the icy floor and shut it before anyone became sick.

Dariya suspected Elena, who shared our room, but I believed it was the headmistress, who insisted night air was beneficial for young girls' growing lungs. I could never find any medical studies proving her theory. I felt a little rebellious closing the window against Madame Tomilov's wishes. But I hated waking up with frost on my quilt.

～◎◇～

The following week, everyone swarmed around Elena with a thousand questions about the tsarevitch. The teachers were just as curious and excited as the girls were. Madame Tomilov asked her to lead the younger girls in the mazurka during dance lessons. At tea, the servants gossiped with her about the tsarevitch's favorite foods. Elena enjoyed the attention.

I tried to put the ball out of my mind. Especially everything Princess Militza had said to me. She had called me a necromancer. It chilled my heart to think of it—especially since I knew it to be true. Even more terrifying, I was not sure of the scope of my abilities. I'd never wanted to experiment. It frightened me to imagine what I might be capable of. What I'd done at the ball was horrible. I'd resurrected a dead insect. But there were certainly worse acts I could have committed. A thousand times worse. It wasn't as if I'd meddled with a human soul. Deep in my heart, though, I feared that I had the power to do so.

The last time I'd purposely used my powers, I was ten years old, and I'd believed it was for a noble cause. I resurrected Maman's poor cat Sasha. I'd found him in our garden, his neck broken from a fall from a tree. I knew that the loss of her beloved Sasha would break my mother's heart. Not wanting Maman to be sad, I wished Sasha back to life. Maman never noticed the subtle difference in him afterward. Not the dull look to his eyes, nor the way he hissed every time I came near. Even at that age, I'd known what I'd done had been terribly wrong. I'd sworn I would never do such a thing again. But I had.

I was traveling down a dangerous and dark path. I had to stop myself. But I knew that if faced with the same choice again, I'd do exactly the same thing. I wasn't sure if that meant my soul was at risk or my allegiance to the imperial family was such that I'd gladly brave the worst to save them. Maybe I was just hopelessly stupid.

I focused on reading the Latin book Madame Orbellani had given me. She knew my dreams of studying medicine, and without the headmistress's knowledge, she had begun to encourage me. She'd seen me struggling with the medical books I'd liberated from my father's library. Even though I was supposed to be reading Pushkin and Tolstoy, she found me a musty-smelling textbook of beginning Latin. She told me stories about the first Russian women to receive medical degrees, in the 1860s, Maria Bokova and Nadezhda Suslova. As a young girl, Madame Orbellani had idolized them as pioneers in women's higher education.

Elena did not forget about my invitation to Montenegro, much to my dismay. She cornered me several weeks after the ball. "You made quite the impression on my older sister," Elena whispered as we were passed by several Browns. "She told me that you have some . . . unusual talents."

"Princess Militza is imagining things," I managed to say,

my heart beating hard. I did not want Elena to think I had anything in common with her.

"Don't worry," she said. "Your secret is safe with me, of course. Militza has written to our mother and Mama is anxious to meet you. She is also sending a letter to your mother to formally invite you to our home in Cetinje for Christmas. I know my brother is eager to meet you as well!"

"Your brother?"

Elena smiled ominously. "Yes. Danilo. He is nearly eighteen, very handsome, and is Papa's heir. Very exciting, no?" She pulled a golden locket out of her bedside table drawer and handed it to me. Inside was a portrait of a dashing young man with dangerously black eyes.

"There's . . . a strong family resemblance," I said, nearly at a loss for a reply. I had no desire to know any more of her wicked royal family. It was bad enough that they were plotting to steal my uncle George Maximilianovich for Princess Stana.

Now Elena wanted me to meet her brother. I had to come up with an excuse to remain at home for Christmas. If Maman found out about the handsome crown prince Danilo, she would no doubt ship me off to Cetinje with my wedding trousseau already packed.

CHAPTER FOUR

I t was Dariya's idea that I enlist my brother Petya's help.
She knew I had no desire to go to Cetinje with the Montenegrins. And she did not think it wise for me to do so.
"Have him speak with your parents, Katiya," she told me.
"I'm sure he has heard the gossip about them." I was too
scared to tell Dariya everything that Militza had said, and I
had not mentioned the grand duke's warnings. I didn't want
my cousin to think that I was a monster.

Petya's regiment was headquartered at nearby Vorontsov
Palace. If I could get word to him, he could intervene with
Papa on my behalf. He and his fellow officers frequently
walked in the Tauride Gardens, near our school. Elena and
the Bavarian princesses, Augusta and Erzsebet, joined me
and Dariya the next afternoon as we set out.

Bundled up, we strolled along the iced-over fountains as
Augusta asked Elena and Dariya endless questions about
the tsarevitch and his younger brothers. I pretended to be

more interested in the barren bushes and birch trees along the sidewalks.

"His brother George Alexandrovich is not so handsome," Elena said. "He is sharp-tongued and mean-spirited. I should like to introduce you to the youngest one, Mikhail Alexandrovich. He is a true gentleman. Wouldn't it be wonderful if I should marry the tsarevitch and you should marry Mikhail?"

I wanted to laugh out loud. The youngest grand duke was only ten years old. He had not even been at the Smolny Ball. Princess Augusta was a few years younger than us, but she would still have to wait for her grand duke to grow up.

"Are you going to the children's Christmas Ball?" Erzsebet asked. "I've heard the grand duchess Marie Pavlovna is a more gracious hostess than the empress herself."

Elena shook her head, her black hair flying in the breeze. "Sadly, I shall be back home in Montenegro for the holidays. You must tell me everything about the ball when I return. I did want to meet the grand duchess, but I'm so happy that Katerina is coming home with me."

Augusta sighed. "Going abroad for the holiday? You are so lucky, Katerina!"

I did not feel lucky at all. But then I spotted my brother laughing with other members of his regiment. "Pyotr Alexandrovich!" I shouted, and ran toward him.

"Brat!" He grinned when he saw me, and spun me around in his arms. "Are you giving your instructors a hard time, as I taught you?"

I rolled my eyes. "I must speak with you, Petya," I whispered. "There is a dreadful plot here at Smolny to ruin my life."

He glanced at the girls behind me, who were shyly speaking with the other officers. We strolled farther away from them. "What the devil are you talking about?" Petya asked.

"Elena and her sisters want me to visit Cetinje with them for Christmas," I explained. "They are trying to marry me off to their brother." I grabbed Petya's arm. "Please talk to Maman and Papa and beg them not to make me go."

"A crown prince, eh? What's so dreadful about that?"

Across the street, Dariya laughed as she flirted with one of the captains. Elena vied for their attentions as well. I turned back to Petya. I couldn't tell him everything about the Montenegrin witches. Then I would have to tell him about me. "I do not want to move far away to some dark country in the mountains," I said, which was partly true. "What am I going to do?"

"Don't be ridiculous. And don't worry your pretty little head about anything. I'll be dining with our parents this evening. Perhaps they already have a more suitable match planned for you."

For some absurd reason, the blue eyes of the grand duke George passed through my mind. I shook my head. "You know I want to study medicine first," I told my brother. "There will be plenty of time for a husband later. Look at Madame Curie."

"Yes, but who wants to marry an old woman who's smarter than him?" said one of the other officers, who had come swaggering up to us. He gave me a salute and a roguish grin.

I was well bred enough to know I shouldn't respond to the officer's taunt, but I could not help myself. "I'm sure no smart woman would want to marry you, anyway, Count Chermenensky. That's for certain."

Petya laughed and put his arm around me. "Do not worry. Everything will work out. Katiya, I see that you remember my friend."

"Of course," I said, holding out my hand for the count, even though he did have a low opinion of educated women. "Petya brought you to our parents' home once."

"*Enchanté, mademoiselle,*" the count said gallantly.

They walked me back to my companions and bid us adieu just as the snow began to fall. Elena was most curious about Petya's friend. "And who was the handsome officer talking with you and your brother?" she asked on our way back to the institute.

"Count Chermenensky."

Elena scoffed. "Only a count? Why should your brother waste your time with someone like that? Surely he doesn't expect your parents to approve of a count as a suitable match for you."

I stopped walking and stared at the princess. "Elena, there is much more to life than finding the richest husband possible. My brother was simply being cordial. Besides, the count is a close friend of his."

Elena rolled her eyes. "You are so bourgeois, Katerina."

Dariya linked my arm with hers. "Of course there's more to life than finding a rich husband," she said. "I want a rich and handsome husband, with a title. He must be a prince or better." She led me back to Smolny with the Bavarian princesses and Elena laughing behind us.

We shook the snow from our cloaks as we entered the front gates. Madame Metcherskey was standing at the top of the stairs glaring at us. We were late to dance practice. Again.

I stayed awake in bed until late that night, worrying about Maman's answer to Elena's mother. Of course she would want me to go to Cetinje. She would think it such an honor. Rumors of the princesses and their dark magic would only intrigue Maman, if she did not know already.

When I did drift off to sleep, my dreams were troubled, full of dark chanting by candlelight in a strange stone castle.

CHAPTER FIVE

❧

"Mademoiselle? The headmistress wishes to speak with you." One of the servants from downstairs awoke me early the next morning. She looked over at Elena, who was still sleeping, and made the sign of the cross.

A feeling of dread clenched my stomach. What had I done now? I quickly dressed and followed the servant to Madame Tomilov's parlor.

I was shocked to see my brother, sitting on the green rosewood sofa. "Petya!"

He stood immediately. "Katiya, I have unfortunate news. I'm to bring you home immediately. Our mother is ill."

"Mon Dieu!" Was this his brilliant plan to help me?

"Can you be packed and ready to leave immediately?"

It was easy to play along with him. I tried to look concerned. "Yes, of course. Is it serious?"

My brother frowned. Oh, he was such a good actor! "I'm not sure, but she has been calling for you."

Madame Tomilov put her hand on my shoulder. "Be strong, child. I shall say a prayer for the duchess."

"Thank you, madame."

I hurried back upstairs to our room and threw my things together in a trunk. I grabbed my cloak and muff too. I did not bother to wake Elena or Dariya. They would hear soon enough.

"That was very clever," I told my brother as we dashed away toward Betskoi House, our family home on the Palace Embankment. It was not an enormous mansion, but Maman loved being close to the Winter Palace. "I cannot believe you kidnapped me to rescue me from the Montenegrins."

My brother shook his head, looking grim. "Maman is truly confined to her bed and has been calling out for you," he said.

I stared at him in disbelief. "You're teasing me."

"I'm sorry, dear sister. I wish it were just a joke."

My face burned with shame. I felt horrible. Deceiving the headmistress would, of course, be devious, and my brother was a good person. Unlike me. Maman's illness could even be my fault. What if Princess Militza had spoken to her about the ball? I was silent the rest of the journey, with knots of worry twisting inside.

As the sleigh pulled through the iron gates into our court-yard, I jumped out without waiting for it to come to a complete stop.

I threw my cloak off as I ran up the marble staircase. "Maman? Maman?" I called.

Her pink boudoir was dark with the heavy curtains pulled shut. Maman was indeed confined to her bed, as my brother had told me. Dr. Kruglevski, our old family friend, stood over her, taking her pulse. Papa sat on the other side of the bed. He looked anxious.

"Hello, my dear," Maman said, holding her hand out to me. She didn't seem to be feverish, but she did look rather pale. Her fingers were like ice.

"Your mother is going to be just fine," Dr. Kruglevski said, tucking his watch back into his coat pocket. "She had an attack of hysterics last night after her card party. Rest is all she needs right now."

"But she's so pale. Is she anemic?"

The elderly doctor smiled. "Still reading your father's books, I see. Do not be troubled; your mother does not suffer from anemia. Time will put the color back into her cheeks soon enough. I'm going to leave her in your hands now, Katerina Alexandrovna." He patted me on the shoulder as he followed Papa out. He smelled of iodine.

Maman let go of my hand. "Oh, Katiya, I'm so glad to see you. But I do wish you wouldn't bother the doctor so about medical things. He does not have the time to indulge a young girl's silly ideas."

"Dr. Kruglevski has always been kind to me, and has even promised to let me see his lab one day."

Maman rolled her eyes. "Katerina! What shall I do with you? And I am so sorry that my sudden illness means you will not be going to Cetinje with your new friends. I'm sure you were looking forward to it."

I patted her hand as I sat on the edge of her bed. "No, Maman. Actually, the Montenegrins are not my friends. I can't imagine why they'd want me to go to their homeland with them."

"You shouldn't say such things, dear. When Princess Militza marries Grand Duke Peter Nikolayevich, she will be very influential in the Romanov court. Besides, what if Princess Stana does marry my brother? Then she will be part of the family!"

Actually, Grand Duke Peter was my cousin on my father's side, so both of the older princesses could end up as relatives. I frowned at the thought. "Now, Maman, tell me what happened to you last night. Why does Dr. Kruglevski think you are hysterical?"

She waved her hand. "Oh, he knows how silly I can become. I was having my cards read by Madame Marina, and I drew the Queen of Swords. It struck my heart with dread, and suddenly I was worried about you. But now that you're here, I feel so ridiculous."

I felt a little queasy. "What does the Queen of Swords mean?" I asked. "Why did you think it has anything to do with me?"

"When you were born, Madame Marina read your cards for you, and she told me that you were the Queen of Swords. And that I should watch over you carefully, for you had a wonderful gift."

"But I don't. . . ." The panic already started to rise in my throat. I could not bear it if my mother discovered my secret. And if she was actually *pleased* . . .

Maman grabbed my hand. "Perhaps not yet, but when I

saw your card last night," she went on, "I was frightened, for above it was the Devil card."

"The Devil?" I quickly crossed myself.

We lived in the strangest of times. Russia was steeped in mysticism and the occult, and science was struggling against superstition to pull the country into the future. It was like dreaming you were in a fairy tale and knowing you should wake up but not being able to. Unfortunately, I knew for a fact that monsters and faeries existed. I might even be one of the monsters. And there was nothing science could do about it.

As soon as Maman fell back asleep, I went to Papa's study, where he and Dr. Kruglevski were talking. "Katiya, come in!" Papa said, smiling. "You'll want to hear this too. The tsar has given me his consent to build a new medical institute here in St. Petersburg!"

"That's wonderful!" I kissed him on the cheek before settling into one of the overstuffed chairs. Dr. Kruglevski handed me a cup of tea from the samovar. "Thank you, Doctor."

"Your father wants to open an institute of experimental medicine, for research on various diseases, just like Dr. Pasteur's institute in Paris."

"Yes, and there's also one in Berlin," Papa added, stirring his own cup of tea. "Russia needs one as well if we're to keep up with modern science."

"If only he would allow women to attend the Medical Surgical Academy again," I said with a pout. "The tsar's minister of education and his cronies refuse to listen to reason."

"They believe the ghastly rumors about female medical students," Dr. Kruglevski said.

"What rumors?" I asked.

"That the women are ghouls who cut up corpses at night and walk the streets of St. Petersburg with intestines in their pockets."

"How ridiculous!" I said. "Papa, can't you speak with the tsar? Or the minister?"

"Be patient, Katiya," my father said. "You are still young. Perhaps next year the minister will change his mind. In the meantime, you should focus on your studies."

"And how was His Imperial Majesty?" Dr. Kruglevski asked. "Nasty business, that train accident last month."

The tsar, his wife, and his five children had been badly bruised several weeks before when the imperial train derailed near Borki in the Caucus region. Terrorism had been almost completely ruled out by the tsar's men, but I had overheard people at the Smolny Ball saying it had been an assassination attempt on the imperial family. "Poor Vladimir must be very disappointed," the tsar reportedly had joked to his wife, knowing that his brother and the grand duchess Miechen had come so very close to inheriting the Russian throne.

"That man is as strong as a bear," Papa said. "He insists on carrying out his duties, no matter how much pain he is in. Perhaps that is why he was so quick to approve the institute."

Dr. Kruglevski nodded. "Your Highness, I know a doctor who would be very interested in working at your institute. His name is Pavlov. I think his main area of research right now is the circulatory system."

"Excellent. We must have him over for dinner soon. Right, Katiya?"

I nodded, hoping I would be able to meet Dr. Pavlov as well. I knew I was very lucky for my close relationship with my father. Most of the students at Smolny saw their parents only once or twice a year, and only on special occasions. My father had always encouraged me to learn and to think for myself. I knew if it weren't for the tsar's edict and Maman's protests, Papa would let me attend medical school.

"We must start searching immediately for the perfect site," he said. "Unfortunately, the tsar could not provide any funds for the institute, so I will pay for everything myself."

Dr. Kruglevski finished his tea. "I might be able to help you with a suitable site, Your Highness." He stood up and bowed. "I shall call on you tomorrow, if that is convenient, when I come to check on the duchess."

Papa stood too. "Very good, Doctor." He took my hands in his as the doctor left. "She's receiving the best care, Katiya."

Papa did not think much of Maman's occult dabblings. To his mind, it was just a fashionable hobby. He was a practical man, who wasted no time on superstitions and fairy tales. If he ever knew the truth about me, it would break his heart. That night, I said two prayers before I went to sleep—one for Maman and one for Papa. Once again, I dreamed of the strange little moths flying in my bedroom. But this time, I was hunting them down with a sword.

CHAPTER SIX

For the next few mornings, Maman was still feeling weak, so she stayed in bed. I was allowed to remain at home, missing the last days of classes before the Christmas holiday. Maman was resting when Princess Elena and her sisters came to pay a call. They were leaving that afternoon on the train back to Montenegro and had come to tell me goodbye.

"We're so sorry to hear about your poor mother," Princess Militza said. "Was her illness sudden?"

"Oh, yes," I answered as they followed me into the sitting room. "Dr. Kruglevski is taking excellent care of her, though."

"Has she never tried any of the Tibetan doctor's herbal medicines?" Militza turned to her sister as we all sat down. "Stana, what is his name?"

"Badmaev, I believe. He is wonderful. He cured the princess Orlova of her female hysterics."

I had heard of the Tibetan doctor. Although he had come

to St. Petersburg to study Western medicine and had received his medical degree, he also practiced his Far Eastern methods of healing. Dr. Kruglevski had recommended some of his tonics for Maman but generally dismissed his healing methods as quackery.

Our servant brought in a tray of tea things. Stana and Militza sipped daintily from their teacups while Elena and I indulged in the sweet biscuits the cook had prepared.

"Oh, Katerina Alexandrovna, I envy you so much!" Elena said, abruptly changing the subject. "You shall be attending the opera and the ballet and all the wonderful Christmas parties here in St. Petersburg while I'm at home missing you terribly."

"Our brother shall be disappointed as well," Militza said. "Perhaps you would permit us to take him a lock of your hair, to show him what a beautiful golden color it is?"

"My hair?" I laughed nervously. "Why on earth would he be interested in the shade of my hair?" It wasn't truly golden, anyway, but more like a dull wheat color.

"We have told him all about you, and he is most anxious to meet you. Elena already drew him a miniature of you in your Smolny dress. He was quite taken with it."

I bit my lip. "Indeed?" It was disturbing that Elena had been drawing pictures of me, and even more disturbing that she had mailed one across the continent to someone I'd never met before.

But a part of me, the silly girl, was actually pleased. Just because his sisters were witches did not necessarily make him evil, did it? Had I been too hasty to judge him before I met him? Still, I would not be so stupid as to willingly give my own hair to a witch.

"Of course he is, Katerina," Elena said. "Please let me take some of your hair to him, as a friendship token."

"My mother would be horrified," I said, trying to think up another excuse. Militza smiled, but it was not a friendly smile. "Come, Elena. We must not frighten your poor friend with our own country's customs. They must sometimes seem barbaric to society here in St. Petersburg."

"Forgive me," I said, blushing. "I don't think it barbaric at all. I just . . . My mother would think it improper. I have no wish to upset her when she is unwell."

As scared as I was to let them possess even one strand of my hair, insulting the Montenegrins terrified me even more. I was anxious for them to leave. I would feel much safer when they were miles away from St. Petersburg.

Militza stood up, her two sisters following. "We have imposed upon you far too long, Katerina Alexandrovna. We must go to the train station soon, and we do have other goodbyes to make."

Elena embraced me. "You must write to me about the parties I am missing." She reached up, pulled a stray hair of mine off my shoulder, and grinned wickedly. "Look what I have found. Danilo will be able to see the color of your hair after all!" She tucked my hair in her handbag.

I fought the rising panic inside. Perhaps no harm would come of this. In fact, I prayed no harm would come of it.

Stana smiled. "Farewell, dear. We will certainly see each other again soon."

As I watched their sleigh drive off down Millionaya Street, I grew worried. How would I be able to protect myself from the Montenegrins' magic? I could not tell Maman everything I knew about the wicked princesses. I did not want her to grow hysterical once more.

I found my mother in her rose-scented boudoir, studying her deck of tarot cards. "Maman," I said with a sigh. "You'll get yourself worked up again."

She waved a hand at me. "Don't be silly. I think it was Madame Marina's deck that caused me such discomfort. These are my own cards, from a gypsy woman in Biarritz. These have never lied to me." She pulled one card after another, carefully laying them in a cross-shaped pattern on her quilt.

Maman's cat Sasha glared at me from across the room. His scraggly gray tail twitched nervously. "What if Papa discovers your fortune-telling cards?" I asked.

It was Maman's turn to sigh. "I know he thinks it's nonsense, but I see problems for your father," she said, "and many obstacles and delays in his projects. Sometimes I can help him forestall them. These cards have been a boon to our household. Here." She laid down the Hanged Man.

It was best to humor her. "I thought the cards were telling you about me," I said as Sasha began to purr. "Where is my knight in shining armor?"

Maman smiled at me. "I've already seen your future this morning. And my deck has told me that you're going to meet your handsome knight very soon, if you haven't already." She gathered up her cards and put them back in their silver-plated box. "Have I ever told you the story of the bogatyr?"

I shook my head, trying in vain to remember. "Is this another fairy tale?" Our library was full of fairy tale collections, from many different countries. When I was little, I'd spent hours gazing at the beautiful illustrations.

"Yes, Katiya, but this one is very important. Long ago, the bogatyr was a very strong warrior-tsar who protected Russia from evil wizards. He also fought and killed a wicked dragon named Vladimir. The bogatyr lived for more than a hundred years, and it is said that he returns from time to time when Russia has need of him. But for him to return, the current tsar must pay a great price."

"A great price?" I asked.

"A secret ritual must be performed in order to transform the current tsar into the bogatyr," Maman explained. She took my hand in hers. "The reason I am telling you this is that I dreamed last night of the bogatyr's return."

"Why would Russia need him now?" I asked. "We're relatively at peace with all of Europe. Even Germany. Even Turkey."

"The bogatyr does not protect us only from our political enemies, but also from the forces of evil. The last time was in 1825, when my grandfather Tsar Nicholas defended us from the vampire uprising. Some kind of evil has returned, Katiya. I wish you could sense it as I do. There was a time, when you were younger, I truly believed . . ."

She looked away, out her window into the snow-filled garden below. "Anyway, even if you cannot feel it, there is a great evil presence growing in St. Petersburg. We need the bogatyr to return and protect us. I believe the dream I had last night was a sign that he will return." Her eyes were bright, as if she was holding back tears. She squeezed my hand.

I didn't want to believe my mother's wild tale. "Vampires do not exist, Maman."

"Certainly not," Maman said. "Not since the uprising. The bogatyr banished them and their Dekebristi minions from St. Petersburg."

I had a sick feeling in my stomach. I knew faeries and witches existed, as well as necromancers. What other monsters walked the streets of St. Petersburg? What if the bogatyr believed I was the evil presence in the city? Would Maman have seen that in her tarot cards?

CHAPTER SEVEN

M iechen's Christmas Ball was an annual tradition for the younger set, who were allowed to dance polonaises and mazurkas and quadrilles but no waltzes. I was hoping this would be the last year Maman dragged me along, as I was now attending the grown-up balls, which were silly enough.

"Come along, Katiya!" Maman called up the stairs.

Anya was finishing my hair.

"Please be careful, Highness," she whispered. "Even with the Montenegrins out of the city, there is always evil about. I overheard the footmen talking about recent grave robberies. Who would do such a wicked thing?"

I frowned at myself in the looking glass. I'd heard Papa discussing the same thing with my brother. The graves had belonged to two princes, both decorated war heroes. I couldn't fathom what possible good could come from digging up someone's grave.

Even more distressing, what possible evil could come of it? I shivered with disgust and then sighed. I could not contemplate such things now. I had a command performance to attend.

I stood up, twirling my skirts a little. "I'm sure it is quite safe to attend a ball at the Vladimir Palace," I said.

The grand duchess Maria Pavlovna, wife of Grand Duke Vladimir, was known as Miechen to her family and friends. A fierce rival of the empress, the faerie was a German princess from the darkest Brothers Grimm story. No one threw a more spectacular party than Miechen. And the empress knew it.

Maman loved any excuse to see and be seen, and the Christmas Ball was no exception. Maman had long been friends with Miechen and the empress and had managed all those years to remain cordial with both. She tried to stay neutral, but her fondness for séances and the occult drew her to the Dark Court's favor. Both faerie queens scared the skirts off me. I tried not to draw either one's attention.

Maman's deep red gown matched the ruby tiara sparkling in her dark hair. She looked paler than usual in the rich-colored velvet. Maman had her mother's Romanov features: the piercing dark eyes and the long, narrow nose. I had my mother's eyes but my father's pudgy nose. My cousins had teased me mercilessly about it when I was younger, knowing it disturbed me. I wore a white velvet gown, similar to my Smolny dress. I looked forward to the day when I could wear any color in public other than white. White was innocent. My soul was not.

Miechen was dressed in a dark purple ball gown, with her

famous Vladimir tiara, which dripped diamonds and pearls. She saw Maman as soon as we were announced, and came toward us.

"Yevgenia Maximilianovna, darling, I am so glad to see you." She held out both of her slender gloved hands for Maman to take. "And your daughter, Katerina Alexandrovna," she said, smiling down at me.

"Your Imperial Highness," I said with a curtsy.

"Your daughter is growing up," Miechen said, studying me with her dark violet eyes.

"She is, indeed," Maman said with a dramatic sigh. "We have been so fortunate with both of our children."

"And how is the younger Duke of Oldenburg?" Miechen asked.

I glanced across the crowded ballroom as the women chatted. The orchestra was playing Tchaikovsky. Some of the youngest Romanovs were dancing a quadrille with my cousin Dariya. She caught my eye and winked.

"And how are your children?" Maman was asking.

Miechen glanced across the ballroom. "Kyril is over there, talking with his uncles. And Boris and Andrei are torturing their poor sister."

From the way my mother's eyes lit up, I could guess she was wondering about a marriage between me and one of Grand Duchess Miechen's sons. Never mind that the eldest, Kyril, was only thirteen. He wasn't bad-looking, as far as thirteen-year-old distant cousins went. But I would not marry just to satisfy my mother's social ambitions.

I envied Petya that he did not have to be here with us. He was attending a dinner party with his fellow officers, having a much more amusing time, I was certain. Maman was still scheming, however, even as she perused the young guests. If my brother wasn't careful, she might match him up with Miechen's pasty seven-year-old daughter, Helena.

The grand duchess looked at me. "Katerina Alexandrovna, I am sure Kyril will be looking for an expert dance partner for the quadrille. I heard the empress was most impressed with the way you danced at the Smolny Ball. Would you be a dear and accept when he asks you?"

"I'd be honored, Your Imperial Highness," I murmured with another curtsy. The empress had noticed me? *Mon Dieu*. I took a glass of punch from the silver tray a nearby servant offered. This would be a long night.

As I looked for my cousins, the imperial family was announced, and the empress appeared at the entrance to the brightly lit ballroom. The orchestra immediately began to play the empress's favorite procession, the cortege from Rimsky-Korsakov's *The Snow Maiden*. As everyone present curtsied and bowed, Miechen glided away from Maman toward the empress.

Both faerie queens were the perfect illusion of grace, pretending to forget their usual hostilities toward each other. Miechen's son, Kyril Vladimirovich, followed his mother. I realized then that all five of the empress's children were standing behind her.

Dressed in a white velvet gown embroidered with silver thread, Grand Duchess Xenia looked almost exactly like her mother. They shared the same dark eyes, but there was something mischievous in the daughter's glance. She was only thirteen, yet already beautiful enough to break some poor prince's heart.

Maman and I made our way to the empress so we could give our greetings. I noticed Xenia laughing at something her brother George was telling her.

I sensed the empress's gaze on me as my mother and I curtsied. "Good evening, Your Imperial Majesty," Maman said. "We hope you and your family are well this holiday season."

I trembled a little under the empress's piercing stare. She was using her faerie sight. I could feel it shimmering over me, illuminating even the darkest stains on my soul. I grew slightly dizzy. And a little sick.

The orchestra began to play a Christmas carol. Kyril Vladimirovich stepped up and asked the grand duchess Xenia to dance. I had been spared for now. "Of course," she said, eyes twinkling as she allowed him to lead her to the dance floor.

The empress turned and spoke a word to her three sons before moving on to greet the next noble family waiting to speak with her. The tsarevitch remained with his mother, greeting Miechen's guests, while the younger two grand dukes strolled out to the floor, immediately choosing partners. George Alexandrovich's eyes met mine, briefly, and then he took Dariya's hand and swept her across the ballroom.

"Your Imperial Highness, will you do me the honor of this dance?" I turned to see Miechen's twelve-year-old son, Boris Vladimirovich, looking at me solemnly.

"Of course," I said with a polite curtsy. *Angels and ministers of grace, defend me.*

Many of my distant relatives, and even my closer cousins, whom I only saw on occasions like this, were present. I glanced around the room as Boris and I danced. Uncle George's son Alexander Georgevich looked uncomfortable, unable to excuse himself from chatting with the elderly princess Cantacuzene.

"I hope we get to eat soon," Boris murmured as he stepped on my foot a third time. "Aren't you hungry?"

"Katiya!" Dariya rushed up to me, out of breath, as the dance concluded. Boris bowed, thanking me graciously, then skipped off to find something sweet to eat. The servants had just laid out a tray of iced pastries and sugar-frosted fruits. Dariya was dressed in a white silk dress embroidered with tiny pearls. She wore large ostrich feathers in her hair and in the bustle of her skirt. My cousin was so much more beautiful than I was. Her long dark blond hair was a tumble of curls down the back of her head. All the young men flocked around her.

Dariya and I made our way out of the overheated ballroom and walked through one of Miechen's elegant parlors. Here several small tables were heavy with canapés and caviar. We helped ourselves to cups of punch and sat on the damask-covered settee to catch up.

"I am so glad you did not have to go to Cetinje," Dariya said. "I don't see how Elena could possibly think the crown prince is the man of your dreams."

I shrugged. "Please do not mention him again. Or Cetinje. It is all Maman talks of."

"I'd rather go to Paris," my cousin said. "I hear it is a beautiful city."

We'd both been to visit our grandmother's villa in Biarritz, a resort town on the Atlantic coast, but neither of us had seen the capital of France. Dariya and I used to play French Revolution when we were little. We'd take turns being Marie Antoinette. Our grandmamma caught us once and had us whipped for revolutionary sentiments. We were six years old at the time and had no idea even what revolutionary sentiments were.

I tried to avoid the imperial family during the ball, but Grand Duchess Xenia was getting punch in the grand rotunda and spotted us. She gave us a knowing smile. "If the two of you are together, there is mischief in progress," she said. "Are Auntie Miechen's dogs safe?"

During a children's ball Maman had thrown many summers earlier, Dariya and I found a kitten that had wandered upstairs and we tried to get it to dance a mazurka with Maman's French bulldog, Lola. The kitten wanted nothing to do with the mazurka or Lola and scampered up Maman's silk curtains. Lola ran downstairs, in the opposite direction, then straight through the orchestra and under the violinist's legs. Fortunately, Dariya and I did not get punished, but we were not allowed to play with Lola anymore. The curtains, alas, were never the same.

Xenia was still laughing at us when her brother walked over. "Georgi, do you remember when Katerina Alexandrovna and Dariya Yevgenievna brought the kitten to a ball?"

I hadn't noticed the grand duke approaching. Dariya

curtsied prettily. "Katiya's mother wouldn't let us play together anymore after that," my cousin said.

"I thought *your* mother disallowed it," I said, surprised.

"Both mothers were very wise," George Alexandrovich said, his lips pressed tightly together, almost as if he was trying not to smile. "You two are an extremely dangerous duo."

"Nonsense." Dariya smiled. "Nothing bad has happened tonight."

The grand duke was looking straight at me when he said, "But the night is young."

I met his eyes evenly, expecting to see disdain, or even hatred. Instead, there was heat, an intense but strangely wonderful fire. It frightened me even more.

Xenia giggled and then squealed with delight. "Sandro is here!" she said, running off to dance with her older cousin.

Her brother frowned. "If you will excuse me." He bowed slightly and followed his sister.

"How disagreeable he is!" Dariya murmured as we both watched him leave. "Though he does dance well."

It felt as if the wind had been knocked out of me. I shook my head, trying to get the grand duke out of my mind. "We should rescue Alexander Georgevich from Princess Cantacuzene," I said. "She will talk him to death."

⧼⧽

The elderly princess sat on a velvet sofa in the rotunda outside the main ballroom. Alexander was grateful when we offered a cup of punch to her.

"Thank you, dears," the ancient woman said. Still in

mourning for her late husband, she was wearing a black high-necked ball gown. He had died long before I was born.

Princess Cantacuzene patted Alexander on the knee. "Young man, you must go and dance with one of your pretty cousins! Take Dariya Yevgenievna. Katerina Alexandrovna will be happy to sit with me."

Dariya smiled as she and our cousin hurried away, glad to escape back to the dancing. I sat down next to the princess, cursing my luck. There would be no one to rescue me from the addled woman's rambling stories. She was a frequent member of Maman's séance parties.

"My dear, I fancy a turn in the gardens. Would you oblige me?" she asked.

"Of course, Your Highness."

She rose regally and took my arm as we exited the ballroom. "You have drawn the attentions of the Montenegrins, I hear," she said.

I let out a heavy sigh but remembered not to slump. "My mother has been gossiping."

The princess cackled. "I heard it from others, my dear." She grabbed my arm with an icy, bony hand. I could feel the cold even though she wore the softest black kidskin gloves. "You are in grave danger, Katerina Alexandrovna."

"I beg your pardon, Your Highness?"

"The crown prince Danilo is in line to follow his ancestors, the Vladiki. They have ruled their kingdom for hundreds of years."

"The Vladiki?"

She nodded. "They use the darkest magic to hold on to their throne. They are blood drinkers."

57

Surely I had not heard her correctly. I looked at her in disbelief. The old princess had gone mad. "Vampires?" I whispered.

Princess Cantacuzene nodded. Her silvery white hair was pulled into a severe knot high atop her head, tied so tightly I wondered if it hurt her. "The females are the blackest of sorceresses," she went on.

We stopped as we approached the orangery. The heavy scent of orange blossoms perfumed the humid air.

I had to sit down, feeling a little queasy. I never once had thought such repulsive creatures still walked the earth. Maman's tale about Tsar Nicholas and his treaty with the vampires seemed so long ago. "Why would a vampire prince want to marry me?" I asked. "My family is not that important."

The princess laughed as she joined me on the ornately carved garden bench. "Katerina Alexandrovna, who said anything about marriage? Still, I'm glad to see that you sense it is not your bloodline that makes you so valuable." She took one of her rings off her finger and placed it in my hand. "This will protect you. You and your special talent are a threat to the Vladiki."

Marble statues of griffins glared at us from under the potted palm trees. Only the grand duchess Miechen could have such a sinister-looking garden room.

"I—I have no special talent," I stammered. The ring she offered was a shiny black obsidian in a gold setting.

The princess's eyes flashed. "Do not be ashamed of it, Katerina Alexandrovna. You have the power to defeat the

Vladiki. I have long suspected this, even when you were younger. You can stop their quest for dominance and save the lives of many innocents."

"How can I save anyone?" I asked softly. I carried a curse and the princess had known all along. There was no salvation to be found in my horrible talent.

"You alone are the secret weapon against the blood drinkers. The heir of the Vladiki cannot drink blood until his ceremony of ascension, on his eighteenth birthday." Her fingers were icy as she clutched my left hand and slid the ring onto my finger. "Kill Prince Danilo before his ascension and you will save many, many lives."

I gasped. "I could never kill someone, Your Highness." I was now certain Princess Cantacuzene was thoroughly and utterly mad. She was thin and ancient. The poor woman must be senile. I glanced around for members of her family who would be able to take her home. Married to a long deceased and forgotten Prince Cantacuzene, she had no children of her own, but spoiled all her nieces and nephews. Perhaps one of the latter had escorted her to the Christmas Ball.

We walked back toward the rotunda. "There is your dear mother," the princess said. "She has recently been ill, has she not?"

"Yes, but she is much better."

"You must be on guard, Duchess. I have attended many séances with your mother, and she has attracted the attentions of many unhappy spirits. The cold light of the dying surrounds her."

Princess Cantacuzene gathered her black skirt as my mother approached us. "We will speak again soon, Katerina Alexandrovna," she said. "I can tell you much more about the Montenegrins."

"Your Highness, it is so good to see you." My mother curtsied before the princess. "How are you?"

My mind was reeling. A cold light? The madwoman spoke as if she saw the same things I could see. I stole a glance at Princess Cantacuzene and searched her cold light. It shined brightly, much as any other elderly person's would. I could see nothing unnatural about her. But then again, the empress and the grand duchess Miechen had cold lights that appeared ordinary to me as well. I was unable to distinguish human from fae, which put me at a disadvantage to the faeries in the ballroom.

While my mother and the princess chatted, my cousin Alexander Georgevich asked me to dance the cotillion with him. The Gypsy orchestra was playing a lively piece by Rimsky-Korsakov. My cousin was a perfectly elegant dancer, like his late mother, Aunt Therese, who had died when Alexander was only two. Aunt Therese had been one of my father's sisters, so Alexander was my double cousin. He told me his father planned to announce his engagement to Princess Anastasia of Montenegro after Christmas.

"I hope she makes a kind stepmother," I told him. I worried about the disturbing stories Princess Cantacuzene had told me. But I did not want to alarm my cousin. Surely the princess's tales about the Montenegrins could not be true.

"Father intends for me to enter the Corps des Pages

next year, so I will not be around the princess that often." Alexander smiled. "When Father introduced me to her last month, she was very kind."

"Give him my best wishes, then," I said, smiling politely. He led me back to Maman after the dance ended. It had been the final dance of the night. I said goodbye to my cousin, then followed Maman to make our adieus to the grand duchess Miechen.

As I curtsied, the grand duchess spotted my ring. "What a beautiful trinket," she said, seizing my hand. "A family heirloom?"

Maman did not notice, as she was speaking with the grand duke Vladimir.

"No, Your Imperial Highness. It was a gift from a family friend." I knew Maman would insist I return it to Princess Cantacuzene if she saw it. The ring seemed to glow, reflecting the lights of the ballroom chandeliers.

"You must be careful with such a precious stone. Obsidian protects one from evil spirits and vampires." There was a certain malice in the grand duchess's smile. "It makes me curious. Why would your friend believe you need such protection, Katerina Alexandrovna?"

"An old woman's superstitious nonsense, I'm sure," I replied, my heartbeat pounding in my ears. I was aware the grand duchess could see much more in my aura than I could see in hers. Still, I noted a strange thing when I saw her cold light. Two smaller, brighter lights were entwined with a larger, dimmer light, like a delicate, shimmering braid of light, coiling around her. It was beautiful, but frightening to look at.

I fretted over everything on the sleigh ride home. Princess Cantacuzene was the second person to refer to my curse as a gift. And she spoke as if she too possessed this terrible gift. No one else would see it that way. Certainly not my parents. And not the imperial family.

CHAPTER EIGHT

❧

The holiday passed quickly. Our family broke the Christmas Eve fast in the usual fashion: as soon as the first stars could be seen in the cold night sky, we ate the traditional twelve-course feast, which included mushroom soup and baked fish. The table was loaded with plates of apricots, figs, sweet almond cakes, and rice pudding.

We would not be able to eat most of the Christmas treats, made with butter and cream, until the next day, after the Christmas Mass. But Papa had talked the cook into making his favorite blini with sour cream. The house was cozy, with a fire burning in every fireplace. The familiar scents of tea brewing in the samovar and Maman's warmed cherry brandy smelled like love to me.

After the midnight Mass, my parents decorated the family Christmas tree. Petya and I acted like infants, squealing and giggling as we unwrapped our gifts beneath its heavily scented branches. Petya received a new saddle for his horse from our parents, since he was going into the cavalry, and I gave him a fashionable silk cravat for his favorite white shirt. Maman received a beautiful ruby necklace that Papa had commissioned by Fabergé to match her tiara. There were happy tears in her eyes as she kissed Papa on his whiskered cheek.

I received a number of books: the latest romance by Marie Corelli, a book of poems by Lermontov, and a book of medical drawings by Leonardo da Vinci. Maman enjoyed reading Corelli, which was much too light and ethereal for me. Maman had once told me *A Romance of Two Worlds* was Queen Victoria's favorite book, and said the Romanian queen was also fond of Corelli's work. I never felt quite as much admiration for either queen after that.

I preferred dull scientific tomes to romances and was eager to retire to my room and delve into the da Vinci book. There was secret knowledge to uncover in science. All romances ended exactly the same way: a girl realized the surly boy she had hated all along was the only person in the universe who could complete her soul. I did not believe for a minute that my soul could be completed by some surly boy.

And I would not wish my curse to harm anyone else. So how could I dare long for love?

Maman smiled as she handed me a package with a Montenegrin postmark. "This came for you earlier this week," she said. "I thought you should wait until we opened the rest of the presents."

I opened the brown wrapped package with dread. The

card had the Montenegrin royal seal but was not signed, so I could not tell who had sent the gift. It could have been Elena or her sisters, or even the king and queen themselves.

"Hurry up so we can see!" Maman was so excited about my gift that I considered letting her open it. But something told me not to.

It was a beautiful onyx box, decorated with tiny pearls. Worth a small fortune.

"*Mon Dieu*, Katiya!" Maman said. "You must write a thank-you note immediately!"

I opened the lid and immediately shut it again, sick from what I'd seen. A single tarot card. The Queen of Swords.

"Is there a note inside? A picture of the crown prince, perhaps?"

"Nothing," I lied. Did the Montenegrins know of my mother's superstitions? Or was it just a coincidence?

◦◦◦

There was another feast later that morning with even more treats. Apricot creams and strawberry zephyrs. Chocolate babas and gooseberry puddings. And Petya's and my favorite: an enormous marzipan torte. I ate until I thought I would be sick.

We presented gifts to our small household staff after breakfast: the male servants received new shoes made of the finest Parisian leather, while the female servants received silver-handled hairbrushes. I had knitted a pair of mittens for Anya.

"Did you make these yourself?" Anya asked incredulously as she inspected the delicate needlework. A red rose adorned each mitten.

"Of course," I said, more than a little proud of myself. A surgeon needed to be dexterous to execute fine stitches. When Maman taught me knitting and embroidery, I imagined I was sewing up sick and injured people.

Late that afternoon, I accompanied Maman as she delivered presents to distant cousins, and then we visited the Oldenburg Hospital with baskets of oranges for the patients. It made for a long day. I almost fell asleep in the sleigh on the ride home.

I opened the onyx box again before bedtime, staring at the tarot card. It looked much older than the one in my mother's deck. This queen was dressed in a crimson robe and the lettering was in Italian. According to Pushkin's short story "The Queen of Spades," said queen, along with the Queen of Swords, signified secret ill will. I wasn't sure if the card was meant to be a warning. Or a threat. Either way, it seemed like a bad omen, so I threw it into the burning logs in my fireplace.

The flames leapt up and turned a deep violet. I stepped back, dropping the box to the floor.

I heard a gasp from the doorway behind me. Anya.

"What strange, unholy fire is this?" she asked, making the sign of the cross hastily. "Are you practicing witchcraft, Duchess?"

I'd never felt more terrible in my life. She was frightened of me. "No, Anya. Of course not. I was getting rid of an old card. It must have been the chemicals in the ink."

She stared at the fire, which once again appeared normal. "Perhaps your father should come and see. In case it's dangerous." She opened the window a tiny bit to freshen the air.

"No, I'm sure everything is fine. I don't want to disturb him or Maman." The last thing I wanted was my mother to become ill again. And though Anya didn't care for the Montenegrins, I thought she would be safer if she didn't know everything about them. I hoped I was protecting her by lying to her.

For the rest of school break, I went to bed every night curled up with my medical journal. After having argued with Papa once more about the stubborn minister of education, I had decided to write a letter of application to the University of Zurich. That was where Maria Bokova and Nadezhda Suslova, Madame Orbellani's idols, had received their medical degrees.

Every night I fell asleep to articles about childhood diseases or advancements in cranial surgery. I'd like to say I dreamed about finding a cure for meningitis or scarlet fever, but I didn't. Nor did I dream about surly boys. Less than two weeks after Christmas, the Black Mountain nightmares began.

CHAPTER NINE

❧

I was standing in a temple, which appeared to be carved from deep within a mountain. The temple torches were lit all along the walls, with an especially large fire burning behind the altar. A priest in a black robe chanted something in an ancient language I could not understand. Was it ancient Greek? It did not sound familiar. I tried to move and realized my arms were pinned behind my back by someone I could not see. As I struggled to free myself, I found that I could not remember how I had gotten there.

As the chanting went on, it grew dark outside the bloodred stained glass windows. The wind howled through the temple, shrieking like a banshee battered by a summer storm. Three figures, which stood around the altar behind the priest, wore black hooded robes. The sight of their hoods frightened me more than anything. I knew that they were important people in my life, but I could not determine their identity.

The priest held his chalice up to the fire, seeking some sort of unholy blessing from whatever being they worshipped. The cup was beautiful: golden with colorful enamel in the pattern of a phoenix. As the priest turned to me, I stared at the chalice, trying to see what was inside it.

He smiled at me, his teeth small, white, and pointed. I felt a sudden wave of nausea. Instantly, I knew what he planned to do to me. The person behind me let go abruptly and the priest grabbed my arm, raking one of his sharp fingernails down my wrist. I gasped in pain and tried to fight down the panic welling up inside.

The wound was far too deep. I would bleed to death if it wasn't stopped soon. I began to pray silently, for I was sure only God could save me while I was in this place. I thought about my parents, regretting that I hadn't had the chance to say goodbye to them. I was terrified, but determined not to show it to my captors.

The priest held out the chalice as my blood fell in fat crimson drops into it. I smelled the copper taint of blood on the air. My very life essence was flowing from me; I knew it would not be long before I felt faint.

The priest took the chalice and turned back to the three hooded figures. I would have fallen if not for strong arms and hands that suddenly reached out to hold me up. I did not bother to struggle anymore. I could only look on as the three figures joined in the chanting with the priest. The figure in the middle pulled back his hood to reveal himself as a handsome dark-haired, dark-eyed young man. Stepping forward, he took the chalice from the priest and drank my blood. Suddenly, a thousand white-winged insects flew out from under the altar and ascended toward the temple *vault. The moths flew above the flames and the smoke, swarming the darkness.*

⋙⋘

I woke up stifling a scream. I was shaking. Sweat dampened my white cotton nightclothes. I took a deep breath and tried to calm myself. *Mon Dieu*, what had just happened to me? Had it been merely a dream? Or a prophecy?

Anya was at the foot of my bed, staring at me in horror. "Duchess? Are you ill?" she asked anxiously.

I flinched as a single moth fluttered from under my bed and out the open window. Despite the cold air, my chest was burning. I was still shaking.

Anya poured me a glass of water from the bedside table. "Here, drink this." She had to help me hold the glass so I didn't spill anything.

The water made me feel a little bit better. "Thank you," I said, sinking back down to my pillows.

"Do you want me to call for your mother?" Anya asked. "I'm worried about you, Duchess."

I shook my head. "I don't want to trouble her. What time is it?"

"Half past eight."

I groaned. I had to get up. It was Theophany, twelve days past Christmas. We were to attend the annual Blessing of the Waters, when the metropolitan bishop would cut a hole in the frozen waters of the Neva River and bless it. Slowly, I sat back up. The room was spinning slightly, but really, I

70

couldn't complain. A spinning room was certainly a better place to be than a cave where I would become a human sacrifice.

Thinking about the nightmare made me nauseated. I felt a terrible pressure in the back of my throat.

I jumped out of bed to retch in the washbasin. I held the sides, shaking still, as the spasms seized me.

"Duchess! Allow me to call your maman!" she begged. "You're too sick to be going anywhere today!"

"No, Anya, please! I'll be fine. I ate too much rich food last night—it's nothing."

"Duchess, I—"

"It was just the food, which caused another bad dream," I insisted. "I'll be fine." I cleaned myself up and walked over to my wardrobe. Anya had already laid out my silver court gown trimmed in pearls and Venetian lace.

I splashed cool water on my face, and Anya helped me get dressed. When I looked at my reflection in the mirror, the bags under my eyes were a somber reminder of my miserable night. I could not see my own cold light, but I imagined it to be shimmering brightly, with Death looming close by. After such a dream, how could it not?

Anya arranged the velvet *kokoshnik* on my head, watching me in the mirror carefully. She was still afraid of me, I realized sadly. My strange behavior that morning had done nothing to allay her fears.

"Katiya?" Maman's voice floated down the hallway. "Are you finished getting ready? We have to leave soon for the Winter Palace! Anya, where are my gloves?"

Anya turned away from me and nearly ran from the room. She was grateful for the interruption.

I took a deep breath, preparing for the day ahead.

～◎～

It was a short sleigh ride from our house to the palace, which was situated at the end of Millionnaya Street. The morning was sunny, but freezing. Crowds were already gathering along both banks of the frozen Neva River as we went inside to the palace's Grand Chapel for the divine service.

The chapel was hot and crowded with all St. Petersburg's aristocracy. They all wore their finest court attire. The heat from the candles and the packed bodies made the ceremony almost unbearable. I had to remember not to lock my knees so I would not faint.

After the prayers, I followed Maman in the long formal procession through the palace from the chapel to the Jordan Staircase, leading outside to the snow-covered riverbank. The procession was silent except for the quiet swishes of the women's elaborate court dresses. The empress and the grand duchesses wore long heavy trains that had to be carried by their pages. My mother's page looked as if he were no older than I was.

Hundreds of servants in smart crimson liveries stood at attention along the magnificent staircase. I lifted my skirts slightly, praying I would not trip as I descended the stairs.

When we reached the ground floor, many of the empress's ladies-in-waiting remained inside the enfilade, along with the entire Diplomatic Corps, watching the ceremony from the grand windows. Maman and I followed the procession outside to see Papa and Petya. I was happy to breathe the frigid air, even though it hurt my lungs. After the closeness of the chapel, it was fresh and bracing.

The metropolitan stood in front of the Imperial Pavilion, his silver-and-gold robes blazing in the pale sunlight. He prayed silently over a small hole that had been cut into the ice. The waters of the Neva, warmer than the ice above it, caused steam to rise out of the hole.

We stood behind the pavilion, next to the beautiful young grand duchess Elizabeth Feodorovna and her husband, Grand Duke Serge Alexandrovich, one of the tsar's uncles. The grand duchess turned to greet us. "Katerina Alexandrovna, you attend the Smolny Institute, do you not?"

"Yes, Your Highness." I tried to curtsy, and wobbled slightly on the frozen, uneven ground.

"And you have already been presented to court?" Her breath fogged in the crisp winter air.

"Just this past summer, Your Highness," Maman answered. "I believe you were in Darmstadt at the time."

The grand duchess ignored my mother and kept her unsettling eyes on me. Both of her eyes were grayish blue, but one had a circle of brown. "You must be the same age as my sister, Alix. She is coming to stay with me this winter. I hope you will get to meet her."

"I'd be honored."

Tall and slender, the grand duke Serge leaned over and whispered something to his wife. "Please excuse us," she said, following him to the Imperial Pavilion, where the tsar and empress stood with their younger children. Their older sons sat astride their horses in full dress uniforms.

All of the imperial family looked solemn. And, not surprisingly, cold. The tsarevitch and the grand duke George were dressed in the uniforms of the Preobrajensky Regiment. Even the young grand duchesses were wearing their own regimental insignia.

"There is Petya!" Maman whispered, clapping her hands as my brother's regiment marched past the Imperial Pavilion. The regiment stopped to salute the tsar, who saluted back, before they continued their march toward the river.

We could see Dariya and her stepmother standing at the other side of the pavilion, close to Miechen and her family. I had not had a chance to talk with my cousin since Miechen's ball. I wanted to tell her about Princess Cantacuzene and her warnings about the Montenegrins.

When all the troops had marched or ridden across the frozen river to the opposite side, a hush fell on the crowd. As the priests chanted a hymn, a faint scent of frankincense and myrrh wafted through the pavilion. The tsar kissed the large golden cross in the metropolitan's hand. The metropolitan then lowered the cross into the river, dipping it three times to bless the water that flowed through the streets of St. Petersburg. When the cross was raised the third time and held high above the metropolitan's head, the troops would fire canons from the other side of the river in salute.

Maman spoke in hushed tones with the elderly princess Orlova, standing next to her. They were discussing the Anichkov Ball, which would be held in a few weeks. It would be the first imperial ball of the year, which started off the St. Petersburg winter season. I watched the excited troops and their horses eagerly awaiting their signal to return across the river.

At that moment, the golden cross was lifted, glittering in the pale winter sunlight.

A canon shot fired and the horses charged across the ice in front of the crowd. A great cheer went up but was drowned out by the thundering of hooves. The cavalry raced to the near side of the river, pulling their horses up short before they reached the Imperial Pavilion. It was a dangerous maneuver. The onlookers held their breath as snow and chunks of ice flew up.

Suddenly, there was a shout. The cavalry circled around one fallen horse. A man was down. Maman put her hands to her mouth, worried about Papa. After several minutes, two men rode back toward the Imperial Pavilion to update the tsar. The men wore grim looks on their faces.

Maman and I both sighed with relief when we realized one of the men speaking to the tsar was Papa. After consulting for several minutes, Papa and another soldier rode back across the field. The Preobrajensky Regiment's orchestra started playing their march as the hussars lined up to approach the tsar. In one long line they rode forward, then fanned out in a semicircle.

I glanced back to the far end of the field and saw the fallen soldier being carried off in a sleigh, followed by my father and several officers on horseback. They were taking the injured man to the hospital. Papa's interest in medicine had begun when he had served in the war against the Turks and he'd wanted to get the best medical care for his troops. That was how he had met Dr. Louis Pasteur.

The crowd started to thin out after the ceremony ended. Maman remained in her seat, talking to Princess Orlova and Princess Cantacuzene. We were joined by Dariya and her stepmother. I searched across the ice, looking for Petya. He sat on his horse in front of the Imperial Pavilion with two fellow officers, speaking with the tsar. I made my way over so I could ask Petya what was happening.

As I stepped out in front of the pavilion, my brother's horse reared. I flung my arms up instinctively to protect my face as muddy snow flew everywhere. I was too scared to do anything else. I heard Maman's scream behind me.

Petya fell to the ground, his boot caught in the stirrup by the heel spur. He would have been dragged by the beast if his companion had not grabbed the reins quickly. It was the grand duke George Alexandrovich who saved my brother's life with his quick action.

Everything happened so fast I found myself rooted to the spot. I realized then that I had not been close enough to be in any real danger, but my brother had almost been killed. My heart pounded. And I was shaking with fear.

Maman sobbed as she raced down the steps past me to see Petya.

I tried to follow her, but the tsar's men had him surrounded and were herding the crowd away as they placed him on an army stretcher.

Maman pushed her way through the people, but I was only able to catch a glimpse of my brother as he slowly sat up on the stretcher. He was banged up pretty badly, with several bruises and scratches, but otherwise seemed uninjured. Awake and alert, he still looked dazed. He was searching the crowd for someone, and then I realized he was looking for his horse.

I saw the stupid beast still acting skittishly on the other side of the pavilion. My poor brother. His cold light looked benign now, but there had been a brilliant flash as he'd fallen.

I tried again to push through the soldiers, but they ignored me completely. No one would let me by. Maman was already at Petya's side, hovering over him with her handkerchief.

Frustrated, I found my brother's horse, pawing the ground nervously. The animal snorted as I reached out to touch his neck. His large brown eye stared at me fearfully. Agitated, he was about to rear again.

"Are you so determined to get yourself killed this morning, Duchess?" Grand Duke George Alexandrovich said as he held firm to the horse's reins. The horse seemed finally to quiet down under his gentle command.

Annoyed, I curtsied to the grand duke. "That was a very brave thing to do, Your Imperial Highness," I said. "Thank you for saving my brother's life."

His blue eyes swept over me. "I wonder what frightened your brother's horse, Duchess. He seemed fine until you approached."

I blushed, horrified by and furious at his insinuation. I was too mad to think sensibly before I opened my mouth. "I did not know his horse was afraid of young girls, Your Highness."

He bent his head down so only I could hear him. "Not all young girls, Duchess," he said softly, "but they can sense supernatural malice." He jerked on the reins of his own animal and led Petya's horse back to the imperial stables.

His words stung. What kind of a monster did the grand duke believe me to be? I might be cursed with a tainted gift, but I bore malice toward no one. Fortunately, Maman was still fussing over Petya and had not heard a word of our conversation.

But someone else had. "Pay him no mind," Princess Cantacuzene whispered in my ear. She had been standing behind me all along. "The young Romanov thinks he sees everything with his faerie eyes, and yet he is blind. Do not let yourself be troubled."

That was easier said than done.

Petya insisted that he was fine, and refused to go to the hospital. Then he learned that the soldier who had fallen was his friend Count Chermenensky, and he hurried to accompany Papa there.

I rode home in the sleigh with my mother, worrying about Petya's friend and wishing I'd never have to see the arrogant grand duke ever again. And praying that he would not tell the tsar the disasters that day were all my fault.

❧

That evening, Papa returned home from the hospital looking exhausted and grim. Count Chermenensky had never woken up. Papa said Dr. Kruglevski did not expect the count to live through the night. My brother had refused to leave his friend's side.

Papa was livid when Maman recounted Petya's fall. "I told him to ride one of the other horses today," he said, taking the vodka the servant handed him. Papa knocked the drink back in one gulp and placed the glass on the servant's tray. "Another mount would have been much more suitable."

Reading the Corelli book she'd given me, Maman sat in her chair opposite Papa. I wanted to ask Papa more about the fallen soldier, but he looked tired. I sneaked a glance at the cold light surrounding Papa, then looked at Maman as well. They both appeared healthy, and the dying light that caressed each of them promised that death was far off. With a small sigh of relief, I curled up in the corner chair with my medical book and read.

A while later, the footman announced a visitor. The officer asked Papa to come to the hospital quickly. I jumped out of my chair and begged him to let me go with him.

My father only shook his head sadly as he took his coat and hat from the footman. "Do not wait up for us tonight, my dear," he said to Maman.

She stood up as well, placing her hands on my shoulder in comfort. I turned around and embraced her, saying a silent prayer for Count Chermenensky's family. Twisting the obsidian ring around my finger nervously, I wished that he had not died so young.

After Anya talked us into one more cup of tea, we all went to bed.

And I dreamed.

The nightmares I had after Theophany were nowhere near as lucid as the first one, the night before the Blessing of the Waters, but were far darker. The night before I went back to Smolny, I dreamed of being cold, as if I'd been buried deep in the winter earth. I awoke several times, still shivering, certain I could smell the damp dirt in my skin and hair.

Was I going mad?

I prayed for warmth and daylight.

I prayed for my sanity.

CHAPTER TEN

I tried to forget about the terrible dreams when I returned to Smolny. Madame Tomilov greeted us all and provided a wonderful welcome-back feast.

Elena was happy to be in St. Petersburg again. "I have a present for you," she told me at dinner. "I'll give it to you when we are alone."

I'd already written a thank-you note to her parents for the onyx box. But I still did not know who had sent the tarot card—whether Militza had added the card to the gift. Or perhaps the crown prince himself.

My cousin, who seemed a little paler since I'd seen her at the Christmas Ball, rolled her eyes. "What superstitious trinkets are you trying to scare Katiya with now?" she asked.

A shudder ran through me as I remembered that Elena had taken a strand of my hair back to Cetinje with her. What had she done with it?

She ignored Dariya and laughed. Her eyes seemed so

much brighter since her trip home. Suddenly, I remembered my nightmare, and I wondered what kind of dark magic Elena had been dabbling in over the holiday. What rituals did the Montenegrins practice in their kingdom? I took a nervous sip of my water.

After dessert had been served, one of the Bavarian princesses leaned over and whispered, "We heard about the tragedy at the Blessing of the Waters. How sad!"

I nodded. "It was Count Chermenensky, my brother's friend." I regretted my unkind words to him when we'd met in the park. I wanted to cry all over again. My poor brother was still grief-stricken.

The girls were horrified to hear this. "We spoke with him in the gardens!" Augusta said. "How terrible!"

Elena shrugged, finishing her lemon tart. Erzsebet gazed longingly at my plate. Glancing at the mistresses' table and seeing them deep in conversation, I slid my tart onto Erzsebet's plate.

"*Merci*, Katerina," she said happily.

After dinner, we returned to our rooms to get ready for bed. Elena pulled a small silver box out of her trunk. "Happy Christmas, Katerina!" She opened the box as she held it out to me. Inside was a lock of black hair. "Go on, take it!" she said, nudging me.

I stared at the black curl, tied with a leather cord. "What is that?" I had an ominous feeling in the pit of my stomach.

"Danilo's, of course! It's yours now."

"It would not be proper to accept such a thing." I pulled back my covers and climbed into my bed.

She closed the box and set it on her bedside stand. "You

are no fun, Katerina. You sound just like your cousin, suspicious of everything."

"She's not suspicious of everything," I protested.

"Just Montenegrin witches," Dariya said as she entered our room and crawled into her bed. "You'd best leave Katiya alone. And keep that blasted window closed tonight."

I saw a flash of pure hatred in Elena's eyes, but it was gone quickly and she smiled sweetly and ignored my cousin. "Katerina, my brother has come to St. Petersburg with us," she announced. "You will be able to meet him soon."

"Lovely," Dariya grumbled. "There are too many of your meddlesome family members in Russia already."

"I would watch what I said if I were you." Elena's voice was still sweet but carried a threat. "We come from a family of old romantics, my brother and I. He wishes for my happiness, as I wish for his. I would hate for anyone to stand in the way of true love. Including you, Dariya Yevgenievna."

Dariya snorted and rolled over. "And what could you do about it?" she mumbled sleepily. "Turn me into a toad?"

"My father would be very unhappy to hear that some stupid girl at Smolny was accusing his daughter of witchcraft," Elena said, not missing the chance to remind us she was the daughter of a king.

Then I heard her mumble something in what must have been Montenegrin.

But Dariya was already asleep, her breathing even and easy, with the faintest carefree snore.

Elena yawned dramatically. "Good night, Katerina. May you have wonderful dreams about a handsome, dark-eyed prince. I am certain he is dreaming about you."

I pretended to be asleep and said nothing. But my heart was pounding. I wondered what sorcery Elena was trying to work with her brother's lock of hair. I remembered everything the princess Cantacuzene had told me. If I was truly a threat to the blood drinkers of Montenegro, why would Elena and her sisters want me to grow closer to their brother?

CHAPTER ELEVEN

⁓

Dariya could not get out of bed the next morning. She looked pale and her limbs trembled when she tried to sit up. "Katiya, I am so cold!" she said.

The window was still closed. A pale moth flapped against the inside glass frantically.

Elena rolled her eyes as she cracked the window to let the insect fly away. "Must you always complain?" she asked as she quickly finished getting dressed. "Hurry, Katerina! I'm famished!"

"Go to breakfast without me," I said, sitting on the bed and taking my cousin's hand. "Can you ask Madame Orbellani to come and see Dariya? She is ill."

"What a shame," Elena said. "Of course. I will send her right away."

When she had left, I looked more closely at my cousin. Dariya's pupils were large, and her breathing seemed labored.

"What is wrong with me? My stomach—oh, the cramps!" she whispered. "I feel as if I'm dying!"

"Hush, Madame Orbellani is coming," I said, rubbing her cold hand between my warm ones. Her right arm was floppy, like a rag doll's. I saw a cold light wrapping around her. It was growing steadily brighter and stronger. I was terrified for her. "The headmistress will send for a doctor."

My cousin's eyes rolled back in her head, and she slipped into unconsciousness.

"Dariya!" I shouted, shaking her. Her eyes opened briefly. With a moan, she passed out again. "Dariya!"

"What is this nonsense?" Madame Metcherskey asked severely. "Girls, get down to the dining room at once, or you will be punished."

"Madame, Dariya is ill!" I stood up so she could see for herself. "You must call the doctor!"

Madame Metcherskey's eyes narrowed. "Katerina Alexandrovna, go downstairs immediately. I will deal with her. It is not your concern."

I didn't think I'd ever hated anyone more than I hated Madame Metcherskey at that moment. Her words stung, but I did not dare argue with her. I swallowed hard and squeezed my cousin's pale, limp hand. "I promise I will be back, Dariya."

I ran downstairs and found Madame Orbellani, who sat at the teachers' table, eating breakfast with Madame Tomilov. "Did Elena tell you about Dariya Yevgenievna?" I asked.

I saw confusion in their eyes. "Dariya?"

I gripped the chair in front of me. Of course Elena had not told them. "She passed out!" I explained. "She's extremely cold and complaining of stomach pains. Madame Metcherskey would not allow me to stay with her. I fear something terrible will happen to her!"

Madame Tomilov stood up immediately. "Madame Orbellani, send for the doctor. Katerina Alexandrovna, take me to your cousin."

The headmistress took one look at Dariya, still lying unconscious in her bed, and had her moved to a separate room, quarantined from the rest of us. Dr. Gallitzin arrived and I was shooed into the hall. "She could be contagious," the doctor said. "Keep all the other students away from her."

I tried to argue that both Elena and I had breathed the same air as she had all night long, but Madame Tomilov would not listen. She sent me to class after assuring me that Dariya was in good hands.

I grabbed Elena in the hallway on her way to algebra. "What did you do to her?"

Elena's eyes grew wide and innocent. *"Moi?"*

"Whatever spells you're trying to cast on me with your brother's hair, whatever hateful spell you're casting on Dariya, you're going to stop immediately."

"You say the most bizarre things." Elena shook her head sadly. "Perhaps you feel unwell too. Do you have a fever?" She reached up to touch my forehead.

I knocked her hand away. The girls in the hallway moved quickly to their next classes, making a deliberate effort to ignore us. Out of the corner of my eye, I saw one of the Brown Form's teachers staring at us nervously. Lowering my voice, I said, "I will not let you hurt Dariya or any of the other students here."

Elena rolled her eyes. She had noticed the teacher's attention as well. "Enough of your foolishness, Katerina. You are making me late for class." She turned and disappeared into her classroom.

I needed to see for myself what Elena was up to. I sneaked back upstairs to our dormitory, the chilly hallway now empty. I searched under Elena's cot for proof that she was working dark magic against Dariya. I found nothing under her bed, nor under her pillow, nor in her unlocked storage trunk. Nothing but the wrapped lock of her brother's hair and a single tarot card: the King of Swords. It matched the Queen of Swords that had been sent to me at Christmas. Was it part of a love spell Elena was trying to cast on me? I shuddered, glad that I'd burned the queen card. But there was no evidence here of spells against Dariya.

I headed to the sickroom and peeked inside. Madame Tomilov was bent over Dariya's bed, her hand on my cousin's cheek. Dariya's breathing was slow but even. The headmistress looked up and frowned when she saw me. "Go to class, Katerina Alexandrovna. There has been no change in her status."

Sighing, I went back downstairs and hurried to my next class before I was missed.

❧

It wasn't long before everyone in the school knew of Dariya's mysterious illness. Later that morning, Aurora Demidova passed out in French class, and during the lunch hour, two of the servants fell ill. I tried to return to the sickroom to check on Dariya, but Madame Metcherskey would not excuse me from my music lessons. She glared at me for an agonizing hour as I practiced my scales on the harp. With a rebellious, and possibly devious, impulse, I played the chords as loud as I could. If I had to play the harp, I would make sure the angels in heaven heard me.

My fingers were bleeding by the time the class was over and I could finally leave and visit the sickroom.

Dariya was lying as still as death in her bed, but her cold light had not changed. The bright swirls wrapped around her like a snowy-white cocoon. Beside her, Madame Orbellani sat reading a book. She looked up and smiled sadly. "No change, my dear," she said. "Have you visited the chapel to light a candle for your cousin?"

I shook my head sadly. "I wanted to see her first." I picked up Dariya's cold hand. She was still breathing, but it was very shallow. "What did the doctor say?"

Madame Orbellani shrugged. "Dr. Gallitzin said only that he believes the girls have influenza, and that he would return in the morning to check in on them."

Aurora Demidova slept on a nearby cot, her face as pale as Dariya's and her hands even colder.

"What does he recommend as treatment?" I asked. I noticed a porcelain bowl with dried blood in it slid partially under Aurora's cot. Had the doctor decided to bleed them both? I drew the blanket back to search my cousin's arms, but there were no cut marks. I sighed in relief.

Madame Orbellani put a hand on my shoulder. "I know

you are worried for Dariya Yevgenievna. And the other girls. But you must allow the doctor to do what he thinks is best. No meddling, Katerina Alexandrovna."

~§~

I was awake all night, my thoughts racing in my head. Elena slept soundly, I noticed. She seemed remarkably healthy. The cold light that surrounded her was nothing but a faint gray mist.

I did not believe for one moment that Dr. Gallitzin was right. My cousin was not suffering from flu. There had been no fever or cough, no other reports of influenza in St. Petersburg.

I knew Elena was responsible somehow. She'd been mad at Dariya for disparaging her family. But I couldn't make sense of Aurora and the two servants. I doubted Elena even knew the servant girls existed. And why hadn't I become ill? I was the focus of her attention more often than not. She wanted something from me. Was she trying to frighten me?

I could not sleep, so I saw no point in lying in bed any longer. I pulled on my wrap and looked out the window at the pale gray sky. Creeping quietly down the hall, I peeked in the room where Dariya and Aurora were both sleeping. The cold light enshrouding them had not changed in its intensity overnight. The light gave me no clue to the nature of the illness. Was it caused by a contagion or by a Montenegrin spell? Without any firm evidence of supernatural causes, I had to assume that it was a natural illness, and that it could be cured. Dariya was moaning softly in her sleep, and I could see the glistening beads of sweat on her brow. Madame Orbellani dozed in the chair beside them, oblivious to the world.

I didn't like the way Dariya looked. She did not seem to be improving at all.

The large clock downstairs chimed five. It would be hours before breakfast time. Returning to my room and quietly getting dressed, I decided to sneak out to speak with Dr. Kruglevski. Whatever was wrong with the girls, surely he would be the best man to examine my cousin and the other patients.

The large front hall was dark and quiet. The heavy front door locked from within and was guarded by an elderly doorman, who still wore his faded black uniform from his younger days in the regiments. I waited until he left his post to make his rounds, then quietly unlocked the door and slipped outside.

The late-January morning was bitterly cold, but I did not mind. The Smolny Gardens were beautiful in their icy barrenness. I skipped past them and turned down Slonovaya Ulitsa. Crossing through the Peski District, I passed sleeping town houses and newly constructed apartment buildings. There were few sleighs about this early in the morning. I hoped I looked like some poor factory girl on her way to work. Nobody bothered me.

The Oldenburg Hospital was just beyond the Greek church. Dr. Kruglevski liked to make rounds on his patients before going to his research lab every morning.

The nurses, in their flowing white habits, did not look

happy to see me. A stout, grim-faced nurse met me at the front door. "Our patients are sleeping! Come back during visiting hours!" she told me.

I shook my head, teeth chattering. "I am here to see Dr. Kruglevski."

"Are you ill, child? Where are your parents?"

I wasn't sure if being the daughter of the hospital's patron would help me or hinder me at this time of the day. I coughed a little. "Please, madam, I am from the Smolny Institute. I've been feverish and restless all night." I had no idea who would be maddest when they discovered my charade: the nurses, my parents, or the headmistress at Smolny. I shivered.

The nurse noticed and quickly hurried me inside. "Come along, then. It's much warmer in here, by the stove. Dr. Kruglevski is already making rounds. He can see you in just a moment." She sat me by the fire, wrapped me in a woolen blanket, and handed me a hot mug of tea before bustling off to take care of the patients on the ward.

The doctor recognized me instantly. "Duchess! What in heavens are you doing here at such an hour?" he asked. "Is your mother well?"

Drawing the blanket closer around me, I said, "Doctor, some of the students at Smolny have been afflicted with the strangest illness. I've come to beg for your assistance."

The doctor took a cup of tea one of the nurses handed him, and sat in the chair opposite me. "A strange illness? Tell me of the symptoms."

"It starts with stomach pains and general malaise, followed within several hours by coldness in the extremities and muscle weakness," I said. "So far only four girls have become sick, including two servants."

I'd spent my entire study hour the day before trying to discover what the sick servants had in common with Aurora and Dariya. Something that would explain why they were the only four in the school who were ill. I'd not been able to come up with anything.

"It could be food poisoning," the doctor mused, stirring his tea thoughtfully.

"But the illness seems to strike randomly. Madame Metcherskey called for Dr. Gallitzin but he thinks it is a touch of influenza."

"Bah! Gallitzin is a fool. Believes leeches can still cure everything."

I nodded in agreement. The man wasn't open to modern thoughts or treatments.

"Very well, I will come and examine your sick friends. What did your cousin eat last?"

I struggled to think. She had walked with me in the gardens, where we had eaten pieces of rock candy, and then we'd had cold mutton and borscht and lemon tarts for our welcome-back dinner. Dariya had eaten with the rest of us, but she and the others had not become ill until the morning—and had not come into direct contact with any of the other sick girls until they were all confined to the sickroom.

"Come, let us check on your Dariya Yevgenievna," the doctor said. He gave the head nurse instructions to call for his carriage. "I must say it is perplexing," he told me as we waited by the front door. "None of my patients at the hospital have presented with quite the same symptoms that you describe."

The sun was just beginning to come up as we raced through St. Petersburg. I knew Madame Tomilov would frown upon me for leaving the school grounds with no chaperone. I hoped, though, that if my parents were informed, Papa would not be too angry. Sick people needed proper medical care. And there was no way they would get it without my interference.

Madame Metcherskey and Madame Orbellani both met us at the front gate. Madame Metcherskey looked contemptuous, her upper lip curling in disapproval as I hastened out of the carriage. Madame Orbellani, however, seemed relieved to see me. "Katerina Alexandrovna, thank goodness, we have been so worried about you," she said, embracing me before Madame Metcherskey could say anything.

Madame Metcherskey's eyes widened as she saw Dr. Kruglevski exit the carriage. "Young lady, what is the meaning of this?" she asked.

I stepped forward and introduced the doctor to my instructor. "He is Papa's favorite doctor," I said. "I'm sure he can discover what is wrong with Dariya Yevgenievna and the others."

"Please forgive this foolish girl, Doctor, for disturbing you," Madame Metcherskey said, glaring at me. I knew I was going to be punished for this stunt. Severely. But I did not mind, as long as Dariya got better. I had faith that Dr. Kruglevski would know exactly what to do.

"There is nothing to forgive, madame," Dr. Kruglevski said. "If there are ill students within this institute, I must be allowed to examine them. Or I shall consult the tsar to ask permission, and tell him I was denied entrance. Will you be so kind as to take me to them right away?"

Madame Metcherskey began to retort something but closed her mouth into a thin line and turned around. "Follow me, then, if you please. Madame Orbellani, take Katerina to the headmistress's office, if you will."

Madame Orbellani laid a hand on my arm as the doctor followed Madame Metcherskey. "Oh, Katerina, why would you run off and do such a crazy thing? Running down the streets of the city before sunrise? What were you thinking?"

"I was thinking of my sick cousin, and a doctor who I know can help her."

Madame Orbellani sighed as she led me to the mauve sitting room to wait for my scolding. I glanced up at the large portraits hanging in this room. Many princesses had been educated here, and the halls were covered with their likenesses. In this room was a picture of a very young Madame Metcherskey, in her court gown. She had been a beauty when she was younger, and had been a lady-in-waiting for the dowager empress Alexandra Feodorovna. My great-grandmother.

I hated not being with my cousin while Dr. Kruglevski examined her. I was anxious to learn his diagnosis. And what his recommendations for treatment would be.

I glanced at the golden clock on Madame Tomilov's desk, anxious most of all about my scolding. The longer I waited, the more I was convinced that I would be expelled from Smolny. Thoroughly disgraced, my family would send me away to the South of France and I would never have to worry about Danilo or his sisters again.

A sudden thought struck me.

Perhaps there was a school of medicine that accepted women somewhere in the South of France? Somehow, exile from Russia did not sound so bad.

CHAPTER TWELVE

❧

"N ow, Katerina Alexandrovna," Madame Tomilov said, sweeping into the room with her black skirts swishing noisily. "I have been informed of your reckless actions of this morning." The heels of her boots clicked against the wooden floor as she hurried over to the windows and threw open the curtains, letting in the bright midmorning sun.

"Please, madame, could you tell me what Dr. Kruglevski discovered about Dariya?"

"I would not presume to know," she said. "The doctor has deemed it prudent to admit your cousin at the hospital for further examinations."

"Oh! Please let me see her!" I begged. "She will be so frightened in the hospital by herself."

"Certainly not. I have already sent word to Dariya's family. In the meantime, we must discuss your inexcusable behavior this morning with your parents. I have also sent them a message, asking them to come and speak with me immediately."

"My parents are coming here?" That was unheard of, except in extreme cases of misbehavior. Which, of course, applied to me. I wondered if I should start packing up my belongings.

"You are to return to the classroom until I send for you. Do not discuss either your cousin's illness or your own behavior. I would prefer that you not distress the other students with this news right now. They will learn about Dariya soon enough." With that she picked up a fountain pen and began writing, ignoring me completely.

Quietly, I got up and walked down the hallway to the large classroom. Augusta stopped me in the hall on her way to her German class. "How is Dariya?" she asked.

"They won't tell me," I said, which was partially true. It had been years since any of us had been so ill that we weren't cared for in the sick wing. Even Princess Marija, Elena's older sister, had been tended to here at Smolny instead of taken to a hospital. Perhaps that was why she had not survived.

If I tried to stop worrying about Dariya, I began to worry about myself. I was not sure what my parents would say when they arrived and heard what I had done. I took a deep breath as I opened the classroom door.

Augusta was about to ask me another question when Madame Orbellani beckoned me inside. She did not bother to stop the French lesson as I slid into my desk next to Elena's.

Elena smirked. "You must be mad, Katiya!" she leaned

over to whisper. "I cannot imagine being brave enough to sneak out of Smolny like that!"

"*Mesdemoiselles!*" Madame Orbellani warned. "*Écoutez, s'il vous plaît!*"

I bent my head down and pretended to study my tattered copy of Voltaire. Madame's French droning made me sleepy, and I found myself daydreaming, staring out the large half-moon window at the gray January sky. I wondered if Dr. Kruglevski had found out what was wrong with Dariya yet. If it wasn't influenza, why had it come on so suddenly? Food poisoning came on rapidly—but it seemed to me that more of the students would have been affected. At least none of the other girls had been ill enough to be taken to the hospital. If they all shared the illness, perhaps that boded well for my poor cousin. I hoped that she was on the road to recovery.

"Katerina!" Elena was whispering, trying desperately to get my attention.

Ignoring her, I looked back up at Madame Orbellani, then down at my textbook, and sighed. This was going to be an impossibly long day.

But not as impossibly long as I feared. We were eating lunch in the dining hall when one of the servants summoned me to Madame Tomilov's sitting room. My parents had finally arrived. Erzsebet looked at me sadly and gave my hand a squeeze. "I'll say a prayer for you."

My stomach was twisted into knots. My time of reckoning had come.

Papa was sitting in the red parlor, along with Dr. Kruglevski.

"Where's Maman?" I asked.

"She has taken to her bed," Papa said, his voice short and not a little tired. "What is this all about, Katiya? Madame Tomilov says that you left the institute without a chaperone before breakfast and walked all the way to the hospital?"

I nodded. "Yes, Papa. Dariya was taken ill. I've been so worried about her."

"And Dr. Kruglevski tells me that your good sense has probably saved your cousin's life. Madame Tomilov, I would not have my daughter punished for taking such wise action."

The headmistress was speechless. Her lorgnette fell from her shaking hand. "Your Highness, our rules are meant to be enforced, for the safety of your daughter, and all of the other girls."

I was speechless as well. I'd never heard anyone speak to the headmistress in such a manner.

Dr. Kruglevski spoke up. "Madame Tomilov, Dariya Yevgenievna is in stable condition right now, recovering from a very potent poison. If Katerina Alexandrovna had not called for me, her cousin would have certainly succumbed to the poison's very lethal effects."

The headmistress looked stricken. "Poison? *Mon Dieu*, not here at the institute. That is impossible!"

Dr. Kruglevski nodded. "I'm afraid it is so, madame. I have not been able to detect all the components of the poison yet, but I am sure we'll be able to come up with an antidote soon. I will need to obtain blood specimens from the other sick girls as well to make a comparison."

Papa leaned forward. "Madame Tomilov, I suggest you

move quickly to determine the culprit, before any more girls are harmed."

The headmistress turned pale as a ghost. "What shall we do? What if it is one of the cooking staff?" She rang a little brass bell on her desk, and soon Madame Orbellani came in.

"*Oui*, madame?"

"His Imperial Highness and Dr. Kruglevski believe that there is a criminal within the walls of Smolny. Possibly in the kitchen. Dariya Yevgenievna has been poisoned."

"That cannot be!" Madame Orbellani said with dismay. "Our cook staff has been working at Smolny for years. None in our kitchen would do such an evil thing."

Papa and Dr. Kruglevski exchanged looks. They must have already discussed this between themselves. "What about the rest of the staff? Has anyone been newly hired?"

Madame Tomilov nodded, frowning. "We took on several new staff members for this school year. However, they all came with excellent references."

"They must all be brought forward for questioning," Papa said.

❧

Of course the interrogation of the staff at Smolny revealed nothing and only upset the servants. The cook was indignant and refused to make anything but porridge and brown bread for two days. The truth about the strange illness spread quickly through the institute. Everyone knew that Dariya and Aurora had been poisoned. No one else displayed any similar symptoms after that.

By that evening, Aurora had begun to show some signs of color and was able to eat a little broth. The servant girls quickly showed signs of returning to normal as well. Their cold lights were barely visible to me when I visited the sick-room that night.

I needed to visit the hospital and see Dariya. But now I was forbidden even to take afternoon walks away from the institute. Papa said I was not to leave the school unless accompanied by him or Maman. I would be going home in a few weeks to attend the Anichkov Ball with my parents. It was the one ball of the season where both Light and Dark Court members paid homage to the empress.

In the meantime, I feared Elena would poison someone else. I had to find a way to stop her.

CHAPTER THIRTEEN

❧

As it happened, I got permission to leave the institute that Friday. The empress's permission, no less. The grand duchess Elizabeth was entertaining her Hessian family members for the season and wished to organize a skating party for her sister Princess Alix. Maman said I'd been invited because the grand duchess had noticed me at the Blessing of the Water.

Elena was most vexed. "The tsarevitch will be there!" she wailed. "Promise that you will speak of me to him. Say something like 'The princess Elena is the most graceful skater I have ever seen. She looks like a swan gliding across the ice.'"

I rolled my eyes. "I will do no such thing," I said as I dressed in my warmest Smolny outfit, a white woolen dress with red braiding. I wore my thickest wool stockings, the ones that scratched my legs like mad. I wished the grand duchess had not spoken with me at the Theophany ceremony.

Dariya, I thought mournfully, *would have truly enjoyed an outing like this*. At least Madame Orbellani said they'd received a note saying my cousin was doing better. She'd been able to sit up and take a little broth the previous day. I hoped she would be able to return to Smolny soon.

Anya twisted my hair into a low chignon, so as to keep it out of my face while I skated. "Best not anger her, Your Highness," she whispered, referring to Elena. "You don't want to be her next victim."

We were both certain of Elena's guilt, but what could I do? I had no proof. I could not go to the headmistress and accuse a king's daughter of attempted murder. Anya was right. Elena could well decide to poison me next. And the Montenegrins could cause far more harm to my family than I could to any of them. I needed to speak with Princess Cantacuzene again. Perhaps she was not so mad after all.

The grand duchess and her sister were in the sleigh waiting for me. The footman held my hand and helped me in. "Your Imperial Highness, Your Highness," I said, trying to curtsy before I sat down.

"Alix, this is Katerina Alexandrovna of Oldenburg. Katerina, my sister, Princess Alix of Hesse."

Alix looked just like her older sister, with hair slightly lighter than the grand duchess's. But her eyes were a clear gray-blue, whereas the grand duchess had one clear blue eye and one with a large brown spot.

Princess Alix smiled shyly and took my hand. "It is a

pleasure to meet you," she said. "Please forgive my English. My French is not so good."

"Not at all, Your Highness. How do you like Russia?"

She smiled again. "It is very beautiful. Do you like to skate?" She twisted the pearl ring on her finger, then switched to fiddling with the kid gloves in her lap. She looked painfully shy.

I nodded. "I love to skate, but unfortunately I am extremely uncoordinated. You will be able to laugh at me, for I shall fall many times."

A look of something like relief passed across the princess's face and then was gone. Suddenly, I realized why I'd been invited on this outing. The grand duchess had noticed my clumsiness at the Blessing of the Waters. I was here to make Princess Alix look graceful.

"The rest of our group is already at the gardens," Grand Duchess Elizabeth said. She reached over and patted her sister's hand comfortingly.

They had closed the gardens to the general public for the afternoon, with four large Cossacks standing guard at the front gate. The grand duchess Xenia Alexandrovna stood with her chaperone and her two older brothers—the tsarevitch, Nicholas Alexandrovich, and the grand duke George Alexandrovich. Him again. I would no doubt have to listen the entire time to his accusations that I was filled with dark magic.

The grand duke did not look happy to see me either. After a short, civil greeting, he stayed as far away from me as possible.

A string quartet, bundled in their furs, sat at the pavilion and played music from *Swan Lake* while we skated across the frozen pond in the center of the park. When I finished buckling on my skates, I took a deep breath, inhaling the chilly air deep into my chest, and wobbled steadily onto the ice.

I skated better that afternoon than I usually did, but I was still able to make Princess Alix look like an angel of grace—until Xenia Alexandrovna decided to show off her fae bloodline. She made both me and the German princess look as clumsy as bears on skates.

Xenia's eyes twinkled from their normal brown to a startling icy silver as she tossed her fur muff onto the bench. She took off across the ice, her slender arms stretched out as if she could take to the air at any minute. "Nicky!" she called out. "Race me!"

Princess Alix had not noticed the eerie change in Xenia's eyes, which was most fortunate. The change in the tsarevitch's eyes from a steely blue to silver was much more subtle. And she missed that as well, because she and Grand Duchess Elizabeth were talking to George Alexandrovich, who was still not wearing any skates.

With his brother and sister racing around the frozen pond at almost inhuman speeds, he was telling Alix and Elizabeth that one of his skates had a broken buckle and that he was more than happy just to stand and watch the rest of us. He glanced directly at me as he said this.

I turned away from him, preferring to watch the tsarevitch and Xenia. The ice sparkled as they roared past me. I smiled and waved to them.

On her next pass, Xenia let go of Nicholas and grabbed

my arms. "Your turn to race me!" she cried. Once again, her eyes were their normal chocolaty brown. Had I imagined the silver earlier? She tore off with me at speeds I dared not contemplate under my own power. I wobbled and wavered but stayed upright.

I survived. I didn't even fall. But nobody on the ice that day would have given me compliments on my style.

Thank goodness Elena had not been invited. I shuddered to think what kind of mischief she would have caused. Especially if she had seen the way Nicholas Alexandrovich looked at Princess Alix.

The tsarevitch did not leave the princess's side for the rest of the afternoon. The grand duchess Elizabeth watched over them approvingly. George Alexandrovich watched them as well, with obvious dismay. He took a break every now and then only to scowl at me.

Xenia and I had fun racing back and forth from one end of the pond to the other. Our cheeks were red and chapped before long, our breathing heavy from the vigorous exercise and from laughing so hard. My ears were so cold they hurt. Xenia, of course, beat me every time, even without her fey gift. I was not destined to be an artist on ice, ever.

We stopped after what seemed like hours and sat down at the pavilion in front of the samovar the servants had brought with us. Instead of tea, we had steaming cups of hot cocoa with freshly baked pastries.

"Will you be coming to the ball at Anichkov Palace next week?" Xenia asked me.

"Yes, Your Imperial Highness," I said. I took a sip of cocoa. "I will be attending with my parents."

"Wonderful!" Then she pouted. "Maman says I will be able to attend for a little while but will not be allowed to dance." Xenia still had a few years before she would be old enough to be out in society.

"But you will have a wonderful time nonetheless," Elizabeth said. "You will get to wear your beautiful dress and hear the music. And you will see Alix in her lovely Worth gown." Elizabeth looked at the tsarevitch over her cup of cocoa. "Alix looks lovely in lavender, don't you think, Nicholas?"

"Oh, yes," Nicholas said dreamily.

Alix blushed and smiled shyly.

"Have you ever written a love poem?" Xenia asked me in a whisper.

I smiled and shook my head. "No. I've never met a boy that inspired any poetry," I whispered back. "Have you?"

She nodded, her eyes twinkling. "Many times! I adore poems!" She sipped her cocoa and looked at her brother thoughtfully. "Do you think Alix might write a poem for Nicky? They seem to like each other a lot, but Nicky is twenty. She is closer to George's age."

I almost choked on my pastry. A poem to the tsarevitch, I could understand. A poem to his surly brother, I could not. Everyone looked up at me. I could feel my face flushing. Why was I so socially awkward?

Grand Duchess Ella hurried to refill my cup. "Here, drink this, dear."

I stopped coughing long enough to swallow the cocoa. "Thank you."

Xenia had turned to ask her aunt if she had a favorite poet. They were discussing French and English Romantics.

I looked at Alix and Nicholas, still in their own little world across the table from us. Grand Duke George Alexandrovich would never do for her. I glanced over to see him staring thoughtfully at his brother as well. I could see the concern in his eyes. Xenia still believed in love. George was old enough to understand that tsarevitchs were not allowed to marry for love. And neither were most grand dukes.

The string quartet began to play again, and Alix and Nicholas stood up to return to the ice.

One of the imperial guards approached George Alexandrovich and bowed. "Your skate has been repaired, Your Imperial Highness."

Grand Duchess Elizabeth smiled. "Excellent! Now you can skate a turn with Katerina Alexandrovna!"

It pained him, I could tell, but he put on his skates and bowed to her, then offered his arm to me. "It would be an honor, Your Highness," he said.

I stood up and curtsied and took his arm, much to Xenia's merriment. I heard her giggling as we glided out across the ice. The grand duchess skated with Xenia so she would not feel left out.

The grand duke was silent as we completed our first circuit, his arm stiffly linked with mine. Ahead of us, Alix and Nicholas were smiling and chatting gaily in English.

We managed to make our spins around the pond with no body contact other than our linked arms—something I was grateful for, but also a little sad about at the same time. "How kind of the grand duchess Elizabeth for organizing a pleasant afternoon for us," I said finally, to break the silence.

"Are you truly enjoying yourself? Is this your idea of a pleasant afternoon?"

I immediately thought of a thousand better ways to spend my afternoon. Cleaning up after my brother's horse came to mind. Instead, I said, "It is a beautiful day. I greatly admire the grand duchess and your sister is very kind. I never met Princess Alix before, but she seems kind as well."

"You don't find her enigmatic?"

"What do you mean?"

"In some ways, she is much like you. Her aura is also tainted with dark secrets."

"Do you think my aura is really so dark?" I gave a little laugh, even though there was nothing amusing about his words. "And have you discovered what it is that I conceal?"

"I will discover your secret one day, Duchess."

Something in me snapped. I pulled my arm away from his and skidded to a stop. "May I enlighten you, Your Imperial Highness?" I hissed, hoping no one could overhear us. "The princess Alix and I are witches from hell. We have come to collect the souls of both you and your brother to give to the devil himself." The sad thing was that it didn't sound quite as ridiculous as I had intended.

I stared at him, horrified that I could have said something so stupid to the tsar's son. Why did I always seem to lose all sense of reason when I was around him?

Fortunately, he looked amused. "You are such an odd girl," he said, taking my arm again and coaxing me to skate forward. I relaxed a little, knowing he was not taking my inappropriate jest seriously. "Be careful, though, Duchess."

110

His voice was hushed, but icy in my ear. "They still burn witches in Russia."

I couldn't keep myself from shuddering, though whether it was from his threat or just from the closeness of him I couldn't be sure.

I tried to steer our conversation away from witches. "Anyway, I do not believe the Hessian princess conceals anything, except her own shyness," I said. "Her infatuation for your brother shines on her face." I saw nothing unusual in her cold light. It was the same intensity as the tsarevitch's.

"Perhaps," George said as we made one last turn around the pond. Alix and Nicholas had already returned to the pavilion, and they waved to us. "But I see a soul in despair when I look at the princess."

"She lost her mother when she was eight, did she not? As well as her younger siblings? Surely that would cause a lasting despair."

"Perhaps."

"Your sister likes her," I pointed out as Xenia and her aunt skated toward us.

George frowned. "Xenia is a hopeless romantic." His sister's eyes flashed again as she broke free from Elizabeth and sped past us in a silver blur. "And extremely irresponsible," he added with a sigh.

The grand duke led me gracefully back to the pavilion, one of his hands barely touching the small of my back. "That was most enjoyable, Your Highness," he said, lying beautifully.

"My pleasure," I answered with a quick curtsy. I could

sense his relief that our skating had come to an end. His rigid posture seemed to relax as he sat down close to his brother and the German princess.

I felt the same relief as I sat near his sister. Xenia was pouting at the table, holding a cup of cocoa.

"I wish I could have skated longer, but Aunt Ella thought I was getting too cold. You two looked lovely together. Did you see Nicky and Alix?"

"They skate together beautifully," I said wistfully. They did make a handsome couple. I envied the German princess just a little, because she belonged here so much more than I did. I would never be accepted by the Light Court. Not with the darkness inside me.

The servants were gathering up our things as we took off our skates. Grand Duchess Elizabeth was already in her fashionable footwear and was speaking with Alix by the park gate, where Elizabeth's imperial carriage waited beside the impressive black imperial carriage, with its golden crest of a double-headed eagle on the door.

"Thank you so much for coming!" Xenia said to me. "We shall see you next week!"

I made one last quick curtsy to her and her brothers before following Elizabeth and Alix into Elizabeth's carriage.

Alix seemed to relax on our drive back to Smolny. Her smile came a little easier when I asked if she'd had a pleasant time. "I love being outdoors, especially in the winter," she said.

"Will I see you at the Anichkov Ball next week?"

"Of course, my dear," the grand duchess said, though I could have sworn I saw Princess Alix frown.

And then it was gone and she smiled again. "I am looking forward to it. I have only attended a few balls in Darmstadt."

"Au revoir, Your Imperial Highness," I said to the grand duchess, as I got out of the carriage at the Smolny gate. "Auf Wiedersehen, Your Highness," I said with a final wave to Princess Alix.

❦

Elena pounced on me as soon as I returned to our room. "Did the tsarevitch ask after me? What did you tell him? What did he wear? Did he skate with you?"

I ignored her until I could hear from Augusta that there had been no further word from the hospital on Dariya's condition. Augusta pointed out that that was a good sign. We'd have heard instantly if Dariya had taken a turn for the worse.

She was right. Reassured, I patiently told my friends everything about the outing and everything I knew about Princess Alix of Hesse. Except for the grand duke's suspicions. The girls immediately seized on my description of how well Alix and the tsarevitch had gotten on together. Elena's dance with him at the Smolny Ball was long forgotten.

Elena was not happy. She threw her hairbrush across the room, and it hit the wall with a loud thud. "No!" she cried. "He belongs to me!" She flung herself down on her bed and sobbed.

I looked at Elena, then at the other girls, who quickly left our room. I hoped Elena would not make a scene at the Anichkov Ball. Or cast another spell on the tsarevitch.

CHAPTER FOURTEEN

❧

Several mornings later, the Smolny dining room was buzzing over breakfast with alarming news. Crown Prince Rudolfe of Austria had killed his lover and himself! Although no one knew the whole story, rumors were flying throughout the school.

The Bavarian princesses sobbed as they packed their trunks and were hastily dispatched back to Austria-Hungary for their uncle's funeral. Erzsebet was upset she would miss the ball. "I didn't even like the crown prince," she sobbed as she and her sister, Augusta, climbed into the carriage to take them to the train station. "Please write and tell me all about it," she called out the window. Elena and I both promised.

"There may not be a ball, girls," Madame Orbellani said as we all walked back inside after seeing them off. "St. Petersburg should go into mourning out of respect for the Austrian emperor and his wife."

"No ball?" Elena cried. "That would be horrible!"

Madame Orbellani shrugged. "What if it was your own brother who had died in such a tragedy?"

"He would never do anything so dishonorable," Elena said, stomping off to the dance hall.

Madame Orbellani sighed as we followed her. The servants had already draped the front parlor with black crepe.

"Does anyone know why he did it?" I asked her. I couldn't imagine killing someone you supposedly loved, then killing yourself.

Madame Orbellani shook her head. "No one knows. I am certain we will hear many stories, though, in the weeks to come, before anyone ever discovers the real truth. It is not your concern. You have other responsibilities. Now hurry along, or you'll be late for dance lessons."

"But if there's not going to be a ball, why do I need lessons?" I protested. I had a new medical journal from Papa that I was eager to read. An article about the circulatory system looked particularly interesting.

"There will always be balls, Katerina Alexandrovna. Perhaps not this month, or even the next, but soon St. Petersburg will dance again. And my girls will be the best dancers there."

Mon Dieu, she spoke as if it were our patriotic duty to dance. I thought about it and sighed. Perhaps it was. It was certainly one of the things most expected of us.

Madame Metcherskey handed everyone a black armband. Then she played a waltz by Strauss in honor of the crown prince. So much for our remembrance of the dead.

Elena looked as if she'd been crying heavily. Her eyes

were puffy and red. "What if there is no ball?" she whispered to me. "Do you really think the empress will cancel it?"

"It would be the right thing to do," I said.

"Yes, but the empress hates the Austrians. Do you remember last year when the tsar's great aunt died and the Austrian ambassador held the ball the night of her wake? The empress was furious. She will not forget their callousness."

"But this was the heir of Austria-Hungary! And she is the empress—not some mannerless ambassador."

Elena shook her head, trying to keep time in the waltz. "I hope she is vindictive. I know I would be if I were empress."

I sighed inwardly, praying I would never see the Montenegrin princess as empress of all the Russians. Elena could be extremely vengeful indeed. The very thought of her with the full power of the Russian throne behind her frightened me. It would not be bad just for me—it would be bad for all of Russia.

❧

There was one bright spot on that dark day. My cousin Dariya had returned that afternoon from the hospital. She looked much thinner and paler than ever before, but I was relieved to have her back at Smolny again.

She smiled as I hugged her, but seemed distant. She was anxious to talk with Aurora Demidova, however. After saying hello to everyone else, she disappeared with Aurora for a walk in the gardens.

The dinner hall that night was somber, even though the

servants had not bothered to drape it in black crepe. Everyone was depressed and worried that there would be no dancing, no ballets or operas to attend.

"*Mon Dieu*, there is more to life than dancing," I said over our bland and watery vegetable soup.

"Oh, no, Katiya, surely you are joking!" Aurora said from the end of the table.

"The Anichkov Ball was the only thing that gave me hope while I was lying in that dismal hospital," Dariya said. "I might as well have died if there won't be a ball."

"Dariya!" I said. "Don't even joke about that!"

She laughed. I took it as a sign of recovery and let the moment pass.

In the few hours since Dariya had returned from the hospital, she and Aurora had fast become close confidantes. They sat together now, whispering and giving Elena dark looks. But neither one dared accuse her of anything openly. I felt left out, even though I realized that both girls had been poisoned, and I had not. It troubled me that so much had changed between my cousin and me in such a short time.

That night, Elena stayed up late, reading what looked like her book of French poetry. But I heard her mumbling softly by candlelight as I drifted off to sleep, and the words she chanted were not French.

CHAPTER FIFTEEN

Whatever dark magic Elena had worked during the night, if it had involved the ball, it appeared to have been successful. For the next morning, everyone at Smolny knew that there would still be an Anichkov Ball. Empress Marie Feodorovna insisted that it not be canceled, but that everyone come dressed in proper mourning attire—all black. Women were not to wear colored gems, but only diamonds and pearls. Elena was ecstatic. Her sisters brought a seamstress by that afternoon to take her measurements for a proper black ball gown.

My mother also sent for me and brought me to the house, where her favorite dressmaker could fit us both. With her dark coloring, a black gown would look dramatic on her. Maman could not wear her beloved ruby tiara, but she had a delicate diamond one from Cartier that was just as lovely.

My dress was short sleeved and off the shoulders, with jet beading and black lace across the bodice. Maman called me to her boudoir on the evening of the ball and gave me a pair of my grandmother's diamond earrings to wear.

"These will draw attention up toward your eyes," she said. "Grandmaman Marie would be so proud of you."

"For what?"

Maman sighed. I knew it gave her grief when I did not act as excited about glamorous occasions as she expected. I did not see how dressing up like a painted doll was an accomplishment to be proud of. Would my grandmother have been proud of me if I had discovered a cure for consumption? Or would she have preferred me to look pretty and decorate the arm of a husband with a title?

I shrugged. I was certain I knew the answer to that question. And it wasn't an answer I liked. "They are beautiful, Maman," I said to appease her. I spun around a few times before sitting down to have my hair done. The dress truly was stunning, even though it did make me look paler than normal.

Papa and my brother were both attired in their finest regiment blacks. Petya was still sad about the death of Count Chermenensky, and the mourning wear he sported, a black silk armband against his dress uniform, had deeper meaning to him than any of ours did to us.

I wanted to cheer Petya up, so I promised I would find him a partner at the ball.

He gave me a wistful smile. "There is no one I would dance with tonight. Besides you, my dear sister."

"You shall have it," I said, disappointed that I could not lighten his spirits.

We rode to Anichkov Palace in the black Oldenburg

carriage. It was drawn by four spirited black horses that looked as if they'd driven straight out of hell. The night was icy cold, even with the hot-water bottles in our laps, the fur-lined coach rugs, and the warmed bricks at our feet. The streets were crowded, as most of St. Petersburg was on its way to the ball.

"I don't want you stashing yourself away with your Smolny friends tonight," Maman said. "I want to see you dancing with lots of handsome young princes and grand dukes."

I rolled my eyes and stared out the window at the snow-covered city. I resolved to dance with the ugliest and the poorest men in the ballroom—if they should ask me.

Our carriage approached the northern entrance of the palace, where the nobles were to arrive. There were four separate entrances to the palace, one for the princes, one for the other court ranks, one for the officers, and one for the civil servants. The gates of the palace were draped in heavy black crepe, as were the marble corridors leading inside. Even the candelabras along the walls and the chandeliers were swathed in black gauze.

Papa took Maman's arm, and my brother took mine. We slowly proceeded up the enormous marble staircase behind other noble families, waiting to be announced by the dance master. I noticed the Cantacuzene family being introduced. "Isn't the princess looking lovely and spry tonight?" Maman whispered. "She looks younger than she did before Christmas. I wonder what medicinals she takes."

Seeing the princess made me realize I was not wearing her ring that evening. The black stone would have gone well with my gown, but I'd left it in my trinket box at Smolny. I hoped the princess would not ask me about it.

When it was my family's turn, we stopped at the entrance to the grand ballroom. The master of ceremonies banged his large wooden baton against the floor as he stood in front of the archway and announced us to the crowd.

"Prince Alexander Friedrich Constantine von Holstein-Gottorp, Duke of Oldenburg; his honorable wife, Princess Yevgenia Maximilianovna von Leuchtenberg; his son, Duke Peter Alexandrovich von Holstein-Gottorp; and his daughter, Duchess Katerina Alexandrovna von Holstein-Gottorp."

It sounded impressive, but we were far from the most illustrious of families present that night. Very, very far. I was able to claim Catherine the Great as my great-great-great-grandmother, but so could hundreds of others present. Even Princess Elena, the fifth daughter of a minor sovereign, outranked me.

Elena and her two ebony-clad sisters pounced on me immediately. "Katerina!" Elena said breathlessly. "There is someone we want you to meet!" The Montenegrins' dark coloring looked beautiful against their black gowns. The elder princesses wore jet beaded *kokoshniks*, but Elena wore her hair up simply, with a few flirtatious curls cascading down the back.

My stomach twisted into knots as she grabbed my arm. I suddenly remembered Elena telling me her brother had come to St. Petersburg for the season. I tried to smile. I would not let them see my fear.

"Danilo, may I present the duchess Katerina of Oldenburg? Katerina, this is my brother Prince Danilo." She placed my gloved hand into his.

"I am charmed," the young man said.

Mon Dieu, he looked more dashing than his portrait. His smile was dazzling. It took my breath away. He had an instant pull on me. I could feel the attraction that his good looks and something more stirred in my heart.

Then I remembered my nightmares of chanting and blood, and stiffened my resolve. I would not be so easily charmed, I hoped.

I curtsied. "As am I, Your Highness." Despite my determination, I felt a little bit dizzy as he touched my hand to his lips. Every bone in that hand tingled. Every carpal. Every metacarpal. Right down to the tips of every phalanx. It must have been the heat of the room. I fanned myself just to get some air.

"Would you do me the honor of the first dance?" the prince asked. His eyes gleamed under the brilliant candlelight, and my pulse took off racing as he looked at me.

"Of course," I said without stopping to think. I smiled, then saw the princess Cantacuzene staring at me across the ballroom. She looked very concerned. But I couldn't believe that Danilo was the heir of the Vladiki, or that he was the dangerous prince she believed I must kill.

"Come with us," Elena said as she grabbed her brother with one arm and me with her other. "We must find the best spot on the dancing floor. We want everyone to see us!"

"Do you have a partner for the first dance?" I asked her. "If not, I am sure my brother would be honored—"

Elena shook her head and let go of both of us. "Do not worry about me! I have the most handsome partner here tonight, besides Danilo, of course!"

Danilo smiled again, showing perfect white teeth. There were no fangs, I noticed. But would he not grow fangs until his . . . ascension, as the princess Cantacuzene called it? It seemed a ridiculous story, and I wondered why I'd ever thought such dark thoughts about the crown prince. Even when I knew his sisters had done terrible things in St. Petersburg, I did not want to believe he was anything but the handsome young royal he appeared to be.

I felt his closeness, the warmth from his body. It made me shiver a little. That was when I told myself he might be an even greater spell caster than his sister, without even trying. He stirred my senses. I found myself wanting to know more about him.

As the first sounds of the polonaise played, I realized Elena was no longer standing next to me. The tsar and the empress glided around the ballroom, taking the first turn of the first dance. The ballroom was beautiful, and very elegant, draped in its black crepe. There were no flowers to decorate the tables, only white candles. The room sparkled with the candlelight reflected by the thousands of diamonds worn by all the ladies. In a severe way, it was even more beautiful than usual.

As the tsar and his wife finished their first sweep around the hot and crowded ballroom, the tsarevitch stepped onto the floor with his partner on his arm. Elena. I wondered why in heaven he'd asked her for the first dance when he most likely wished to dance with the princess Alix.

I looked around for her. The Hessian princess was nowhere to be seen.

The grand duchess Xenia joined in next, dancing with her Greek cousin, Prince Nicholas, and then soon everyone was swarming the dance floor. I wondered where the grand duke George was. Why was he not dancing the polonaise?

At the far end of the ballroom, I saw my cousin Dariya, on the arm of a sharply dressed cadet from the Corps des Pages. She gave a little wave, but her smile faded and her eyes grew wide as she noticed my partner. Then she disappeared from my view behind the hundreds of dancing couples.

"Shall we?" Prince Danilo asked. I noticed that his piercing black eyes were fringed with the longest lashes I'd ever seen. All thoughts of everyone else flew from my head. I felt a dizzying rush of delight.

"Of course," I said, taking his arm. My heart beat wildly as our hands touched.

Prince Danilo was devastatingly handsome. And he danced well. I found myself reveling in the feel of his arms around me. Dancing with him was almost like flying. I saw the faces of several people as we twirled around: I noticed Maman and Papa dancing. Papa looked as if he'd rather be shot, but Maman was very happy. Petya was dancing after all, with one of the Stroganova princesses. I could not remember her name, but she was very pretty. The princesses Militza and Anastasia were dancing with their fiancés. Uncle George looked happy and in love. As much as I distrusted the Montenegrins, I had to thank Anastasia for helping him get over his late wife. He'd been mourning her death for far too long.

But I had better things to think of now. I looked up at Danilo and felt all my senses swimming as he smiled at me.

As the polonaise ended, I stepped back, a bit lost as Danilo moved away. His arms were no longer around me, and I wished the dance had gone on forever. Prince Danilo and I clapped politely for the musicians and wandered toward the rotunda, where a wine punch was being served. He brought us both glasses.

"Thank you, Your Highness," I said, grateful for the cold drink. My throat was dry and I was out of breath. But I was certain that it was more than the exercise that had left me so dizzy.

"Thank you, for the wonderful dance," he said, his voice low and hypnotic. "This is my first ball in your beautiful city, and I will never forget it."

I strained to take in his every word. "It is unusual, to be sure," I said. "Most are more colorful than this."

The crown prince pulled my fingers to his lips. "Do not make excuses. The night has been perfect. And my dance partner has bewitched me." He looked at me with his sleepy black eyes as if I were a queen.

I thought I would melt into the floor. I'd never been looked at like that before. It was thrilling and terrifying at the same time.

My heart raced until I thought it would burst. I would have sworn I could feel the heat from his kiss on my gloved hand. The fire raced up my arm and down my spine.

I shook myself as if to break a spell.

That was when I saw the grand duchess Elizabeth with her husband, the grand duke Sergei Alexandrovich, passing us in the hall. I needed some sort of distraction before I lost all my senses.

"Your Imperial Highness, is your sister here tonight?" I asked. "I have not seen her yet."

The grand duchess shook her head. "I am afraid Alix is very unwell today and has stayed in her room resting. We went ice-skating again yesterday, and she is quite fatigued."

"*Mon Dieu*," I said. "Please give her my greetings. I hope to see her again soon."

"Thank you, I will tell her," the grand duchess said kindly. She nodded regally as I introduced her and her husband to the crown prince. Grand Duke Serge Alexandrovich, one of the tsar's younger brothers, was a slim, wiry man with a mustache and beard. He was very possessive of his young wife. Taking her by the arm, he retreated with her to the grand hall.

"I suppose it would be presumptuous of me to ask for a second dance?" Prince Danilo said, smiling his charming smile again.

I couldn't help laughing. He made me feel reckless. Almost enthralled. "It would be very presumptuous," I told him. "But I shall accept, as you are new to the ways of St. Petersburg society."

He grinned and took my arm to lead me back to the ball. Elena was now dancing with one of the officers from my brother's regiment. She was having a grand time.

It was a waltz by Tchaikovsky, a dizzying, breath-stealing

dance, and I was elated to be flying across the ballroom with the heir of Montenegro. The rest of the world fell away from us. I was conscious of nothing except his arms around me, his hands gently holding on to my waist. I wanted the moment to last forever.

But as the waltz ended, I saw Dariya whispering with Aurora Demidova. Surely they knew by now whom I was dancing with, and the speculations would soon start. They saw us heading toward the rotunda and quickly intercepted us. "Katiya!" Dariya said. "I don't believe we've had the pleasure of meeting your beau."

Neither girl was smiling. Both looked at the crown prince with icy disdain.

"Your Royal Majesty, may I present my cousin Dariya Yevgenievna and one of our fellow students, Aurora Demidova? This is Danilo of Montenegro." I looked at Dariya a little guiltily and added, "Elena's brother."

"*Enchanté, mesdemoiselles*," the crown prince said, bowing gallantly with a click of his heels.

Dariya and Aurora both curtsied politely. "How are you enjoying St. Petersburg?" my cousin asked.

"I am enjoying it very much," Crown Prince Danilo said, staring at me. I could feel my cheeks burning with embarrassment. "But perhaps I have monopolized your beautiful cousin for too long?" He turned his dazzling smile on Dariya.

She must not have been quite so immune to his charms, for she finally smiled. "There are so many other girls here tonight eager to dance with you, Your Majesty," she said.

"Then I would not want to break their hearts. Katerina Alexandrovna, I regret that I must leave you now."

I curtsied to the crown prince as he gallantly kissed my hand once more and disappeared back into the throng.

Dariya linked her arm with mine, saying in a low voice, "Really, Katiya! What were you thinking? Elena's brother!"

I sighed. "He's so much nicer than she is." I caught myself searching the crowd for him. I couldn't help wondering who he was dancing with now. Was she prettier than I?

"Elena poisoned me!" Dariya whispered. "And Aurora and who knows how many others at Smolny. Now she wants her brother to get to know you? What do you think her motives are?"

I shrugged, but I promised my cousin that I would be more careful around Elena and her handsome brother. Aurora accepted the hand of a Serbian prince for the next dance, so Dariya and I went in search of refreshments. We ran into my mother and the grand duchess Miechen.

Maman did not look happy. "Please do not cause a scandal tonight, Katiya. Princess Radziwill and the rest of the gossips are already talking about you and that young man. Two dances? Really!" She shook her ebony-handled fan in agitation.

The grand duchess said nothing but looked down her nose at me with her violet-blue eyes. I was certain she already knew my mysterious partner's identity. She probably also knew whatever it was his family wanted from me.

With a heavy sigh, I decided to be prudent and dance with as many different eligible bachelors as I could the rest of the evening. Unfortunately, none of them were terribly ugly. Or terribly poor.

When it was time for dinner, I was not at the same table as my parents but seated instead with my older cousins the grand dukes Nicholas and Peter Nikolayevich, and the princess Cantacuzene. Elena was the only other young person seated with us.

"Whoever made the seating arrangements should be exiled to Siberia," Elena said, pouting. She gazed longingly at the imperial table several times as the tsarevitch frequently laughed at his brother's jokes. George Alexandrovich, I noticed, never looked my way once throughout dinner. The grand duchess Elizabeth and her husband were seated at the same table as Tsar Alexander and his wife. The grand duchess's father and brother were seated at the same table as my parents and Petya. Dariya was seated with them also and laughed as she spoke with the Hessian prince. She looked up at me and gave me a little wave.

I told Elena to hush; our fate could be much worse. At the table next to us sat at least seven elderly dames, all shouting and grumbling loudly because they could not hear each other speaking.

Elena rolled her eyes but kept her peace.

The meal was delicious, served by men in crisp black liveries. Even the china was a formal mourning pattern, with a wide black band around the imperial crest. Elena was silent through most of the meal, as was I, for we were not seated next to each other and had little to say to the older grand dukes.

Princess Cantacuzene fussed over her vegetables and complained that her meat was overcooked. She was favorably impressed with the dessert course, however, and tried to eat the grand duke Nicholas Nikolayevich's sorbet when she had finished her own. I sighed, thinking she truly was senile. I decided to ignore her dire warnings about the handsome crown prince of Montenegro.

Elena and I were grateful to escape when we saw the tsar and the empress stand at their own table. With relief, we hurried back toward the ballroom.

"So what do you think of my brother?" Elena said. She had been bursting to ask me this all night.

I could feel my cheeks growing hot. "I think he is very nice. I am glad he came to the ball tonight."

Elena laughed. "He thinks you are very nice too."

I cannot explain the way my heart made a funny little jump when she said that. Perhaps I was having a palpitation? I placed my hand over my chest to calm it down. "Will he be staying in St. Petersburg long?" I asked her.

"At least for the next month. He is going to visit our sister Zorka and her family in Geneva at the end of February."

The orchestra began to play again, and I danced the rest of the night with young officers in Petya's regiment. They were all very handsome and very respectful, but none danced quite as well as my first partner. By the end of the evening, my skirt had several tears where their spurs had caught the hem. Elena complained that her dress shared a similar fate.

I remembered my promise to Petya and danced the last dance with him. Despite his protests, he had overcome his reluctance and had danced with several beautiful princesses and countesses. It did not appear as if any young lady had caught his eye, though.

"Your heir of Montenegro seems to be meeting with your approval after all?" he said, nodding toward the crown prince, who was dancing with his sister Militza.

I blushed. "Perhaps I was too hasty to judge him without meeting him first." But it was as if a fog had lifted once I was away from the crown prince. He did not seem quite so irresistible anymore. "He is handsome enough. But I don't trust him or his family," I whispered. "Princess Cantacuzene said they are blood drinkers. Vampires."

Petya laughed. "Don't be ridiculous. She is a senile old woman with a wild imagination."

I glanced around the room, startled to see the elderly princess staring straight at us—as if she could hear my brother and me talking in the middle of the dancing crowds.

"I've heard nothing about him, good or ill, but I can't say the same for his sisters," Petya went on. "Perhaps you should stay away from that whole family."

"Elena was the one who poisoned Dariya. I'm sure of it."

My brother looked at me in surprise. "You have proof?"

I shook my head. "Of course not," I said. "She's too clever for that."

"Then leave it alone. Elena is the daughter of a king. All the more reason you should not be encouraging the crown prince's attentions."

"I wasn't!" I protested. But I saw that Petya was only half serious, and I pretended to pout. "Maman will be so disappointed. I am sure she is already planning my wedding to the crown prince."

131

Petya rolled his eyes. "She has been plotting your wedding since before you were born."

"Before I was born? With whom?"

My brother's grin was wicked. "The Archduke of Bohemia."

"The prince who is always digging in his ear with his pinky finger?" I asked, cringing. I was glad I'd heard no mention of this growing up.

As the ball ended, I did not see the prince Danilo but found myself a little sad he had not bid me good night. Petya and I found our parents and we slowly followed the crowds down the long grand staircase outside to wait for our carriage. *Le Bal Noir* had been an amazing success, and now the full moon shone brightly across the snow-covered streets, casting a ghostly light.

"Your Highnesses," Princess Militza said as she bowed to my parents. The Montenegrins were standing behind us as they waited for their own carriage. I saw Elena smile and wondered how they had managed to push their way through the crowd.

I introduced my parents and my brother to the crown prince, and my mother hurried to invite him and his sisters over to the house for tea the next week. Petya was polite but cool as he shook Prince Danilo's hand, as was my father. I was thankful no one would notice my blush even in the bright moonlight. A huge full moon had risen high in the clear winter night sky.

Papa did not seem to be impressed one way or the other with the Montenegrins as we chatted, but on the ride home he spoke up. "I hope that young scoundrel does not expect you to live in Montenegro if you marry him," he said.

"Papa!" My voice, to my dismay, was much higher than normal. "No one has said a word about me marrying the crown prince." I settled back into my seat, wrapping my cloak tighter around me. "Besides, I would never leave the two of you, even if I married the Prince of Wales."

My brother snorted at that. He quickly regained his composure as Maman shot him a look that we both could see, even in the dim carriage.

"Let's not be too hasty," Maman warned my father. "I hear Cetinje is a beautiful city."

"I just wanted to make my feelings known on the matter," Papa said gruffly.

I patted his hand. "Do not worry about such things, Papa. It will never happen."

As we made our way down the Palace Embankment, the horses reared, and the carriage shuddered and stopped.

"Good heavens!" Maman said, crossing herself. "What is wrong with those beasts?"

Petya stuck his head out to speak with the driver. He agreed to get out and help calm the horses. As I looked out my window, I saw a silver blur streaking past. "A fox!" I said.

Papa leaned over. "Too big. It looks like a wolf. No wonder the horses are spooked."

It was a beautiful creature, whatever it was, running across the frozen city at midnight.

What surprised me most was the creature's cold light, trailing behind it. I'd never seen an animal with a cold light before.

CHAPTER SIXTEEN

❦

"Balls, balls, balls! I am sick to death of balls!" I let out a large breath as Anya helped me undo my dress and corset and freed me from the elegant torture device. "Much better," I said with a deep sigh. I could finally breathe again.

I had attended three balls in the past two weeks, not to mention a ballet and an opera. I was exhausted. I had an essay on Pushkin due first thing Monday morning, as well as a chemistry test, and I had not studied for it yet. And the winter social season still had two months to go.

"Anya, I'm going to move to Siberia and live in a hut!" I was lying on my bed at home, staring up at the ornate gilded plasterwork on the ceiling. No more balls for me.

"I thought you wanted to be a doctor, Duchess," Anya said, carefully folding my ball gown away. "What about medical school?"

"No medical school in Russia will admit a woman," I said.

"But I could go to Paris. Or Switzerland." I sat up. "Anya, let's run away together."

She shook her head, her eyes wide. "Oh, no, Duchess. We'd get whipped by your father, for sure. Maybe you could marry a doctor and help him out in his office?"

"I don't think I could ever be happy just being a man's helper. And I doubt any suitable husband Maman picks out for me would be the progressive sort who would allow me to attend medical school. No, I think I must run away."

I was only half serious, knowing it would throw Anya into fits. Still, I did worry that my dream might never come true. To enter the University of Zurich's program, one had to prove proficiency in Latin and Greek. I had doubled my efforts in my Latin studies. Madame Orbellani had also found a beginner's Greek textbook for me. It was more difficult than Latin, but I was struggling through it. I was determined to succeed.

⁓≥⁓

I'd seen the handsome prince Danilo and his sisters several times over the past weeks, dancing with him often at the balls. He had been a perfect gentleman and did not act like a blood-drinking vampire at all.

I mentioned the prince to Princess Cantacuzene when Maman and I were invited to a small dinner party—"small" meaning only one hundred or so guests—at the Vladimir Palace. All members of the Dark Court, of course.

"He has not reached the age of his ascension yet," the

princess Cantacuzene told me. "When does he turn eighteen?"

"This June," I told her. We strolled together through the great hallway from the grand Russian-styled dining room to the more intimate and more exotic Persian room. "But what if he doesn't turn into anything? I do not want to kill anyone, Your Highness."

"Are you willing to lay down your own life, then? For he will surely kill you. Or worse, turn you into one of his undead mistresses. You put others at risk as well. Your servants, your family, your children, even."

"Children?"

"If you marry the Montenegrin prince, you will be required to produce heirs for him, Katerina Alexandrovna. Your daughters will become witches, and your sons will become blood drinkers upon their eighteenth birthday. Will you condemn your own children to such a life?"

She stopped walking and grabbed my hand. "You are not wearing my ring! *Mon Dieu*, child! You will not be able to resist his charms if you do not wear the ring!"

The old woman was mad. Even though I suspected the Montenegrins of black magic, I found it difficult to believe Prince Danilo could be capable of any evil. Even Dariya had warmed to him a little, and no longer frowned when she saw the two of us dancing together.

The old woman grabbed my chin with her cold hands and snorted. "Bah, I can see it in your eyes," she said. "You are already in his thrall."

I did not want to believe it. The thought of being under

someone else's control frightened me. I promised her I would wear the obsidian ring from then on.

"Do not eat or drink in the Montenegrins' presence. They will trick you with one of their herbal potions. They put something in that poor man's sorbet at the Anichkov Ball."

I stared at Princess Cantacuzene in shock. Her supposed senility that night had been just a ruse to protect the grand duke! It would not surprise me at all if the Montenegrins had been trying to cast spells on many eligible bachelors that evening. I hoped the tsarevitch was safe. And his brother. I'd not seen Grand Duke George Alexandrovich at any of the recent balls. Of course, we had not attended any that belonged to the Light Court.

But Princess Cantacuzene was still talking about Prince Danilo. "Before his ascension, he is merely a mortal and can die easily. After his ascension, he will not be immortal, but more difficult to destroy. You will have lost your chance."

If only I had some proof that the ancient princess was telling me the truth. My troubled thoughts kept me awake for hours that night. *Think rationally*, I told myself. How would I find scientific proof that my handsome prince was going to turn into a blood drinker on his birthday?

I thought about my dreams.

Dreams are not proof, I reasoned. But Princess Cantacuzene's words had frightened me. I got out of my bed, poked through my jewelry box, and put on the obsidian ring.

CHAPTER SEVENTEEN

⁓⊙⁓

I t was a quiet week at Smolny. There were no social obligations, and I had time to think about Princess Cantacuzene's words. On a cold and gray afternoon, while the
others were huddled in the warm parlor, drinking hot tea
and reading Pushkin's fairy tales, I stayed in the drafty library with my anatomy book. But the tiny print was giving
me a headache and made it difficult for me to concentrate.
I needed fresh air. And solitude.

Grabbing my cloak, I persuaded the elderly doorman to
let me out into the snow-covered gardens, and went for a
walk to clear my head.

But I did not stay on the school grounds. I did not pay
attention to where I was headed. I ignored the passing
sleighs and carriages. I walked past the Tauride Gardens
and along the frozen Neva River. The bitter winds swept
across the ice and stung my face. I pulled my cloak closer
around me. As much as I loved winter and its late-afternoon

opal-colored skies, I would be happy to see the spring return.

I took the shortcut through the thicket back to the gardens. In the winter, the trees were bare, and the forest was not so dark. I heard no sounds but the crunching of my boots in the snow.

And then I heard another set of boots crunching behind me. Slower, heavier footsteps than mine.

I stopped behind a tree, holding my breath to listen more closely. I could hear my heartbeat thumping in my throat.

Slowly, the footsteps got louder. The person was getting closer, and soon I could hear a soft grunting.

Mon Dieu! I looked around, realizing I was still in the middle of the thicket, too far away to run in any direction. And no one would hear me if I screamed for help.

"Duch-essss," a young man's voice whispered. His footsteps were right behind my tree. "My mis-tressss."

I peeked around the tree at him. I felt sick as I recognized him. It was the soldier who had fallen at the Blessing of the Water. Count Chermenensky. His face was ashen, his eyes a milky white. "Oh, no," I whispered, shaking my head. "It cannot be. . . ."

"Duch-essss," he said, holding a frostbitten hand out to me. "Help meeee."

"What has happened to you?" I whispered. I wanted to run, but I was so scared my legs refused to budge. "You were dead."

He bowed his head. Some of his black hair had fallen out. "You called me."

"No," I said hoarsely. I felt like retching. "No."

"My mis-tressss, please help meee."

This could not be happening. I was going to hell. This was much worse than reanimating a dead cat or an insect. "What can I do for you?" I asked him. "How can I help you? I'll take you back if I can only figure out how."

He moaned. It was a horrible, painful moan. "Pleasssse! Do not send me back! There are . . . terrible things there. . . ."

I did not know what to do with him. I didn't even know how I had summoned him, though I vaguely remembered wishing that he had not died. Could one be a necromancer and not consciously work at it? I wanted to scream and cry and run away, but I felt sorry for the poor soldier. And responsible. He had been one of my brother's best friends. Who could I turn to for help?

There was only one person I could think of, the only person who knew what I was and had not judged me. I knew I was taking an enormous risk. But the poor count had to find somewhere safe to hide.

"Let's get you out of the cold. We can find you something warm to eat."

"Eat? Am I . . . hungry . . . ?"

The Cantacuzene Palace was on Millionaya Street, only a few blocks away from my family home. But it was a good distance away from the woods, and of course, I did not have any rubles to hire a carriage. We would have to walk.

It was already starting to get dark. I would be in trouble when I did not show up for dinner at the institute.

I began to hum as we walked, a piece of melody from the polonaise Prince Danilo and I had danced to the week before. It seemed to appease my new friend's moaning.

We had gone a short distance when I heard silver sleigh bells approaching behind us. Suddenly, I felt alarm. How could I explain walking unchaperoned with this unkempt-looking young man?

"Duchess von Oldenburg?" I heard a familiar voice in the carriage as it slowed to a stop beside us. *Oh, merde.*

It was the grand duchess Xenia and her brothers, the tsarevitch and Grand Duke George. Princess Alix and her brother were with them. Everything would not be all right.

I curtsied, trying to stay calm. "Good afternoon, Your Imperial Highnesses. How are you today?"

"Good Lord, is that poor creature with you?" the tsarevitch said, standing up in the carriage.

"Yes, Your Imperial Highness. I found him in the woods and I need to get him to the hospital." My swift change of plans was necessary. If I asked to be brought to the princess Cantacuzene, I knew I would arouse suspicion. And perhaps Dr. Kruglevski would be able to deal with an undead patient. I prayed so.

Grand Duke George stepped out of the carriage to check on Count Chermenensky. The count moaned softly to himself, since I was no longer humming. "Sir, are you all right?" the grand duke asked. "Can you tell me your name?"

Before the count could say anything, I responded quickly, "The poor man does not know his own name. I think he has a fever." I hoped no one would notice the count's lifeless eyes. Or the slight smell.

"He is as cold as death!"

"No, no, I am sure he has a fever, for he is delirious," I insisted.

"And you are a medical doctor?" the grand duke asked arrogantly.

Before I said something that would land me in Siberia, I bit my tongue. "Your Imperial Highness, would you send for a carriage to take this man to the Oldenburg Hospital? I would be eternally in your debt."

"The military hospital is much closer. We are just down the road."

"That will do fine, then." As long as the military doctors did not recognize the dead count. Or ask questions I could not answer. "We can walk from here. I thank Your Imperial Highness." I offered my arm to the count, and said, "Come along, sir. It is just a little bit farther."

"Heavens, Georgi, we must not let them walk," the tsarevitch said. "Duchess, please let us take you and your companion to the hospital. There is plenty of room in our carriage."

"You are too kind, Your Imperial Highness." I curtsied, wishing their carriage hadn't stopped at all. "It will be all right, sir," I said to the count. "These people are going to help us."

The count moaned softly but allowed Grand Duke George to help him into the carriage. He behaved until he saw Princess Alix. Then something strange came over him. He began to sniff her.

"Sir!" The tsarevitch tried to push the count away from Princess Alix. "You must not come any closer to her!"

Princess Alix gave a cry of shock.

Count Chermenensky moaned louder. "A . . . monster!

Like . . . me!" With a moan that turned into a growl, he leapt at her. The carriage erupted into chaos.

The Romanov sons pulled the count off the princess and wrestled him out of the carriage. Grand Duchess Xenia and I slid over to comfort Alix.

"I am so sorry, Your Highness," I said. "This is all my fault."

"How could you have known?" the grand duchess asked. "You were only trying to help the poor creature."

Outside the carriage, I heard the tsarevitch and the grand duke struggling with the undead count, who was shouting bizarre things.

"Unnatural! Smelled . . . her skin!"

"He called me a monster!" Princess Alix was pale and trembling. She was descending into hysteria fast.

"Your Highness, take deep breaths for me," I said. "You are not a monster. No one believes that poor, deranged man."

The footmen helped the Romanovs subdue Count Chermenensky. He howled as they tied him up with a belt. I couldn't be sure, but I thought I heard a fist connecting with a head. A deep thud. Could an undead person be knocked unconscious? Was he truly conscious to begin with?

"You, send for the imperial guard," I heard the tsarevitch order in his calm, quiet voice. "Have him taken to the hospital and question him after he is seen by the doctor."

Princess Alix was shaking, as if to stop herself from crying. "Please breathe, Your Highness," I said. "Deep, slow breaths."

Grand Duchess Xenia was beginning to look scared. It was easy to forget that she was just a thirteen-year-old and had probably never witnessed such an altercation before. Or a hysterical princess who'd been accused of being a monster. For that matter, neither had I.

I grabbed hold of both Xenia's and Alix's hands. "Grand Duchess, why don't you take a few deep breaths with us? Slowly, slowly breathe in—that's good—and now slowly, slowly breathe out."

We kept taking deep breaths, and I was starting to feel a little light-headed. The tsarevitch stuck his head in the carriage. "All right there, ladies?"

Grand Duchess Xenia giggled. "My head feels funny, Nicky."

Princess Alix was still pale but she had regained her self-control. She nodded shyly. "May we go back to my sister's palace soon?" she asked. "My head is beginning to hurt."

"Yes, of course," the tsarevitch said. "Are we finished here?" he asked his brother.

Grand Duke George nodded. "Nicky, you can ride back with the ladies. I'll stay here with this poor fellow until the guardsmen arrive."

"No!" I shouted, climbing out of the carriage. "We mustn't wait for any guards. Let me take him to the hospital. It is not much farther down the road."

The grand duke looked at me. I could tell he suspected something. And he was right, of course. This was all my fault. Not that I compelled Count Chermenensky to attack Princess Alix, but still, I felt responsible. I had to make it up to the princess. And to the count.

"Please, Your Imperial Highness," I said quietly. "I must see this through."

He nodded and told his brother to go ahead and leave us. "We shall be fine. Send the carriage to the hospital to pick us up."

The grand duke had a hand on Count Chermenensky's arm and was already leading him down the street. "Sir, can you tell me your name? Where do you live?"

"I think he has amnesia," I said again, over the count's incomprehensible moaning. At least, I hoped it was incomprehensible. Would the grand duke remember the name of the soldier who had died at the Blessing of the Waters?

It was a windy day, and we were all frostbitten by the time we reached the hospital. The portly guard recognized the young grand duke immediately.

"Your Imperial Highness! What brings you to our military hospital? It is truly an honor to have you here!"

"This man with us needs medical care immediately. He was found wandering in Tauride Gardens."

"Of course, right away, Your Imperial Highness." An orderly helped Count Chermenensky into a wheelchair. We followed down the hallway as he was pushed into a large and cold examination room.

"Mis-tresss," the count moaned, looking at me pitifully. He reminded me of my father's favorite hunting dog.

"Have faith, sir. The doctor will make you feel better." I patted Count Chermenensky on the shoulder.

In a low voice, the grand duke, behind me, said, "I wouldn't be too sure of that."

I turned to him in alarm. I was afraid that he saw

something with his faerie sight. Surely he could not see the cold light as I did. The dead count was bathed in a blue glow, his cold light completely uncoiled. Before I could ask the grand duke what he meant, a short Austrian doctor walked in.

"What have we here?" He grabbed the count's hand to check his pulse, and I held my breath. The count wouldn't have a pulse. Or a heartbeat. Or a breath.

"This man was found half frozen in the woods," the grand duke explained again. "We, er, believe he has amnesia."

"Amnesia, eh? What is your name?" the gruff doctor practically shouted at the poor count.

"Count Alexander Eframovich Chermenensky," the count said. My heart sank. So much for amnesia.

"Open your mouth," the doctor said, and held the count's tongue down to look at his gray throat. Then he looked into his yellowed eyes, and at his blackened fingernails. "Ja, ja, I see now." He turned away from his patient to wash his hands in a basin on the washstand.

"Do you know what is wrong with him?" the grand duke asked.

"Of course I know what is wrong with him. This man is suffering from hepatitis and will continue to deteriorate slowly if not properly treated. He must be sent to the Crimea for the fresher air immediately."

"Hepatitis?" I asked. I knew I should be thankful for the misdiagnosis, but I was shocked at the doctor's incompetence. "Shouldn't you conduct blood tests or examine the man's urine before you determine what's wrong?"

The doctor looked at me with disdain. He would have

looked down his nose at me if he had not been two inches shorter than I. "And what would I find if I examined his water, young lady?"

"Tea-colored urine, with a strong odor, if he indeed has hepatitis."

The doctor shook his finger at me. "Mind your own business, fräulein. I have practiced medicine for thirty-six years. I have never made a wrong diagnosis."

The grand duke stepped forward. "I beg your pardon, Doctor, but you are certainly not speaking with a mere fräulein. She is the daughter of the Duke of—"

"Mis-tressss!" Count Chermenensky whimpered, and knocked the doctor over with a large clumsy swipe of his arm. I couldn't help feeling just the tiniest bit proud for a brief second.

"*Monsieur!*" the grand duke said firmly. "You must control yourself."

The furious doctor stood up with my help, straightening his glasses in a huff. "Take him to the Crimea and be gone with him! Ungrateful, wretched young ruffians . . ." He stormed out of the exam room muttering to himself.

"Mis-tressss," Count Chermenensky whimpered again.

I sighed and patted him on the shoulder. "Do not worry. We will think of something."

Grand Duke George leaned against the exam table, arms crossed. "I do not see why you found it necessary to insult the doctor. Why all the nonsense about tea and blood tests?"

"It wasn't nonsense," I said, crossing my arms too. I suddenly felt drained. Emotionally exhausted and physically tired. I slid down the wall to a sitting position. The count hunched down next to me. I sighed. "Since I was a little girl, I have wanted to be a doctor."

"A doctor?" The grand duke looked at me as if I were crazy. "You?"

I nodded. "Women are allowed to attend medical schools in Paris and Switzerland. I know I would make a good doctor."

He smirked. "Better than the one you just insulted?"

"No one should make a diagnosis of a fatal disease by merely glancing at a patient. It was irresponsible of him." Even though it really had been in the count's best interests. I should have kept my mouth closed. If I could just get him safely to the Crimea, maybe everything would be all right.

"We must leave the man here, Duchess. I must see you back to your home safely."

"I am grateful, Your Imperial Highness. But I must return to Smolny this afternoon, and it is only a short walk from the hospital." I had no idea what to do with the count. I had a feeling he would become agitated if I tried to leave him.

The grand duke reached out a hand to help me stand up.

I hesitated. His hand dropped to his side. "You waltz with vampires and parade about town with undead monsters, and yet you are afraid of me, Duchess?"

"He's not a monster," I whispered, staring at the grand duke in horror. He knew. All along, he had known. And he'd seen me dancing with Danilo at *Le Bal Noir*. I'd been too wrapped up in the crown prince's attentions even to notice. "How did you know?"

"I recognized the poor man the moment I laid eyes on

him. Thank God my brother did not, or he would have told the guards."

"I found him in the woods," I said, starting to sob. I had always hated girls who cried in front of boys. And here I was. "He called me his mistress."

"I knew you had dark powers, but I never suspected something this terrible," he said softly. "You brought a dead man back to life. Why would you do such a thing? Did you hate him? Had he scorned your love for another?"

"How could you say such a thing? No, it was nothing like that at all!" I closed my eyes, wishing the grand duke would just leave. He always saw the worst in me. The parts I couldn't change, no matter how hard I tried. I took a deep, ragged breath. "I did nothing to bring him back. I had no idea it had even happened. Until today. When he found me."

"You could not have done this without some sort of incantation or ritual."

I shook my head. "I swear on my life, I have never performed any rituals. Even the moth at the Smolny Ball . . . I did that on purpose, but I had only to focus on the insect, and it just happened."

The grand duke sighed, crossing his arms. "You know what must be done."

"No, I do not know what must be done. I do not routinely summon people from the grave and have them follow me around!"

"Lower your voice, Duchess. Or you will have more guards on your hands than you would prefer."

I wiped the tears off my face. "I should find a way to get

him to the Crimea, as the doctor suggested. Even if he doesn't have hepatitis, he would probably like the warmer climate."

"Are you mad? He must go back where he came from."

My blood went cold as I realized what he was saying. "No," I whispered.

"Duchess, look at the poor creature." The grand duke ran his hand through his hair. "It's no longer human."

"Don't speak of him like that. He wouldn't hurt me."

The grand duke shook his head. "Perhaps not, but he can hurt others. He attacked Princess Alix. And the doctor."

I sighed. I knew deep down he was right. But that didn't make it any less painful. "Did the princess smell odd to you?" I suddenly asked.

"That is not the point." He offered his hand to me again, and this time, I took it, standing up with his help.

I looked into the grand duke's blue eyes, pleading. "Couldn't we hide him somewhere safe? Where he will not harm anyone?"

"Duchess, where in this entire city would he be safe?" He knew it was breaking my heart. "You know this must be done."

I sobbed, hating myself, and hating to admit the grand duke might be right. "There must be another way," I pleaded.

Count Chermenensky was quietly gnawing on something, which, upon closer inspection, appeared to be his own tattered clothing. *Mon Dieu.*

"He is no longer one of us, Duchess," the grand duke said in a low voice.

"Mis-tresss," the count whimpered, apparently not capable of saying much more than that. "Home."

My heart was breaking for the poor creature, and I deserved every stab and pain I felt. I wished to heaven there was some way I could rid myself of this curse. How many more lives would I ruin? None if I could help it.

"Home," the count said again in a mournful voice. For an undead soldier, he had been relatively docile, and I wondered how much military action he had actually seen. Since he was the same age as my brother, probably none.

The grand duke stood at the doorway with his hand behind his back. He had his saber drawn and hidden. "Leave, Duchess."

The count only whimpered and began to nibble on his own hand. "Hungry," he said. "Home."

I did not move.

Apparently, the undead count was lucid enough to see what the grand duke was planning. Or perhaps he thought my life was in danger. With a sudden snarl, he leapt up and would have separated the grand duke's imperial head from his imperial shoulders if the grand duke had not been faster. George Alexandrovich spun out of the count's way and swung the saber, nicking the count on the ear.

"No!" I cried.

With a howl of pain, Count Chermenensky swung another time at the grand duke, sending him careening into the glass cabinet. The glass shattered all over the floor.

The guards pushed me out of the way as they rushed into

the room. "He is mad!" the grand duke shouted, holding his arm, which had a large gash.

Count Chermenensky growled as he saw the guards approach him. They had him backed into a corner like a wild animal. With another snarl, he turned and crashed through the window, landing on the frozen hospital grounds below.

"No!" I cried, running to the window. The count had already scrambled to his feet and dragged himself into the thicket.

The leader of the guards ordered the rest of the men to form a search party and find the missing patient. The Austrian doctor came back to the exam room and was angered when he saw all of the broken glass. "What is the meaning of this?"

As the doctor left the room muttering to himself and yelling for his nurses, Grand Duke George looked at me. "You explain to him. I've got to go after Chermenensky."

"You cannot! Your arm is bleeding!" I reached behind him into a cabinet and pulled out a bundle of gauze and a bottle of iodine. "Let me see that."

The grand duke frowned. "There's no time. You know it's too dangerous to leave that creature running around the city!"

"I know it is too dangerous to let you run off losing blood like this. Give me your arm." I ignored the short little doctor, who was pitching a fit about regulations in the doorway. The gash on the grand duke's arm was long. "You are going to have a nasty scar," I said as I gently held pressure to stop the bleeding.

"All true warriors wear their scars proudly," he mumbled. "How can I be proud of this one?"

I looked up at him, horrified, as I realized what he meant. "What will your parents say?" I would be sent to Siberia. My whole family would be exiled. If not executed.

He shook his head. "They will know about the count before too long. My father will think that I failed to protect the public from this danger. It is I who fear being sent to Siberia."

"But . . . wait. I didn't express my fears out loud, did I?" I dropped his arm and backed away, suddenly spooked by his silvery faerie eyes. "Can you read my thoughts?"

"Sometimes, when I concentrate." He winced and grabbed the bandage from me to apply pressure to the bleeding himself. "You are very easy to read. Most of the time."

I blushed and could think of nothing more to say. When the bleeding had stopped, I cleaned the cut with iodine and wrapped it in gauze for him without saying another word.

The Austrian doctor returned to the room with a suture kit, wishing to sew up the grand duke's arm. But the grand duke shook his head. "Thank you, this will do, sir. Is my carriage outside?"

The guard behind him nodded.

The grand duke's face was grim and pale, but he refused any morphine, though I pleaded with the doctor to medicate him. "No, it is not necessary. I thank you for your help. We must hurry, Duchess."

I quickly followed him into the carriage. "Are we going after the count?" I asked as we drove away from the hospital.

"No, you are going back to Smolny."

"But what about the count?"

"The guards are searching for him in the woods right now. He will be found soon, no doubt, taken for a madman, and dragged away to the asylum."

"No." I could see the grand duke was fighting the pain in his arm. "We can't abandon him like this. He needs our help."

"Duchess, I believe you might belong in the asylum as well." The carriage stopped at the Smolny Institute's front gate. The brief daylight of winter was already starting to fade. "Good day, Duchess. I hope you enjoyed our carriage ride in the woods this afternoon. My sister tells me she enjoys your company. She hopes you will join us again sometime soon."

He said this loudly, for Madame Metcherskey was standing in the portico, glaring at me with her pinched mossy-green eyes. I knew whatever punishment the grand duke was going to face, mine would most likely be worse.

CHAPTER EIGHTEEN

◦⁄◦

I was wrong.

Apparently, being the guest of the tsar's son gives one special privileges. Madame Metcherskey did not scold me after the grand duke nodded in her direction. She did manage to lecture me about the importance of modern propriety and the dangers of appearing in public without a chaperone, no matter how high-bred a gentleman my companion was. Never mind that we had actually been with chaperones for most of the afternoon. Both living and undead.

By that evening, the entire dining hall had heard that I had skipped dance lessons to visit with the imperial family. Elena pouted, wishing I had asked her to walk with me. I was most glad I had not. She need know nothing about Count Chermenensky. Aurora Demidova asked me if the grand duke let me call him by his Christian name, a sign to her that we were close to being formally engaged. Dariya gave her approval. "A much better choice for you than the crown prince," she whispered.

Mon Dieu! As if the grand duke thought of me as a potential grand duchess! I almost choked on my spiced fruit compote. "Not at all. I was only invited to join them because of Grand Duchess Xenia," I told them. "She decided to accompany Princess Alix back to her sister's palace when the princess became ill."

Elena seemed to perk up at that information. I did not know who the tsarevitch favored of the two princesses, Elena or Alix, but I suspected he would be much happier with the latter. Not to mention that she would probably make a better empress.

I did hope I had changed the grand duke's mind toward female doctors after we'd seen the old Austrian physician's gruff incompetence. Perhaps he'd been a little impressed with the way I had handled his injury.

I fell asleep that night with my head on the Latin textbook again. I'd still received no word from the University of Zurich, so I'd sent a letter to the University of Paris as well. Madame Orbellani told me their admission requirements were even stricter. But I was too stubborn to give up hope.

I dreamed once more of the unholy temple in the Black Mountains of Montenegro. I dreamed of Prince Danilo. He had completed his ascension and had become a Vladiki. And there was nothing I could do to stop it.

CHAPTER NINETEEN

∾

There was no word on the fate of Count Chermenensky. I heard nothing from George Alexandrovich. Nothing from the gossips at the school. Nothing in the newspapers I read in the library. As each day passed without news, my nerves twisted tighter and tighter in my stomach. I had unleashed a monster on the streets of St. Petersburg, even though I didn't know how. And I was worried about the poor creature's safety.

I received an invitation to go sleigh riding on Saturday with the Montenegrin sisters and their brother, followed by tea at the Tauride Gardens pavilion. The thought of seeing Prince Danilo again after my latest horrid dream put my stomach in knots. I was both repulsed and confusingly attracted to him.

Saturday morning was cold and crisp, with pale Russian sunshine casting a weak light across the snow. Dariya was worried about my going on an outing with the

Montenegrins. "Perhaps you should pretend to be ill, Katiya?" she asked nervously.

"Do not worry about me. Princess Cantacuzene gave me a ring that I wear. She says it will protect me against their spells." I showed her the ring on my finger before donning my kidskin gloves. I wore it all the time now, mostly on a ribbon around my neck, hidden under my dress. It certainly wouldn't hurt anything.

Dariya crossed herself and muttered but still tried to be helpful and told me the blue woolen dress looked better against my winter-pale skin than the brown dress.

Elena, looking particularly rosy, was entirely too chatty as we took breakfast in the nearly empty dining hall. It was a simple breakfast of bread and jam with tea, just enough to warm our bellies. I usually returned home each weekend, as did most of the St. Petersburg students. The foreign students remained at the institute unless invited home with another classmate. I rarely invited my friends home, never wanting anyone to witness one of Maman's séances. I did not think Madame Tomilov would approve if one of my classmates became possessed. Such things had been known to happen before—at my aunt Zina's one and only séance, for example.

One of the Smolny servants came to the dining hall to tell us Elena's siblings were at the front gate. She helped us both into our woolen cloaks.

Prince Danilo smiled at me, his white teeth dazzling. "Katerina Alexandrovna," he said, extending his hand to help me into the sleigh. "It is good to see you on this beautiful morning." He smiled at Elena too. "And you as well, my sister."

She rolled her eyes as she climbed in and sat next to Militza. The grand duke Peter Nikolayevich, Militza's fiancé, sat on the other side of Militza. I bowed to the grand duke and said hello to Militza and Anastasia.

We rode through the Summer Gardens, which were just as beautiful in the wintertime, at least to me. The sleigh was pulled by four handsome black stallions.

Elena was eager to tell her sisters about my outing with the imperial family. "Our Katerina must find our company too dull for her when the Romanovs call upon her so often."

"They did not call upon me the other day." I felt I had to confess. "I was walking in the woods and found a soldier who was ill. I was trying to help him when the Romanov party came upon us and helped me get the man to the military hospital."

"What a kind thing to do," Militza said. "That man is most lucky that you happened upon him."

"I'd like to believe that" was all I could diplomatically say. I doubted the count would agree if anyone should ask him.

"You were lucky he was not a dangerous man," the grand duke Peter Nikolayevich said to me.

I nodded. "I realize walking alone in the woods was rather foolish, but I cherish winter days like this." I'd go insane if I did not have some fresh air and solitude every day. Though if every day was like that one, I'd go insane even faster.

The horses were lively, trotting past the frozen ponds along the main garden path. I hoped the count had found a safe place to hide. Did he even realize he was in danger? He'd had the sense to run away from the guards at the hospital.

"And tell us, what do you think of the mysterious princess Alix?" Stana asked. "I have heard so very little about her. Is she much like her sister, the grand duchess Elizabeth?"

I nodded. "I think she is a good deal younger, but she favors the grand duchess very much. Although she is shy, she seems to be enjoying her visit to St. Petersburg."

Stana looked at her older sister and smiled wickedly. "I do hope we get to make her acquaintance soon."

"Maybe she will be at the ballet tomorrow night," Elena said. "I wonder what she thinks of Tchaikovsky."

"She certainly cannot be as beautiful as any of you," Prince Danilo said. "I am surrounded by the most beautiful women of all of Europe. What lucky men we are, Peter Nikolayevich!"

Elena laughed. "Dani, you are not even a man yet! Quit teasing us!"

The prince glowered at his sister. "And you are not yet a woman, but I praise you nevertheless."

The siblings got into a pushing match, making the carriage wobble from side to side.

Princess Militza sighed. "Children, behave."

The grand duke smiled as Militza took his arm in hers. They made a very handsome couple but did not act like a young couple in love. Not at all like the tsarevitch and Princess Alix.

Elena shoved her brother playfully, pushing him into me.

"I am so sorry, Duchess," he said, his dark eyes boring into mine. He took my hand gallantly. "Have I injured you?"

"Oh, not at all!" I said, even though I secretly wanted to box Elena's ears. I knew she had shoved him toward me on purpose. She looked positively gleeful. *Be careful*, I told myself. *This family is dangerous. All of them, even Danilo.*

We stopped at one of the pavilions within the garden to rest the horses. There was no one else visiting that day, and the gardens had a barren, deserted appearance. Their naked branches and snow-covered grounds gave them a stark beauty, and I wandered off from the group to breathe in the crisp air. Away from the chattering of Elena and her sisters, it was as silent as a tomb.

A rabbit hopped out of the thicket, saw me, and ran back into hiding. He reminded me of poor Count Chermenensky.

"A ruble for your thoughts, Duchess," Prince Danilo said, his voice low behind me.

Believing my thoughts were truly worth more than that, I merely shook my head. "It is so beautiful out here," I answered.

"You are a true snowbird," the crown prince said, taking my hand. "I prefer the more temperate climates of my home. Yet it does grow bitterly cold in the winter in our mountains."

I could not help shivering as I remembered my dream. Was there really a temple in Prince Danilo's Black Mountains?

"You must come and see my beautiful country," he said as we walked farther away from the others. "The trees and the flowers bloom in the spring, and Cetinje is full of fragrant blossoms. We celebrate St. Yuri's Day when the earth opens up and everything blooms. There is a magnificent church festival."

"It sounds lovely," I said.

The prince took my gloved hand and held it up to his lips. Even through the leather, I could almost feel his warm breath on my skin. I tried not to shudder, because I realized then that the ring was indeed protecting me. I felt nothing for the prince—except fear. "I hope you will join us in Cetinje for St. Yuri's Day. Nothing would please me more, Katerina Alexandrovna."

He smiled, and his teeth gleamed in the cold winter light.

I managed to make some noncommittal remark, and the moment passed.

But my fears stayed. If anything, they grew stronger.

CHAPTER TWENTY

❦

"St. Yuri's Day? Heavens, child. Why would they want you present on that day of all days?" Princess Cantacuzene paced back and forth in her mauve wallpapered parlor. She looked at the calendar on her writing desk, then continued to pace and mumble to herself.

I was finally able to visit the princess on Sunday afternoon. The headmistress at Smolny believed I was at home with my parents, and my parents believed I had already returned to the school. I had many questions about the Montenegrins, and the princess was the only one I felt I could trust. "He says it is when the earth opens up in the spring and sends forth the flowers," I told her.

"Yes, and it is traditionally known as the day when the earth spews forth all sorts of foul things as well. Vampires, and other forms of the undead."

"Other forms? What other forms?" I sat down on the sofa.

I wished there were a textbook of undead creatures. Or a field guide. It would make my life so much easier.

The princess sat down next to me. "You already know there are several kinds of vampires. First there are the Vladiki."

"There are other kinds of vampires?" This was getting more and more complicated.

The princess called a servant to bring us tea in the parlor. "Of course, Katerina. The Vladiki and the female veshtizas are found in the southern Balkan countries, but there are also the Russian upyri, who are savage blood drinkers, more animal than man. And then there are the Dekebristi, who have not been seen in Russia for many, many years."

"The Dekebristi were vampires?"

Princess Cantacuzene closed her eyes. "Their undead servants. Created by Konstantin's beloved to serve him."

Maman had told me about the vampires Tsar Nicholas had defeated, but I hadn't wanted to believe it. "The history books tell us that Grand Duke Konstantin signed away his claim to the throne because he wanted to marry a Polish commoner," I said. "But if she created the Dekebristi, what did that make her? What kind of powers did she have?"

"A commoner is what the Romanovs call her," the princess said with a bitter laugh, waving her hand absentmindedly. "But you are wanting to know about the different kinds of undead. Besides the vampires, you may find a revenant, or a ghoul. Flee from the both of them, because they are mindless and violent. More so than the normal peasant.

"They both like to come out under the full moon," she continued, "when there is plenty of light, for they are almost blind and their eyes are not accustomed to daylight. A revenant will haunt the graveyard in broad daylight, however, if there is reason. The ghoul likes to devour human flesh, while the revenant often prefers to eat its own flesh. He is usually not too particular, however. A revenant is always hungry."

I started to feel hollow inside. Hollow and nauseated at the same time. Poor Count Chermenensky. "Your Highness, is there any way to cure an undead, like a revenant, for example?" For that was what the count appeared to be.

"Of course, dear." My shoulders relaxed when I heard her say this. There was hope for the count. If I could just find him and administer the cure before the tsar's guards found him, everything would be fine. The princess took her tea from the servant's tray and stirred her sugar slowly. "The cure is very simple. Remove the revenant's head from his body. *Voilà*. Revenant is cured."

My heart sank. This had been the grand duke's plan all along—what he still planned to do when he found the count again.

"But do not dwell on such creatures. The Vladiki are the only ones you should be concerned with. And not only the crown prince. You must be wary of Princess Militza. She is more ambitious than she seems."

"What do you mean?" I asked.

"You must become better acquainted with them, I believe, in order to uncover their secrets. My ring will keep you safe from them." She rose from her chair and approached the bookcase. "You should also begin learning more about your abilities. Here we are." She selected a thick, dusty book from the bottom shelf and pressed it into my hands. *A Necromancer's Companion*. The black leather cover had Egyptian hieroglyphics imprinted down its spine. "I don't need to tell you to keep it hidden. Share it with no one."

"Your Highness, I want no part of this. Please take it back."

Her dark eyes flashed. "I insist, Duchess. It is the only way you can protect your precious imperial family from the vampires."

"If the tsar is in danger, he must be warned!"

"Your tsar, the Bear, believes that the king of Montenegro is his staunchest ally. We cannot go before him without proof. You must discover their treachery by befriending the Montenegrins. Or kill the crown prince yourself."

I wanted to remind the grand duchess that the Bear, as the peasants called Alexander III, was her tsar as well. But I held my tongue. Reluctantly, I took the book and hid it within the folds of my cloak, silently promising myself I would never open the foul thing or read one unholy word. There had to be another way to keep the tsar and his family safe.

CHAPTER TWENTY-ONE

～～

For weeks, I heard no news of the missing count Chermenensky, not from servants or family members. My brother appeared to have finally gotten over his friend's death, and had returned to his raucous parties with fellow officers. Dr. Kruglevski had not seen any strange frostbitten patients with yellowed eyes and black fingernails. But he was seeing more patients who had been poisoned. Another maid from Smolny was currently resting in the women's ward. And the doctor had identified the poison at last: hemlock. "It is the strangest thing," he said. "I do not understand how so many people can be ingesting such a poison."

I had finally decided that Elena could not be responsible for all the poisonings. It was happening all over the city, not just at the Smolny Institute. But I knew she was involved somehow.

"Do not worry," Dr. Kruglevski told me, patting me on the shoulder and giving me a new medical journal to borrow.

This issue contained an article about sterile and clean techniques in the hospital setting. I took the journal back to Smolny with me and read the entire thing from cover to cover before dinner. The book Princess Cantacuzene had given me I still refused to open.

When I had a chance to speak with my cousin alone, I told her about Dr. Kruglevski's discovery. She deserved to know what kind of poison had made her ill.

"Hemlock! But how would Elena get a hold of such a thing?"

We were whispering together on our way to geography class. Elena glared at us as she brushed past us. I shook my head. "I don't think she was acting alone," I said. "There are people being poisoned throughout the city, the doctor says."

"By her and her sisters?" Dariya asked suspiciously. "Why would they be poisoning so many people?"

"Princess Cantacuzene wants me to find out," I said unhappily. "She said we need to be able to prove to the tsar that he is in danger."

Dariya frowned. "Do you think they could have caused the train wreck at Borki last fall?"

"How?" I couldn't imagine the Montenegrin princesses being capable of causing such a horrible accident. Besides, I'd overheard my father saying it had most assuredly been due to the train's traveling at unsafe speeds. The Montenegrins could not have achieved such destruction merely with their poison.

"Please be careful," my cousin begged. "Princess Cantacuzene has no right to ask you to spy on Elena and her siblings."

"If I don't do it, who will?" I asked. We had reached our classroom, where Madame Metcherskey hurried us all into our seats before Dariya could answer.

❧

The Bavarian princesses had returned to St. Petersburg, their mourning period for their uncle, Crown Prince Rudolfe, officially over. Erzsebet told me her grandmother the empress Sissi had gone completely mad with grief over her son's death. She walked the halls of the palace spouting morbid poetry. Erzsebet was more than happy to get back to the institute, but Augusta would have preferred to stay on. Dariya and I tried to raise her spirits with card games and gossip.

"Tell us about the infamous Black Ball," Erzsebet said that evening as we sat in the Smolny parlor, playing a game of tarock.

"It was beautiful, with everyone in black dresses!" Elena said. "The ladies' diamonds and pearls showed up like moons and stars against the night sky. The ballroom looked celestial."

Aurora Demidova nodded. "Princess Yussopova wore a pearl that was larger than her hand!" she exclaimed.

"And the music was wonderful," I added, studying my cards carefully.

"I danced with the tsarevitch. He was very, very sweet."

Elena sighed. "Such beautiful blue eyes he has. And Katerina danced with my brother twice!"

Erzsebet and Augusta teased me mercilessly for this. "You are almost engaged now! What did your mother say?"

I rolled my eyes, thinking of my father's words on the carriage ride home that night. I did not want to share that with Elena, who would know my parents were taking Prince Danilo's suit very seriously.

Augusta said shyly, "I should have liked to dance with every last cadet from the Corps des Pages. They look so handsome in their dress regiments!"

"Then you shall dance with every last one of them next week, at the grand duchess Marie Pavlovna's ball," Elena said. "It is a children's ball, so you will both be allowed to attend."

"Oooh!" Augusta said, smiling. "I shall dance all night long! I shall wear a beautiful white dress embroidered with diamonds, and ermine, and velvet slippers with diamonds on my feet."

I was glad to see the young princess cheered a little. She had looked so glum earlier. As much as it pained me to dress up again for yet another ball, I caught myself wondering if the grand duke George would be there. Not that I hoped he would dance with me, but I did need to speak with him. About my undead friend.

CHAPTER TWENTY-TWO

⌇

The gown I wore to Miechen's ball was white, of course, with a pale blue ribbon around the waist and tiny seed pearls sewn into the bodice with silver thread. I had the same diamond earrings I'd worn to *Le Bal Noir* and a delicate silver tissue wrap. I could not find the obsidian ring, despite turning my room at home upside down. It had not been in my jewelry box at Smolny either. I resolved to be strong if I saw the crown prince. I promised myself I would not fall under his spell so easily.

The empress and her family were not in attendance at Miechen's ball. I heard whispered rumors that she and the grand duchess were feuding again. I would not see Grand Duke George, so I had no way of knowing if he had found the count.

Prince Danilo was his charming self again, daring to ask me for a third dance, which I declined with a smile. "We mustn't!" I said as he took my arm and strolled through the fragrant jardinière with me. "The old ladies will talk and my mother will know, and I will never hear the end of it."

Being with the prince again made me forget everything else. There was something I needed to do that evening, but for the life of me, I could not remember what.

He handed me a cup of warmed wine from the samovar. "Why should you care what the old hags say? Their world does not concern you; I have seen that in your eyes. You would rather be anywhere else than here. Tell me, Duchess," he said, his black eyes burning into mine as his fingertips gently rubbed the inside of my wrist. "Tell me where you would rather be tonight. Tell me, and I will take you there at once."

I tried hard not to tremble; I was afraid he could hear my heart pounding in my throat. I was falling under the prince's spell all over again. And it felt delicious.

I could think of nowhere on earth I would rather be at that moment, and I told the prince so.

He smiled and whispered, "I am glad," before kissing me.

Mon Dieu! He kissed me! And I kissed him back. His grip on my hands tightened. I could have sworn I heard his heart pounding too.

I broke away first, dazed, with my legs feeling weak. His arms circled me and held me up. He smiled down at me. "Katerina, I want to bring you back to Montenegro and make you my bride. I shall speak to your father in the morning, yes?"

"Yes," I said breathlessly without stopping to think. What would my father say? I did not care. All I cared about was the prince holding me in his arms. I sighed happily, resting my head on his shoulder. His hand caressed the back of my neck. I trembled all over again.

"Katiya! I have been looking all over for you!" Dariya shouted as she hurried toward us. She stared at me and the crown prince in shock. "Where have you been?"

I blushed, still foggy. I could not think to answer her. I was in Danilo's arms. How had that happened?

"Katiya, please come with me back to the ball," Dariya entreated. "Your mother is looking for you." She glared at Danilo.

"That's all right," I said, smiling slowly. "Do not worry about me."

"But—"

I looked back up into Danilo's eyes, still smiling. I was hopelessly lost.

"I found something that belongs to you, Katiya," my cousin said. "Come and talk to me if you'd like it back." Dariya gave me a frustrated look before storming off.

"We must rejoin the others, my love," the prince said, sighing heavily. "Will you tell your mother that we have talked?"

"Of course," I said, leaving his embrace to walk back to the ballroom. I took his arm with a smile, suddenly feeling shy.

"Shall I bring her a gift tomorrow when I come to visit? Does she like flowers?"

"Roses," I said, not really paying attention to what he was saying. I was intoxicated by the sound of his voice, by his warm touch, by his hypnotic eyes. He led me back to my Bavarian friends, but I honestly cannot remember anything more about the ball other than Prince Danilo's standing at my side throughout the evening. He had whispered, "Do not dance with anyone else tonight," low enough that no one else could hear. And I did not dance any more after that. Who else could I have danced with? I didn't think there was another soul in the world who could make me feel like the prince did. Wasn't that love?

CHAPTER TWENTY-THREE

The next morning I slept late, exhausted from the previous night. It all seemed a blur. Wasn't I to do something today?

I dragged myself out of bed with a horrible migraine and rang for Anya to bring tea. Then crawled back into bed.

My mother burst into my room, shouting and crying. "Katerina Alexandra Marija! Why did you not tell your *maman*? Shame on you, you wicked girl!" But she was crying tears of joy. "Who do you think has just left your father's study?" She sat down on my bed, causing it to shake. I felt nauseated.

Suddenly, I remembered. I sat straight up, feeling as if the room were spinning. "Oh, Maman, what have I done?" I burst out.

The smile on her face faded. "You have consented to marry the crown prince Danilo of Montenegro. He has just received permission from your father. It took plenty of convincing on my part, I'll have you know. Anya, bring Katiya some cold water, please. She looks ill."

"Oh, poor Papa. He said he didn't want me to leave Russia."

"Yes, but a crown prince cannot be expected to simply pack up and move to his new wife's country. You will become queen someday. You must get to know your new country and its people."

"Queen?" The consort of the Vladiki. How had I gotten seduced into this? Had I been drugged the previous night? Or was it just that I was infatuated with the first young man to pay attention to me? *Mon Dieu*, I'd let him kiss me! I had kissed him back! There was truly no way to refuse the prince now.

"But I don't want to be a queen," I said, a lump catching in my throat. "I want to be a doctor."

"Enough of that nonsense," Maman said. "We have so much work to do. We shall plan a trip to Cetinje within the next month to meet Prince Danilo's parents. I shall have to order a new wardrobe for you. And for myself." She kissed me on the cheek. "Why don't you try to rest some more, dear? You do look rather pale."

"I do?" Had the prince drunk my blood the night before? No, he'd not become a blood drinker yet, at least not according to Princess Canta— Oh, *mon Dieu*, what would she say when she heard about the engagement? *Zut* and *merde*. What had I done with my ring? I remembered Dariya telling me she had something that I had lost. It must have been the ring. I hoped she still had it.

I flopped back down on the bed, covering my head with a pillow. "*Merde! Merde! Merde!*"

CHAPTER TWENTY-FOUR

✎

I returned to Smolny on Monday. My parents had decided I would finish out the school year before my marriage in the fall. The prince would turn eighteen in June, and I would turn seventeen in October. My father forbade a wedding before my seventeenth birthday and would have postponed it until my thirtieth if not for Maman. I tried to ignore all the attention at school, but everyone congratulated me and asked about the moment the prince had proposed. I had to tell my story over and over, making the kiss seem much more chaste than it had actually felt.

My cousin was furious with me. "How could you be so stupid, Katiya?" She grabbed my hand and placed the obsidian ring in my palm. "I found this on the floor by your cot. If only you'd been wearing it at the ball!"

I felt miserable. "I will think of something," I told her. "There has to be a way."

As soon as I could slip off, I visited Princess Cantacuzene. I dreaded telling her about the engagement. She swept into her parlor in a bloodred tea gown. "I believe congratulations are in order, my dear," Princess Cantacuzene said, kissing me on the cheek.

"I know you are disappointed in me, but I have not—"

"Disappointed?" She laughed. "Why, my dear, it's the cleverest idea possible! You will be able to go to Cetinje and murder the prince in your marriage bed! It is perfect!"

It must have been one of her off days. "Your Highness, the marriage isn't to be until October, long after the prince's ascension. Besides, if I murdered him in our bridal bed, wouldn't I be the only suspect in his death?"

"Remember your gift?" The madness was returning in her eyes. "You have the power of life and death. A necromancer can not only raise the dead, but can also destroy the living. Your blasphemous prince is still one of the living until his ascension. You must destroy him before he becomes one of the immortals. Before he can harm the tsar."

"I don't know how." And I didn't ever want to know either. I promised myself I would never kill anyone, no matter how evil the person was. "Your Highness, you spoke to me before of ghouls and revenants. How are they created?"

She frowned. "Have you not been studying the text I gave you?"

"I do not intend to study it!" I stood up, shaking. "Please forgive me, Your Highness, but I only ask because I believe there is a revenant loose in the city." I was surprised to feel my eyes flooding with tears. "I believe I may have created him. I swear before God I do not want to do it again."

The princess stared at me with her piercing black eyes. Her hair, piled up on her head in a bun, was streaked with silver, but I could tell it had been Gypsy black when she was younger. She was still a beautiful woman at her advanced age. "Dear Katerina Alexandrovich," she said. "It is quite impossible to raise the undead without consciously working at it. Do not worry your head about such things. Tell me, where did you see this revenant?"

"In the woods near Smolny, at the park at Tauride." I sat back down on the settee, gratefully accepting a cup of tea from my hostess. "Thank you."

"Did he see you? Did he try to say anything to you?" The princess took her tea and sat opposite me in a large over-stuffed chintz chair, watching me closely.

"Yes, he called me mistress and said I had called him. He never tried to hurt me, and I wasn't afraid of him." I sipped my tea mournfully. "I just felt so sorry for him."

"That is impossible," the princess said softly. "It simply cannot be." She grabbed my hand, staring at the obsidian ring. I knew I would not take it off again.

There was a strange look in the princess's eyes. Fright, I thought. But no, it was simply astonishment.

"I am so sorry, Your Highness. Please help me understand. I do not want this to happen again."

"No, of course you wouldn't, my child." She set her teacup down on her table and rang the bell for her servant.

179

"Come, Katerina Alexandrovna. We must go and see the grand duchess Maria Pavlovna, immediately." She asked her servant to send for her carriage.

I felt all the blood drain from my face. A cold, clammy sensation clenched my belly. "Miechen? You wish to tell Miechen about my curse?"

Princess Cantacuzene smiled, hustling me out the door and into her carriage. "We're going to tell her about your gift and your revenant. My dear, we are going to tell her everything."

CHAPTER TWENTY-FIVE

❧

I fretted all through the ride across town to the Vladimir Palace. It was an enormous residence, not far from our own home on Millionaya Street. We walked through ornately arched hallways, up the marble stairs, past several silent and impeccably dressed servants. The grand duchess received us in her parlor, opulently decorated in shades of deepest red. She did not look happy to see Princess Cantacuzene. Or me. Her smile was cold, but polite. "Princess Cantacuzene, Katerina Alexandrovna, it is always a pleasure."

We all sat down as the servants provided tea from the samovar.

Princess Cantacuzene stirred the spoon in her cup slowly. "Katerina Alexandrovna has been telling me the most interesting stories," she said. "My dear, won't you tell the grand duchess?"

I didn't know where to begin. I felt small, like a little

child. I wanted to go home. Or back to Smolny. Instead, I took a deep breath and told Grand Duchess Miechen everything.

Princess Cantacuzene sat with a fiendish gleam in her eye as she watched Miechen's face. The grand duchess looked as astonished as the princess had. She also looked furious.

When I finished telling her about Count Chermenensky, I was in tears. Again. Miechen stood up and stared out the window across the frozen Neva River. The spires of the Pyotr and Pavel Fortress could be seen in the distance. "Ruxandra Mikhailovna, you should not have brought her here," Miechen said as she turned to face us.

I didn't think I'd ever heard Princess Cantacuzene's first name before. I wasn't even sure if Maman knew it. Why did she and Miechen suddenly seem to hate each other so much?

"We want nothing more to do with your kind," Miechen went on. "The family cannot be involved with this."

Princess Cantacuzene laughed. "Grand Duchess, your family is already involved. Perhaps I should have taken the poor girl to the empress instead?"

Miechen's lips pursed into a thin line. She appeared cold and calculating. "And what is the extent of my family's involvement, Your Highness?"

"The Dekebristi are returning," the princess said. She was calmly stirring her tea. It looked as if she was enjoying herself, while I sat wondering what the grand duchess meant when she'd said "your kind."

Miechen's face went white. "And the Bear?"

"He does not believe they, or the vampires, exist anymore."

"The tsar will not put up with any such foolishness."

The princess glanced at me, giving Miechen one of those "not in front of the children" looks. The grand duchess rolled her eyes. "You are the one that brought her here, Ruxandra. She already knows too much for her own safety."

What was she talking about? I knew nothing of the Dekebristi's return. Was she implying that I was somehow to blame?

The princess smiled. "No doubt you have heard the happy news of Katerina Alexandrovna's engagement? She is going to marry the heir of the Vladiki."

"Poor child, you fell under their spell, did you?" Miechen said. "You do realize the prince plans to kill you on your wedding night, do you not?"

My mouth was dry. "Princess Cantacuzene said I must kill him before his eighteenth birthday, before we are married."

"Ruxandra, what lies have you been spreading?"

The princess laughed wickedly. I was starting to feel very cold, and short of breath. "Katerina Alexandrovna is much more powerful than I ever dared to hope. How do you think she turned the dead knight?"

"He is not one of the Dekebristi!" I cried. "I did not bring him back on purpose!"

"Of course you didn't," Miechen said, pacing back and forth and pausing to study me intently. "Child, do you know why it is so important that the prince does not live to see his own ascension?"

Was this a trick question? Why was it so cold in here? I shivered. "He will become a blood drinker," I said. "By killing him, we can prevent him from killing many more people."

Miechen's smile was grim. "Ruxandra, shame on you. You have not told her everything, have you?"

I did not hear what Princess Cantacuzene said to her then, for at that moment, I fainted and slid out of my chair onto the floor.

CHAPTER TWENTY-SIX

❧

"The Ten of Wands! *Mon Dieu.*" I heard my mother's voice, at a near hysterical pitch. "Burdens, and responsibilities. You have an uphill battle ahead of you. My poor baby has been overtaxed with these wedding plans. You have worn yourself out."

"Maman?" I opened my eyes and realized I was not in my own bed at home, but in a green ornately decorated room. "Where am I?"

Maman put her tarot cards down and ran a cool hand over my head, pushing my hair back as she had done when I was little. "My poor Katiya. You are still at the grand duchess Miechen's house, in one of her bedrooms. They sent for me as soon as you fainted. Do you remember anything?"

"I remember drinking tea with the grand duchess and Princess Cantacuzene," I said. They had been having the most terrible argument.

Maman sighed. "You bumped your head. Miechen

185

thought you looked overwrought." She smiled and kissed my forehead, clearly happy that she thought she could fix everything for me. "Planning a wedding can be a difficult thing. You just relax and let me worry about the preparations. That is what mothers are for."

I closed my eyes again, trying to remember what had happened. My nerves had been on edge, I supposed. Miechen and Princess Cantacuzene had been discussing the return of the undead Dekebristi, and I had fainted when they had implied I might be involved. Or had the grand duchess put something in my tea? I tried to sit up. I needed to see Dr. Kruglevski to be certain. "The doctor . . ." I tried to speak, tried to get out of bed. The room was spinning around in circles.

"The doctor has been sent for, Katerina Alexandrovna," Grand Duchess Miechen said, entering the room and sitting at my bedside, opposite my mother. "How long has she been awake?"

"Not but a few minutes," my mother said.

"How long have I been out?" I asked. It still looked like morning to me.

"Two days. We sent for your mother when you first fell, as we were afraid to have you moved anywhere in a carriage."

"Two days?" I tried to sit up again. The room was still spinning and the back of my head throbbed. "Has Dr. Kruglevski been to see me? Did I have a concussion, or some sort of seizure?" Or . . . or had they wanted me to remain unconscious all that time for a reason? I stared at

Miechen's blue-violet eyes, wishing I could read minds, like Grand Duke George. Could Miechen read minds, with her dark-faerie blood? I shuddered as she gave me a wicked smile.

"Yevgenia Maximilianovna, why don't you take a short walk through the orangery?" the grand duchess asked. "You have been at your daughter's bedside all this time. I will sit with her."

Maman refused at first, but she looked so very tired I begged her to get up and get some fresh air. "I shall be fine, Maman," I promised, although I was wary of being left with Miechen. "Take your time, and enjoy the grand duchess's garden."

When Maman had gone, Miechen picked up the tarot card that had been left lying on the bedclothes. "Ten of Wands. It usually means that someone is overburdened, but it can also mean a dangerous trial, whether by fire or by pain. The card is ruled by Saturn, the planet of necromancy. The number ten is the number of the end of things."

"The end of a dangerous trial?" I asked. "What am I being tested on?"

"Your wits, girl. For good or evil, you have been given a terrible power. Now that certain groups in St. Petersburg know it, you have become a very desirable pawn. The Montenegrins want you. And the St. Petersburg vampires need you as well."

I shivered. "The Montenegrins want me alive, but what about the others? Is my life in danger? Do I know any of the St. Petersburg vampires?"

"Your life has always been in danger, Katerina Alexandrovna," Miechen said. "From the vampires, from the faeries, from the tsar. It is a delicate balance the humans in this city dance."

"What should I do?" I asked, closing my eyes, not sure if I should trust the dark faerie. "What role does Princess Cantacuzene play in all of this?"

Miechen smiled. "Clever girl. You are right to worry. You are right not to trust Princess Cantacuzene completely, for she is not what she seems. Nor should you trust me completely, for my interests in all matters are self-motivated. But you may believe me when I tell you this: the Montenegrins must not be allowed to gain too much power in St. Petersburg. Princess Elena will never become empress, no matter how many rituals or spells she, or her sisters, or her mother casts. Militza believes she will gain powerful influence when she marries a Romanov, but she underestimates her rival."

"The other vampire families in St. Petersburg," I guessed. "They are the ones who hate the Montenegrins so much. But why?"

"You are very wise for such a young girl, Katerina. I would protect that pretty little neck of yours if I were you."

"But who are the St. Petersburg vampires?" I asked. Surely not anyone in the imperial family, whose light and dark faerie factions plotted and intrigued. "A member of the Order of St. John of Jerusalem?"

Miechen shook her head. "The families who make up the Order are the knights who have sworn to protect the imperial family and the rest of Russia from the vampires," she said. "Rather, it is one of the oldest vampire lines in all of Eastern Europe, with a family branch that has been living here in Russia for many generations."

The grand duchess frowned. "Unfortunately, they are under my protection. I am bound by the Dark Court's treaty to keep their names secret, but their leader is known to you. Do you still have the obsidian ring that the princess gave you? Do not lose it, as it will protect you from the thrall of any blood drinker."

"What do you mean?" I was determined to learn more, but Maman returned at that moment with Dr. Kruglevski.

"There's the patient!" the doctor said kindly. "My dear child, I'm always finding you and your friends afflicted with the most unusual ailments!" He set his black medical bag on the dresser and picked up my hand to feel my pulse.

Miechen stood up. "I will leave you in the doctor's good hands, Katerina Alexandrovna. We can speak again later, my dear. Yevgenia Maximilianovna, did you enjoy your walk?"

"Of course. The fragrance in the orangery was heavenly." Maman stood at the doorway, chatting with the grand duchess.

Dr. Kruglevski inspected my head for bruises and swelling. "I believe you will be fine," he said. "A few days' rest is all you need, my dear."

In a low voice, so Maman wouldn't hear, I asked him, "Could you please test my blood?"

"What on earth for?"

"I was drinking tea right before I fainted. There have been so many strange deaths, and then with my cousin being poisoned . . . well, I would feel safer just knowing for sure."

He nodded, even though he chuckled a little. "I have never had a patient ask me to draw their blood before, Duchess. You know it will sting a little?"

"Yes," I whispered. I was afraid of the large syringe, but I needed peace of mind.

It did sting, a lot, so I turned my head and stared at the portraits and paintings on the wall. One was of Miechen and her siblings as children. Another was of her and the grand duke Vladimir dressed for one of the famous imperial costume balls, given many years earlier. The couple were dressed like a Russian boyar and his wife from the time of Pyotr the Great. Grand Duke Vladimir was a large man who wore his beard and sideburns in the old Russian style.

The doctor had already finished and had given me gauze to hold over the puncture site when Maman returned. She caught a look of the syringe of blood the doctor held in his hand. "*Mon Dieu!* Do you think there is anything seriously wrong, Dr. Kruglevski? Oh, I cannot stand the sight of blood!" She waved her fan quickly, to prevent herself from fainting.

"It is all right, Maman. Here, sit down on the bed next to me. I am well, truly."

The doctor packed away the rest of his things. "I must take the sample to the hospital and run a few tests. We should have results by this evening." He patted me on the arm. "Do not worry, young duchess. Everything will be fine, I am sure." He turned to Maman and asked, "Will she be staying here or do you plan to take her home this afternoon?"

"What do you suggest, Doctor? Do you think it is safe to move her?"

Dr. Kruglevski looked at me, and I nodded ever so slightly. "Yes, I think she would do much better in her own bed, surrounded by her own things. It is more than safe."

"Thank you, Doctor. I'll let the grand duchess know immediately."

After the doctor and my mother had left, I breathed a sigh of relief. I lifted the gauze from my arm and was happy to see the bleeding had stopped.

I still felt as if I had no one to trust, and no one to give me any rational advice. I couldn't discuss vampires and faeries and revenants with Dr. Kruglevski, and I couldn't discuss any of this with my family. Dariya was already mad at me for agreeing to marry Danilo. If I told her about my curse, she would think I had become a monster just like the Montenegrins. Grand Duchess Miechen and Princess Cantacuzene had their own subtle agendas, as did the Montenegrins. Who did that leave me with?

No one.

CHAPTER TWENTY-SEVEN

Maman called for the largest of our family carriages and told Miechen she was taking me home with the doctor's blessing. The grand duchess looked unhappy to see me go. "Are you quite sure?" she asked Maman. "She looks so fragile."

"I believe she needs to be in familiar surroundings," Maman said, gathering up her things. She had apparently sat at the side of my bed and knitted an entire coverlet while I had been unconscious. "Are you ready, darling?" she asked me.

The pale winter sunshine outside seemed painfully bright to me after I'd been indoors for so long. I had to shield my eyes. "Into the carriage, dear," Maman said.

I turned to say my goodbye to the grand duchess. "You have been most kind, Your Highness. Thank you for everything you have done for me."

She smiled. "It has been a pleasure, Duchess. I hope you

are feeling better soon. Perhaps we will see you at the ballet this weekend."

That evening, Prince Danilo and his sisters came by to see me. Maman insisted I dress and receive them in the parlor. The prince gave me an exquisite four-carat diamond Cartier engagement ring. "I've been so worried about you, my love," he said, kissing my hand. "It has seemed like forever since I've seen your beautiful face."

"I am fine, honestly." There was something in his touch, his eyes that was so mesmerizing! I could feel myself slipping under his spell again, even with Princess Cantacuzene's ring, now hidden safely on a ribbon around my neck. I stood up and took a deep breath, trying to shake my senses. "You will be attending the ballet?"

"Only if you are feeling quite better, my dear."

"I wouldn't miss it for the world. Jelena Cornalba is dancing." The enchanting ballerina from Italy had such a following that when she performed in Moscow, the front six rows of the Mariinsky Theatre were usually empty, as several of her fans traveled to Moscow to see her there as well.

I was extremely fortunate that the Montenegrins left before Dr. Kruglevski made his visit that evening. He talked jovially with my father and mother before coming in to examine me in my bedroom. Maman huddled over him. "Do you think she is much improved from this morning? Her fiancé came to visit earlier. I hope he did not tire her out."

The doctor smiled warmly and felt my pulse. "Do not fear, Duchess. Your blood is free of any poison," he said in a low voice. Aloud, to my mother, he said, "I think she needs a few more days' rest. I do not suggest any more social outings for the week."

"But the ballet!" Maman said. "Oh, well, if it must be, it must be. Your prince will be so disappointed."

The doctor said his goodbyes, and Maman kissed me on the forehead before following him downstairs. "I do hope your prince is not having second thoughts about the engagement. That he does not think you have a poor constitution. You are to be the mother of the future heirs of Montenegro! You should be healthy as a horse!"

I rolled my eyes. Maman had the strangest priorities.

CHAPTER TWENTY-EIGHT

The next day was back to the flesh and bone world of St. Petersburg, for I was feeling slightly better. I begged Maman to let me attend the ballet that Sunday evening, even though Dr. Kruglevski had advised against it. It would be my only chance to see Jelena Cornalba that season.

She was dancing the lead in the premier of Riccardo Drigo's *The Talisman*. We dressed in our Sunday finest, heavily beaded, thick woolen dresses, and set out that evening for the Mariinsky Theatre.

The Mariinsky had been named in honor of our previous empress, Marie Alexandrovna, wife of Tsar Alexander the Second. It was a very beautiful building, with a wide, sweeping staircase that rose three whole stories. We were seated in our family box, and I noticed that members of the imperial family were seated in the majestic, central imperial box, next to ours. I could not see Grand Duke George

Alexandrovich from my seat, however. I did not know if he was even present that evening.

Prince Danilo and his sister Elena visited our box before the ballet started. The prince met me with a gallant bow and a kiss on my gloved hand. Something deep down inside me trembled. I hoped the obsidian ring's magic would protect me.

Grand Duchess Elizabeth was attending the ballet, with her sister, Princess Alix, and their brother, Prince Ernest Louis of Hesse. Their father, Grand Duke Louis IV of Hesse, was enjoying a stay at the imperial hunting lodge with the tsar. The two men were getting along splendidly, as they both detested balls and ballets. Princess Alix had a little more color in her cheeks than she'd had the last time I had seen her. I could tell she doted on her older brother, whom she called Ernie, and he in turn doted on her.

Grand Duchess Elizabeth frowned with concern when she saw me. "We had heard that you had taken ill recently," she said.

"I am much better now, thank you," I replied. Actually, I was still feeling rather weak and wobbly, but I refused to let Maman know. She would have rushed me back home to bed.

Princess Alix stepped forward and clasped my hands. "We have heard the good news of your engagement. I am so happy for you!" She smiled shyly.

"We thank you," Prince Danilo said, stepping in beside me, with a protective hand on my waist.

A cold nausea washed over me. I could not wait much longer to break off the engagement. Miechen had frightened me more about the Montenegrins than Princess Cantacuzene had. "Princess Alix, may I introduce you to my fiancé, Prince Danilo of Montenegro? Prince Danilo, this is my friend Princess Alix of Hesse-Darmstadt."

"*Enchanté,*" the prince said, gallantly taking her hand and kissing it. I did not think the princess approved of this. She blushed deeply. I hurried to introduce him to Prince Ernest and the grand duchess Elizabeth, neither of whose hands, I noticed, did he kiss.

"We should get back to our family's box before the ballet starts," Grand Duchess Ella said. "It was a pleasure meeting you, Your Highness," she said to the crown prince with a polite bow. Her sister smiled shyly at us before hurrying after Ella.

"Your Highness, we must speak tonight," I whispered. "Alone." Enough was enough. I would not take any part in Princess Cantacuzene's plans, and I would not risk my life dallying with the Montenegrins any longer.

"Indeed?" he said, bringing my hand to his lips. I shuddered, realizing he had a different kind of conversation in mind than I did.

I smiled, hoping I looked seductive and coy at the same time. "During the second act? Can you get away and meet me in the lobby?" It was a grand room, covered with gold and enamel and enormous ornate chandeliers that sparkled.

He kissed my hand once more before leaving me with my family. His sisters were sitting in the box of Grand Duke Pyotr Nikolayevich, Militza's fiancé. Maman and Papa frowned as I sat down. "You must take care. You must not be seen with the prince alone," Maman said.

The orchestra began to play and the curtain rose, so she could say no more to me.

That night was the ballet's debut, and I was intrigued by the Indian costumes. The music was beautiful, the choreography somewhat on the simple side. Several times during the first act, a group of university students in the general-seating area below us caused a ruckus, applauding and yelling bravos so loud that His Excellency the Governor General of St. Petersburg turned around and shook his finger at the students.

"*Mon Dieu*," Maman whispered. "The ballet is not *that* good."

In the imperial box, I could see Grand Duchess Xenia looking bored. Her brother leaned over and whispered something to her that made her giggle.

I waited impatiently for the second act so I could speak with Prince Danilo. I hoped to use reason with him. I would tell him that I would not make a good queen for him, and that he needed to find a more suitable princess. I was still determined to accomplish important things with my life. Becoming a doctor was one of them. Rescuing Count Chermenensky was another.

Jelena Cornalba was beautiful onstage, as usual. I regretted having to miss her pas de deux, but I wanted my conversation with the prince to be over. I slid my gloves off and looked down at my hands, one wearing the engagement ring, and the other the obsidian ring. I whispered to Maman, "I need some air. Do not get up. I will be right back," and slipped out of our box. I hurried to the lobby, where my prince was already waiting. "You are impatient, Your Highness," I said. I did not smile coyly anymore.

We walked over to a dim corner of the lobby and sat on a black velvet upholstered settee. We were half hidden from the rest of the lobby by a large palm tree in a Chinese vase.

Prince Danilo took my hand, once again pressing it to his lips. "It is torture to be apart from you, my love. I want to hear you call me by my Christian name."

"Danilo," I whispered, wondering how much power there was in a name. His seemed to hold sway over me. "We must discuss something very important."

"Yes, Katerina?" His thumb rubbed over the inside of my wrist. "I am delighted that you have come to me."

I shook my head. "This is not what you think. Danilo, I want us to have an understanding. I know you are the heir to a kingdom, and I will assume certain responsibilities by becoming your wife. But I want other responsibilities. I want to become a doctor and study diseases and their cures. I want to care for sick women and children."

Prince Danilo looked at me silently. His black eyes showed no emotion at first, and I was suddenly more afraid of him than ever before. Perhaps I should not have discussed my ambitions with him.

Then something in the prince's face changed. He picked up my hand again, caressing it gently. "You are a very special woman, Katerina. When you are my bride, I will build hundreds of hospitals throughout Montenegro in your name. You may spend your days visiting and comforting the sick."

I pulled my hand out of his. "Your Highness, that is not my wish. I do not want hospitals named after me."

"Becoming a doctor is not an option. My queen shall never have an occupation."

"But—"

He stood up, pulling me with him by the elbow. "We have been absent from the ballet long enough. You must return to your family, and I to mine."

"We must talk about this," I protested.

"No." His eyes flashed with anger. "There will be no more discussions. You are to start behaving like a proper fiancée."

I saw red. How dare he tell me how to behave? I calmly pulled the engagement ring off my finger and placed it in his hand. "Then I can no longer be your fiancée." How could I have fallen under his spell? He was an arrogant young man, not charming at all.

Prince Danilo grabbed my right hand, turning it to reveal the obsidian ring. "I see someone has been filling your head with lies about me."

"I don't know what you're talking about," I whispered, pulling away from him. "Please leave me alone."

The crown prince smiled. "Just because you are protected does not mean those closest to you are safe."

I gave him the frostiest gaze I could summon. "Stay away from me. And stay away from my family." I turned on my heel and walked off before he could grab me again. I was shaking as I heard the crown prince laughing behind me.

Maman turned to look at me as I slipped back into our box and sat down. "Where on earth have you been?" she whispered.

"I needed fresh air," I hissed back, still seething inside. I knew she would be hysterical when she discovered the engagement had been broken off, but I would let her know in the morning. Princess Cantacuzene would be disappointed as well, since it would interfere with her own schemes. As for Princess Militza, I was no longer afraid of her. Not much, anyway.

Maman took me to see the empress and Grand Duchess Xenia after the end of the second act.

The empress's brown eyes twinkled and she smiled kindly. "My dear, we have heard news of your engagement. Congratulations, Katerina Alexandrovna."

"Thank you, Your Imperial Majesty." I curtsied. She would have more gossip the next day when she heard of the engagement's being broken. I could not tell the empress without telling Maman the bad news first.

Grand Duchess Xenia followed me to the anteroom behind the imperial box, where servants stood ready to pour wine or tea. There was a feast of hors d'oeuvres, called *zakuski* in Russian, laid out on a white linen–covered table. We each took a small glass of wine and sampled some of the caviar. "Tell me about the prince's proposal!" the grand duchess said. "Was it in the moonlight? Did he get down on his knees?"

I smiled weakly. "Not at all. It was at Grand Duchess Miechen's ball. And he most definitely did not get down on his knees."

"Did he kiss you?" the grand duchess asked. *Mon Dieu,* she was a nosy thirteen-year-old.

I blushed. "I cannot tell you that, Your Imperial Highness."

"He did!" she exclaimed, laughing.

"He did what?" the tsarevitch asked as he and his brother appeared, taking glasses from the impeccably dressed servant's silver tray.

I almost choked on my wine.

"Katerina Alexandrovna was telling me about the night her prince proposed to her." Their sister giggled. "And the prince kissed her!" I felt my face burn scarlet.

"Congratulations, Duchess," the tsarevitch said warmly. "It is a wonderful match. And we will be calling you Your Majesty one day!"

I should have confessed right then the engagement had been broken. But instead, I said, "Thank you, Your Imperial Highness," with a feeble smile. I could not bring myself to look at the grand duke's face.

"Will you be married in St. Petersburg or in the prince's country?" Grand Duchess Xenia asked.

"Most likely Cetinje, though it upsets my mother so." This conversation was ridiculous. I was discussing a non-existent engagement and wedding plans that were no longer valid.

"You leave many responsibilities behind in St. Petersburg," the grand duke said in a low voice while Xenia asked the tsarevitch something about the ballet.

I glared at him. "You know nothing of my responsibilities, Your Imperial Highness," I whispered back.

"Don't I?" he said softly. "Your troubled friend was sighted, not four days ago, across the Neva River."

"The count?" I whispered. I almost dropped my plate of blini. "Why did you not send me word?"

"What would you have done? Run after him? That would not be safe, Duchess. I am merely pointing out the fact that you have created a mess that you would leave behind for your new life in Cetinje. Besides, would your fiancé approve of your traipsing through the woods after an undead count?"

I almost told him right then and there about the Vladiki, and Princess Cantacuzene and Miechen. I almost told him that I had just broken off my engagement. That I would not give up on saving Count Chermenensky.

The empress and my mother entered the anteroom at that moment. "Katerina! We must hurry back to our box, dear, before the next act. Ooh, chanterelles? *Merci!*" Maman said, picking up an hors d'oeuvre. "These are divine!"

I risked a glance at the grand duke before following Maman out. He raised his glass to me but did not smile. I looked away in a hurry.

Slipping into my seat next to Maman, I settled in to watch the remainder of the mediocre ballet. Fortunately, the Montenegrins did not visit our box the rest of the evening. I did not know what Danilo had said to his sisters, if anything. They would be coming to call on me as soon as they found out; I was certain. I wanted to be the one to tell my parents, but I did not want to spoil their evening. I promised myself I would tell Maman and Papa first thing in the morning.

Ah, well, some other girl could be the prince's fiancée. Let her become queen and have hospitals named after her. It was not for me.

CHAPTER TWENTY-NINE

❧

I dragged myself out of bed the next morning, dreading the day I knew I was going to have. Before anything else, I had to tell my parents about my broken engagement. Somehow I did not think Papa would be terribly disappointed. Maman might take to her bed, however. We would have to send for Dr. Kruglevski.

Anya's friend Lyudmila had been hired to help out while Anya was recuperating from a late-winter cold. She was not as friendly as Anya, but I thought she was just shy, having traveled from Kiev and leaving her family to come here. I tried to put her at ease. "Do you know Anya's brother?" I asked her. "He attends the medical school in Kiev."

She cast her eyes down, her face a deep scarlet. Lyudmila must have known him rather well, but she said nothing.

She fixed my hair in a slightly different fashion, more Russian than European, but I liked the change. The curls framed my face, making my cheeks seem thinner. "This looks beautiful, Lyudmila. You'll have to show Anya how to do my hair like this."

"Thank you, Duchess," she said, finally smiling.

I gave myself one last glance in the mirror before going to face Maman.

She was in her boudoir, having tea and toast. "Katiya! You are up early this morning! I expected you to sleep until noon. Sit with me and have some tea."

"Maman, I must tell you something and I do not want you to be upset." I slumped into a peacock-blue velvet chair. "I broke off the engagement with Prince Danilo last night."

She let her butter knife slip, and it hit the table with a loud clang. "Katiya! What on earth would you do that for?" She turned to her maid, who was putting several dresses away in the wardrobe. "Please send for my husband at once! Oh, Katiya, how could you?" She was going to be hysterical again.

I helped her to her bed, sighing. "Please understand, Maman. I am not consort material. The prince and I had a disagreement and I realized that he is not someone I would be happy with."

"Happy? Being queen would not make you happy?"

"Would you have married Papa if he did not make you happy?"

"Well, that was different. I should have married him for his title, even if he hadn't made me happy. We were extremely fortunate that our personalities were so . . . agreeable to each other."

"Agreeable? Is that what you call it?" Papa said, catching

the tail end of our conversation. "You were hopelessly in love with me."

"It was you who were hopelessly in love with me," she said indignantly. "Anyway, it is not our marriage I'm concerned about. Katiya has broken off her engagement with the crown prince!"

Papa raised an eyebrow. "And?"

"And? And you must convince her to change her mind— if the prince will take her back."

"Did the prince try to take advantage of you?" Papa's face looked grim. "I'll challenge him to a duel if he did."

"Heavens, no, Papa! It was nothing like that." I sat down on the bed beside Maman. "I told him I wanted to be a doctor and he said he forbade it. He said it would not be proper for a crown prince's consort to have a career outside of the home. So I told him I could not be his consort."

"Oh, Katiya! This foolish nonsense about medical school again?" Maman wailed. "Alexander, please talk some sense into your daughter!"

"My dear, are you sure you'd give up the chance to be queen? You would have the money to open a hundred hospitals and fund more medical research. A doctor can only do so much in his lifetime."

When he put it that way, I felt almost selfish. But I shook my head. Not as the wife of a blood drinker. "I don't want hospitals named after me. I want to be the one finding new cures and antidotes."

He shook his head and smiled. "Then I suppose you would not make a very good queen. How did the prince take it?"

"Alexander!" Maman said. "You are not taking this seriously! Do not encourage this foolishness!"

"Shenia," Papa said, using his pet name for Maman and taking her hand. "The world is changing. Our daughter does not belong to our old ways. She is going to be one of the brightest women of her age. The Russian Medical Council has filed a petition requesting that the minister of education reopen the women's medical courses. Dr. Kruglevski was one of the doctors here in St. Petersburg who signed the petition." Papa winked at me as he said this.

"However," he continued, "if Katiya cannot attend medical school here in Russia, we can take her to Switzerland. Or Berlin. And if she never finds a husband that accepts her and loves her for who she is, then she can live at Betskoi House with us forever."

I wanted to cry with happiness. "Thank you, Papa!" I flew into his arms as Maman pulled away from him.

"We are not finished discussing this!" Maman said. "Alexander, I must put my foot down!"

"Maman, please think about it," I said.

"And what will all of St. Petersburg say? My daughter threw away a crown to dirty herself with the sick and the dying?" She sat straight up, her face pale. "What did the prince say?"

"The prince was not happy when I handed his ring back. I expect we shall have a visit from his sisters sometime soon."

Maman wiped her eyes with her handkerchief. "The

Montenegrins will tell everyone that he broke off the engagement."

"It will all blow over, my dear," Papa said, squeezing her shoulder gently. "Have courage. Katiya, I think I shall name my medical institute after you. That way, you can be a doctor, and have your own hospital."

I couldn't help smiling; I loved my father so much. I thought he'd been unhappy when I had accepted the prince's proposal. "That would be wonderful, Papa."

Maman blew her nose loudly. "Well," she said, getting out of bed as soon as my father left us. "The only thing to do is to leave immediately for France. Even though I hate to abandon St. Petersburg in the middle of the season, we must go and let the scandal die down. In a few months, no one will be talking about it anymore."

"Maman, do you really think that many people care about what a silly little Oldenburg girl does? There won't be much of a scandal."

Maman looked astonished. "Katiya, you are the great-granddaughter of a tsar! Of course people will care! And you are rejecting a crown prince!" She told her maid to begin packing. "We must make plans to depart immediately."

"What about my lessons at Smolny?"

"I will send word to the headmistress, and we will hire a tutor for you. I must go and speak to your father about our trip."

I did not want a tutor. As much as I dreaded lessons with Madame Metcherskey, I liked my classmates (most of them) and I loved Madame Orbellani. I did not think a personal

208

scandal was a good enough excuse for not attending my classes.

I started to pack my bags, but there was one person I could still not abandon. Count Chermenensky. I did not know where he was hiding, but the grand duke George was right; I could not leave my messes behind for someone else to clean up. I wished I could find the count and take him with us to France. I needed to speak with Dr. Kruglevski.

Perhaps he would have some kind of tranquilizer we could inject Count Chermenensky with, subduing him for travel. I told my parents I was going to visit the patients at Oldenburg Hospital and tell the doctor goodbye, since we would be leaving soon. Papa let me take the family carriage but insisted that I bring Anya with me and have the doctor give her medicine for her cold.

Anya was reluctant to leave the house, but I made sure she was well bundled in furs and I let her keep the hot brick under her own feet. "Thank you, Duchess," she said, snuggling into the warm fur. "I went to the healer in the Gypsy quarter, but I haven't felt any better since her treatment."

"What did she do to you?" I asked.

"She prayed and rolled an egg up and down my arms. She—" Anya's fitful cough interrupted her story. It was several moments before she could talk again. "It seems to me the illness is in my chest, though. Why wouldn't she have rolled the egg there?"

I frowned. "Because she knew nothing about proper medicine. Dr. Kruglevski will know what to do."

Anya sat back, worn out by her coughing. "I just hope I'll be well in time for Rudolf and Lyudmila's wedding."

No wonder Lyudmila had blushed when I'd asked if she knew Rudolf. I patted Anya on the shoulder. "I'm sure you'll feel better in no time. And if not, perhaps they will wait with the wedding until you are."

"Oh, no!" Anya said, distressed. "The date has already been set. If they don't marry on that date, it would be bad luck for them to marry at all."

I tried to soothe her, reassuring her that she would be healthy again soon. I shivered, wondering what my wedding date would have been. Thankful that I was no longer the crown prince's fiancée, I did not worry about superstitious wedding omens. I had enough to worry about.

CHAPTER THIRTY

The nurses at Oldenburg Hospital were much happier to see me when I arrived with my maid in the carriage bearing the Oldenburg family crest. We were ushered into the doctor's office and each given a cup of hot spiced tea. Dr. Kruglevski came in and listened to Anya's chest and gave her a small vial of cough syrup.

The doctor looked happy to see me as well. "Duchess! What a pleasure! You are looking much better than when I saw you last. How are you feeling?"

"Actually, I wondered if you have any medicine that will help me sleep more deeply at night. I have been having horrible nightmares lately, and I've not slept well in over a month." Not including the two days I was unconscious at the Vladimirichi Palace.

"Hmmm." He scanned through his glass cabinet full of brown and green glass bottles. "Here is one I feel comfortable with you using. But only take one dropperful each

211

night before going to bed. And it would be better if you do not use this every single night, as you will become dependent upon it."

"Thank you, Doctor," I said, taking the green bottle he handed me, feeling only a little remorseful about deceiving him. If one teaspoon would knock me out, I wondered how much it would take to knock out an undead soldier.

As Anya and I were preparing to leave, the head nurse rushed in. "Doctor, you must come quickly! They have brought in Prince Demidov!"

Princess Aurora's cousin. I set my things down and followed Dr. Kruglevski into the triage area, where they had laid the prince on a stretcher. There was blood everywhere. Anya began to swoon.

"I need a bottle of saline and some gauze, quickly!" Dr. Kruglevski barked out orders to his associates.

"What has happened to him?" I asked. The prince was still breathing, but it was very shallow. His face was snow-white.

"Katerina Alexandrovna, you should go home now," Dr. Kruglevski said. "You should not have to see this."

"I want to help," I said. "Tell me what I can do."

The doctor did not waste any more time arguing with me but handed me a large bundle of gauze and told me to place it over the young man's neck. "Hold pressure on the wound," he said grimly. "There is a major artery there that is bleeding out."

The gauze bloomed a bright red and became saturated. I still put as much pressure on his neck as I could.

The doctor cut the patient's clothing off, revealing a

young, muscular chest. I sucked in my breath. I had never seen even my brother's chest before. The room was getting a bit warm. *Fight it, Katiya*, I told myself. *You are not going to pass out just because there is a half-naked, bleeding man in front of you.*

The doctor handed me more gauze, and I used it to reinforce what I already had pressed up against the severed blood vessel. The doctor started an intravenous line in the prince's arm and attached the bag of saline, trying desperately to replace the blood the prince was losing.

Suddenly, the prince awoke with a cry and a spasm. His eyes rolled back in his head and he stiffened.

"He's seizing!" the nurse cried.

But the prince did not seize. He fell limp with a rattle in his chest. There was no more shallow breathing. He had just died. In my arms.

I swooned. I tried not to, but I did. One of the nurses behind me held me up. "It's all right, dear," she said calmly, as if she was used to seeing young men die. She tried to lead me to the bench in the hallway, where Anya was sitting. But I didn't want to leave.

"I'm fine, thank you," I said, angry at myself. I was angry at the doctor for not being able to save the young man. And I was angry at whoever had killed him. "What kind of wound is that on his neck?" I asked. "It almost looks like an animal bite." But there was so much blood I really couldn't tell.

"It does appear to be an animal bite," the doctor said, cleaning away the blood with saline. "Who brought this man to the hospital?"

"His companions are out in the lobby," one of the nurses said, and hurried off to find them.

I did not recognize the soldiers who had accompanied Prince Demidov, but I was certain they knew my brother. I hoped he was not in any danger. I could hear the doctor asking them questions, but I could not hear the soldiers' answers. They were in shock. One of them was pale and shaking. He didn't look much older than I was.

Feeling steadier now, I moved closer so I could hear the conversation.

"We were walking in the woods, behind the palace," said the first soldier.

"Something jumped out at us," the younger one finished. "It was enormous."

The doctor looked skeptical. "In broad daylight? You must have gotten a very close look at it."

"It was dark in the woods," the first soldier said. "I cannot say for sure, but I believe it was a wolf."

I felt a little nauseated. Had a wolf caused all that damage to the prince's neck? Wolves were normally too shy to approach humans, especially in broad daylight. I thought about the slender silvery gray wolf we had seen coming home the night of *Le Bal Noir*. The wolf's fur had gleamed in the light of the full moon.

"I'll test the body for rabies. This is the first wolf attack I have seen in years. Were either of you bitten as well?"

They both shook their heads. I felt sorry for the soldiers, knowing they could do nothing to save their friend. As they turned to leave, I saw a white cross flash from a bearded soldier's chest. The Order of St. John of Jerusalem. I rushed back to the room where the dead soldier was. Dr. Kruglevski had ripped the soldier's clothing off to inspect him, and I found the tattered, bloodstained uniform on the floor. There, on the right breast, was the white Maltese cross. This prince had been one of the tsar's knights. Like Count Chermenensky.

CHAPTER THIRTY-ONE

∽◈∾

I had to get a message to the grand duke George. He most
assuredly already knew about Demidov, but I wanted to
tell him about the Dekebristi. I suspected they were behind
these attacks on the Order. According to Grand Duchess
Miechen, the Romanov family was certain the Dekebristi
had been eradicated. If they had indeed returned, I needed
to find out where they were hiding.

Elena was not at school. I breathed a sigh of relief, not
eager to face her.

Dariya was helping a grieving Aurora Demidova pack her
things. Her family was coming to take her home later that
day for her cousin's funeral. The princess did not expect to
return to school for some time.

Erzsebet and Augusta walked with me in the snow-
covered gardens of the school, discussing the ballet of the
previous weekend. They wanted to know what plans I'd already made for the wedding. I sighed. Maman would not let

me say anything publicly about my broken engagement just yet. So I merely said something vague about flowers. And cake.

"Ooh! Our cousin Princess Sophia had a lemon cake at her wedding that was twenty feet high!"

"It was not!" Erzsebet said. "It only looked like that to you, because you were only five years old."

"Maman said it was twenty feet," Augusta said, pouting.

The princesses' chattering was giving me a headache, and I wished I could go for a walk in the woods alone. The attack on Prince Demidov frightened me, however, and soon enough Madame Tomilov would learn of it and forbid anyone from leaving the school grounds.

"Is your handsome brother coming to visit you soon?" Augusta asked. "He always brings his handsome friends with him."

I winced, remembering Demidov's last breath. And Count Chermenensky's swagger. No more of the tsar's knights would die if I could do anything about it.

"Did you know your brother's friend told us about their scary school? The count said that there is an enormous portrait of Tsar Pyotr the Great in the Great Hall of the Corps des Pages, and the portrait comes alive and walks the palace at night."

"It wasn't Pyotr the Great," Erzsebet said. "It was Pavel."

"Or was it Alexander the First?" Augusta asked. She was arranging rocks in a pretty pattern in the snow. A heart.

I stopped walking. It was definitely Tsar Pavel. My brother had mentioned the portrait before. And if the tsar walked the Great Hall at night, I needed to speak with him. I stopped in my tracks. "I've forgotten something important," I said as I turned to head back to the school. "I must send a message to my brother."

"Oh, do ask him to come," Erzsebet said. She and Augusta giggled as they skipped along behind me.

❦

I needed to see the portrait of the tsar in the palace of the Corps des Pages. Women were not allowed in the palace, but I wouldn't let that stop me. I could borrow my brother's clothes and disguise myself as a boy to get past the guards.

Never had I wanted to speak with the dead, raise the dead, touch the dead, or even think about the dead. But it was imperative that I speak with the tsar's ghost. He could tell me how to protect the Romanovs from the Dekebristi.

I returned to my room to compose my letter. Elena was there, waiting for me. She was not angry, as I had expected, but was very upset.

"Oh, Katerina! How could you?" There were large tears pooling in the corners of her eyes.

I sighed as she rushed forward and embraced me. "I'm so sorry," I told her. "As much as I admire your brother, I don't believe we could be happy together."

"But you were happy!" she said. "Did he say something to upset you? Tell me and I will make him apologize."

I shook my head. "He cannot apologize for being who he is." *An arrogant and dangerous soon-to-be blood drinker.*

Hastily, I added, "He is the crown prince and needs to

218

have a bride who will be a proper consort for him. I'm afraid I am not the right choice."

"But who wouldn't want to become a queen?" Elena demanded. She looked sincerely puzzled. It was her only ambition in life to become a queen or a tsarina herself.

"Me." I smiled sadly.

Elena sighed. "I do not understand you, Katerina. I think you will change your mind when you realize how much you love Danilo."

My cousin walked in as Elena left. They had been cool toward each other ever since Dariya had returned from the hospital. Her father and stepmother had wanted to withdraw her from Smolny, but Dariya had wanted to come back. "Who else is going to look after you?" she had asked me. I was glad to have her here, but I still worried. We had no way of proving Elena had done anything wrong. And what was to prevent her from poisoning Dariya again?

Dariya's stepmother, Countess Zina, was as fond of séances and tarot cards as Maman, and had given Dariya her own card deck for Christmas. Dariya had thought the occult was merely a fashionable hobby until she met the Montenegrins. Now she knew better.

I told my cousin about the ghost in Vorontsov Palace.

She agreed that we should try to speak with the ghost. "The opera is this Friday night," she said. "We could sneak away from the performance." My cousin was devilishly clever sometimes.

❧

Dariya came home to Betskoi House with me for the weekend. We sneaked into my brother's room after dinner and I
opened up his wardrobe. "Help me find an outfit to wear."

My cousin shook her head. "Katiya, dressing as your
brother to get into the palace might work, but there is something else you can do that would be far more stylish."

Mon Dieu. My cousin always had her own priorities. She
was so much like my mother.

Dariya pulled a small torn book from behind her. "Your
mother told me I could borrow any book I found in the library, and I picked this one up, thinking it was a new Marie
Corelli novel."

I took the book from her and shivered as I read the cover.
A Necromancer's Companion. How could she have possibly
thought it was a romance? And how had it ended up in
the library? Maybe one of the maids had found it under my
bed and placed it on the shelf, thinking that was where it
belonged.

I opened the *Companion* and began leafing through the
pages, but Dariya stopped me. "There are things in this book
that we probably shouldn't know, Katiya," she said. "Talismans, incantations, rituals for terrible things."

I wanted to tell her that Princess Cantacuzene had given
the book to me, but then I would have to tell my cousin
everything. About me. I dreaded how she might react. And
I believed she was safer not knowing. For the moment, at
least.

Then Dariya smiled mischievously. "But there is a spell
for creating a shadow around oneself. Wouldn't that make a

clever disguise? Of course, you're no necromancer, but what if it works anyway? We could use it to sneak into Vorontsov Palace!"

We hurried back to my room. Dariya rang for Lyudmila and opened the door to my closet. "We shall dress for the opera and go with your mother. We can slip out during the first act and take the carriage to the palace."

I nodded, scanning through the pages of the book. There was a spell for a *sheult*, which was Egyptian for "shadow." There were incantations to Egyptian gods and goddesses. Drawings of talismans and sigils. A ritual for letting the dead rest in peace. My heart stopped as I looked up at Dariya.

I couldn't tell her about the count. But there was a ritual in the book that might be able to help him. I berated myself for not consulting it sooner.

"Where on earth did your mother find the *Companion*, Katiya?" my cousin asked. "Should I ask her tonight at the theater?"

I swallowed in alarm. I couldn't allow Dariya to mention the book to Maman. "I don't even know if she's seen it," I said, trying to sound casual. "Princess Cantacuzene gave the book to me, though I certainly can't imagine why. I had forgotten all about it."

My cousin shrugged nonchalantly as Lyudmila entered and started to fix Dariya's hair. "I found a drawing in there of something called the Talisman of Isis," Dariya said. "Don't you think that would make a wonderful title for a romance novel?"

I rolled my eyes and flipped through the book again. Something had been written in the margin of one of the pages. I had no way of knowing if it was Princess Cantacuzene's handwriting.

You must always, always return from the darkness. Always return to the light.

CHAPTER THIRTY-TWO

M y mother nodded off in our stuffy box at the Mariinsky Theatre, making it easy to slip away during the
second act of Tchaikovsky's *Eugene Onegin*. Dariya told the
footman we were to pick up my brother at Vorontsov Palace, and the poor footman believed her.

I twisted the obsidian ring around my finger as our carriage made its way through the streets of St. Petersburg. The
Vorontsov Palace, which housed the Corps des Pages, was
one of the oldest buildings on Nevsky Prospekt and sat back
on enormous gated grounds. Our carriage rolled through the
imposing gates and up to the chapel entrance on the eastern
side. Dariya held the *Companion* open on her lap. "Say
'*Sheult Anubis*' three times and you will be protected by your
own shadow." She looked up from the book. "Are you sure
you want to go through with this? Your mother's séances are
diverting, but this might be dangerous if it works."

"I believe it will work, Dariya. It has to. Think of my

brother and the other members of the Order. The ghost must be awakened to look after his knight-commanders."

Dariya shrugged. "You don't even know if there's anything a dead tsar can do for the Order."

"But there's a chance. I have to try." I whispered the spell three times. I felt the darkness begin to close in and fought a surge of panic rising inside. This was my first conscious experiment of my powers as a necromancer. I was a bundle of nerves—especially as I understood the importance of what I needed to accomplish. It was strange how I could feel the shadows enveloping me and yet I could still see everything.

"*Mon Dieu!*" Dariya said, crossing herself. "How frightening! You just vanished! It worked!"

"Now you try!" I said, wondering what would happen.

Dariya looked down at the book in her lap. "*Sheult Anubis,*" she whispered. She repeated the words rapidly twice, but nothing changed. She held out her hands and wiggled her fingers. "I'm still visible! Perhaps that's best. What if your mother wakes up to find us both missing?"

I opened the carriage door and stepped out into the frigid February night. There must have been a new moon, for there were millions of stars in the inky-black sky.

"Good luck," Dariya whispered. She was heading back to the theater, where she could keep an eye on Maman. "I'll see you in a few hours."

I pulled my cloak closer around me, thankful to be shrouded in shadows, and stepped into the portico in front of the chapel as the carriage pulled away. There had been no guards at the outside gate, and the pale young man on watch at the chapel entrance was hiding just inside the portico, snoring loudly. He never stirred as I tiptoed past him and hurried inside.

I knew the younger cadets were in the far western wing of the palace, sleeping, so I had to be very quiet. I hoped the tsar's ghost would not speak loudly.

The chapel was very beautiful, added on to the palace at the tsar's request by the same architect who had designed my parents' Betskoi House. Gold icons depicting the twelve apostles decorated the walls, flanking the arched Gothic windows. The stained glass in the windows portrayed the Holy Family, guarded by several seraphim. I crossed myself before approaching the altar, then exited through the side door into the Great Hall. This was where the portrait of Tsar Pavel stood, watching over his cadets and the future knight-commanders of the Order.

The painting loomed at the end of the hall, the very romantic-looking tsar in the robes of the Grand Master of the Order. The Maltese cross on his insignia gleamed in the dim candlelight.

I sat down on a cold mahogany bench to wait. After what seemed like an eternity, a clock somewhere began to chime, announcing midnight. I held my breath, not sure that His Imperial Majesty, the rumored ghost, would even deign to speak with me. He would not be pleased to hear what I had to say. I discovered I was able to drop the shadows around me by repeating the Egyptian spell again.

The clock chimed a twelfth time and the Great Hall grew silent again. There was no sign of the tsar. No movement from the portrait at all.

Several long minutes passed. I heard nothing but the soft ticking of the clock. I had the growing feeling that the ghost story was nothing more than a legend. I had put Dariya and myself in danger for nothing.

I stared at the portrait, silently willing the tsar to come forth. Did I dare attempt to conjure the Grand Master on my own? I shuddered, with a sick, cold feeling in my stomach. No. I would never do such a thing.

Yet he alone could tell me how to save the members of the Order. My brother would be safe.

The sound of footsteps stopped my heart. I backed up against the wall, wishing I were still cloaked by the shadow spell. I tried to hold my breath, but gasped in surprise when I recognized Grand Duke George Alexandrovich approaching the portrait of Tsar Pavel.

He heard me and drew his saber immediately. "Show yourself!"

I took a step closer to him, my hands out. "Your Imperial Highness."

"You!" he snarled in a low voice. "What are you doing here?"

"I would ask you the same question," I hissed back. "Are you not here to speak with the ghost of the dead tsar?"

He put his weapon away but still frowned. "You have no right to be here! I insist you leave immediately."

"But the members of the Order are in danger!" I said. "If the tsar's ghost can offer any advice . . ."

The grand duke shook his head. "There is no need for you to taint the halls of Vorontsov Palace with your dark rituals. The ghost walks on his own."

A chilled breeze swept through the hall. I saw wisps of spirit flowing from the portrait. "Look," I whispered, taking several steps backward. Even the grand duke stepped back cautiously, managing to put me a little behind him. I was not sure if he was trying to protect me from the ghost or trying to protect the ghost from me.

The powerful tsar stepped outside his painting, all seven feet of him. His white-hot eyes stared down at both of us. "Who disturbs my vigil?" he bellowed.

The grand duke stood at attention. "I am George Alexandrovich Romanov, son of Tsar Alexander the Third."

I bent my head. "I am Katerina Alexandrovna von Oldenburg, Your Imperial Majesty. We've come to tell you about the Knights of the Order. They are in great danger."

The tsar roared, his spirit quickly forming flesh and bone. I took another small step backward as the grand duke glared at me.

"Tell me more of this danger to my knights," the ghost tsar said.

"Three knights of the Maltese cross have died since the new year." I did not think I needed to mention that one of them had been turned undead by me. "And there have been several grave robberies, all of them belonging to Knights of the Order."

Grand Duke George spoke up. "We fear the vampires, Your Imperial Majesty."

"The supreme enemy of the knights is the House of

Bessaraba, descendants of the Dragon," the tsar bellowed. "Find the Dragon's descendant, Koldun, and you will find their enemy."

Koldun? That was a word Maman had used to describe ancient Russian wizards when she'd told me bedtime stories long before. But I had never heard of the House of Bessaraba.

"Yes, Your Imperial Majesty," the grand duke said.

The tsar turned toward me. "You are very brave, young lady, for seeking me out in the darkness of night. I can see that you are protected by the shadow. But you must be strong, and not give in to the shadow's seduction."

"Yes, Your Imperial Majesty," I said, frightened and bewildered by what he said. I remembered Maman's tarot cards and her dream. "Can the bogatyr return to fight the House of Bessaraba?"

The seven-foot-tall ghost laughed. It was a terrible laugh. "Do you know what you ask of your living tsar?" he said. "To invoke the bogatyr means to accept an enormous physical burden. Though the bogatyr imparts supernatural strength, the tsar pays a great price. It is . . . debilitating."

The grand duke simply bowed his head. "Yes, Your Imperial Majesty."

Tsar Pavel began to pace in front of us. "The living tsar has more problems than he realizes. Cursed members of the Order are rising from the dead, blood drinkers are stalking young girls, even the wolf-folk are running loose on the streets of St. Petersburg. The House of Bessaraba and its allies are growing too strong." He spun around and looked at the grand duke. "Why is the Bear so soft on the Dark Ones?"

My head was swimming. Wolf-folk? Dark Ones?

The grand duke was silent, but I saw him stiffen.

"Koldun, we must not let the Dark Ones win."

"I understand, Your Imperial Majesty." The grand duke clicked his heels together and inclined his head slightly.

"In the meantime, you must pledge to me that you will protect this girl." He nodded toward me. "Her powers place her in great danger from the House of Bessaraba."

"Your Imperial Majesty," I said hurriedly, "that is not really necess—" But I was silenced by the tsar's frosty stare.

"I pledge to protect her with my life," the grand duke said grimly. "I serve at the pleasure of the tsar."

"As do you, young necromancer," the ghost tsar said. "You must be prepared to summon the bogatyr if he is needed."

"I do pledge this, Your Imperial Majesty," I said with a curtsy, even though I had no idea what he meant.

"Good." The tsar looked at us both. I saw the grand duke's shoulders relax slightly, even though he still stood at attention.

It was time for the tsar to return to his resting place. He turned and walked back to his portrait, his boots sounding heavy beneath him. Just when I thought his corporeal body would bump into the wall, he disappeared into the painting.

I suddenly wished I'd asked the ghost about the Dekebristi. I asked the grand duke instead.

"It is not possible," he said. "Those not executed were exiled to Siberia. The vampires and their minions are forbidden to return."

"But what if they are behind the attacks on the Order? Who else would rob graves?"

"The tsar said to find the descendant of the Dragon."

"How will we find him?"

He didn't answer, and I knew that he wasn't going to tell me. I knew too that he would honor his pledge to the tsar and protect me, even if he despised me.

"Let's go," the grand duke whispered. His black cloak swirled around him as he walked, surrounding him in his own waving shadow. "We must leave quickly."

"My carriage will be outside."

"In the middle of the night?" He rubbed his forehead, an action I'd seen his father do often when he was weary of his social obligations. "Your life is in danger," the grand duke said. "You must stay at home, where it is safe. The House of Bessaraba will not be able to harm you there."

He put his hand on my arm to drag me away. "Hurry, Duchess."

I heard footsteps in the hallway behind us. The young guard I'd seen earlier must have woken up and resumed his duties. We did need to leave quickly.

My mother's carriage was waiting for us outside the chapel gate.

"Hurry!" the grand duke shouted to the driver as he ushered me inside and climbed in after me. We sat across from my mother and my cousin.

Dariya had told Maman that I had received a message to meet Petya at Vorontsov Palace and had hurried ahead of them to find out if he was in danger.

"Katiya!" Maman cried. "You should not have done anything so foolish! You were fortunate the grand duke was there to look out for you. Where is Petya?"

"He received orders from the general and had to leave," the grand duke said, catching on quickly.

Maman seemed surprised and a little nervous to have the tsar's son in the carriage with her, and she spoke the whole ride home about our planned trip. "We will probably be in Biarritz for the rest of Lent, and most of spring," she said, fanning herself with a paper fan made with pressed lilacs. "I hope we will see your mother at the ball tomorrow night so we may say our goodbyes."

Grand Duke George nodded politely. "Of course, Your Highness. And what takes you away to France this early in the season?"

Maman looked at me. "Katerina has not told you? Our Katiya has argued with her fiancé and broken off the engagement. We must leave St. Petersburg to ignore the scandal."

Dariya snorted in a most unladylike fashion.

I wanted to vanish like the ghostly tsar right then and there. The grand duke had no business knowing about my engagement—or ending of the engagement. But he seemed very interested.

"You shall not be marrying the crown prince," the grand duke said thoughtfully. Our carriage was drawing nearer to Anichkov Palace. As the carriage slowed, he told the driver he wished to accompany us to Betskoi House, as he wanted to see us home safely. The carriage driver nodded and drove on.

"Your Imperial Highness, that is not necessary," I said.

"I have given a promise. And so have you, Duchess."

I sighed. Maman was staring out the window into the

231

darkness, and Dariya had fallen asleep against her. "Why did the tsar call you Koldun?" I asked in a low voice.

"I cannot tell you. It is a secret only for the members of the Order to know."

"But I thought a *koldun* was a sorcerer. Why would he think that you were—"

"Do not ask me again." His voice was soft, but firm.

I kept my voice low, even though Maman seemed to be dozing off now as well. "You are to be the Grand Master, then, when your brother becomes the tsar," I said softly. Although much of the inner workings of the Order was secret, Grand Duchess Miechen had once said that the Grand Master of the Order was a sorcerer, who performed the arcane rituals that protected the knight-commanders. If she knew who the current Grand Master was, she kept that secret to herself.

"Yes," the grand duke said, closing his eyes. He looked tired, and I had the urge to comfort him.

I wished there were something I could do to help him. "I promise I will never tell another soul."

The grand duke merely nodded.

The carriage approached Betskoi House, all dark except for the lamps at the entrance. The grand duke helped my mother and cousin out of the carriage. "Thank you, Your Imperial Highness," Maman said. "We are so grateful for your escort. Our carriage will see you home."

The grand duke turned to take my hand. It was awkward, for just a moment, and then he was the tsar's son again, regal and overbearing. "I must ask that you not return to

Smolny in the morning," he said. "When do you leave for Biarritz?"

"In a few days, Your Imperial Highness."

"Will you stay here at Betskoi House until then?"

"I cannot promise that. Maman and I have provisions to deliver to the hospital, and we must say our goodbyes to Princess Cantacuzene and the grand duchess Maria Pavlovna."

His eyes narrowed. "You know that the grand duchess Miechen is a very dangerous woman. As is her friend, Cantacuzene."

"They are friends of my mother."

"Cantacuzene is a descendant of the House of Bessaraba."

That stopped my blood cold. "What?" I whispered.

"Katerina!" Maman was standing inside the front door. "Hurry along! It is freezing outside!"

I ignored her. "Her family is the enemy of the Order?" I asked the grand duke.

His smile was grim. "You truly should pay more attention to the ancestry of your friends. Cantacuzene, the Montenegrins. You and your mother travel in some rather nasty social circles, Duchess." He closed the door of the carriage, and our driver headed back to Anichkov Palace.

I stood in the snow, chilled from the inside out. There was something ominous about the darkness now that the grand duke had left. The night seemed to be pressing in on me. I raised my hand and examined the obsidian ring more closely. Exactly what kind of black magic did it contain?

CHAPTER THIRTY-THREE

❧

Of course I didn't stay home as the grand duke had instructed. Of course I went to see the grand duchess Miechen—without Maman. I wanted to ask her more about the princess Cantacuzene.

Dr. Kruglevski was leaving the Vladimirichi Palace. He smiled when he saw me. "Duchess Katerina Alexandrovna!" he said in greeting. "What a pleasure!"

"Good morning, Doctor," I said, alarmed to see him. "Is the grand duchess ill?"

He shook his head. "Not at all. But I shall let her tell you the news. How are your parents?"

"They are well. Papa is excited about his plans for his new medical institute. And we shall travel to Switzerland this summer to look at the medical schools there."

"Excellent! Good day to you, Duchess."

I hurried inside and up the stairs to the grand duchess's parlor. I waited as her servants announced me.

"Katerina Alexandrovna, what a delight." The grand duchess did not exactly look pleased to see me. Her voice dripped with sarcasm. "How is your mother?"

"She is well, thank you. And you are well? I saw Dr. Kruglevski leaving."

"Yes, I am fine, my dear. As are the babies."

"Babies?"

She smiled slightly, though the smile did not reach her eyes. "They are due in the fall."

"Congratulations, Your Imperial Highness. I did not know. Twins? That is wonderful."

The dark faerie's youngest child, Helena, was already seven years old. Her oldest, Kyril, was thirteen. It must have been a surprise to find herself expecting again. She sat down in the velvet chair opposite me. "And what has brought you here today?"

"I need to ask you about Princess Cantacuzene," I whispered. I was never sure when the princess would be at Miechen's palace. This would not be a good day to run into her.

"Yes?" the grand duchess said, turning to pour herself some tea. From the side, I spotted a slight swelling in her belly that I had not noticed before. "What can I tell you about the princess?"

"Her lineage," I said, holding my breath. "Is she a descendant of the House of Bessaraba?"

"Of course, dear."

I felt cold and slightly nauseated. I grabbed the chair in front of me as the room tilted slightly.

"Do you know the history of the House of Bessaraba?" Miechen asked.

"Only that its descendant is the person responsible for killing the members of the Order of St. John."

"Indeed?" the grand duchess asked. "Where did you hear such a thing?"

I did not think the grand duke George would want me to let Miechen know exactly how I had come across that information.

Miechen's violet eyes narrowed like a cat's as she stared at me. "Then you do not know that one of Princess Ruxandra's ancestors was Vlad Dracul of Wallachia."

I almost dropped the cup of tea she had given me. "No," I whispered. Princess Cantacuzene was a vampire. She was their leader. "You have been protecting her secret from the tsar?"

Miechen nodded. "I am bound by an oath. But now you have discovered it on your own."

"Why would she want members of the Order dead?"

"She must believe them some sort of threat. She and I will discuss this. I will not allow it to continue." The dark faerie's face was grim.

"She wanted me to kill Prince Danilo."

"So you told me before. It would be the most prudent way for her to deal with the Montenegrin threat. They are close allies of the tsar." Miechen stirred her own tea thoughtfully. "And Princess Militza is an ambitious young blood drinker, who wants to rule the St. Petersburg blood-line."

"But what about Princess Elena and the tsarevitch?"

"Somehow, I do not see that union coming to pass, no matter how fond the tsar is of King Nikola. Elena is still a

236

blood drinker, and the Romanov line cannot be tainted with their like."

I must have breathed a sigh of relief, because Miechen smiled. "You perhaps thought of marrying the tsarevitch yourself?"

"*Mon Dieu*, no!" I said, blushing. "I would never want to be empress." I shuddered, imagining the burden. "Besides, I believe the tsarevitch has already found his bride."

Miechen smiled. "Do you have a touch of the faerie sight as well? You have a precarious situation, child. Your future is very unclear to me. I wonder what you will do with your gift."

"Why does the tsar allow the Romanian vampires to live in St. Petersburg?"

"A truce that his grandfather Nicholas made with the most powerful vampire house. The House of Bessaraba is strong enough to keep the other houses in line."

"How many houses are there? Does Princess Cantacuzene rule the Dekebristi?"

Miechen shook her head. "The Dekebristi minions do not exist anymore. But the House of Bessaraba has absorbed many of the smaller families, especially the Bulgarians and the Moravians. There is a small family of upyri in Siberia, but they are watched carefully by the Old Believers. And there are the houses in Rome, India, Egypt."

I shuddered, wondering how many blood drinkers there were in the world. I had heard before of the Old Believers, who kept to the beliefs of the Byzantine Orthodox Church. "Princess Cantacuzene told me about the Dekebristi," I said. "She said the wife of Grand Duke Konstantin Pavlovich was a vampire and had created the Dekebristi from members of the Order of St. John."

Miechen nodded. "But I imagine she did not tell you Konstantin's wife, Johanna, was also from the House of Bessaraba."

"She was related to Princess Cantacuzene?" A chill slid down my spine.

"Distantly, or so she has told me. Johanna was defeated with the Dekebristi by Tsar Nicholas."

"He had summoned the bogatyr," I guessed. Why did they not teach us the true version of history in school? It would be ever so helpful.

"Yes, and that is why you have become so valuable, Katerina Alexandrovna. Only a necromancer can evoke the bogatyr for the tsar. The Koldun is forbidden from performing such rituals. The Dekebristi would kill you to prevent the bogatyr from being summoned. If they still existed."

Now I did not know who to fear more—Princess Cantacuzene or the Montenegrins. Or the Dekebristi. I had planned to visit Princess Cantacuzene, to say goodbye to her before we left for Biarritz. I had never felt threatened or in danger when I was with her. I could not imagine the aged princess drinking someone's blood. She was too elegant. Too delicate. And yet I remembered Princess Cantacuzene's tale of the veshtizas. They were beautiful women who turned into insect-like creatures and sucked the blood of sleeping victims.

My breath caught. How could I have forgotten? Flying insects, like moths.

CHAPTER THIRTY-FOUR

∼◦∽

I decided not to visit the princess Cantacuzene, and returned home instead. There was a carriage with the imperial family crest in front of my house. As I walked inside past Papa's study, I heard a familiar voice. Grand Duke George Alexandrovich. I swallowed back fear and a little bit of irritation.

I went to Maman's parlor and started working on a piece of embroidery, something to keep my fingers occupied, even though my mind wandered. I craved to know what Papa and the grand duke were discussing. Maman chattered away about the latest gossip concerning the deaths of the Austrian crown prince and his mistress. Something about lycanthropy. I rolled my eyes. Surely Erzsebet and Augusta would have told me if their uncle and his mistress had turned into werewolves.

I stared out the window onto the snow-covered grounds below. It was a dreary gray day, with months to go before the spring thaw. I sighed. At least it would be pretty and warm in Biarritz. Maman and I expected to leave that Friday, with Papa joining us the following week.

One of the house servants appeared at the door. "Your Highness, forgive me, but His Imperial Highness would like to speak with his daughter in his study."

I put my needlework down and quickly went to Papa's study. I hoped the grand duke was gone.

He wasn't. He was sitting in Papa's favorite leather chair.

My father was standing at the window. "Katerina!" He did not sound happy. "Come in here, my dear!"

"Yes, Papa?" I asked, standing at his doorway. I curtsied to the grand duke. "Your Imperial Highness."

"The grand duke has informed me that you took it upon yourself to help a strange man who was clearly insane."

I hated the grand duke. "Forgive me, Papa. He was injured and I did not feel I was in danger."

"Next time you come across an injured person who needs medical attention, have the carriage driver take him immediately to see Dr. Kruglevski. Until you have graduated from medical school, you are not allowed to practice medicine on any human being, and furthermore—"

The grand duke cut him short. "Katerina Alexandrovna cleansed and dressed one of my own wounds, when the injured man attacked me." He pushed his sleeve back for Papa to see what was left of the deep gash Count Chermenensky had given him. The scar would heal nicely, and it gave the grand duke a wicked look to him. I noticed the grand duke's hair was slightly longer that day than it usually was, as if he hadn't had time for a trim in over a month. It made it look softer, and I had to fight the urge to run my fingers through it.

"May I look at the scar?" I asked, trying to distract myself. I unceremoniously grabbed the grand duke's arm and slowly ran my finger along the groove in his skin. "It's healing so quickly. How fascinating!"

The grand duke sucked in his breath, gently grasping my hand and removing it from his arm. "Yes, one of the gifts my mother gave me," he murmured low enough so only I could hear.

"Katerina, I am sure you handled the bandages expertly, but you cannot practice medicine on the tsar's son!" my father said, exasperated. "What if something had gone wrong?"

The grand duke smiled. "At the time, Your Highness, she was the most competent person available. There was no harm done."

Had the grand duke just given me a compliment? I blushed pink with pride. I wanted to look at his scar again.

Papa rubbed his eyes and sighed. "I thank you, but I will feel much safer when she attends medical school for proper training."

"You do realize what a struggle it will be to change the law? My father is a traditionalist and does not see the value of women working outside of the home. A girl of your daughter's station should be content with raising a family and keeping a household."

I fumed. But before I could open my mouth and say something both my family and I would regret, my father rushed across the room and hurried me to the door. "Yes, we are aware, Your Imperial Highness," he grunted as I moved to strangle the grand duke. Fortunately, for my sake, Papa pushed me into the hallway before I could reach my target. "But times are changing, and I believe women physicians will become common, perhaps after the turn of the century."

"Content? Would you be content keeping a household if you were a woman?" I shouted from the hallway.

"Katiya? What on earth are you going on about?" Maman hurried up the staircase, clutching her needlework.

I sighed as I turned toward her. It didn't matter. The grand duke was right, at least about some of it. Tsar Alexander the Third was extremely conservative; he would never allow women to return to medical school in Russia.

"I shall have to live elsewhere when I grow up. Perhaps Berlin or Vienna," I told my mother. I shuddered, wondering what family of vampires roamed those beautiful cities. "Or maybe I will move somewhere exotic and tend to the poor." The previous tsar, Alexander the Second, had allowed several young women to obtain medical degrees in exchange for pledging to take care of the indigent in Siberia.

"*Mon Dieu*, Katiya, the things you say," Maman said with a sigh. "I wish you would just make up with Prince Danilo and let him build you all the hospitals and orphanages you want."

"Maman," I said, exasperated by having had the same argument with her hundreds of times. "I will never marry someone who does not accept me for who I am!"

I turned to stalk off to my bedroom, and almost ran into

the grand duke, who had been standing there listening. I was not sure who blushed more, me or His Imperial Highness. Curtsying hastily, I brushed past him and hurried to my room.

Was I being stubborn and foolish? By dreaming of doing something outlandish and forbidden with my life? I did not want to be a necromancer. I did not want to be killed by vampires. And I most certainly did not want to be stuck in a loveless marriage with nothing to do all day but change dresses and take tea with other bored women. It made defying the tsar seem as pleasant as a walk through a grove of lilacs.

CHAPTER THIRTY-FIVE

❧

It was getting close to dark, and my parents were planning to attend a dinner party at Miechen's that evening. I was supposed to go with them, but pleaded a headache and begged to stay home. Maman told Anya and Lyudmila to have a sandwich and tea sent up to my room.

I asked Anya to let me sleep through the night undisturbed so my head would feel better in the morning.

As soon as everyone left, I dressed quickly in one of my plainest brown dresses. I wrapped my head with a black woolen scarf, grabbed my warmest, fur-lined black cloak, and quietly slipped out of the house. It was a short walk to Vorontsov Palace. I wanted to know what was happening at the Order. I spoke the Egyptian magic words, veiling myself in my own shadow. Once again, I felt the darkness closing in around me, but I knew to expect it this time. I took a few deep breaths and hurried down the street.

I was freezing by the time I reached the palace, but I tried not to let my teeth chatter too loudly. In shadow, I easily slipped past the guards, who were very much awake and heavily armed this time. Several members of the Order had gathered in the Great Hall before the portrait of Tsar Pavel. I could hear anxiety and fear in their voices. There were whisperings about an old curse on the Order. The youngest pages were not present. They had been sent to bed.

General Tcherevine led the assembled men, reminding them that they had pledged their lives to serve the tsar as well as Mother Russia. That they had made this pledge before God. He did not discuss what had prompted the gathering. I moved through the crowd cloaked in shadow, trying to pick up some conversation from the nervous soldiers.

"Did you see him?"

"Count Orlov did. Said it was Demidov, all right. He looked a little pale, but he knew it was him."

"And he attacked him?"

"Yes. Said he tried to bite him."

I felt a little weak but leaned up against a wall to breathe. Prince Demidov had returned from the dead now too? Was that what had happened to all the stolen bodies? They had all been members of the Order. Was someone making revenants out of them? It would have taken a powerful necromancer to perform such black magic. The only other necromancer I knew of was the vampire princess from the House of Bessaraba. What in the holy name of God was Princess Cantacuzene doing?

It was several hours before midnight, but I wondered if the ghost of the tsar would speak to the men. I hoped they knew what they were going after.

There was a stir of murmurings as a small band of men pushed through the crowd and reached the front of the room. "Make way for His Imperial Highness Grand Duke George Alexandrovich," someone said.

The grand duke looked tired but grimly determined. He wasn't addressing the crowd but stood off to the side of the general, listening to what the older, wiry-haired man had to say. I stayed far away. I did not want the grand duke's faerie eyes to see me under my *sheult* spell.

General Tcherevine nodded and then spoke to his regiments: "Unfortunately, I have just received confirmation on the attack on Count Orlov," he began. "The doctors are working on him as quickly as possible but say he has lost an enormous amount of blood. It does not look well for him. His family is being notified as we speak."

"How are we to fight this monster?" someone asked.

"Fire will kill it," the grand duke said. "As will decapitation. Or preferably both."

Why had Demidov attacked a former comrade in arms? Bitten him, no less. Count Chermenensky was not running around St. Petersburg biting people, was he? No one had seen him in several weeks, but I feared the worst. I had to sneak closer and hear what the grand duke was saying.

"Search the woods behind Smolny, as well as the Tauride Palace," the grand duke was telling the other men. "As soon as this monster is caught, his body must be brought to the Koldun."

"He has to have been called forth by a powerful necromancer," General Tcherevine said. "Who is the prince's master?"

"Or mistress," the grand duke said grimly. He suspected Princess Cantacuzene, just as I did.

The crowd stirred as a messenger arrived. They had cornered the undead Prince Demidov in a small abandoned building along the river. Close to the Field of Mars. I swallowed hard, thinking how near my home this monster was.

"Commander Oldenburg has his men in position, sir," the messenger said.

"Very good." The general nodded. "We shall join him immediately. Men!"

Petya. He was in the building with that monster. If anything happened to my brother, it would devastate my mother. And my father. I huddled against the wall, trying not to sob out loud.

The grand duke brushed past me on his way out with the members of the Order. I held my breath, but he stopped, as if he could sense my presence. He frowned, shook his head, and continued on.

I stayed hidden until the last man left the Great Hall. Then I was alone with the giant portrait of Tsar Pavel. His eyes seemed to find me, even though I was cloaked in the shadows. I wondered if I should speak to him again and ask more questions about the bogatyr. The ghost had said that becoming the bogatyr was not pleasant. But who else would be able to fight an army of undead soldiers running amok in St. Petersburg?

An army of undead. That was a chilling thought. Princess Cantacuzene was creating such an army out of the tsar's own elite knight-commanders. Just like the Dekebristi in 1825. I couldn't fathom why she needed this army. Or whom she was planning to attack.

CHAPTER THIRTY-SIX

❧

I slipped back outside and hurried toward home. I followed the general direction of the soldiers, thankful that I did not hear any sounds of fighting. A carriage came up behind me as I walked along Nevsky Prospekt. I thought it was more soldiers until strong arms grabbed me and pulled me inside. A hand covered my mouth before I could scream for help.

"Be very careful, my love. I wouldn't want you getting hurt," Prince Danilo said, his voice grazing my ear as his gloved fingers held my head against his. I could feel myself wanting to melt into his arms. Even with the obsidian ring on a ribbon around my neck, his spell was washing over me again. Spell. Why had I not kept the *sheult* spell around me? I struggled to get my arms free, but he had me pinned with his arms.

"Let me go!" I said as soon as he lifted his hand from my

mouth. I was fighting against his attraction. And I was failing fast.

"Ah, Katerina," he whispered into my hair, caressing the back of my neck. "I was so concerned for your safety. There are dangerous things about tonight, and here you are out, walking the streets, when you should be safe at home."

"I was on my way home." His fingers on the back of my neck were making me sleepy.

"Allow me to escort you, my love," he purred. "We have been apart for too long."

"We are no longer engaged, Your Highness."

"You were too hasty, my love. And I was arrogant. Please reconsider." His lips moved from my hair to my temple, brushing my skin lightly. I shivered. It made him laugh. "See? I knew you missed me as much as I missed you."

"What do you want from me?"

"I told you, I want to keep you safe. There are monsters on the loose."

"What do you know about them?"

"Mmm, I know that you have been a very naughty girl, but I can protect you, my love. The tsar's men will not harm you. Nor will your creatures."

"My . . . I had nothing to do with those . . . those poor men."

"Tsk, tsk. My sisters have been keeping their eyes on you, love. They know what you have been up to."

I started to tell him about Princess Cantacuzene, but I hesitated. He was evil, even if his adversary was as well. I didn't really want to back either side.

"What would I do with an army of undead soldiers?" I asked finally.

"A gift for your fiancé, I would hope?" he said with a sly grin. One of his hands slid down my throat and traced down the side of my arm. I shut my eyes and counted to ten in Latin, trying to ignore his seductive touch. With a low laugh, he said, "Forgive me for teasing you. Of course the creatures do not belong to you."

"Please let me go," I said.

"Katerina, I do not wish to hurt you, my love. But you must stay with me while the soldiers fight the revenants. Many men will die tonight, and I do not want to see you blamed."

"Why would the tsar's men suspect me?"

"Because you are the one whose handkerchief was found at the hospital where Prince Demidov died."

My heart froze with a sudden thought. Could it have been me and not Princess Cantacuzene? How could I know for sure? I still did not know how I'd caused the count to return. But the count definitely considered me his mistress. If I'd raised Prince Demidov as well, wouldn't he have sought me out?

"Yes, I was at the hospital when he died, but I did not see him after that. I don't even know when Prince Demidov was buried."

"He was never buried. The body disappeared from the morgue the day after his death."

Something cold gripped my stomach. "How do you know this?" I whispered.

His smile was equally cold. No longer the loving fiancé,

he said, "Nothing is hidden from me, Katerina Alexandrovna. Not your visits to the good doctor, not your visits with the princess Cantacuzene, not your cozy visits with the tsar's son. You must start behaving like a proper fiancée. Or your family will suffer, beginning with your brother. I would hate for him to be the next victim within the Order."

I tried to pull away from him, but he did not let go.

"What do you think your brother would prefer, Katerina? Being turned into a vampire or becoming an undead ghoul? Being a blood drinker is much more fun, I can promise you."

"Leave my brother alone."

He laughed and gave my arm a vicious squeeze. I knew it would leave a bruise in the morning. "As you wish. But remember this: you belong to me, Katerina. Me, and no one else."

❧

The prince returned me to Betskoi House. As we pulled up through the front gates, I said, "You really don't have to see me inside, Your Highness. It isn't necessary."

"Ah, but it is, my love. You must have witnesses that you were with me this evening and not causing the undead soldiers to raid the city. And I must speak with your parents, to reassure them that we have smoothed over our disagreements and the wedding is still on. Come along, my love." He pulled me roughly out of the carriage, bruising my other arm.

My parents were bewildered to see me arriving home with

the crown prince when they had not even known I had sneaked out. Papa glared at Prince Danilo frostily. "What the devil are you doing with my daughter?"

"Please accept my apologies, Your Highness," the prince said. "I sent a message begging for her forgiveness and a chance to talk over our differences. I am happy to say she has consented once again to marry me."

"Oh, wonderful, Katiya!" Maman said, her eyes tearing up with joy. "I am so happy for you!" She tried to hug both of us at the same time.

"Did you now, Katerina?" Papa asked me. I wanted to scream and hide behind him and have him make the crown prince go away forever, but I feared what the Montenegrins would do to my family.

Avoiding his eyes, I nodded. "Yes, Papa. I am sure."

Papa looked from the prince to me and slowly nodded. "All right, then may I offer my congratulations, again?" He shook the crown prince's hand.

Danilo smiled. "I thank you, Your Imperial Highness. I promise to take very good care of Katerina. She is most precious to me." He held my hand to his lips before saying good night.

"Good night, Your Highness," I said, looking him right in the eye and forcing a smile. I knew he would have my family killed if I did not play along with this madness. Or worse— could he turn them into blood drinkers? "I am glad we talked things out."

"As am I, my love." With one last kiss on my hand, he left me standing in the foyer with my parents.

"Oh, Katiya!" Maman gushed again. She embraced me and led me upstairs. "I am so happy! Now we can get back to the wedding plans!"

I turned and fled to my room. I could not face Papa yet. He would be disappointed in me, and he would no doubt call me into his office in the morning to make sure I knew what I was doing. I didn't want to break his heart, but I couldn't risk his life either. Or my brother's.

CHAPTER THIRTY-SEVEN

⚬⚬⚬

"Did Petya come home last night?" I asked at breakfast the next morning. He continued to keep his rooms at Betskoi House, but he often slept at the barracks with his friends.

"No, he must have stayed at Vorontsov Palace," Papa said. "How are you feeling this morning?"

"I'm fine," I said. Taking a deep breath, I picked up a warm piece of brown bread and coated it with strawberry jam. "Papa, I'm truly happy with my decision. I want you to be happy for me as well." I gave him a smile, and I saw his face relax.

He said nothing but raised his cup of tea to me.

"We have so much work to do," Maman said. "Instead of hiding in Biarritz, now we can go to Paris to look at wedding dresses. Do you remember the gown Grand Duchess Elizabeth wore? Very simple, but elegant. You would look better in something a little more daring. Your neck is one of your best features."

I tried not to blush, thinking of Prince Danilo's hands on my throat the night before. "I liked the grand duchess's dress."

Maman laughed and continued chattering. "What about the gown your aunt Zina chose? The Worth gown with all the little white feathers?"

I wondered what she would say if I admitted I detested feathers, but Papa already looked as if he were being tortured. I winked at him. "I am sure we will find something hideously expensive and horridly tasteless, which will have all of St. Petersburg talking for years." I stood up and kissed both of them on their cheeks.

I was on my way back to my room when my brother returned home, looking very haggard. It had been a rough night for him. "Petya!" I ran and hugged him, relieved that he was unhurt. "What has happened?"

"I cannot discuss it, Katiya," he said with a tired sigh. "The actions of the Order are secret."

But he did discuss it with Papa. I wrapped myself in the *sheult* spell and stood outside my father's office while he and Petya argued about the safety of the Order.

"Demidov was poisoned," Papa said. "I read the report myself. By hemlock."

"What sort of a creature uses hemlock?" Petya asked. He sounded incredulous. "Is the Order truly cursed, as the cadets say?"

"Of course not," Papa said. "You're being superstitious. But it's the damnedest thing. The girls at Smolny who took ill were poisoned with hemlock as well."

"Is Katiya safe there?"

"Yes, for now." I heard Papa chuckle. "Kruglevski told me she had him check her blood to be certain."

"She is too headstrong to stay out of trouble," Petya said. "She should be here at home, where you can keep an eye on her."

"I must say, I'm unhappy about her marrying the crown prince. I thought she wanted to focus on her education. But if it's what she wants, I cannot forbid the marriage."

I could hear my brother's boots clomping on the floor as he paced back and forth. "There are rumors of the royal family having dark powers, Papa. I think you should look into their bloodline before agreeing to the engagement."

"King Nikola has pledged his loyalty to the Bear. If his family uses their powers to support the tsar, how could Katiya be in danger?"

"Perhaps she will be safe," Petya said, but he did not sound convinced. I leaned back against the wall. My brother cared more about me than I'd ever realized. I didn't want him to get hurt—or worse—trying to protect me.

"The War Ministry has been receiving reports of an increase in animal attacks," he went on. "People have been seeing wolves in the city at night."

"The tsar has always tolerated the wolf-folk as long as they behave." I heard Papa set his glass down. "But if they become a danger to the people of St. Petersburg, he will force them to leave."

"But the teeth marks on Demidov's neck were not animal but human bite marks," Petya said. "The general fears it was another of the creatures that attacked him."

I wanted to tell my father and my brother about the Montenegrins, but I couldn't endanger them by revealing the secrets of Danilo and his family. I wondered if Grand Duke George knew of Prince Demidov's blood test. I was eager to discuss it with him at the ball that evening.

I smiled, wondering what the chances were of the grand duke asking me to dance that night. Then my stomach lurched as I remembered. I was engaged to Prince Danilo again. I could not dance with anyone but him.

CHAPTER THIRTY-EIGHT

~⚬~

The palace of the grand duke and grand duchess Serge was beautiful. A brilliant brick-red on the outside, it had been bought by the grand duke as a wedding present for his bride. On Prince Danilo's arm, I followed my parents and my brother up the elegant grand staircase to the ballroom. My father and brother treated the crown prince cordially enough, though I could feel they were still wary of him. My father was willing to place his trust in the tsar's judgment. I wondered if the empress could see the Montenegrins for what they truly were with her faerie sight. Did she approve of the tsar's friendship with King Nikola?

The crown prince's sisters were not in attendance, as they were journeying back to Cetinje in the morning to be with their sister the princess Zorka and her new baby.

Although it was nowhere near as large as the one at the Winter Palace, or even the one at Anichkov, the ballroom was very beautiful. The pale blue walls were decorated with plaster angels and scrollwork, and huge arched mirrors along the walls created the illusion of an even larger space. The room sparkled with the light from several chandeliers.

I stood at the entrance, waiting with dread as the dance master announced us. "His Imperial Highness Crown Prince Danilo Petrovic-Njegos of Montenegro, with his fiancée, Duchess Katerina Alexandrovna von Oldenburg." I saw the grand duchess Elizabeth standing with her sister, Princess Alix, who smiled shyly at me. My father spoke with Alix's father, Grand Duke Ludvig of Hesse, and Alix's brother Prince Ernest.

The crown prince left me with a kiss on the hand, saying, "I will return shortly, my love. I must go and speak with the grand dukes Serge and Pavel."

"You look beautiful, dear," Grand Duchess Elizabeth said to me. "The faint blush of love blooms on your face."

This only caused me to blush more. It was not love that bloomed on my face, but shame. And misery. I wanted more than anything to run away to another country where the Vladiki would never find me.

The orchestra struck up the imperial theme as the empress arrived with her children. I was surprised to see the tsar arriving as well. Everyone knew he detested balls, but this one was being given by his favorite brother and sister-in-law. He must have felt honor-bound to make an appearance. We bowed low as the members of the imperial family swept into the room. The tsar wore his dress regimentals, with the empress, on his arm, wearing an ice-blue gown. The tsarevitch followed him, looking just as handsome, and then the grand duke George escorted his sister, the grand duchess Xenia, who wore a gown of white heavily embroidered in silver. The youngest Romanov children were still too young to attend even family balls. The tsar and the empress led the first dance as the tsarevitch and his siblings made their way to where we were standing.

"Aunt Elizabeth," the tsarevitch said, smiling. "It would give me great pleasure if you would honor me with the first dance."

The grand duchess curtsied, her hand placed over her heart dramatically. "I'd love to, Your Imperial Highness, but I have promised that dance to my husband."

The tsarevitch's eyes twinkled. "Then I must humbly ask Princess Alix for the pleasure."

The princess blushed, embarrassed by his gallantry. "Of course, Your Imperial Highness." She took his hand as he led her onto the floor.

The grand duchess Xenia smiled at me and whispered something to her brother the grand duke George. "Ooh, there is Sandro!" she said excitedly, and ran off after her Romanov cousin.

The grand duke George bowed politely to me. "Your Highness, would you honor me with the first dance?"

He must have had some information to tell me. Something about Count Chermenensky or about the princess Cantacuzene. I couldn't turn the tsar's son down, and yet I could not dance with anyone other than my fiancé—who showed up precisely at the wrong moment.

"Are you ready to dance, my love?" the crown prince said, placing his arm around my waist possessively.

Anger flashed in the grand duke's eyes. And something

else I could not place. He bowed curtly, to both me and the crown prince, before turning around and walking away. My heart ripped. I realized I actually wanted to dance with the grand duke. Not with Danilo.

Prince Danilo swept me onto the dance floor for the last strains of the mazurka. I let him twirl me around and around, not paying attention to anything but the music. As I was dancing in his arms, I realized that I had fallen in love with someone else. Someone who most likely hated me more than anyone else in the world did. I felt miserable.

"Are you happy, my love?" the crown prince asked, looking down at me. The mazurka ended, and we clapped politely before the orchestra started up a polonaise.

"Of course," I said, not even attempting to smile. How had I ended up in this nightmare? There was no way I could speak privately with the grand duke anymore if I was engaged to the crown prince. I could not believe how utterly miserable that made me feel.

As we danced around the room to the polonaise, I saw the grand duke dancing with Princess Erzsebet. I felt a stabbing pain in my chest. Jealousy? What a strange feeling. I did not want the grand duke holding any girl in his arms but me.

I wished Dariya were there. I needed to explain to her that the engagement was back on until I could find a way to protect my family from the Montenegrins. And from Princess Cantacuzene. My aunt had chosen to spend the evening at Miechen's Dark Court dinner party instead, taking my uncle and my cousin with her. I hoped Dariya would learn more news of Cantacuzene at the Vladimirichi Palace.

When it was time for dinner, Prince Danilo led me to our

table. We sat with my parents and brother, along with Princess Alix's father and brother. The food was delicious: roast duck and salmon aspic, followed by leg of lamb and a wonderful salad of beets and beans. My brother and Prince Ernest got along well, trading jokes and stories of an officer's life. Prince Ludvig asked Papa about his correspondence with Dr. Pasteur and wanted to know if Papa had ever met Dr. Koch, the German bacteriologist.

"No, but I have read his work," Papa said. "Brilliant job he did with the tubercle bacillus."

"Indeed. Now if he could only discover a way to cure it!" Prince Ludvig replied.

Maman kept up a lively conversation with Danilo, asking him about the wedding traditions of his country. I wanted to choke on my salad. Still, I was glad she was talking. I did not feel chatty that evening at all.

Danilo had noticed, for he bent low and whispered in my ear, "What is wrong, my love? You seem a million miles away tonight."

"Just tired." I tried to perk up when the impeccably dressed servants whisked away our dinner plates and returned with orange and strawberry sorbets. I sighed, knowing the night would soon be over and I could go home.

I glanced at the table where the imperial family sat. Grand Duke George was staring at me, a frown etched between his eyebrows. He was not enjoying the evening either. *Rescue me*, I thought with another sigh. *Why can't you be my knight in shining armor?*

His blue eyes narrowed, and he whispered something to his sister. The grand duchess giggled and nodded.

The empress and the tsar rose from their table shortly afterward with their host and hostess. This signaled that it was time to return to the ballroom and the dancing.

I took Danilo's arm, and then the grand duchess Xenia was beside me, pulling on my other arm. "Duchess Katerina, would you please join Princess Alix and me in the drawing room for a game of cards? We don't wish to participate in the contredanse, and we desperately need one more player." She smiled at the crown prince and batted her eyelashes. "Your Highness will not mind if I steal her away from you? Princess Alix has left poor Nicky as well, but we are determined to sit out the next dance and rest our stomachs. You may have Katerina back for the quadrille."

Prince Danilo could not resist the grand duchess's smile. "I cannot refuse you, Your Imperial Highness," he said with a pompous bow. He kissed my hand, saying, "Enjoy your game, my love."

The grand duchess grinned and linked her arm with mine, leading me toward the golden drawing room. It was a dazzling room, with its golden walls and gold-leafed furniture.

"I did not know that Princess Alix enjoyed cards," I said.

"She detests them," the grand duchess whispered gleefully. "You will see!"

In the drawing room, it was not Princess Alix waiting, but the grand duke George. Grand Duchess Xenia gave me a push into the room. "I am going to show the princess and Aunt Elizabeth how to play tarock in the sitting room next door. We do not need a fourth person just yet," she said, winking at her brother.

The grand duke and I were left alone. "Why do you need to be rescued?" he asked me finally.

I had forgotten he could read my thoughts. I blushed. I had never felt so vulnerable before. "Please forgive me. If I had remembered . . ."

The grand duke took my hands in his, gently. It sent delicious shivers up my arms. "Katerina, I cannot read all of your thoughts. Especially when your mind is racing a million miles a minute, like it is now." He stared into my eyes, looking unsure about something. "But I heard your message across the dining room loud and clear. Tell me what has happened. I thought you'd broken your engagement with the crown prince."

"I thought I had too. I mean, we . . ." How much could I tell the grand duke? Not that the crown prince had threatened my brother. It had occurred to me that the grand duke was a member of the Order as well. Which meant his life was also in danger. "We had a long discussion, and . . ."

"What about your dreams of medical school? Will your crown prince allow this?" The grand duke looked skeptical. "The Montenegrins are dangerous, Katerina, even if King Nikola is a friend of my father's. You should think long and hard before allying your family with theirs."

I tried to cloud my mind, which was not too hard to do, actually, as confused as I was feeling at the moment. I shook my head. "I will be happy with the crown prince." It killed me to say it, and it left a bitter taste in my mouth.

"Do you need to be rescued or not?" he asked.

I wanted to run away with him right then and there. I wanted him to protect me from the Vladiki. But I knew he could not. And I could not see him get hurt. If the grand duke died, it would kill me. "No," I said finally.

"Katerina," the grand duke whispered, still holding my hands. "Who are you trying to protect?"

Who was I protecting? Who was I hurting? "Everyone," I whispered back.

The grand duke's eyes grew cold, and he let go. "Fine, Duchess. Keep your dark secrets, and let yourself be seduced by the crown prince. It will be the death of you."

He turned around and walked away. I had never felt so alone before.

❧

I did not want to go back to the ballroom. I was not ready to see Prince Danilo just yet. I wandered down the hallway toward the glass garden. The grand duchess Elizabeth had a magical touch with flowers. Orchids and roses and angels' trumpets bloomed with wild abandon. The air was heavy with their fragrances. I could have stayed in there all night, listening to the babbling fountain. But I noticed a door leading outside into the courtyard, so I pulled my wrap around me and stepped out into chilly night air.

I had been wrong. It was not a courtyard, but a tiny patio that looked out into the wooded patch along the still frozen Fontanka River. It was a silent night, and I loved the cold. I walked a little bit away from the lights of the house so I could look up and see the starlit black sky. I hugged myself, wishing hopelessly for a happy ending.

A branch rustled in the stand of trees, startling me. My

heart began to pound. *Silly girl*, I told myself. *It is only the wind. Or perhaps a fox, hunting at night.* Another branch snapped, and I fought the surge of panic rising in my chest. I had strolled too far away from the house to run without tripping in my ridiculous ball gown.

Slowly, I backed away from the stand of trees. Another noise, closer to me this time. And then a whimper: "Mis-tresss . . ."

"Count Chermenensky?" I whispered. What was he doing here outside the grand duke and grand duchess's palace?

"Mis-tresss . . ." I heard him stumbling through the thicket of dried and dead branches. "Hide . . . I have been hiding. . . ."

"You've done well," I told him. "And you need to stay hidden, for your own safety. Do you need me to get you anything?"

He kept to the shadows of the woods. "Hungry . . . ," he whimpered. He sniffed the air. Perhaps he could smell the leftovers from the feast, which the cooks would sell to the poor at the end of the ball.

"I can get you something warm to eat. Wait here."

I started to head back to the house. I hoped I would be able to sneak into the kitchens and come outside again without anyone seeing me.

"Wait . . . Mis-tresss . . ."

"I shall return shortly, Your Excellency. Let me bring you something to eat."

"Hungry . . ."

"You need to stay in the woods and hide."

"Hide . . ."

The kitchens were in a smaller building apart from the main palace. The back door was open, and I could hear the servants cleaning up and preparing to sell the leftovers. I opened my purse, finding a few rubles that Papa had given me. "Do you have any of the duck left?" I asked one of the servant women, a ruddy-faced peasant, who looked at me suspiciously.

"No duck. We have plenty of lamb, though," she said. I paid a dear price for it, probably more than they would sell it for to the poor, but I didn't mind. I wasn't sure if that would fill an undead count's belly, so I also purchased a baked potato and some pastries. She wrapped the food in a cloth napkin and handed it to me.

"Thank you," I said, and hurried back to the wooded area, where I hoped the count had stayed hidden. I had no idea if revenants even ate real food. Perhaps there was a chapter in *A Necromancer's Companion* on their care and feeding. I hoped a warm meal would at least keep the count from gnawing on his own arm.

"Count Chermenensky?" I whispered, not really wanting to wander into the trees to search for him. "Your Excellency?"

A rustle of the dry branches answered me. "Count Chermenensky!" I whispered. "I have some food for you."

The rustling grew louder. And then someone lurched out of the trees. It was not Count Chermenensky. With a low growl, he grabbed for me, knocking the napkin of food out of my hand.

"Mis-tresss!" That was the count, and he came running out of the woods at my attacker. I could not see who the other creature was, but he growled and whined like the count. I realized it was another of the undead knights of the Order. One who did not call me mistress.

The two struggled, not fighting over the food as I'd half expected, but fighting over me. If I had been a smart girl, I would have run back into the palace. But terror had me paralyzed. I did not want Count Chermenensky to get hurt by the other creature.

"Stop it!" I cried. "Leave him alone!" There was nothing I could pick up to throw at them or hit the other one with. It was like watching two wild dogs fight, bloody and vicious. I knew it would be dangerous for me to try to separate them. Still, I felt astonishingly useless.

With a snarl, the other knight tore into the count's shoulder. He howled out, and I knew the poor creature could still feel pain. He ripped at the other knight's face, tearing a bit of his already rotting skin away. I bit back a scream. I couldn't look anymore.

Suddenly, I heard a loud crack of gunfire over my head. I dropped down to the snow. The creatures did not stop fighting. "Cease!" a loud voice boomed. It was the grand duke, sounding more like his father than I'd ever noticed before. His revolver was aimed straight at the undead soldiers.

CHAPTER THIRTY-NINE

❧

"Protect . . . Mis-tresss . . . ," Count Chermenensky muttered, clawing at the other knight once more. His opponent either had not heard the grand duke or hadn't cared. He was still trying to tear Count Chermenensky apart.

"Katerina, get inside. Now!" the grand duke barked. I stood up, my dress covered in wet snow. I was freezing.

"Do not hurt the count," I begged. "He was only trying to protect me."

"Now, Duchess." His face was hard. He looked years older at that moment. I nodded finally, tears running down my face, and headed toward the palace.

The sound of another shot made me stop and turn around again. "No!" I ran back down to the edge of the woods. A lone creature lay in the snow, whimpering.

"He got away," the grand duke said grimly. "Your count. What the devil were you doing out here, anyway?"

I wiped the tears from my cheeks. "I heard him in the woods and I was bringing him food."

The creature on the ground had merely been slowed down by the bullet hole in the side of his head. He was already dead, so the grand duke could not have killed him. The grand duke rolled the knight over.

"Demidov," he said. "He must have smelled your food too."

"Demidov?" I grabbed the grand duke's jacket sleeve. "Dr. Kruglevski's toxin screen! He'd been poisoned with hemlock."

"Poisoned? That makes no sense." The grand duke stared at the revenant's body. "He seemed perfectly healthy before he died."

I shook my head. "It's the same poison that made my cousin and the others at Smolny ill."

The creature began to stir, and the grand duke pulled me back protectively. "You must leave, Duchess."

"But the hemlock—"

"I'll look into it. But you must return to the ball."

Demidov moaned and started to stand. The grand duke pulled his saber from the scabbard at his side. "Go back to the ball, Katerina. Before your fiancé misses you."

His words stung, but I knew he was right. I had to play the infatuated young girl. For the grand duke's safety as much as for my brother's. I nodded sadly and headed back inside the palace.

"Unless you still need to be rescued," the grand duke said softly over his shoulder.

I turned around to face him, holding back more tears. I

tried to keep my mind blank so he couldn't read my true thoughts. My true feelings. "I thank you, Your Imperial Highness. But I can take care of myself."

I returned to the ball, not wanting to watch him complete his grim task. The grand duchess Xenia and Princess Alix were sitting in the drawing room still, nervously waiting for me. Princess Alix jumped up when she saw me. "What happened to you?" she cried. I looked down and noticed the mud on my skirts.

"*Merde!*" How was I going to explain that? I sighed.

"Forgive me," the princess said. "My French is very poor and I have learned very little Russian since we have been here. What is '*merde*'?"

The grand duchess giggled and whispered into the princess's ear. Princess Alix blushed. "I see," she said. "I thought it looked like mud."

I shook my head. The princess asked a servant to bring us some rags and a bowl of water. She helped me sponge most of the dirt from my gown. Perhaps in the dim light of the chandeliers, and on the carriage ride home, no one would notice the other smudges. I sighed. "Thank you for helping me," I told the princess.

"Did you and Georgi talk?" the grand duchess asked eagerly. "Did he kiss you?"

"What? Of course not!" I couldn't help blushing. "Why would he do such a thing?"

She looked disappointed. She leaned closer, whispering so Princess Alix could not hear. "With my mother's faerie sight, I can see glimpses of the future," she said. "And I see you and my brother embracing. I thought tonight he would tell you to get rid of that black-hearted prince Danilo and run away with him instead."

If only he had. If only I could have told him yes. But I had made it quite clear to the grand duke that I was committed to the crown prince. He would not ask me again. It was not safe to have such fantasies about the grand duke. Not for him or for me.

I shook my head.

"Is that what this was all about?" Princess Alix asked, looking shocked. Her hearing was extraordinarily acute. "You were walking in the woods with the grand duke?"

"I went for a walk for the fresh air. The grand duke must have decided he needed fresh air as well, for he came upon me after I slipped on the wet embankment. He behaved like a perfect gentleman."

"Who behaved like a perfect gentleman?" my fiancé asked, entering the drawing room. I glanced at the grand duchess and princess, silently pleading with them not to say anything about the grand duke. "I do hope you are speaking about me." He took my gloved hand and pressed it to his lips. I squirmed with revulsion.

"Of course, Danilo." I slipped my hand out of his grasp. "Do we have time for one last dance?"

"They are about to begin the cotillion. That is why I came looking for you. Did you enjoy your card game?"

"Yes, very much," the grand duchess Xenia said, stepping on Princess Alix's foot before she could say anything. George's sister looked at me reproachfully with her huge dark eyes. But she would help me keep my secret.

"Then we shall have the princess and the grand duchess

over every night to play cards with you when we are married." Which of course was not true, since the heir of Montenegro and his bride would have to reside in his home country. I would probably never see the princess or the grand duchess ever again. Danilo placed my arm in his with a possessive smile. "This way, my love."

I knew Grand Duchess Xenia was shocked, and probably more than a little peeved that I would choose the crown prince over her brother. If only she knew that I preferred to keep the grand duke alive and safe, she would understand. Perhaps one day the grand duke would understand as well.

That was the last large ball before Lent. There would be no more dances or operas or ballets for the season, and in a way I was relieved. I hated parading around on the crown prince's arm. Especially when I saw the way it disturbed the grand duke. How I wished it were his hand on my waist.

CHAPTER FORTY

※

The Lenten fast was upon us, which meant no meat during the week. Our days and nights were quiet, spent reading or doing needlework. Maman even gave up her tarot cards for forty days and forty nights. Princess Alix and her father and brother returned to Wulfgarten. The Montenegrins left for Cetinje, with Prince Danilo promising to return before Easter.

"It is only for a little while, my love," he said. "You must write me every day." I did no such thing, and I burned all the letters he sent me.

With my royal wedding back on, our trip to Biarritz was, of course, postponed. Maman now made plans for us to journey to Cetinje in the summer. She was eager to meet the King and Queen of Montenegro.

Once a week I went with Maman to the hospital to visit with the sick and to the Oldenburg Infant Asylum to bring food and clothing to the orphans.

Papa was still busy with the planning of his institute of experimental medicine. He had been corresponding with several leading scientists across Europe for their suggestions. The building of the institute had already begun. Papa hoped it would be completed within two years. In the meantime, he was collecting a massive medical library, which he kept in his own library at Betskoi House. I'd heard no word from either Paris or Zurich, but it was just as well, I told myself. A crown princess could not become a doctor. I continued to study the medical journals and textbooks, soaking in the knowledge, all the same.

On a cold and dismal day in March, we were visiting the hospital when Dr. Kruglevski received another patient with his throat ripped out. The smell of the blood was horrible.

Maman would have swooned and fallen to the floor if the head nurse had not caught her and settled her down onto an empty cot nearby. I fanned her while another nurse brought her a cup of tea.

The nurses gave Maman a cool wet rag for her forehead, and I went to see the body. "Do you think it was an animal?" one of the nurses was asking. She crossed herself and prayed for the poor man's soul.

Dr. Kruglevski shook his head. "No man could do something this hideous," he said. There was a hole in the victim's neck bigger than my hand. The jugular had been shredded and mangled. The doctor pulled me back. "Don't look, my dear. I wouldn't want you to have nightmares."

"But a doctor must be objective," I said. "And truly, it doesn't bother me much." Not anymore, at least. I realized with shock that I sounded like a coldhearted monster myself. Perhaps that was what I'd been all along. Just another monster.

"Seeing men injured by war or disease is one thing," Dr. Kruglevski said. "Cold-blooded, senseless violence like this disturbs even an old man like me, Duchess." He patted me kindly on the shoulder. He pulled a silver flask out of his pocket and took a long drink.

The dead man's hand was clenched shut with rigor mortis. I could see something shiny hidden in his fingers. I took a handkerchief and wiped away some of the blood and tried to pry his hand open. His fingers were cold and already a bluish gray.

"Duchess, what are you doing?" the doctor asked.

"He's holding something. He must have struggled with his attacker." I gently opened his fingers and pulled the shiny object out, holding it to the light. It was a button. From a military jacket.

"*Mon Dieu.*" The doctor frowned. He took the button from my hand and held it against the buttons on the man's torn coat. It was a perfect match, yet none of the man's buttons were missing. There was some sort of crest on the button. The shape of a Maltese cross.

I sighed sadly. Another Knight. "Do you know who the victim is?" I asked.

"No, but I am sure another member of the Order can make an identification."

"Will you send for the commander?"

"Yes." He asked the nurse to send a message to Vorontsov Palace requesting General Tcherevine's presence for the identification of the body. He took another long drink from

277

his silver flask. I'd never seen the doctor look so tired and old before. It appeared as if he hadn't slept in days.

"Is there anything I can do for you, Doctor?" I asked. "Can I get you a cup of tea? Or something to eat?"

He shook his head and smiled. "I thank you, but no. And I hope you are getting a good glimpse at the unglamorous side of being a physician. It is not all glory and praise for medical breakthroughs."

"Of course. This is where the real heroism is seen," I said quietly. I laid a hand on the doctor's shoulder before leaving him to check on my mother.

I sat with her until General Tcherevine arrived with several of his officers. Petya was with him. "Mother?" he said, rushing to her side.

"She's fine," I told him. "We were here when they brought the young man in, and she swooned. She should be feeling well enough to ride home soon."

"When will this nightmare end?" Maman asked, starting to grow hysterical again. I gave her my handkerchief.

Petya and I both followed the general to the exam room, where the dead soldier lay. I heard my brother draw in a sharp breath. I turned and grabbed his arm, squeezing his hand. "Who is it?" I whispered.

"Troubetsky," he whispered back. "He and I have served together since we first started at the Corps."

"Do you think Demidov killed him?" I whispered, not wanting to disturb the general. He was covering the dead soldier with a clean white sheet. His grandfather's body was one of those that had disappeared from its tomb several weeks earlier.

Petya shrugged with an uneasy frown. "Why is this happening? Some of the men are saying the Order is cursed."

I wished I could tell him. But it would be safer if he did not know.

The general glanced at my brother, who quickly snapped to attention.

"Commander Oldenburg, I want you to place your troops here in the hospital to guard this man's body."

"Yes, sir." He efficiently dispatched two men to guard the front door of the hospital and two to patrol the grounds. Once everything was settled, he returned to Maman's bedside. "Are you feeling better? Ready to go home?" he asked her.

"Of course, dear." She enjoyed having everyone making a fuss over her, and it was during times like this that I suspected he was her favorite child. He always did what she expected of him. Unlike me.

Petya helped me and Maman into the carriage and refused to let the driver take us home alone. I was about to tell him everything I knew, but as soon as the carriage took off, my brother scowled at me.

"What on earth do you think you were doing back there?"

"What do you mean?" I asked innocently, glancing at Maman, who was quietly sniffling in her handkerchief.

My brother's eyes narrowed. "You were meddling."

"I was only trying to help. Does anyone really know what is going on?" I leaned closer to him and lowered my voice. "Someone, or some*thing*, is raising an army of undead soldiers to attack the other members of the Order. Your knights are destroying each other. Does your general have a plan to stop this?"

Petya frowned and stared out the carriage window. "No. We do not know how to stop them."

I sat back, brooding. Who would know how to stop them? I knew there was nothing in *A Necromancer's Companion* that could help. After I'd discovered the *sheult* spell with Dariya, curiosity had gotten the better of me. I had read the book with the strange Egyptian markings several times, looking for a way to help the count or a way to protect the remaining members of the Order. I had found nothing useful.

I reached over and covered my brother's hand with my own. "Please be careful, Petya."

He said nothing, but nodded. Maman sobbed softly.

That night the nightmares returned, more vivid and more horrible than before. Fires and women screaming. Young men dying. And so much blood.

CHAPTER FORTY-ONE

~∽◑∽~

Maman had taken to her bed upon returning from the hospital, and refused to leave her room the next day. Dariya and her stepmother, Countess Zina, paid a call and asked if I'd like to visit the Vladimirichi Palace with them. Maman had no objections. "Do give your aunt my love," she said. "I simply cannot get rid of this headache."

I remembered the sleeping drops Dr. Kruglevski had given me. He had told me to take a dropperful, so I knew it was perfectly safe for Maman as well. I left Maman sleeping comfortably and rode with my aunt and cousin in their carriage to see the grand duchess.

Dariya was furious with me when I told her the wedding was back on. "Are you mad?" she asked as we rode down the muddy streets of St. Petersburg. The snow was almost completely gone, and spring was just around the corner. "What did George Alexandrovich have to say about this?"

I felt a stab of pain in my chest as I thought of the tsar's son. "He thinks I'm foolish, just as you do. But please believe me, Dariya. I have to uncover the Montenegrins' secrets in order to protect the tsar."

"There must be another way," she said. "Perhaps Miechen will be able to help."

❧

Grand Duchess Miechen took my aunt's hands in hers, kissing her on each cheek. "Welcome, Zina. Have you told Katerina already?"

"No, Your Imperial Highness. I wanted to wait until we were here." They both turned to face me and my cousin.

I suddenly felt like a rabbit looking at two very hungry wolves. I started to back away toward the door. "Aunt Zina?" I asked. Dariya grabbed my hand. She looked as surprised as I was.

The countess smiled. "Do not worry, my dear. The grand duchess has planned an amusing diversion for this afternoon."

Grand Duchess Miechen gestured to the table, which held numerous candles and a heavy, ancient book. "We want to speak with someone with vast knowledge of the occult. An Egyptian necromancer, Ankh-al-Sekhem."

"A necromancer?" I repeated softly. "He would know how to defeat the undead soldiers?" I said.

Miechen nodded. "I believe so." She clasped my hand and added in a low voice, "Katerina, my husband is a member of the Order. I fear for his life too."

Of course. And the grand duchess's sons would be expected to serve when they grew up as well. She had very dear reasons for stopping the revenants.

"Does the tsar know of this necromancer?" I asked. "Why hasn't he sent for him in Egypt?"

My aunt laughed. "My dear, Ankh-al-Sekhem lived over three thousand years ago. We must hold a séance to channel his spirit. Isn't that delightful?"

This was what I had feared. This was why Miechen needed me. To make sure the séance was successful.

A three-thousand-year-old necromancer would not be a pleasant person to speak with. I sighed. "Are you certain this is the only way?"

"It may not be the only way, but it is the most expedient, Katerina," Miechen said as she drew the curtains shut. My aunt began to light the candles.

I glanced at my cousin. Dariya nodded, her eyes gleaming with excitement. She was actually looking forward to this. I took a deep breath and glanced at the pages in the book. They were not in hieroglyphics, as I'd half expected, but had been translated into Latin. Wonderful.

There was a knock on the door before we could begin. The maid announced the arrival of the princess Cantacuzene.

With a swift move, Miechen pinched out the candle and threw open the curtains. If she was afraid, she did not show it. She stood regally, waiting for the Romanian princess to enter.

"Your Imperial Highness," the elderly woman announced, entering the parlor on the arm of a young man. A nephew, I believed.

The grand duchess nodded graciously. "Your Highness. It is a pleasure to see you again. We have missed you."

Princess Cantacuzene looked around at Aunt Zina and me with her shrewd eyes. She leaned in and whispered something to her nephew. He smiled at us pleasantly and, with a bow, left the room. The princess did not wait for an invitation but sat down on one of the velvet cushioned chairs. "Strange things are happening in the city at night," she said.

"Indeed," Miechen answered.

Aunt Zina nervously sat down in a chair next to the princess. She folded her hands in her lap but played with her handkerchief.

Dariya looked from her stepmother to me. She and I both could feel the frosty tension in the room between the princess and the grand duchess.

"Katerina, sit down, my dear," Miechen said, retiring to her own chaise by the window.

I obeyed, noticing the smell of burnt candle in the air and hoping the princess would not comment. I settled in the chair next to my cousin.

Miechen rang the maid for tea. "Have you been ill, Ruxandra?" Her violet eyes gazed serenely upon the Romanian.

"I have been indisposed," the princess answered vaguely. "The tsar's men have made hunting difficult for my family." She looked directly at me with a gaze that chilled me down to my toes. She knew that I knew what she was. I could not hold her stare. I looked away out the window.

"You missed a beautiful ballet last month," Aunt Zina said nervously. "The young ballerina Cornalba was superb."

"I am sorry to have missed it," Princess Cantacuzene said. "And what news do you have, Katerina? Are your wedding plans going well?"

I tried to swallow the piece of strawberry tart in my mouth, even though I had no appetite at the moment. "Yes, Your Highness." I wondered if she still hoped I would murder the crown prince.

"Indeed," Miechen said. She stirred her tea. If she was eager to get rid of Princess Cantacuzene and continue with the séance, she did not show it. She was so perfectly serene it was eerie. I had heard stories of the grand duchess in passionate yelling matches with the grand duke Vladimir during dinner parties but had never witnessed one. I hoped I never would.

Aunt Zina finally succumbed to her nerves. She stood up and announced it was time for us to return home. There would be no séance that afternoon. I glanced at the grand duchess, but her face gave no hint of what she was thinking. Dariya and I rose from our seats as well. We said our goodbyes to both her and the princess.

"Do come and visit me sometime, Katerina," the princess said, her bony fingers cradling my chin. "We should have much to chat about."

I tried not to shudder. "Of course," I said.

⁓⦿⦾

As we were climbing into our carriage, Aunt Zina cried out, "Oh! My gloves!"

"I can retrieve them for you," I said, hurrying back inside

the palace. As I approached the parlor, I could hear the grand duchess and Princess Cantacuzene arguing.

"Ruxandra, you'll do no such thing. They are not welcome here."

"You cannot stop me. It is already in motion."

"This is treason."

Whatever Princess Cantacuzene said next was too low for me to hear in the hallway. But I heard the grand duchess's reaction loud and clear.

Miechen's voice was cold as steel. "Blood drinker, get out of my house. Do not ever threaten me or my family again."

I heard Princess Cantacuzene's laugh as she came closer to the door. I hurried back down the hallway so it would look as if I were just coming inside.

The princess's face was inscrutable as I passed her. "Always remember, Katerina Alexandrovna. No one has allies in this city. There is no one to trust but yourself."

I found Miechen sitting in her chair, looking a little paler than usual. "Are you all right, Your Imperial Highness? Can I do anything for you?"

She shook her head. "I'm fine. I thought you had left."

"My aunt forgot her gloves." I spotted them on the chair where Zina had been sitting. I hoped the grand duchess did not want to continue with the séance now that Cantacuzene was gone. "Are you quite sure you are well?"

The grand duchess's smile was frosty. "You are very kind, Katerina Alexandrovna. But the princess was right. There are no allies in this city. It's every creature for him- or herself. And you will stay alive much longer if you remember that."

CHAPTER FORTY-TWO

❧

No one attempted another séance after that. As the weeks passed and the days grew warmer, I heard no more about contacting the ancient Egyptian necromancer—which was perfectly agreeable to me. But I still worried about the growing threat to my brother and the rest of the members of the Order. Dariya did not believe me when I said there was nothing useful in *A Necromancer's Companion*—though I had casually admitted to her that the book had been given to me by Princess Cantacuzene. Dariya had barely blinked an eye.

"Somehow the book must hold the key to stopping all of this madness," Dariya said.

"If the princess is the one behind the undead army, then why would she give me a book that shows how to defeat them?"

Dariya looked back at the book. "What if she didn't know what spells were in there? And how would she know you would be able to use any of them?"

I could not answer her question. My cousin was clever, and she was close to figuring out my secret. But I was afraid of losing her friendship once she knew. I took the book out of her hands and closed it. "Besides, the *Companion* is nothing but parlor tricks and ancient myths." But even as I said it, I knew it wasn't true. The magic of the *sheult* spell was old, powerful magic. It felt old when the spell settled around me. It even tasted like old magic.

And it frightened me that I had mastered the spell easily when Dariya could not.

Tired of my cousin's relentless prodding, I once again re-read *A Necromancer's Companion* and found a passage about Ankh-al-Sekhem. Well-known for his ability to raise an army of undead soldiers for his country's protection during the thirteenth dynasty, he fell out of favor with the Egyptian court. He had attempted to bring a powerful but long-dead pharaoh back to life with an artifact called the Talisman of Isis. But when he released the dead pharaoh's soul trapped within the talisman, the necromancer was killed.

It took twelve of the kingdom's most powerful magicians to return the lich pharaoh to the land of the dead. There was a picture of the talisman, shaped like the goddess Isis holding a large black stone above her head, her wings stretched out on either side of her. I shuddered, thankful we'd not gone through with the séance.

There had to be another way to find the answers we needed.

◦⊘◦

Once the Lenten fast and Easter were over, we had a visitor at Betskoi House: Anya's brother Rudolf. He had completed his medical school training in Kiev and was about to begin his internship in St. Petersburg. He and Lyudmila were to be married that weekend. Maman and I helped Anya and Lyudmila with the wedding preparations. Papa kept Rudolf in his study for hours discussing the latest in medical breakthroughs.

Papa and Rudolf argued over the cause of infections in wounded soldiers. Papa believed it due to physicians not washing their hands between patients. Rudolf said it was caused by flies and other insects that crawled over the soldiers. I had to admit both scenarios seemed likely. I asked Rudolf if he had ever met Louis Pasteur, and he nodded.

"I heard the doctor deliver a lecture in Paris last year about bacteria in the blood. It was fascinating."

I wanted to ask him if he'd ever seen corpses reanimate, but decided it was not proper dinner table conversation. It would have to wait, I thought sadly. Besides, Papa kept plying poor Rudolf with a million questions, inviting him to use his medical library anytime. He also issued Rudolf an invitation to join his institute for experimental medicine.

"I would be honored, Your Highness," Rudolf said.

❧

On the morning of the wedding, Lyudmila's mother came to the house with a basket of fresh-baked wedding bread and other treats from their family bakery in Kiev. The quiet ceremony took place in the small St. Katerina Cathedral, with the young bride wearing a simple white gown with a lace collar and a lace veil that had belonged to her grandmother. Maman lent her a pair of diamond-and-pearl earrings, and I gave her my best pair of gloves.

Lyudmila's little sisters looked sweet as pink-clad attendants strewing rose petals everywhere, and Anya was her maid of honor, crowned with a wreath of daisies in her hair. Anya cried harder than Lyudmila's own mother during the ceremony.

A small party was held afterward in our garden. Lyudmila's family had hired a Gypsy band to play, and we danced several folk dances, such as the matryoshka, in addition to a more formal polonaise and mazurka.

The food was simple as well: fresh-baked breads and cold meats, fresh fruits and sorbets. Maman served a sweet spiced punch made with wine from her own family's French vineyards.

❧

Spring was coming to life in St. Petersburg. Everything was starting to awaken out of the cold, sleeping earth. Including things that should have remained deep asleep.

Princess Cantacuzene had told me of the folk tales that said vampires rose out of the earth in the spring and stalked the living between those two holy days: St. Yuri's Day in April and St. Andrew's Day in November. But I knew now that this was just a silly superstition. They stalked us all year round.

CHAPTER FORTY-THREE

❧

The days in May were growing longer. The school year would be over soon, and plans were being made for me and Maman to travel to Montenegro for Prince Danilo's eighteenth birthday. I dreaded the summer. Elena was ecstatic. "You will love it in Cetinje," she promised me. "It is a very beautiful city, in the shadow of Black Mountain. And the people of Montenegro will adore you."

I found that difficult to believe. Did the people know the truth about the Vladiki? Perhaps they lived in constant fear of their king and queen.

"And you will be able to meet the rest of my family," Elena continued as I tried to ignore her and study my Latin. "My oldest sister, Zorka, and her husband live near the palace, since he is in exile from Serbia. She just had another child before Christmas, and he is the fattest baby! And then there are Militza and Stana, then Danilo, then me, and my younger siblings: Anna, Mirko, Zenia, and Vera."

"The palace must be always noisy," I said, not used to such mayhem at home.

Elena laughed. "Of course. But we would not have it any other way."

I closed my Latin book and tossed it aside. There was no way Elena would let me concentrate. "Tell me more about Danilo's birthday plans. What is going to happen?" I asked.

Elena smiled wickedly. "It will be one of the most important days of his life, second only to his wedding day. There will be a ceremony in the church, which you must attend, as his betrothed. Then we will have dancing and feasting like you have never seen before. It will put any St. Petersburg ball to shame!"

Elena's father was indeed very wealthy and enjoyed spending his money more than our frugal tsar. The grand duchess Xenia had turned fourteen the previous month, and there had been no ball or party, since her birth date had fallen during Lent. But there had been a spectacular fireworks display at the empress's birthday celebration the previous fall. And a petting zoo with chattering monkeys at the young grand duchess Olga's fête the previous summer. I still had the scar on my little finger where one of the nasty creatures had bitten me.

I caught myself wondering how the grand duke George would celebrate his eighteenth birthday. I was mostly certain he wouldn't be turning into a blood drinker. But it was no use thinking about the grand duke. "And after the feasting?" I asked Elena.

"That is when you will play the most important part," Elena said all too sweetly. "But the ritual is secret and I cannot speak of it. Truthfully, I've never seen an ascension performed. I've only heard Maman speak of our father's ritual when he was young."

"What makes you think I'll agree to participate?" I asked.

Elena grabbed my hand, squeezing it to the point of pain. "You'll have no choice, Katerina. Your family's safety, and your own life, depends upon your cooperation."

CHAPTER FORTY-FOUR

❧

The next morning at breakfast, we heard terrible news. There had been another death. Another soldier from the Order. Madame Tomilov did not know the dead man's name, however, and quickly sent one of the footmen to find out. I worried about Petya, whom I hadn't spoken to in days. Dariya put a hand on my arm. "I am sure your brother is somewhere safe. Surely he is going after the killer right now."

That thought twisted my stomach even more. I tried to smile. "Most likely, you are right," I agreed halfheartedly. I could not concentrate on my French or history lessons. I ran to the window every time I heard the clip-clop of horses approaching the front gate.

Madame Orbellani was sympathetic, but Madame Metcherskey was not. "Katerina Alexandrovna, return to your seat at once. There are several students here that have family members in the Order. You are not the only one."

I looked around, shocked that I had not realized it earlier.

Countess Orlova and Princess Troubetsky, both younger than I. The poor girls. I knew that Aurora Demidov had withdrawn from Smolny after her cousin had been killed, but the countess Orlova had remained and had been there to comfort Princess Troubetsky when she heard about her cousin. Princess Troubetsky was distantly related to Countess Orlova, and thus the Count Orlov, so her grief had been doubled.

"Forgive me, madame," I said, sliding into my seat. I stared out the window at the darkening clouds passing overhead. I prayed my brother was safe. I worried about my mother, for I knew she must be in hysterics.

The dining hall was like a tomb at lunchtime. Everyone picked at their food silently and got up with relief when it was time to return to class. Madame Metcherskey canceled our dance lessons for the afternoon, and instead, we went to the chapel to pray.

It was late afternoon when a messenger returned with more news. The dead prince was Aleksey Narychkine, murdered in his sleep. He had been the nephew of the elder Prince Narychkine, who had died before Christmas. He had no sister or cousin at Smolny, so we all breathed a sigh of relief, crossing ourselves and saying a prayer for his soul.

"What is happening to the Order?" Princess Troubetsky cried. "Why would someone go after the tsar's men? Why won't the tsar do something?"

Madame Orbellani embraced her. "This nightmare will be over soon, I am sure of it."

The night patrols increased throughout the city. The soldiers always patrolled together, never alone. It made me only slightly less apprehensive for Petya.

Anya looked frightened when she helped me get ready for bed that night. Whispering so she wouldn't awaken Elena, she told me what her brother had seen when the dead prince had been taken to the hospital that afternoon.

"There were two bodies, Duchess! He said that Prince Narychkine managed to stab his killer in the neck before he bled to death." She looked green as she told me this. I knew she didn't like hospitals to begin with, even when there were no dead bodies involved.

"Do they know who his attacker was?" I whispered back. Elena rolled over in her sleep, her breathing slow and regular.

"That is the strangest thing, Duchess! They said it looked just like Prince Ivan Naryshkin."

I racked my brain, trying to place the name. Was he a friend of my brother's?

Anya's cold fingers grabbed my hand as she whispered, "But that is impossible, because they said Prince Naryshkin died over ten years ago. It couldn't have been him."

Mon Dieu. As limited as my knowledge of necromancy was, I did know that it would have taken a powerful necromancer to reanimate someone who had been dead for that long. I shuddered and tried to ignore the wave of nausea I felt. And the other robbed graves—they were all being turned into the House of Bessaraba's undead army.

This horror needed to end. Soon.

I tried to stay away from Elena the next day. I walked in the garden with Dariya. She was looking pale again. "It's the night air," she complained, pulling the budding leaves from the lilac bushes as we passed them. "And those horrible insects that keep flying into our room."

I stopped walking suddenly and stared at her. "Have any of the insects bitten you?" I asked.

Dariya frowned. "I don't think so. But I did wake up once with one on my face. Oh, it was horrid! I screamed into my pillow so I wouldn't disturb anyone."

I looked at Dariya in alarm. Was it a veshtiza that was making her ill? What about the hemlock that had shown up in her blood? I needed to learn more about veshtizas and the other vampires. I didn't dare ask Princess Cantacuzene. Or the Montenegrins. We had to find a way to keep the window closed at night.

Elena found us in the hallway on our way to dinner. "Katerina! Where on earth have you been?" She did not wait for a reply. She was breathless, almost giddy. "You'll never guess what happened. Princess Cantacuzene has been murdered!"

CHAPTER FORTY-FIVE

❧

I felt my blood run cold. "What did you say?" I whispered.
There was a wicked gleam in Elena's eye as she told me.
"Princess Cantacuzene. Has. Been. Murdered."

"That cannot be," Dariya said. "By whom?"

Elena shrugged. "She had enough enemies, I believe. I do
not think she was a favorite at the Romanov court."

"How did it happen?" I asked. How exactly did one
murder a vampire? Surely not with a stake in the heart,
as in the Gothic novels. Although that would certainly accomplish the task, no matter whom one was attempting to
eliminate.

"I heard the headmistress speaking with the guards. Madame Tomilov said she'd been poisoned. But I think it must
have been something stronger than that. Don't you think?"
Elena grinned evilly. "There were no marks on her, though."

"Then why would you think it was murder?" I asked,

wondering how much Elena truly knew about the Romanian princess.

Dariya shook her head. "She could have had a heart attack or choked on a bonbon. Or just passed away from old age, for heaven's sake. The woman was ancient."

"Older than you think," Elena said. "Are you two coming to dinner? I think we are having lamb tonight."

She left us reeling in shock. And apprehension. Was Princess Militza responsible for Cantacuzene's death? If it was true, she was much, much more powerful than I'd believed. The thought of traveling to Cetinje suddenly made me ill, and I lost all appetite for dinner.

"Elena's not only dangerous," my cousin said. "The stupid girl is mad."

I followed Dariya to the dining hall, entering just as the instructors were being seated. I slid into my seat beside Elena, bowing my head for grace. Princess Cantacuzene's death was the talk of the table.

Erzsebet leaned across the table to whisper, "Oh, Katerina, did you hear? It is so awful!"

I nodded, mechanically taking a roll from the bread basket.

"She was such an elegant lady, even if she was a bit strange," Augusta said with a sigh. "Do you suppose the tsar will call for official mourning?"

"Why would he?" Elena asked. "She was no member of the imperial family."

"But she was an important member of society. Didn't she donate one of her palaces for a museum?"

"I did not know that," I said. "How many palaces did she have?"

"Several!" Erzsebet said. "One in St. Petersburg, one in Tsarskoye Selo, one in Moscow, a summer palace in the Crimea, plus all the property she owned in Romania."

"How do you know all that?" Dariya asked.

"Because I heard our mother talking with the princess at our uncle's funeral. I know she did not have any children. I wonder who will inherit all those beautiful palaces."

Princess Cantacuzene had been the mortal enemy of the Montenegrins, and Grand Duchess Miechen had led me to believe that her vampires had been the most powerful of the vampire families. Not to mention the warning from the ghost of Tsar Pavel. Could the dead tsar have been wrong? It seemed to me that whoever had killed the princess was even more powerful.

What this meant for the people of St. Petersburg, I did not know. Were we being caught in the middle of a war for dominance between vampire families? Vampires that were not even supposed to exist?

CHAPTER FORTY-SIX

❧

I was summoned home the next morning to comfort my
mother after the loss of her friend. Maman had taken to
bed again. Dr. Kruglevski told me to give her a few drops of
the sleeping potion he'd prescribed for me. I asked the doctor if he had seen the princess Cantacuzene's body. "Do you
know how she died?" I asked him.

"We have seen far too much death this year," Dr. Kruglevski said, patting me on the shoulder. "It is not good for
young girls to dwell on such things."

"But if I'm to be a doctor, I must learn as much as I can
about the human body." *Even if the princess was not completely human*, I thought.

Dr. Kruglevski smiled kindly. "Katerina Alexandrovna,
you should focus on taking care of the living. Your mother,
for instance."

I sighed and nodded.

After the doctor left, I went into Maman's room to check

on her. I kissed her forehead, noting it was extremely cool. That was when I realized her respirations were slow and very shallow. I grabbed her wrist. "Maman?" I said, feeling a very faint pulse. "Maman!" I shook her by the shoulders.

"Maman!"

She stirred finally, opening her eyes once and staring at me with a drugged gaze, then rolled over and fell back into her coma.

"Maman!" I was frightened. I picked up the bottle of elixir and read the label. ELECAMPANE AND BELLADONNA, TO PROMOTE DEEP, DREAMLESS SLEEP. BOTTLED BY DR. BADMAEV, #72 BETOSKY PROSPEKT.

I remembered that Dr. Kruglevski had mentioned using the Tibetan doctor's herbal remedies. I put the bottle in my purse and ran to find my maid. "Anya! I believe Maman has taken too much sleeping medicine. Make a pot of strong tea!"

We sat Maman up and coaxed her to drink the tea until she was alert. She seemed annoyed that we had disturbed her rest. Anya promised to stay with my mother while I ran an errand.

When I got into the carriage, I gave the coachman the address for Dr. Badmaev's office. I had to find out more about the mysterious Tibetan.

The sun was already making the day warm. Soon it would be time for everyone to remove themselves from the city and take up their summer residences in the country. Most of the nobility would follow the imperial family to the Crimea. Papa swore the air was healthier at our summer residence on the Black Sea. But I knew Maman preferred Biarritz, on the coast of France. There the entertainment carried on all year round.

Dr. Badmaev's pharmaceutical shop and clinic was tiny, tucked into a large building on a crowded, dusty street in St. Petersburg.

Inside, I stared at the floor-to-ceiling shelves along one wall, lined with hundreds of bottles of herbal potions.

There was no place to sit except for an old bench, already occupied by a babushka with a dirty child sitting on her lap. The old woman slid over to make room for me. I smiled gratefully. The child cried and clasped the old woman's neck.

"What is wrong with her?" I asked, trying to make conversation.

"She has been bitten by the upyri."

I looked at the little girl, who must not have been any older than four or five. "What is your name?" I asked her. "My name is Katerina Alexandrovna."

The little girl peeked at me from behind the old woman. "Oxsana Yulievna," she finally said, after deciding I was not going to hurt her.

"Pleased to meet you," I said, smiling.

"Did the upyri bite you as well?" she asked.

I thought of the kisses from Prince Danilo and felt sick to my stomach. I thought of the nightmares about moths I had been having for months. I thought about poor Dariya and her illness caused by poison. I shook my head sadly. "I am not sure, Oxsana. Perhaps the doctor can tell me."

Soon after, the babushka took Oxsana into the exam room to see the Tibetan. The old woman tried to convince me to go ahead of her, but I refused. I did not want the little girl to wait because of me. It was not long before the babushka and Oxsana left the clinic, the little girl smiling. Perhaps the doctor did have a cure for vampire bites.

The afternoon sun was beating down through an open window in the doctor's exam room. The infamous Tibetan doctor Pyotr Badmaev was a middle-aged man with a kind face and dark, hypnotic eyes. He looked at me quietly as I entered and sat down in a chair by the window, clutching the bottle of his sleeping potion in my hand. He seemed to be examining me from head to toe without laying a finger on me or asking a single question.

It seemed like forever before he finally spoke. "Can I ask your name, please?" His Russian was perfect.

"Dr. Badmaev, my name is Katerina Alexandrovna of Oldenburg. I am not ill, but I came because Dr. Kruglevski has given my mother a sleeping medicine manufactured by you."

"Oldenburg? Ah, I have met your father. He is a remarkable man."

"Thank you," I said. As a practitioner of Eastern medicine, he surely scorned Western science, did he not? "Do you remember giving this medicine to Dr. Kruglevski?"

He took the bottle from my hand, turning it around. Without a word, he placed the bottle on the counter and sat down in the chair next to me. "Your Highness, I am sorry, but I am afraid I cannot help you. Dr. Kruglevski has been coming to buy my medicines for several years now. I cannot recall when he was here to buy this elixir."

"My mother was very difficult to rouse after taking this. I believe she has taken too much."

"She will be fine." He took my hands in his, turning my palm up to look at the lines. "The sleep potion is very potent and keeps one in a state of healing."

"From what? I did not know she was sick."

"You did not notice? You have the hands of a healer, Katerina Alexandrovna. But you also have the aura of death around you."

"What is wrong with my mother?" I asked. I had not come here to talk about myself.

"Her aura is cloaked in shadow, just as yours is. You are aligned with the Dark Court, are you not?"

I hesitated. I wasn't sure where I belonged. "How can you tell?"

"I can see the forces of light that surround every living being, and your light force is a dark violet."

I wrinkled my nose, pulling my hand out of his. I hated the color purple. "What does that mean? How can you be certain my mother will be all right?"

The elderly Tibetan laughed. "You who walk the paths of the dead do not believe in the possibility that there are paths of the living as well."

I was growing uncomfortable. "Did you cure that little girl? Was she really bitten by the upyri?"

"Yes, and no. It was a veshtiza that bit her. And that is curable with the right antidote." He must have seen the stunned look on my face, because he smiled. "Come, Katerina Alexandrovna. I have something that may be useful to you." He found a brown bottle on the shelf and handed it to me. "This is an antidote for the poison of a vampire bite."

"How?" I could not believe in folk medicine. I wanted cold facts to back up his claims. I wanted to examine the medicine under a microscope—to identify the herbs and their chemical compounds. "It can't be magic."

He shook his head. "Of course not."

"But the vampires cannot be studied in a lab, or dissected by scientists. How do you know your potion will work?"

The Tibetan smiled. "I know only from firsthand observations. Not all vampires drain one completely of blood. The veshtiza moths only take a tiny bit when they drink. It is their poison that is deadly."

"Poison!" I shivered and thought immediately of the girls at Smolny and the members of the Order. My worst fears about Elena and her sisters were confirmed. Elena was turning into a moth at night and poisoning us while we slept.

"Veshtiza moths are particularly fond of hemlock leaves."

"And the moths inject the poison into whoever they bite?" My mind was reeling. Dariya needed the Tibetan's medicine immediately. "Frankincense is the antidote for the veshtiza's poison," I deduced in a whisper.

He closed my hand over the bottle. "You come back and visit me, Katerina Alexandrovna. I am sure we have much to discuss."

CHAPTER FORTY-SEVEN

I needed to return to Smolny with the antidote right away, before all the girls went home for summer vacation. I decided to believe in the kind-looking Tibetan doctor. But I asked the coachman to take me to the Oldenburg Hospital first, because I had several questions for Dr. Kruglevski.

The doctor was looking more and more like a peasant drunkard. His hair astray, his eyes slightly glassy, the doctor shuffled from patient to patient in the large hospital ward, blinking several times as he tried to read each patient's medical chart. I went and brewed some strong tea in the samovar in his office and found Rudolf.

He confirmed my fears about Dr. Kruglevski. "The poor man is exhausted. He has been working all night."

I convinced the doctor to lie down in the morgue and get some rest. There was no other place for him to sleep. Dr. Kruglevski finally agreed, after admitting he had not left the hospital in several days. I covered him with a blanket, and he was soon snoring softly.

Rudolf shook his head. "I must go make rounds on the patients. Will you excuse me, please?" With a quick bow, he left me alone with the doctor. And with the body of Princess Cantacuzene.

I knew it was her, even though the body was covered with a sheet. I walked over and pulled the sheet from her face, surprised at her coloring. She was pale but did not have the familiar bluish tinge of death to her skin. There were no marks on her body that I could see. I pulled the sheet down farther and picked up one of her hands. It was cool, but decay had not set in yet. I was surprised. She had been dead for over forty-eight hours.

Suddenly, the princess's eyes opened and she awoke with a horrid gasp. "They have taken the talisman!" she ranted. "Protect the Dekebristi!"

I jumped back, dropping her hand. "Your Highness!"

Eyes still fixed straight ahead, the Romanian princess drew in a ragged breath. "Blood . . . I must have blood. . . ."

I backed away to the door, bumping Dr. Kruglevski's bed. The doctor stirred in his sleep.

Princess Cantacuzene sat up, looking at the doctor.

"No!" I screamed. I ran over to the doctor and tried to shake him awake. "Dr. Kruglevski, you must wake up! Hurry!"

The princess stood up off the morgue table.

"Get away from him!" I screamed.

Rudolf appeared in the doorway. "What is going on?" he demanded. His face paled when he saw Princess Cantacuzene upright. "Holy Mother of God," he said, crossing himself.

I managed to wake Dr. Kruglevski, and he muttered the same thing as he saw the vampire princess coming for him. Still groggy, he stumbled off the bed he'd been sleeping on and tried to push me ahead of him to the door.

I turned around to see the princess grab him by his hair. She was trying to bite his neck. I'd never noticed her tiny fangs before.

"No! You mustn't!" I grabbed the doctor's walking cane from the corner and struck her shoulder. This distracted her long enough to let go of the doctor.

"Katerina! No!" Dr. Kruglevski said. He took the walking cane from me and pushed me into the hallway, then shut the door on me. I heard it lock with a click.

"No!" I beat on the door. "Do you have a key?" I asked Rudolf.

He shook his head. "Move aside!" he said. He proceeded to ram the door with his shoulder, but he was not a large man and it didn't give way. He tried a second time, with the same result.

"What is the meaning of this?" a familiar voice asked.

I spun around. It was, of course, the grand duke George Alexandrovich. He had an uncanny habit of showing up whenever bad things happened. "Hurry!" I said. "The doctor is in there with a vampire!" We could hear horrible noises from inside.

He grabbed me by the arm and pulled me away. With one forceful kick, he broke down the door.

It was too late. I could see that Princess Cantacuzene had

Dr. Kruglevski's head in her grasp, and she was drinking blood from his severed neck.

I turned my head.

The grand duke withdrew his saber and rushed into the room.

The princess made a sound like a hiss. I had to see what was happening, so I looked back. The princess Cantacuzene was still draining the doctor of his blood. His eyes were closed. I wanted to cry. Why had I insisted he lie down in the same room with her?

The grand duke did not hesitate. With one clean slice the princess was not expecting, he separated her head from her neck. Blood spurted everywhere. The vampire let go of the doctor's body and they both slumped to the floor.

"It's my fault!" I sobbed. "I never should have told him to take a nap. And I never should have left him next to a vampire. I should have known she wasn't truly dead."

"Katerina," the grand duke said, his voice tired. He wiped the sweat from his forehead with the back of his sleeve. "You are not to blame."

"Your Imperial Highness," Rudolf said nervously. "We have the results back from the toxicology report on Princess Cantacuzene. It was not hemlock, as we first believed, but frankincense."

"Where the devil would someone get that?"

I pulled the small brown bottle out of my purse and opened it. "Badmaev," I said. "The Tibetan doctor." I held the bottle up for the grand duke to see, the heavy scent of frankincense filling the air. "But I don't understand. Dr. Badmaev said this counteracts hemlock poisoning from veshtizas. Would it harm a vampire that was not a veshtiza? I thought the princess was another kind of vampire."

"Obviously, its effects were not permanent on her," the grand duke said as he took the antidote from me. "Perhaps it is poison to all vampires. Or perhaps she is a different kind of veshtiza. Doctor, can you close off this room until General Tcherevine's men arrive?"

"Of course, Your Imperial Highness," Rudolf said.

The grand duke turned back to me. "Duchess, you will be safest if you come with me. We need to discover who poisoned the princess in the first place, and why."

"It was negligence on my part that caused the doctor's death. He was looking so tired that I convinced him to lie down for a rest in the morgue. I should have known that Princess Cantacuzene would—"

"Would what? Return from the dead?"

I sighed and stared out the window. "She was a blood drinker. Who would have wanted to poison her?"

"Can you think of anyone powerful enough to match Princess Ruxandra as her rival?"

I shook my head. "The only enemies she ever spoke of were the Montenegrins. She believed Princess Militza wanted to take over the St. Petersburg bloodline."

"What did the princess do when she awoke?"

I had to think for a moment. Everything had happened so fast. "I was holding her hand, and she opened her eyes and said, 'They have taken the talisman.'"

The grand duke looked puzzled. "Has she ever mentioned a talisman before?"

"Not to me."

We had approached the clinic and herbal shop of Dr. Pyotr Badmaev. The grand duke looked at the sign on the door, which said all patients were welcome regardless of method of payment.

"Are you ready?" he asked me. "Or do you need a minute?"

I took a deep breath. "I am fine. But thank you for asking." He was such an agreeable young man when he tried hard.

He smiled, his faerie blue eyes lighting up. "You can be rather agreeable too, Duchess, at times."

I blushed. I had forgotten about his gift. I thought something very rude about him, and he just laughed out loud. "You should stay here in the carriage. I shall return as soon as the doctor tells me who bought the frankincense."

I nodded. Then I suddenly remembered. "Your Imperial Highness, she said something else when she awoke."

"Princess Cantacuzene?"

"Yes, she said to protect the Dekebristi."

"The Dekebristi?" The grand duke's face went pale. "Katerina, are you sure?"

I nodded. "I know everyone says the Dekebristi are gone, but what if they aren't? What if the vampires brought them back?"

He sighed and rubbed his temples. "It means that we know who she was raising the undead army for. Stay here. I will speak with the Tibetan doctor and then we must hurry back to the palace. I must speak with my father immediately." His face was grim, but he touched my cheek with the back of his hand, only for a moment, before leaving the carriage. My heart began to palpitate. My legs felt weak and shaky. The grand duke caused the strangest effects on my body.

That was the last thing I thought before the grand duke stepped inside the clinic and everything went black.

CHAPTER FORTY-EIGHT

❧

I woke up in someone's warm, strong arms with my head pounding. The grand duke? I had the tiniest happy feeling inside. Then I looked up and was immediately disappointed. And frightened.

It was the crown prince Danilo. I had not known he was back in St. Petersburg. "What am I going to do with you, Katerina Alexandrovna?" he said, a menacing smile on his face. "I leave you alone briefly and you are off gallivanting in another man's carriage."

"What did you do to me?" I tried to sit up and look around but the crown prince held me fast. The only thing I could see was that I was now in a different carriage. Even the horses' hooves sounded different on the street. Were we still in St. Petersburg? "You must let me go."

"Must I, my love?" He stroked my hair. He laughed when I flinched. "We are leaving for Cetinje tonight, for my birthday celebration. Your mother has already been notified and

314

has been invited to join us. She believes you are leaving on the train with my sisters. Your father has already given me your passport papers."

"You cannot do this." I tried to struggle, but it was no use. The pain in the back of my head throbbed. I wondered if the grand duke could hear my thoughts. *Your Imperial Highness? George?* I was desperately trying to stay conscious. But the pain in my head was so intense my eyes closed again.

CHAPTER FORTY-NINE

∽❧∽

When I awoke, I was in a private compartment on a train. "The Sleeping Beauty!" Elena snickered from the sleeping berth above me.

My head still pounded. I shut my eyes again, praying this would all go away. "Where are we?" I whispered.

"Two hours from my homeland," Elena said.

The swaying of the train did nothing to help my head. "I have to go back," I said.

"There will be no going back, Katerina," she said softly. "You belong in Cetinje, at Danilo's side. He needs a powerful bride and you are the most powerful, and richest, necromancer in St. Petersburg."

I realized my hands were tied. The ropes were cutting into my wrists. I'd never felt less powerful in my life. I began to panic. "Please, Elena. I have no wish to marry your brother."

Elena laughed.

I was growing more frightened by the minute, but I decided on another approach. "Who poisoned Cantacuzene? Was it Militza?"

"You think you are a clever girl, Katerina." Elena crawled out of the sleeping bunk and smiled. "Just wait until you meet my mother."

∼❧∽

I smelled fresh air as we stepped down off the train. Prince Danilo held a protective arm around my waist, leading me to the royal family's carriage. Several villagers waved and clapped, held back by guards with bayonets. "They have come to see their future crown princess," Danilo whispered in my ear. "Give them a royal smile."

I forced a weak smile. I heard them shouting in a strange dialect I could not understand.

He helped me into the carriage, where Elena, Militza, and Stana sat across from us. "How far to Cetinje?" I asked. The countryside was beautiful as we rode past fields of wildflowers, but I did not care.

"We will be there by nightfall," Danilo said.

"Thank the saints," Elena muttered, crossing herself.

Militza laughed and stared at me with her dark eyes.

I closed my own eyes, forcing myself to remain calm. Even in a carriage full of vampires, I knew they needed me for their ritual and I was not in mortal danger for the time being. I wondered what my parents had thought when they'd heard I had left. And the grand duke. What had happened to him at the herb shop?

Your Imperial Highness? I tried again to reach him.

317

Perhaps his faerie powers could not reach this far across the continent.

Danilo picked up my hand, slowly tracing the length of my fingers with his own. I fought the bile in my throat. "I can sense her power already," he said with relish.

"That is your imagination," Militza whispered. "You cannot be sensitive to such things."

"Not yet, anyway," Elena said.

"It is strange," Danilo said. "But there is something almost electrical when I touch her."

I pulled my hand away. I did not want him touching me. Ever.

"You imagine things," Militza said. "Do not say such nonsense in front of Mother."

Danilo laughed, settling back in his seat more comfortably. "Do not worry about me and Mother. You are the one who disobeyed her instructions."

"Do not speak of such things right now," Militza hissed. I slowed my breathing, pretending to drift off to sleep.

Danilo was pouting. "You should have waited for me, and then we would have destroyed Cantacuzene completely before she could say anything. We have no way of knowing what secrets she told before the tsar's son finished her off for us."

"There was no way I could have known she was so different from us," Militza said, her voice a whisper. "She should not have been able to wake up from the frankincense." She sighed. "If you had come with me that night, instead of staying in your suite with the bar wench, we would not be having this conversation right now. We could have cut off her head after I poisoned her."

I felt sick. I had never believed, deep down, that the crown prince was actually in love with me. Hearing this hurt my pride more than anything. I rolled away from the prince with my eyes still closed, and tried to snuggle down in the corner of the carriage.

"Sister, you say the most wicked things with that tongue of yours." The crown prince's voice was cold. "Take care, lest something happen to it."

"Don't you dare threaten me," Militza countered.

"Hush! Both of you!" Stana said. A hand brushed my forehead, tucking a strand of hair behind my ear. I tried very hard not to shudder. It was the same way my mother used to brush my hair out of my face when I was little. But it did not comfort me at all.

"I still say we should have killed this one and have done with it," Militza said.

"No," Stana said. "Our parents have been looking for a necromancer like her for a very long time. For your sake, as well as for Danilo's."

"I suppose she will be useful to me," Militza said, sighing.

All these years, I'd tried my best to keep my curse hidden, thinking it made me a terrible person. But Princess Militza had just showed me what true evil could be.

I must have truly fallen asleep after that, for the next thing I knew, Elena was shaking me roughly. "Wake up, Katerina Alexandrovna. Welcome to the Black Mountain."

I did not want to open my eyes. The castle where King

Nikola and Queen Milena lived was enormous: Gothic and intimidating, with huge gargoyles perched over the front entrance. They looked as if they could leap down and rip apart anyone who tried to enter—or leave—the castle without permission.

"Come with me, my love," Prince Danilo said, dragging me from the carriage. "The coachmen will bring your bags in. We must introduce you to our parents. They are anxious to meet you."

"But I am exhausted from the trip. Perhaps I might be allowed to freshen up first?"

Militza frowned. "To keep the king and queen waiting would be disrespectful."

"Will my mother be joining me soon?" I asked.

No one answered my question.

Our footsteps echoed on the parquet flooring in the palace entrance. There was no grand staircase, as in the palaces of St. Petersburg, but there was a grand foyer, with ornately plastered ceilings. Several servants stood waiting to greet us. A regal-looking couple stood behind the servants. My heart began to hammer.

"My children! My children have returned to me!" the large man said, his arms open to embrace his daughters. His voice was warm and booming.

"Papa!" Elena flew into his arms first and planted a kiss on his cheek. She then turned to kiss her mother, the dark beauty standing next to him.

"Papa, we have a very special guest," Danilo said. "May I present Her Highness Duchess Katerina Alexandrovna of

Oldenburg? Katerina, my father, King Nikola; and my mother, Queen Milena."

He did not need to give me a sharp squeeze on the arm. I still would have curtsied politely before his parents. I knew the proper etiquette for greeting a ruling sovereign—even if he was a vampire.

King Nikola was an imposing man, still handsome in his older years, his hair streaked with strands of gray. His dark eyes bore down on me. "What a beauty! Welcome to Cetinje, Katerina of Oldenburg." Before I knew what was happening, he'd embraced me in a crushing hug. He reminded me of the tsar. He did not seem like an evil blood drinker at first glance.

"Thank you, Your Majesty," I squeaked.

When he released me, I looked at his wife, Queen Milena. Something about her frightened me. She was a beautiful older woman, with long dark curls and hypnotic black eyes. I felt as if I already knew her. I curtsied again.

She held out her hands to me. "Welcome, my child. We have been waiting for you for a long time."

I could not say I was glad to be there. I felt a surge of panic in my chest. I had to get out of there. I had to get away from this woman. Her fingers were cold as she embraced me.

"Come, let us dress for dinner," Elena said. "There is a feast tonight in your honor, Katerina." She pulled me away from both her mother and Danilo, leading me deeper into the palace.

The palace was much larger than Betskoi House, but of course nowhere near as large as the Winter Palace or

Anichkov. My room was next to Elena's, which she shared with her younger sister Anna, who would be attending Smolny in the fall. Elena's eldest sister, Princess Zorka, and her husband, the Crown Prince of Serbia, lived in a fashionable house across the street from the palace.

Elena said I would be meeting them at dinner. "Her children are adorable. We will play with the babies tomorrow," she said. "You'll want to sleep late, though, after tonight's ritual. It is . . . exhausting. Especially for the fiancée."

"The ritual is tonight?" I asked. "Before my mother arrives?" I could see no way of escaping this.

"Yes," she said. "Some things are best kept within our immediate family. The ritual, well, you might say it's . . . draining."

I swallowed. I turned to the crimson dress hanging up outside the armoire. "Is this my dress?" I asked. "It's beautiful." Not quite Paris fashion, it had a short red jacket with heavy embroidery. "Your mother was wearing a belt like this," I said, touching the metal beadwork at the gown's waist.

"Yes, it's traditional. We will all be in traditional dress this evening."

I ran to the window, hoping to see a chance for escape. The window was bolted shut, of course. And I was three stories up, with no balcony or other method of climbing down. I tried to stay calm. I would think of something. I hoped.

I dressed myself, without the help of any maid. I did not think anyone would mistake me for a Montenegrin, with my wheat-colored hair and pale eyes, but I did not look quite like myself either. And the dress did not flatter one's waist. I'd noticed that when I had first seen the queen.

After one last glance in the mirror, I left my room and hurried downstairs.

Elena was in the hallway holding a little girl, who looked to be only two. "Katerina! This is my youngest sister, Vera! Maman is going to have another boy in the fall."

"She is expecting?" No wonder her dresses fit her so. "How do you know it will be a boy?"

"Maman always knows."

Princess Vera climbed out of her sister's arms and held her arms up to me. I'd not picked up a child since my little brother's death. Nervously, I lifted her, and she clasped her little hands around my neck.

"You have made a new friend!" Elena laughed. "Come, we must take Vera back to the nursery before dinner."

The nanny had already put the three children of Princess Zorka to bed for the night. Princess Vera went quietly to her nanny's arms. We tiptoed out of the nursery silently.

"You will meet Zorka and her husband, Prince Petar, at dinner."

"A Serbian prince?" I asked.

"In exile, for the time being. But Maman is working on that." Elena smiled to herself and pushed open the swinging doors to the dining room.

The vast room was heavy with the scent of roses. There were several large arrangements down the long heavy wood table. The crown prince came over and led me to the table. "Enchanté, my love," he said, kissing my hand. "You look beautiful in my country's native costume."

I said nothing. He introduced me to his sister Zorka and her husband, Prince Petar Karađorđević. He was an unpleasant-looking man, much older than his wife. Princess Zorka looked a lot like her mother and sisters, dark-eyed and dark-haired, but not quite so deadly. There was a maternal softness to her smile. Perhaps she was not a witch like the others?

"Hurry! Hurry! To the table!" Queen Milena was rushing everyone to stand at their places for the entrance of King Nikola.

The king entered, sat at the head of the table, and signaled for everyone else to sit. A servant appeared at the king's left side and began to pour the wine. It did not take him long to come around the table and fill everyone's glass. Other servants stood waiting at the doorway, ready to bring in the first course.

King Nikola raised his wineglass. "Tonight we come together to celebrate the most important night of my firstborn son's life. Tonight, he becomes a man. Tonight, he becomes more than a man."

I glanced around the table. No one, not even Prince Petar, seemed to be taken aback by this announcement. Except me.

"And tonight we also celebrate the arrival of Danilo's future bride, Katerina of Oldenburg." His dark eyes twinkled like cold stars as he looked at me. "Welcome, Katerina. We have indeed been waiting a long time for you."

I nodded stiffly and raised my glass with the rest of the dinner party. It was a local wine, a rich, sweet red. As soon as the toasts were over, the servants rushed in to serve the first course: a traditional soup with vegetables in a beef broth. This was followed by fresh trout, caught in the nearby Lake Skavda, a smoked ham, polenta, and local cheeses.

"Does your mother have a Russian cook or a French cook?" Queen Milena asked me.

"She has both, Your Majesty," I answered, hoping I did not sound pretentious.

She nodded. "I do not care for French cuisine. It is too rich for my tastes."

"I love French cooking," Elena said. "But our cook's smoked ham is the best."

It was, overall, a pleasant dinner. There was no blood drinking in sight. No black-magic chanting. I glanced around the table at smiling, gay faces. Militza and Stana were laughing at something Zorka's husband had said. Elena was whispering to her sister Anna. Anna and Elena could have been twins, instead of being a year apart.

Danilo was listening to his father discuss his latest work of poetry, which the national theater was staging as a ballet. His father was a great patron of the arts and enjoyed writing plays and poetry. I was not sure I wanted to know any of Queen Milena's favorite pastimes. She gazed around at her children affectionately, and then her gaze rested on me with a wicked smile. I tried to smile back, to show her I was not afraid, but I didn't think I was successful.

The servants began to clear away the table as soon as King Nikola rose from his chair. "Katerina Alexandrovna, I would like to show you the drawing room. Danilo, would you escort the young lady?" The king placed his wife's hand on his own arm.

"My dear," Danilo said smoothly, taking my hand. I would have believed the prince passionately in love with me if I hadn't overheard Militza in the carriage. He behaved like a perfect gentleman. The devil.

We entered a grand room with silk-paneled walls, on which hung several large portraits. "These are my ancestors, Duchess," King Nikola said. "These are the Vladiki of House Peidros-Njegos."

Several black-eyed men stared down at me from their paintings. The earliest men wore the black robes and head-pieces of the Orthodox clergy. The later bishop princes wore only the less formal princely jackets, with various medals on their chests. The last portrait on the wall was the one of King Nikola, in his own jacket. None of them wore crowns denoting their sovereign status.

The opposite wall held portraits of the king and queen's children and a beautiful portrait of Queen Milena when she was younger. Her dark eyes flashed seductively in the painting. "How pretty!" I could not help saying.

"That was many years, and many pregnancies, ago," the queen said with a sigh, one protective hand on her abdomen. She pulled me away from the others, and we walked along the grand hallway, looking at other portraits.

"There is something about your eyes that is so familiar," I said. "I suppose it is just that your daughters favor you. But I could swear it is something more than that."

The princess stared at me silently for a few seconds. "Perhaps it is my sister who you are thinking of?" she said finally.

I shook my head. "I do not think I have ever met your sister."

"But of course you have, dear. Princess Cantacuzene."

I felt the blood drain from my face.

"You seem very surprised," Queen Milena said with a laugh that sounded almost like a cackle. "I don't suppose my dear sister ever mentioned me?"

"Only that your son is about to become a blood drinker. And that your daughters are powerful sorceresses." I hesitated before adding, "I take it you were never close."

Queen Milena laughed some more. "In truth, we were only half sisters, sharing the same father." She stared out the window into the black night. "My mother was the maid for the princess's mother. She was turned out of the house when she found out she was with child. Our father, Prince Drag- omir, married my mother off to one of his noblemen, Count Vujovic, and I carried his own name. But Mother never let me forget I carry the blood of Bessaraba in my veins."

"And so do your children," I muttered. Had the ghost at Vorontsov Palace been speaking of Princess Cantacuzene or Queen Milena that night? Or even her daughter Militza? Why must ghosts always be so ambiguous?

"She was truly an enemy of the tsar, you know," Princess Militza said, joining us at the window. "She has been plot- ting to return her corrupted lover to the throne with her undead army."

I felt cold. And confused. "Ruxandra?" How old had the princess been?

The queen did not notice my shudder. "Ruxandra is the name she lived under for the last sixty-odd years, after one of our ancestresses. Her true name was Princess Johanna Marija Cantacuzene. It is sad that there are still prejudices

327

against blood drinkers in this day and age. Konstantin was turned by Johanna and they attempted to reclaim the throne from his brother Nicholas."

I could not believe what I was hearing. It seemed to me that no member of the House of Bessaraba had our tsar's best interests at heart. "But Konstantin Pavlovich, he is most certainly dead. Isn't he?" I asked.

The queen smiled and shrugged. "He was staked by the bogatyr in 1831. But I believe my dear sister has been raising the undead army for him."

I had to get back to St. Petersburg and I had to warn the tsar. But I had no money, and no way of traveling. There wasn't even a railroad line out of Cetinje. If I managed to escape from the Montenegrins, how would I be able to leave the capital city?

"Come, my dear." Princess Militza grabbed me by the arm. "It will be midnight soon, and it will be time for the prince's ascension. You have a very valuable part to play." Her pretty white teeth gleamed. She steered me back toward the others, where Prince Danilo took my arm.

"But what about the Dekebristi?" I asked. "If you are truly the tsar's ally, you must send him a warning!"

Queen Milena smiled. "Do not worry about your tsar. Johanna is dead and can do nothing more for her precious Konstantin."

I wasn't so sure. What if she had already revived him? What if that was why she had been so ill the past spring? Such a ritual would have required an enormous amount of energy, even if the necromancer had been an ancient and powerful vampire.

The crown prince's smile was as wicked as his mother's. "Tonight will be magical, my love. Soon it will be time to go to the monastery, where a very beautiful ritual is to take place."

"We cannot be married before my birthday, Danilo. You know my parents will not allow it."

"That does not matter," he said with a low laugh. "I shall wait patiently for our wedding night, but tonight is another matter completely." He caressed my cheek in a threatening manner. "Do not forget what will happen to your loved ones if you do not cooperate."

His renewed threat filled me with dread. Militza took me by the arm again. "We're going to be a good girl, aren't we?" she asked.

"Please let me go," I said. "If your family is truly aligned with the tsar, why must you do this?"

"Even the Light Court has need of friends that follow the paths of darkness. With your blood, Danilo will become a more powerful ally for the tsar. Now, if you're not going to behave properly, we shall have to do something about that." She placed a cloth with a sickeningly sweet smell over my face. I tried not to breathe in, but the fumes overpowered me anyway.

The last thing I was aware of was sliding to the floor, with Militza not bothering to catch me.

CHAPTER FIFTY

I awoke, with both my hands and feet bound, in a stuffy, damp chamber. There were two candles lit, and someone circled the room, lighting more candles. I heard a low murmuring, like a buzz or a hum coming from outside. The person lighting the candles was dressed in a black hooded robe. "Hello?" I asked. "Can you help me?"

The robed figure said nothing, but put a finger to his lips. The hairy arm and masculine jaw I saw were the only clues that told me it was a man.

"But I must get out of here," I said, squirming and trying to work on the ropes. My wrists were being rubbed raw.

The buzzing grew louder, and as the large wooden door swung open, I realized it was not buzzing but chanting. A small group of more black-robed men, swinging an incense censer, chanted as they approached the table where I was lying curled up on my side.

I suddenly realized I was lying on a cold stone altar. My heart began to pound. My nightmare was becoming all too real. "No!" I screamed. I was going to be some sort of sacrifice. "Let me go!"

The chanting drowned out my cries.

The wooden door swung open again, and this time, the king and queen entered, followed by the crown prince. He was now dressed in the black robes of the Vladiki. It was time for his rite of ascension.

The prince's sisters followed him, wearing veils, so I could not tell which sister was which. The first one carried a small brass pitcher, and the second a brass chalice. The third sister carried a jewel-encrusted chest. The three women approached the dais as the black-robed men continued to chant. I wanted to scream again, but as I caught a whiff of the incense, all thoughts of escape left me. They were drugging me again, I thought hazily.

Suddenly, the chanting stopped, and the chamber was silent. I looked around at the walls, where iconic images flickered in the candlelight. The temple reminded me of another chapel, thousands of miles away.

The queen turned around to her three veiled daughters. "Bring forth the talisman," she said.

The veiled sister carrying the jeweled box came forward, opening it in front of her mother.

Milena's eyes lit up as she carefully lifted something out of the box. Triumphantly, she cradled an ancient metal disc in her hand. "The Talisman of Isis. Created for our ancestors thousands of years ago, to bring the gift of eternal life to us, her favored children," she said. "But part of the talisman was stolen by my sister, and taken to a distant, frozen land, where it stayed for many years.

"Tonight, we reconsecrate it and put its two pieces back together."

I gasped. It was the talisman from *A Necromancer's Companion*. From what I could see, the talisman was not broken in half but had a large empty spot in the center of the disc, where it looked as if a stone was missing.

The sister who held the brass pitcher stood in front of me and anointed my head with a sweetly scented oil. I was too weak to protest. She moved to Prince Danilo and anointed his head as well.

The second sister bent down in front of the altar, holding up the chalice in front of me. I bent over and peeked down, but the chalice was empty.

The third sister held out the jeweled box to Danilo, who withdrew a golden jewel-encrusted dagger. My eyes grew large, and my mind slowly put together what was about to happen.

King Nikola took my hands and untied them, yet held me down so I could not run.

Danilo took his dagger and sliced my palm open, and I gasped in pain. The sister with the chalice held it up to catch my blood.

"No, please," I whimpered. My hand stung from the cut. I could smell the metallic scent of my blood mixing with the fumes of the incense, and I was growing dizzy. "No . . ."

The veiled sister handed the chalice to her brother.

But his mother held out her hand. "Not yet. We must

restore the two pieces and rededicate the talisman to the Goddess." King Nikola grabbed my hand and held it while the queen ripped the obsidian ring from my finger. I winced as she scraped the skin. "My sister stole the talisman, hoping to place her lover on the throne of Russia. When she failed, she broke the talisman into two parts."

I gasped again. Princess Cantacuzene had given me the stone of the talisman to protect. And the Montenegrins had known I carried the missing piece all along! Danilo had recognized the ring and had relayed the information to his sister and mother. I felt sick and helpless, held down on top of the altar.

Queen Milena set the ring back into its proper place in the center of the golden disc. "It wants a gift from you, Katerina," she said softly, holding the talisman under my hand so that drops of my blood fell on the obsidian. The blood hissed a little as it seeped into the stone.

"No," I whimpered again. But I was too weak to fight them anymore.

The queen held the talisman above Danilo's head. "The blood of Isis, the strength of Isis, the words of power of Isis shall be given to you. May the symbol of Isis act to protect this great divine being from our enemies." She lowered the talisman and held it over Danilo's heart.

He took the chalice of my blood and held it up. "The blood of Isis, the strength of Isis, the words of power of Isis are all mine."

With those words, he drained the chalice and became a blood drinker.

I wanted to retch but was too tired. Tears rolled out of my

eyes. My cursed, necromancer's blood. That was why his mother had wanted a marriage between the two of us. She wanted to use my blood to make him a more powerful Vladiki than his own father. I knew that now that she had her talisman and my blood, I was no longer useful to her. As soon as possible, they would kill me. Princess Cantacuzene had been right.

Queen Milena smiled at her son. "You will now be able to walk both the paths of the living and the dead, my son. For Isis shines her favor upon you."

At that moment, the talisman began to move in her hands. With a cry she dropped it to the floor and stepped back. The walls of the temple began to shake.

We were deep within the Black Mountain, and one of the terrified priests cried out, "Earthquake!" They crossed themselves and ran out the door.

"What is this?" King Nikola roared, letting go of me.

A thin line of smoke, or mist, rose from the middle of the talisman. The walls of the temple stopped shaking as the vaulted ceiling above us filled with the mist.

I sat up on the altar and slid down, hiding on the opposite side of the large block of stone from the king and queen. Everyone remaining in the temple stared up at the mist in horror. "What have you done?" King Nikola whispered to his wife.

The chamber had suddenly grown much colder, even though the torches and candles still burned.

Queen Milena raised her hands up and spoke a prayer to Isis for protection. Her frightened daughters huddled behind her.

The mist began to take shape above us. It glowed a bluish white. I watched in terror as I recognized the familiar glow. It was a pure cold light.

Suddenly, the torches and candles were extinguished, and the temple was flooded with the cold light of the mist. The color drained from Prince Danilo's face. He seemed to wilt, crumpling to the floor in a faint.

A malevolent voice thundered from above us. "WHERE IS JOHANNA?" it said.

"No," the queen whispered, growing as pale as her son. "It cannot be. . . ."

King Nikola drew himself up. "Who are you?" he shouted. "I order you to leave Black Mountain at once!"

The walls shook again. Stones began to tumble from the ceiling. I heard Elena shriek from behind her mother.

"YOU DARE ORDER ME?" the mist roared. "I AM KONSTANTIN THE DEATHLESS! YOU WILL OBEY MY COMMANDS!"

The mist grew, swelling until it filled the temple and closed in on us. And it was painfully cold. The cold I felt in my bones was nothing like the chill it gave my heart. It felt as if the cold light was grasping for my very soul. I heard the others on the other side of the altar crying out and realized that the mist was clawing at all of us.

"Your Johanna is not here!" Elena shouted. "She is dead!"

"YOU LIE!"

I did not think the pain could get any worse, but it did. I fell to the floor, freezing and exhausted and ready to quit fighting. The others must have collapsed as well.

Suddenly, the painful cold disappeared, along with the mist. It did not recede into the talisman. It simply vanished.

My head was throbbing. I tried to get up, to get away from that horrible place. I had to escape. But I did not have the strength to move.

The crown prince was the first to stir. Moaning, he got to his knees and placed his fingers on my neck. "She's alive," he said.

The blackness closed around me again.

CHAPTER FIFTY-ONE

❧

I awoke the next morning in a large bed, my head pounding and my bandaged hand throbbing. The prince had drunk my blood. We would now be forever linked. Feeling nauseated at the thought, I started sobbing miserably. How could I have let this happen?

And now—with my blood—Konstantin had returned. Queen Milena had not realized her sister had been using the talisman to keep her lover's soul safe. He would go after Tsar Alexander and his family next.

I climbed out of bed and tried the door. I realized with relief that it was unlocked. But then, the Montenegrins had what they needed from me. They had no reason to keep me imprisoned.

Princess Militza met me in the hallway. "Awake at last, I see! Mama will be pleased. Would you like something to eat? She is having tea in the parlor."

"No, thank you." To be truthful, I was afraid of eating or drinking anything else in the palace. "Have my parents arrived yet?"

She did not answer. "Follow me, Duchess" was all she said.

Tea was held in the queen's parlor, an elegantly decorated room with red silk wall hangings. The walls were covered with portraits of her children.

"Duchess, good afternoon," Queen Milena greeted me.

Afternoon? I hurried to the window and drew back the heavy curtains. Late-afternoon sun stretched across the courtyard in front of the palace. I saw several carriages slowly driving up and down the street.

"You have been sleeping deeply all day. Sit here and have some tea."

"I am sorry, but my stomach is feeling a little queer at the moment. Please forgive me."

"Oh?" She placed the pot of tea back on its tray and stared at me with her penetrating black eyes.

"We should warn the tsar about Konstantin," I said.

Queen Milena nodded. "Of course. A telegraph has already been sent to St. Petersburg."

"What else can we do? How can he be stopped?" I asked.

The queen shrugged with a helpless smile. "I would not have the slightest idea."

"But—"

"Enough of this. We must discuss your wedding plans."

"Wedding plans?" I felt a sickening, cold wave of apprehension wash over me.

"Of course. I know how young people are these days. So

much in love and in such a hurry to start their lives together." She looked directly at me.

"I am not allowed to wed before my birthday. I believe my father made that clear."

The queen shook her head dismissively. "Nonsense. I was fourteen when I married my first husband. Fifteen when I had my first child. You must marry my son and bear him the heirs that he needs while you are young and fertile."

"Heirs?" I asked faintly. The room seemed to spin.

"Strong sons and plenty of daughters. Heirs to spread our dynasty across Europe. When Elena marries the tsarevitch, her children can marry your children."

"But they would be first cousins. The Church forbids such marriages." Of all the thoughts flitting through my head at once, that was what came out of my mouth first.

The queen waved her arms. "The Serbian Church will grant a dispensation for our dynasty."

I could not think of anything to say to her. The woman was mad. "Your Majesty, what if the tsarevitch marries someone else?"

"You mean the German bitch?" She laughed. "Yes, I know all about that one. She is a Protestant and is not willing to change her religion for her precious Nicholas. Besides, there is the little problem of her supernatural . . . affliction. The tsar and his empress cannot possibly agree to such an alliance. The tsar looks favorably upon our dynasty. Did he not say Nikola was Russia's one true friend?"

I knew nothing of Princess Alix's affliction, but everything else the queen said was true. The tsar still considered King Nikola and his wife close allies. Maman had told me he had been quick to approve my engagement to Danilo. I did not see how he could remain fond of the Montenegrins when he discovered they had released Konstantin. "How can you know so much about the Hessian princess?" I asked.

"I have spies everywhere, Duchess." She stopped stirring her spoon in her teacup. "I even know of your flirtations with the tsarevitch's brother."

"Flirtations?" I sputtered nervously. "Your spies must be mistaken. There is no affection between me and the grand duke." At least, not on his side.

"You are now bound to my son by your blood, and soon you will be bound to him by holy matrimony," the queen said as she continued to stir her tea. "I warn you, Katerina Alexandrovna, if you want your family to remain safe from Konstantin and the Dekebristi, you will do exactly as I say and begin to act the part of the happy bride-to-be. I will see Militza and Stana happily married before the tsar learns of Konstantin. The Dekebristi will pledge their loyalty to Militza rather than the lich tsar. And Alexander Alexandrovich will owe his life to us."

I could not stand it anymore. I was tired of feeling helpless. And tired of my loved ones' safety not being in my own hands. I was still frightened for them, but I was also furious. "Your Majesty, you have no way of protecting my family from Konstantin, and you have no reason to believe the Dekebristi will follow your daughter instead of their old master. You cannot force me to keep your secrets anymore." I was shaking all over, but I did not lower my gaze. "And you cannot force me to marry your son."

The queen did not look in the least shocked at my

outburst. She smiled. "Dear Katerina, I believe your mother feels quite differently." She turned and opened the parlor doors behind her, beyond which my mother stood—with Petya and Uncle George.

Maman rushed to embrace me. I wanted to cry with relief when I smelled her familiar Paris cologne. "Katiya! Why did you run off so foolishly? We came as quickly as we heard. The king and queen have been most kind."

I did not know what my mother had been told, but I was ready to leave for St. Petersburg immediately. "We can leave tonight," I told her. "I have nothing to pack."

"*Mon Dieu,* no! We are here to celebrate the crown prince's birthday. The king has promised to show us around the city himself."

"No, Maman," I begged, looking from her to my brother. "The tsar is in danger. We must return home and warn him."

The queen laughed. "Dear Katerina. Do not trouble your family with such things. It is time for dinner. Come."

We had no choice but to follow her. Queen Milena took my mother's arm and discussed the paintings we passed in the hallway. As quietly as I could, I told Petya about everything. Yes, everything.

My brother was horrified. "Katiya, you should have told me! I would have protected you!"

"How? They told me you would become one of the undead as well. I couldn't let that happen."

"Where did you learn this terrible power? At Smolny? Papa should never have let Maman talk him into sending you to that school."

"Smolny is not to blame. I think I was born with this

curse." I reached out and grabbed his hands. "You must warn the tsar, Petya. Can you get away tonight?"

"And leave you and Maman in the blood drinkers' clutches? The palace is surrounded by guards. We will all leave together in the morning."

"Are you sure they will allow us to go?" I asked.

Petya thought silently as we approached the dining room. "We mustn't tell Maman. Not before we get her safely away from here. She would become hysterical."

"When is she not hysterical?" I asked glumly.

"You're right," Petya said. "Surely at some point tonight, she'll get upset over some nonsense. We will then tell the Montenegrins that Maman is ill and we must take her back home to her own doctor."

I knew it would not take much for Maman to have one of her hysterical fits. Telling her about the Vladiki would definitely serve such a purpose. But I also knew that if the Montenegrins discovered I'd told anyone about the Black Mountain ritual, my family would be killed. Petya I could trust to keep silent. Maman I could not.

We enjoyed more local cuisine that night at dinner. Uncle George was happy to discuss military matters with King Nikola and Princess Zorka's husband.

Young, romantic Anna did not take her eyes off my brother the entire evening. And Danilo never took his eyes off me.

Everyone was excruciatingly polite. My nerves were on edge as I waited for something horrible to happen.

Maman complimented the queen on her beautiful palace. "The grand duchess Miechen has a boudoir decorated in the Moroccan style, very similar to this," she said.

"Does she indeed?" the queen replied, sipping her soup.

The women discussed wedding plans for Militza and Stana. "Now let us discuss plans for Danilo and Katerina's wedding," Queen Milena said as the servants served us glasses of sherry.

Maman did not smile. "I believe this has already been settled. We will not allow Katerina to marry before she is of age."

"Perhaps you may change your mind if your daughter was found to be in a delicate situation."

Maman's face grew white with shock as she realized what the queen was implying. "Katiya, what have you done?"

"Nothing, Maman," I protested. At least, not what she suspected. I felt violated all the same.

The queen laughed. "It could happen, Duchess. They are young and their passions are hot. It has been difficult for my husband and me to keep this pair apart."

I shuddered with disgust.

But the queen's suggestion did frighten my mother. I could almost hear her thoughts.

"I . . . well . . ."

"Maman, you know I would never do anything to disappoint you or Papa. . . ." *Besides raising the dead, that is.*

"I must speak with my husband." Maman's glass of sherry trembled slightly as she raised it to her lips.

"We are already planning two weddings in St. Petersburg for next month. It would be simple to arrange a third as well." Queen Milena smiled. She knew she already had my mother convinced I needed to be married off immediately. "Cost is no consequence, of course."

"Of course. It does seem the sensible thing to do," Maman said. She had a glassy look in her eyes as she sipped her sherry.

The queen smiled at me. I had to break her hold over my mother. I would rather die than marry Prince Danilo.

CHAPTER FIFTY-TWO

My brother was right, of course. It had not taken much for Maman to descend into hysterics. Convinced that I was in danger of being compromised by the crown prince, if indeed I had not already been compromised, Maman took to her bed before the end of the evening. Both Petya and Uncle George apologized extensively but insisted that we return to St. Petersburg the coming morning. The Montenegrins had no choice but to let us leave. They had accomplished everything they had hoped for.

Danilo kissed my hand as our families said their goodbyes. "We will be together again soon. And then it will be forever."

Maman and I argued the entire trip home. She insisted that I be married at Peterhof with the Montenegrin princesses. Uncle George was delighted at the thought of sharing his wedding day with his niece. At least my brother was on my side.

"She is only sixteen, Maman," Petya said. "Let her finish school, at least."

"For what? As young girls grow older, they begin to get strange ideas in their heads. And no man wants that in a wife."

"Oh, Maman." I could not believe she was saying this. She had always prided herself on her education. She was always reading and trying to improve her mind. "Papa does not feel that way," I said, crossing my arms.

But when we returned home three days later, Maman and Papa had the most dreadful of arguments. Maman would not be talked out of a hasty wedding.

⁓

There had been no sign of Konstantin. The attacks on the Order stopped, and everyone seemed to relax a little. However, there were several undead members still left unaccounted for. Whether Konstantin had found them and was preparing them for battle, no one could say.

Danilo arrived back in St. Petersburg not long after us and came to visit my father.

Papa wanted Danilo to promise him I would be allowed to attend medical school, but the crown prince refused. Danilo smiled and dazzled Papa with his new and improved Vladiki charm. By the time Danilo left my father's study, even Papa was joyfully handing over large sums of money to Maman for my trousseau. There was no talking my parents out of this marriage anymore. To cry off now would cause an enormous scandal and no suitor would ever offer for me again. As if that mattered to me at all.

The weddings were to be at Peterhof, the grand summer palace of the imperial family, twenty miles outside St. Petersburg. The grounds were beautiful, especially in summer, with several elaborate fountains over a hundred years old. I had been to Peterhof for the grand duke Serge and Princess Elizabeth's wedding when I was ten. I had fallen into the lion fountain.

The imperial family was currently visiting the empress's family in Denmark. They would return to Russia in time to attend the weddings. I dreaded seeing George Alexandrovich again. He would never forgive me for releasing Konstantin. And he would have every reason to hate me.

I did not cry when the wedding gifts began to pile up in our parlor. I did not cry when Madame Olga came to the house to fit me for my wedding gown and yelled at me to stand still. I did not cry when I saw Papa's sad face as he gazed upon the wedding gifts. He may have been won over by Danilo's powerful charms, but my father did not want his little girl to grow up and move so far away. My heart was breaking.

I did not cry when we visited Dr. Kruglevski's grave and I laid a rose on it. Papa squeezed my hand. It was my fault that he had lost a very dear friend. He had already asked Anya's brother Rudolf to take Dr. Kruglevski's place as head of the Institute of Experimental Medicine. But Rudolf did not have Dr. Kruglevski's years of experience.

"Papa," I said, grasping his arm on the carriage ride home. "Are you terribly disappointed in me?"

He looked surprised. "Katiya, you could never disappoint me. Whether you become a queen or a peasant, as long as you are happy, I will be happy."

I hugged him. "Thank you, Papa."

"Prince Danilo makes you happy, yes?"

I was glad he couldn't see my face. "Of course, Papa." It would make me happy if we were all safe from Konstantin and the Dekebristi. I prayed for Petya and his men as they searched St. Petersburg for them.

Before returning home from the cemetery, we stopped in front of the Tibetan doctor's pharmacy. Papa smiled and squeezed my hand.

I remembered the last time I had been here, with the grand duke. I hoped he had discovered something useful when he'd talked to Dr. Badmaev. What had he thought when I had disappeared? Surely by now he had heard of my trip to Cetinje. And my wedding plans.

The Tibetan doctor smiled when he saw us, and gave us a respectful bow. "It is good to see both of you." His empty shop was heavy with the scent of incense.

"Any new information about our friend?" Papa asked.

Badmaev shook his head. "I am sorry. He does not seem to be affected by anything I give him. It is most puzzling."

"Has he been violent?"

"Of course not. He does not seem to want to leave this area. He doesn't say much—only calls sadly for his mistress."

I'd had no idea whom they were speaking of until that moment. "Mistress?" Surely they couldn't be talking of . . . "Where is he?" I rushed toward the back, behind the beaded curtains.

"Katiya, wait!" Papa called after me. "This patient has some unknown disease. He may be contagious."

"Please, I must see him."

"It is strange," Dr. Badmaev said, looking at me curiously. "This man did show up the same day the grand duke was here asking about hemlock antidotes."

"Which grand duke?" Papa asked.

I pushed past both of them into the tiny courtyard in the back. Badmaev had made a sleeping area for Count Chermenensky, who did not seem to enjoy being inside.

"His Imperial Highness the grand duke George Alexandrovich," the doctor said. "He was investigating the death of Princess Cantacuzene. He seemed to recognize our patient here. In fact, he asked me to take care of him here rather than send him to the hospital."

Tears rolled down my cheeks. "Count Chermenensky?" I whispered. I did not want Papa to know his name yet if he hadn't already realized who the undead soldier was.

The count looked up at me with glassy eyes. He had been washed and someone had given him clean clothes. "Mistress? Back?"

"Yes, Your Highness. I am so sorry I left."

The count remained huddled in his sleeping box, rocking back and forth. "Bad people took you . . . could not save you . . . Forgive . . ."

"No, Your Highness. I must beg your forgiveness for leaving you. Everything is going to be all right now."

"Mistress not safe . . . hunted by shadows."

"Katiya?" Papa stood in the doorway of the courtyard. "Step away from that man, my dear. He is deranged."

"It's all right, Papa. He won't hurt me." I reached out and placed my hand on the count's. "Your Highness, what shadows do you speak of? What can you see?"

"Shadows with wings," he muttered, still rocking back and forth. "Must protect mistress."

"What is he talking about?" my father asked.

"Count Chermenensky, do not worry. I want you to stay here with the doctor. He is trying to help you."

"I'm not sure I can help him, Duchess," Badmaev said softly.

I nodded. What could modern medicine do for the undead?

"Mistress," Count Chermenensky whimpered. "Must protect you."

"I'll be safe," I promised him. With a pat on his shoulder, I turned to follow Papa back to our carriage. Ancient medicine was what the count needed. The Egyptian necromancer. Perhaps there was still an undiscovered ritual in *A Necromancer's Companion* that would help him. But I was running out of time. After the wedding, I would be taken back to Cetinje and would never be able to help the count, or my family, again.

And Konstantin was still out there somewhere, biding his time. Had he found the Dekebristi and persuaded them to follow him? Or did Princess Militza control them?

"That was quite amazing how you soothed that creature," Papa said on our ride home. "You have a healer's touch, Katiya. A gift you are wasting."

I wanted to laugh. Hadn't Badmaev said the same thing? But the life I brought to the dead was not a gift. It was not life at all. Perhaps that was the true reason I'd wanted to be a doctor all those years. I wanted to ease people's suffering and prevent death altogether.

Papa sighed when I did not answer him. "All right, Katiya. I only want you to be happy."

CHAPTER FIFTY-THREE

Queen Milena and her daughters arrived at Peterhof to prepare for the wedding festivities, and Grand Duchess Miechen held a ball in the Montenegrins' honor. All the members of the Dark Court would be in attendance. Dariya told me the gossip she'd overheard from her stepmother as we got ready for the ball in my family's nearby dacha.

"Militza has succeeded in dominating the St. Petersburg vampires," my cousin whispered. "She will take Princess Cantacuzene's place as the head of the House of Bessaraba in Russia. As Cantacuzene's niece, she has a legitimate blood claim."

"But her sister Zorka is older," I said. "Wouldn't she be the rightful heir?"

Dariya shrugged. "Militza has persuaded her sister to support her. She alone knows the secret hiding place of the undead Dekebristi. She believes she can control them with the Talisman of Isis—the same one that was mentioned in your book—and keep them out of Konstantin's hands."

It would make Militza almost untouchable.

"Besides," Dariya said, "the tsar now knows that Cantacuzene broke the treaty of 1825. Miechen thinks Militza will try to renegotiate that treaty with him once she has the undead army in her power."

"I don't think there is anything that Miechen can do, other than smile graciously and dance the polonaise with the King of Montenegro," I said. I hoped I would get a chance to speak with the dark faerie queen at the ball.

"What is the grand duchess thinking?" my cousin said. "She is too far along in her confinement to be dancing in public!"

"Nonsense," I said. "Princess Yussopova danced all night long at one of her own balls and gave birth to her son the very next day. With no difficulties." I looked up at my cousin in the mirror and smiled. "And with no scandals."

Dariya sighed. "I suppose it would be a worse scandal if the King and Queen of Montenegro were snubbed by the Dark Court of St. Petersburg. I do hope you are careful tonight. If only there was a spell you could invoke to protect yourself from the crown prince. I kept searching that book of yours, but I could not find anything that looks practical." She looked at me pointedly. "Nothing that does not involve raising your own undead army."

"That is out of the question," I said, my hands trembling as I fastened pearl earrings in my earlobes. "I couldn't possibly do such a thing."

"But you do have the curse, do you not?" Dariya asked soberly. "Why else would Cantacuzene give you such a book? And the moth at the Smolny Ball. That was something you did, was it not?"

I did not know what to say. How long had she known? "But I didn't want you to think I was a monster!"

"How could I? My mother had the curse as well."

I looked at her in surprise. "How do you know that?" Dariya's mother had died giving birth to her. Had she truly been a necromancer, like me?

"I found my mother's journal when I was six. For years, I secretly hoped I would inherit some special talent from her. Even the curse. It would have kept me connected with her in some small way." Dariya played with the lace in the window. "I know how stupid it seems," she said sheepishly.

"Of course it doesn't. But I wouldn't wish this curse on anyone. I've wanted to tell you for so long, but I didn't want you to be afraid of me!"

She rushed forward to embrace me. "I know you are a good person, Katiya," she whispered in my ear. "I'm not afraid of you."

I tried to blink away the tears. I prayed I would never let my cousin down.

"Girls!" Maman's voice rang through the hallway. "We must leave immediately!"

Hastily, I brushed the tears out of the corners of my eyes and sighed. "I suppose I shall have to dance every dance with the crown prince," I said.

Dariya smiled. "Do not give up hope yet, Katiya. We will think of something before you have to marry him."

Peterhof was a stunning estate, consisting of several palaces and chapels. The Grand Palace was known as the Russian Versailles and had an impressive bank of fountains, called the Grand Cascade, that flowed down toward the sea. Our own family dacha was also close to the water, looking out across the Gulf of Finland.

It was a beautiful white night, the last in July, and the sun had no intention of setting that evening. All the women wore white court gowns embroidered in silver. Maman wore one of her tiaras and I wore an embroidered *kokoshnik*. Once I was married, I would be allowed to wear tiaras to balls and court functions. Maman had already showed me a few of her treasured pieces of jewelry she planned to give me as wedding gifts. I was afraid, though, that after my wedding, I would never see another ball again. I was afraid I would never see St. Petersburg again.

"Katerina, I am so pleased to see you." The crown prince met me at the top of the grand staircase at the Grand Palace and kissed my hand possessively. "You are looking especially ravishing tonight."

I could tell he did not plan to let me out of his sight all evening. With a polite bow to Maman and the grand duchess, he pulled me onto the ballroom floor, making sure everyone saw us as a happy couple.

We spun around and around to Strauss and Glinka. "You look distracted, my love," he said. "As if you long to be elsewhere."

I said nothing. I glanced around the ballroom. The

Montenegrin princesses were all dancing gaily. Princess Anastasia was speaking with her mother and Grand Duchess Miechen. The grand duchess did not look happy. She looked pale.

"What has happened?" I asked.

"Nothing to concern yourself with, my dear," Danilo said. "But Russia's worst fears have been confirmed. Konstantin the Deathless has returned."

I was so shocked I almost tripped over my own feet. I stopped dancing and stared at him. "How do you know this?"

"He has been at the priory here at Peterhof all along. The vampires have seen him and reported this to Militza."

"The tsar! He must be warned!" I tried to pull away from Danilo. His hands gripped me tighter. "The imperial family is here at Peterhof for the wedding ceremonies. We must send word to them immediately!" Tsar Alexander and his wife preferred staying at one of the smaller palaces on the estate. It was tucked far away from the Grand Palace.

The crown prince smiled lazily. "Do not worry your pretty head about this. Montenegro has sworn her allegiance to Russia and the tsar. We have already sent our warrior priests to help the tsar's men defeat Konstantin Pavlovich."

My stomach knotted. When the tsar found out about Queen Milena's ritual, he would know of my involvement. My blood had brought back Konstantin the Deathless. I could be killed for treason.

"Do not be frightened, Katerina. The tsar will never know your part in betraying him." He pushed a lock of my hair back off my shoulder and leaned forward to whisper, "That is what you were thinking, is it not?"

I looked over again at Queen Milena, who was smiling at me and the crown prince. The grand duchess was no longer standing with her. I looked all around the vast ballroom, but Miechen had left her own ball. Maman and Papa were dancing merrily, as were Princess Elena and one of the Georgian princes.

"Your Highness, I am terribly sorry," I said. "I have been overcome with a terrible headache. I must beg you to excuse me for a moment."

"Perhaps you need some fresh air?" Danilo asked as he turned to lead me to the veranda.

I could smell the sea air on the night breeze, but I did not want to go outdoors. I wanted to find the grand duchess. I shook my head. "I need to find a quiet place to sit down."

His eyes flashed darkly as his fingers dug into my arm briefly. It was a painful warning. "Do not try anything foolish."

"Of course not, Your Highness."

CHAPTER FIFTY-FOUR

∾◦∾

I searched the long corridors of the Grand Palace for the grand duchess. The private apartments were on the opposite side of the palace from the ballroom. I knew I wouldn't have much time before the crown prince would come looking for me.

Grand Duchess Miechen was sitting on a couch in the Blue Room, just off the grand staircase. She still looked pale, and was holding her belly.

"Your Imperial Highness? Can I send for anyone?"

She shook her head. "Katerina, do not worry about me. You must get word to the tsar. The foolish Montenegrins have uncovered Cantacuzene's secret and resurrected her dead lover, Konstantin Pavlovich. He is going after the tsar before the bogatyr can be summoned."

"What can we do?"

The grand duchess smiled, despite her obvious pain. "I can do nothing, I'm afraid, except keep the rest of the Dark

Court out of the fight. The Russian vampires will wish to side with Konstantin, of course. He and Princess Cantacuzene created most of them. There are still families in St. Petersburg who are bitter about Nicholas's brutality in crushing the Dekebristi. To revenge themselves against Nicholas's grandson would be too tempting."

"I am so sorry, Your Imperial Highness," I said. "I was there when Queen Milena released him, but she did not realize what she was doing. And then he disappeared, and there was nothing anyone could do."

"Soon everyone will know. The tsar will not be pleased—if he survives."

"Why do you care?" I asked suspiciously. "Would you not be happy to see the tsar dead?"

"Alexander Alexandrovich is a foe I much prefer to Konstantin Pavlovich. What hope would my Vladimir have of inheriting the throne from a lich tsar?" She gave a little grimace as her face drained of all color.

"Is it the twins?" I asked anxiously. "It is much too early, isn't it?"

She nodded and clutched her abdomen with a strained whisper: "Katerina, send for Dr. Badmaev. I cannot let the vampires in the ballroom smell the blood."

I gasped and realized the grand duchess was indeed beginning to hemorrhage. *Mon Dieu.* "Can you walk at all?" I asked. "I can send for our carriage."

The grand duchess shook her head. "I cannot leave the palace."

I helped her down the long corridor to her private rooms. Her maids quickly undressed her and helped her into bed.

They had a footman send for the Tibetan doctor. It would take several hours, however, for the man to reach St. Petersburg and to return with the doctor.

"Shall I get my mother?" I felt helpless as I watched the grand duchess suffer. The cold light that surrounded her seemed to be growing. She nodded, not bothering to open her eyes. Her maids stood at her bedside, bathing her face with cool rags.

I hurried down the corridor, heading back to the ballroom. I needed to find my mother without the Montenegrins finding me first.

CHAPTER FIFTY-FIVE

I slipped into the ballroom and saw my mother speaking with Queen Milena. *Merde*. I looked around for my father instead. He needed to know about Konstantin Pavlovich as well if he was not already aware. My brother and the rest of the living members of the Order of St. John were still in danger.

"There you are." Danilo's voice was low in my ear as he came from behind and grabbed me around the waist. "I was beginning to get concerned."

"What did your mother do to the grand duchess Miechen?"

"She has done nothing." He smiled. "My sisters, on the other hand, consider the grand duchess a friend of Cantacuzene, and therefore an enemy of the tsar."

"She was no friend of the princess!" I hissed. "Let me go!"

He led me out of the ballroom, and into a deserted corridor. "I am afraid I cannot do that."

"She could die!"

Princess Elena sneered behind us. "And what can you do to help her? Pretend to be a doctor?"

If there was ever a moment I wanted to embrace my darkest powers and destroy someone, it was then. But Danilo pushed me into a small sitting room. I heard the door lock behind me.

"What are you doing?" I screamed.

"You must not interfere, beloved. When Konstantin is defeated, we shall be married. There will be no more meddling from the Dark Court."

"What do you plan to do? How will you protect the tsar?"

There was no answer.

"Danilo, you cannot leave me in here!"

But the crown prince and his sister had already left. The hallway fell silent.

There were no windows in this room, decorated in an Oriental style, and only the one door, which was locked. I was trapped. No one would be able to hear me above the noise of the ball.

Except George Alexandrovich, if luck was with me.

"Your Imperial Highness?" I spoke aloud. "Please, Your Imperial Highness. If you can hear me, the tsar is in danger. Konstantin Pavlovich has returned and is here at Peterhof. Princess Cantacuzene was raising the undead army for him."

I tried to stay calm.

"Your Imperial Highness? Georgi?" I whispered desperately.

There was a sudden commotion in the hall. I could hear Elena shrieking.

The door opened, and instead of the Vladiki prince, I saw the grand duke. I wanted to cry. "George," I whispered, forgetting all imperial protocols.

He stared at me for a moment. "Katerina, I—"

"Who dares disturb my bride?" Prince Danilo said as he rushed into the room.

The grand duke turned to face him, his hand going to the saber at his hip. "I dare. And by the order of the tsar, Katerina Alexandrovna must come with me at once."

"What nonsense is this? This is a Dark Court gathering and you have no right to be here."

"I have no intentions of staying. But the necromancer must come with me."

Danilo tried his best to look menacing. "But the duchess and I are about to be married."

"I do not believe the duchess wishes to be married," George Alexandrovich said, glancing at me. I shook my head slightly. There was no reason for me to pretend anymore.

"This is none of your concern, Imperial Highness," the crown prince said.

"Perhaps not, but by order of the tsar, I am required to take the Duchess of Oldenburg to the Peterhof chapel immediately."

"For what purpose?" Danilo said through gritted teeth.

"Urgent matters of state." George turned to me and offered his arm, which I took, gladly.

"This is an insult to my family. I will not allow this." Danilo grabbed for me, his fangs visible.

But the grand duke was faster. He took my arm and swung me out of the crown prince's reach. He threw a punch at Danilo's jaw. The crown prince stepped out of the way just in time.

I was too scared to scream.

I looked around the room wildly as the two princes scuffled. George had managed to land a blow somehow, as I noticed Danilo's lip bleeding. I saw the Oriental vase in the curio cabinet wobble as Danilo shoved George into the wall. I ran to catch the vase before it tumbled off the shelf, and turned around to hit it over Danilo's head.

Something sharp poked me in the back. "Don't even think about it." Elena's voice behind me was menacing. "Tell the grand duke to leave, or I will kill you, Katerina Alexandrovna."

I tried to twist away from her, but she held me by the hair. I let out an unladylike yelp.

Just then, Danilo punched the grand duke in the stomach and he staggered back into the wall. George slid to the floor, dazed.

"No!" I cried, trying to break free. Elena pulled me back, pressing the blade a little deeper.

Danilo turned toward me, his eyes darkening and his fangs growing longer. I couldn't let him have my blood. He would have the power to kill the grand duke. Or worse.

"Your Imperial Highness!" I pleaded. "Get up!" He was still conscious and trying to regain his bearings.

We had to get out of there. I kicked backward at Elena's

shins and she let me go. "Bitch!" she screamed. I pulled away before she could reach me again.

"He cannot help you now," Danilo said. He laughed as he grabbed me by the arm and pulled me close. His breath was warm on my neck. "You belong to me, Katerina."

"No, she does not," George Alexandrovich said grimly, throwing a punch that struck Danilo in the jaw. He let go of me and fell back.

Elena screamed and jumped at the grand duke with her dagger, but I snatched the back of her dress, causing her to stumble. She dropped her blade. I kicked it across the floor and the grand duke picked it up.

"Now," he said, wiping the blood from his lip with the back of his hand. "I am taking the Duchess of Oldenburg to the tsar. And there will be hell to pay if anyone makes another attempt to stop me." He offered his arm to me. "Your Highness."

I felt a little giddy. He *had* come to my rescue. Even if it was only because the tsar needed me. We stepped over the Montenegrin siblings and ran out the door.

Right into my father.

"Katiya! Where have you been? Your mother has been frantic since you disappeared with the crown prince."

"She is safe, Your Highness," the grand duke said. "We have no time to explain, but the tsar is waiting for her."

"The tsar?" Papa asked. "Whatever for?"

"The bogatyr must be summoned."

"The bogatyr?" Papa asked. "But what does this have to do with Katiya?"

"She is the only one who can perform the necessary ritual." The grand duke turned to me. "We must hurry."

I saw fleeting bewilderment on my father's face. But he was a clever man. He knew what the grand duke meant. "Go, quickly, Katiya," he said. "We will have much to talk about when this is over."

"Please take Maman to the grand duchess Miechen at once, Papa. She is in danger of losing the twins."

"*Mon Dieu.* I will see that your mother attends her immediately. And that the doctor has been sent for."

⁓⊘⁓

The grand duke helped me into the carriage. He scowled silently as we rode off across the park. The chapel was only a short ride from the main palace.

"Were you hurt badly?" I asked him.

"I'm fine, Duchess."

More scowling silence.

I sank back into my seat, folding my arms. "I'm fine too, thank you ever so kindly for asking."

He grunted. "Were you really planning to marry that creature?"

"They said they would hurt my family! My brother." I risked a glance at him. "Even you."

The grand duke seemed to relax slightly. He reached over and touched my cheek. I felt dizzy as my world tilted a little bit. "Katiya, they cannot harm your family. Or me. Please believe that. You need never fear them again." He turned his attention back to the road ahead. "Once Konstantin and his army are defeated, the tsar will have nothing more to do with the Montenegrin king."

But how could he be right? There was a horrible bond now between me and the crown prince. I was afraid I'd never be safe from the Montenegrins.

CHAPTER FIFTY-SIX

~⚬~

Members of the Order were stationed around the Gothic Chapel. We were met at the chapel entrance by the tsarevitch. "Georgi! Thank goodness!" he said. "We must hurry."

I took a step back, startled to see the silvery white wolf sitting quietly by the tsarevitch.

"Isn't it beautiful?" he asked. "It just showed up this evening. It won't come inside the chapel, but it won't leave either."

The Gothic Chapel was a tiny square building with beautiful rose windows on each side. This was the imperial family's private chapel when they stayed at Peterhof.

Inside, the empress stood next to her husband in the chapel hall, smiling tightly. "Katerina Alexandrovna," she addressed me. I knew she was terrified for her husband.

I curtsied low. "Your Imperial Majesties." I forced myself to look up into my sovereign's eyes.

The tsar stared at me hard. Even seated in an ordinary wooden chair, he seemed majestic. When he stood up and towered over me, I thought my heart would burst in fright. There was a reason he was called Sasha the Bear by the Dark Court. "The time has come for you to accept your responsibilities as a princess of the imperial blood," he said. "Although your family belongs to the Dark Court, you still owe your allegiance to me, your tsar."

"Yes, Your Imperial Majesty," I whispered.

"A necromancer is the only one able to summon the bogatyr when Russia has need of him. My son tells me you have the dark gift."

I glanced at the grand duke, whose face betrayed nothing. "I have the gift—or curse," I said. "But I do not know the ritual."

"The patriarch will instruct you," the tsar answered.

It was almost like the ascension ritual of the Montenegrin Vladiki. Three priests stood chanting in front of the icon-covered doors. Only they wore white robes, with golden embroidery, instead of black ones. Incense burned, creating a smoky haze.

A heavy wooden chest was carried into the chapel by two young pages.

I was sprinkled with holy water, then anointed with oil as the patriarch chanted prayers over me. He did the same with the tsar and his sons, only the prayers for them were much longer. The tsar, who had been kneeling, stood up stiffly. The empress discreetly assisted him.

The young pages opened the chest and the patriarch

lifted out a bundle wrapped in linen. Inside the linen was a jeweled medallion.

I shuddered. Another talisman.

The patriarch's voice boomed across the chapel. "Katerina Alexandrovna, walker among the paths of the dead, place your left hand upon the amulet of His Imperial Majesty the tsar Pavel and place your right hand in the hand of His Imperial Majesty the Sovereign Emperor, Alexander Alexandrovich."

It was the same medal, a Maltese Cross, the symbol of the Order of St. John of Jerusalem, that I'd seen in the portrait of Tsar Pavel. Trying not to shake or tremble, I did as the patriarch instructed. I felt a tingling as something cold flowed through me from the amulet into the tsar's hand. But I was thankful this ritual did not require my blood.

The tsar let out a roar as the cold hit him. I cringed, and tried to break off but the tsar gripped my hand tightly. He appeared to grow two feet taller, looking even more like a bear than ever.

When the summoning was complete, he finally let go of my hand. I stumbled back into the grand duke, who put out his hands to steady me.

The tsarevitch handed his father a large sword that looked very old. And very deadly.

The heavy wooden doors to the chapel burst open. A bitterly cold wind blew in, extinguishing all the candles.

The patriarch continued his chanting. The other priests rang bells and sprinkled more holy water on the tsar, now imbued with the spirit of the bogatyr.

Making the sign of the cross, the patriarch stepped back. A holy light blazed within the tsar's eyes. I dropped to my knees, bowing my head, as he strode past me.

The bogatyr stormed out of the chapel, his voice booming across the gardens. "Konstantin Pavlovich!" he bellowed. "You are no longer welcome in Russia!"

Grand Duke George Alexandrovich helped me stand before joining his father and brother. The light burned in his eyes as well. A holy light I never wanted to taint with my curse. I hurried after them to the arched doorway and looked out.

Konstantin the Deathless stood unnaturally tall, like the bogatyr. Closing in behind him were the undead knights of the Order of St. John of Jerusalem. The Dekebristi. Johanna's last gift for her vampire lover.

Konstantin had been a short, ugly man in his time. Death, and undeath, had not been kind to his body either. "Alexander Alexandrovich, stand down, or you and your sons will die horribly," he warned. "As did your guards."

"Mon Dieu!" I whispered. Could it be that every last one of the tsar's men who had been guarding the chapel had been killed?

"Your Imperial Majesty! We come to serve you!" the Montenegrin king shouted as he ran toward us. He had arrived in a carriage with Danilo. Queen Milena stepped out of the carriage after them, looking pale, with a bandage wrapped around her neck. She had been fed upon. No doubt by both father and son.

I did not see Militza, who must have been using all her shaky new influence to keep the vampires out of the fight.

Or perhaps she feared losing control of them if they saw Konstantin.

The tsar barely acknowledged the Montenegrin king, who took a position safe behind his wife. The tsar raised his sword high and glared at Konstantin the Deathless. "No blood drinker will ever sit on the throne of Russia," he declared.

The tsarevitch and the grand duke held their swords ready. I was frightened for them as well. The silver wolf kept close to the tsarevitch, fangs bared.

Danilo stood smiling, an evil gleam in his eye. He did not bother to raise his sword as an undead soldier advanced toward him.

Queen Milena muttered some kind of incantation under her breath and the undead soldier fell to the ground, motionless. The queen turned toward me with a vicious smile. I knew no incantations to fight with. Except the spell of shadows. My gift of necromancy would be no help on this battlefield. I shuddered.

A low rumble alerted me that we were about to have company. The undead soldiers were closing in on us. "George!" I shouted, praying that protocol infractions were forgivable in the middle of a life-or-death battle. "The undead!"

The undead soldiers trampled toward us. I wanted to cry when I saw the poor creatures, but I knew they shared no such human compassion. They were intent on feeding and were under the control of the false tsar.

"KILL THEM ALL!" Konstantin Pavlovich snarled, adding what sounded like a spell in an ancient language. He was locked in combat with the true tsar, who, although larger and stronger than the lich tsar, was not as fast. Konstantin had already drawn first blood, piercing the bogatyr's shoulder.

One of the undead tried to pull me away from the fight. It was Prince Demidov.

With a feral growl, he lunged for my throat. His foul breath almost made me gag.

Queen Milena lay on the ground, too weak to get up after expending all her powers, but she smiled as she watched me struggle with the undead prince. She drew something out of the bodice of her gown. It was the Talisman of Isis, which hung around her neck.

I kicked and threw the undead prince off balance. He let go of me only for a moment, but it was enough for me to move out of his reach. I started toward the queen.

Her eyes narrowed, and she whispered something in an unfamiliar language. Two more undead soldiers marched toward me.

My heart pounded in my throat. I realized I was going to die. In a most horrible fashion.

The two soldiers suddenly stopped, and their heads became curiously detached from their bodies. Behind them I saw George Alexandrovich, holding a bloodied sword. "Get the talisman!" he shouted at me.

I did not have time to thank him for saving my life. I ran toward the queen again and we rolled in the dirt. I was hurting, and my dress was filthy, but I did not care. I did not want to touch the tainted talisman, but I couldn't leave it in Queen Milena's hands.

"Foolish girl, you will destroy everything!" she spat. "The Romanov court will never accept you! Your place is with us!"

"I would rather die," I said, prying the talisman from her bloody fingers. I was about to damn myself. To accept the darkness I'd struggled against all my life. In order to save the tsar.

I held the talisman high over my head and shouted as loud as I could, "The blood of Isis, the strength of Isis, and the power of Isis is mine!"

A chilly wind roared in my ears. It seemed to rise inside of me, threatening to overtake me. I closed my eyes and concentrated on the talisman in my hands. When the roaring stopped, I opened my eyes.

Slowly, the undead soldiers in front of me laid down their weapons and turned their pale faces to me. All kneeled, rather wobbly, on one knee.

It didn't stop all the undead, but I was safe for the moment. I turned to see if I could help the tsarevitch and his brother. The wolf was ferociously defending both of them. Snarling and snapping, it tore through the vampire who attacked the tsarevitch from behind.

"THIS IS NOT OVER!" Konstantin the Deathless shouted. Fangs bared, he charged the bogatyr with his sword. The bogatyr anticipated him and stepped back, unbalancing the false tsar. But Konstantin took the bogatyr down with him.

The cold light surrounding Konstantin grew larger. The bogatyr struggled stoically, but I knew he was suffering from the cold touch of the deathless tsar.

Both sons of the bogatyr were fighting another wave of undead soldiers. King Nikola and Crown Prince Danilo were protecting Queen Milena from three more of the Dekebristi. No one was able to help the bogatyr.

I watched Konstantin's cold light wrap around the bogatyr. It was draining his soul.

I wanted to scream. The talisman had not affected Konstantin at all.

But shadows could destroy light.

Even a cold light.

"*Sheult Anubis*," I said, the sick feeling of dark magic beginning to rise in my stomach.

Nothing happened at first. The bogatyr and Konstantin continued to struggle.

"*Sheult Anubis*," I repeated, a little stronger this time as the shadows began to close in around me.

I spoke the words a third time and concentrated on pushing the shadows toward Konstantin.

It was a weak effort, but the shadows distracted him just long enough for the bogatyr to roll away and stand again. Konstantin was caught off guard as the bogatyr charged him.

He slipped in a puddle of blood and slid toward the Montenegrin queen. King Nikola pulled his wife out of the way.

The bogatyr pointed his sword at Konstantin's neck. "Yield, blood drinker."

"NEVER!" Konstantin spat.

The bogatyr drew back his sword to deal the death blow.

The false tsar laughed. "This is not the end, Alexander Alexandrovich. The throne of Russia belongs to me!"

A chilling wind blew and the ground began to shake. I could barely stand up, but Nicholas Alexandrovich held out his arm to assist me. Then, suddenly, the wind disappeared, taking Konstantin the Deathless with it.

The bogatyr swore disgustedly as his sword came down with a heavy clang upon nothing but dry earth.

"What the devil?" the tsarevitch said.

"Konstantin!" the bogatyr roared. But the false tsar was gone. An eerie silence fell across the churchyard.

"Is it over?" I asked.

The bogatyr's gaze swept across the bloody field. With a satisfied grunt, he nodded and sheathed his sword.

I heard a weak voice calling out. "Mistress . . ."

It was not Count Chermenensky, but Prince Demidov. I found him lying in a tangled heap, his left arm sliced off. I was nervous approaching him, but he was under my control now, thanks to the talisman.

Gently, he held something out to me. "He lived to serve you, Mistress."

I stepped back with a cry. It was Count Chermenensky's head in the crook of his right arm. The undead count had been killed while trying to protect me.

George Alexandrovich was at my side immediately and put his hand on my arm to steady me. "He served his mistress well," he said. It took everything I had not to faint. I could not stop the tears from rolling down my cheeks.

The grand duke bent down and clasped the undead prince's remaining hand. "This war is not over yet, friend. We ask that you lead the other undead soldiers and fight for Russia against Konstantin the Deathless."

Prince Demidov nodded and stiffly saluted the grand duke. "If the mistress wills it, it shall be done."

I wiped the tears out of my eyes. I'd hoped to find a way to return the poor count and the others to their eternal rest. At least the count would no longer suffer. But if the tsar wanted the others to remain as revenants, there was nothing I could do. I stood up to hand the talisman to the bogatyr.

With a frown he shook his head. "Only a necromancer may wield the Talisman of Isis. Will you bear this burden? Will you serve your tsar?"

I hesitated. All my hopes and dreams for my future had already slipped away. I bowed my head. "I will, Your Imperial Majesty," I whispered. I would embrace my dark powers, to protect the tsar.

The bogatyr's voice boomed over the bloodied field. "I do hereby recognize the undead knights of the Order of St. John of Jerusalem. From this day forward, you will belong to the Order of St. Lazarus."

The priests who had been standing in the hall of the chapel chanting prayers now rang their bells and said prayers for the newly created order.

The mysterious silver wolf had vanished. If it hadn't been for the ghost of Tsar Pavel mentioning wolf-folk, I might have believed that I'd imagined the beautiful creature. I wondered if the wolf was someone I knew. The creature had kept very close to the tsarevitch throughout much of the fighting.

The bogatyr retreated into the chapel, where the empress waited, and the priests led me in after them to complete the ritual. It was time to send the bogatyr's spirit back and relieve the tsar of his supernatural burden.

CHAPTER FIFTY-SEVEN

I was sitting in a pew in a dark corner of the chapel, crying softly. I did not know if I was crying for Count Chermenensky or just because I was exhausted.

"Katerina Alexandrovna, let me take you home." George Alexandrovich stood over me and held out his hand.

I wiped my face and let him help me stand. "Forgive me, Your Imperial Highness," I said. "Let me collect myself."

In the carriage he asked me, "Were you in love with him?"

"Who, the crown prince? Of course not!"

He frowned. "Count Chermenensky. Before, I mean."

I shook my head. "I hardly knew him. But I felt responsible for him. I never meant to bring him back, I swear to you." I started sobbing again.

"You have been very brave today, Katiya." His voice was tired as he used my family pet name. He slid his arm around me protectively, pulling me closer to him. It made my heart pound.

I closed my eyes and rested my head on the grand duke's shoulder. He smelled like dirt and sweat and tobacco. There was no other place in the world I would rather have been.

When the carriage stopped, he turned to me with those fathomless blue eyes. He wiped the tears off my face with his hand. There was something unreadable in his expression. It vibrated down deep inside me. My palm went to his cheek.

"Katiya," he said, his voice hoarse and battle-weary. He grabbed my hand and pressed it to his lips. "I can give you the sun, my duchess. Marry me."

I was dumbstruck. I had not expected this. It had been a long, bloody day, and now this. I couldn't help crying harder.

It was not the reaction the grand duke had been expecting. He frowned. "Katiya?"

I shook my head, my tears falling too fast for him to catch now. "You promise the sun when you know I belong with the Dark Court. Your parents would never allow such a marriage."

"My father owes you his life. He needs you."

"Not as his daughter-in-law." No matter how dark his path, I could not live with myself if I tainted the grand duke's soul with my own shadows.

He sighed with frustration. "This is about you becoming a doctor, isn't it? I swear to you I will hire the smartest physicians across Europe to tutor you privately."

I smiled despite my tears. He seemed so eager to make me happy. "Georgi, you are deluding yourself. Your parents will never agree to this."

"Then we'll leave Russia. We'll live wherever you wish."

"And what of your obligations? You are to become the Koldun."

"It doesn't matter." He pulled me into his arms and whispered into my hair, "I cannot live without you, Katiya."

I closed my eyes, leaning my head against his chest. "And I cannot come between you and your family."

George sighed. "I'm not giving up, Katiya. Don't give up on me."

I pulled away to look up at him. "Georgi—"

Before I could say another word, he took my face in his hands and kissed me. I had been kissed only once before, and it had been nothing like this. His lips fit mine perfectly. We belonged together. Something inside me uncoiled, filling my body with a strangely wonderful sensation. I placed my hands on his chest and felt his heart beating wildly. My heart was beating just as fast.

Growing dizzy, I kissed him back. The uncoiling continued, the sensation getting stronger and stronger.

George groaned against my lips and started to pull away.

It was my dark magic. My cold light had been set loose and was wrapping around the grand duke. His face drained of its color and warmth.

I was killing him.

With a cry, I tore out of his arms and tried to get out of the carriage.

"Katiya! Wait!"

I couldn't look at him. Sobbing, I climbed out and ran down the lane.

I didn't know where I was headed, but I ended up by one of the fountains in the Upper Gardens.

"Katiya!" George caught up with me, his breathing ragged. "Katiya, look at me."

"Don't you see? I almost killed you! I couldn't bear it if I hurt you."

He took me in his arms once more and I sobbed on his shoulder. "Won't you have a little faith in me?" He took my chin and lifted my face so I could see the silver light in his eyes. "I am to be the Koldun," he said with a confident smile. "I think I will be safe with you."

"You're not taking me seriously."

His smile faded. "Give me a year. Give me a year to prove to you that we belong together. That your darkness won't blot out my light. Promise me."

I could already feel the cold light rising inside me again. I couldn't take any chances. I couldn't trust myself not to hurt him. I kissed the tsar's son on the cheek and whispered, *"Je promets."*

I turned around and walked all the way to my family's villa without looking back.

CHAPTER FIFTY-EIGHT

～❧～

The grand duchess Miechen was dying. She was bleeding heavily from the miscarriage of her twins. Even Dr. Badmaev was worried that he would not be able to save her. My mother stayed at her bedside for two weeks, giving the grand duchess the herb-laced potions the Tibetan doctor had prescribed for her. I stayed at home to take care of Papa and my brother.

Princess Anastasia of Montenegro married my uncle George of Leuchtenberg, and Princess Militza of Montenegro married my cousin Grand Duke Peter Nikolayevich. The double wedding had taken place secretly during the confusion immediately surrounding the battle with Konstantin. The couples had left on their wedding trips and the Montenegrin king and queen had swiftly returned to Cetinje with their son. The tsar's friendship with King Nikola turned frosty when he heard about Danilo's ascension ritual and Militza's new position as ruler of the St. Petersburg vampires. He would not be willing to discuss any treaties with her when she returned from her honeymoon.

I breathed a sigh of relief, praying I would never have to see the Montenegrins again.

Papa found me in Maman's parlor, staring out the window into the courtyard. The roses were just beginning to bloom: deep crimson reds and the palest pinks. I'd brought several of them inside to fill the parlor with their heavy scent.

"Katiya, you have been moping around this house for too long," Papa said. "There will be other handsome young men to catch your eye. I believe the crown prince's proposal was only the first of many for you."

He would never know of the grand duke's offer of marriage. I tried to force a smile. "You truly think so? What if I said I preferred to stay here with you and Maman and never marry?"

His eyes twinkled. "I'd be delighted, but I believe your mother has other plans for you. Plans that involve grandchildren for her." He sat down in the chair next to me with a letter in his hand. "Katiya, the time has come for you to make serious plans about your future. It appears that your years at the Smolny Institute are almost over." He handed me the letter. It was postmarked from Zurich. "You must have applied to the university some time ago?" he asked.

Nodding, I opened the envelope and read the letter. "It's an acceptance from the University of Zurich," I said, stunned. "They have an opening for me in the fall. I'll have to take a course in natural sciences before my anatomy classes begin, but . . . I would be on my way."

Papa looked at me cautiously. "We have a family town house where you can stay, if you like. Anya could go with you. And your mother and I would come to visit often."

"Oh, Papa!" I threw my arms around his neck. I was torn. I wanted to accept, but I hated to leave Russia. Everything I loved was here.

And everyone.

I shook my head. "What about the tsar?" I asked. "Will he allow it?"

Papa released me and looked down at me. "Katiya, you know I was proud to serve the tsar in the Order of St. John when I was younger, and I am proud of Petya as well. I even served a term within the Inner Circle."

I looked at him in shock. "You? A wizard?"

He shook his head and laughed. "Not at all. Only the Koldun has the authority to study the arcane magics. The other members of the Inner Circle are merely loyal members of the Order who show a talent for channeling magic to the Koldun. I helped the Koldun raise protective wards around the city after the assassination of Alexander the Second. What I am trying to say is the Oldenburgs will always perform our duty to the tsar and to Russia. You have a unique opportunity to serve him with your . . . gift." His face looked troubled as he searched for the right words. He took my hands in his.

I sighed. This was the conversation I had been dreading ever since George had spoken to Papa at Peterhof. I pulled my hands away and moved to the window. "I didn't want you to know," I said, looking down at the rosebushes below. "I never wanted anyone to know."

"I will admit, your gift is frightening, and there are many who would try and force you to use it for evil."

I turned to look at him. "Like the Montenegrins. The tsar is a good man, and I will always help him, but I don't want anyone else to find out, Papa."

"I think that is wise. Your brother and I will keep your secret. And perhaps one day, we will tell your mother." He smiled. "But I believe you would be safer abroad. The tsar can always send for you in Zurich whenever he has need of your talent."

"What about Konstantin? He is still out there some-where."

"The Order is searching for him as we speak. Once they find him, the Inner Circle will be ready with a ritual to banish him permanently from our world."

"They won't need the bogatyr to fight him again?"

Papa sat down on the velvet settee and beckoned for me to join him. "Katiya, I do not believe our tsar has the physi-cal strength to become the bogatyr again anytime soon. The Inner Circle must find a way to defeat Konstantin without the bogatyr."

I was filled with fear for the tsar. "Perhaps I should stay here, then. I could protect the tsar with the shadow spell. I could look up more spells to keep him hidden from Konstantin."

"Do you really think the tsar is the kind of man who would hide from his enemy?" Papa laughed. "Katiya, do you want to remain forever in the dark ages with us, or do you want to embrace the new world of modern science? Let go of superstition and backward folk magic." His eyes grew sad. "Your future lies in Zurich, not here in St. Petersburg."

I nodded, realizing he was right. But why couldn't there be a balance? Of old ways and new ways? What would become of the old ways if we forgot them? What would become of the bogatyr? And what would become of me?

AUTHOR'S NOTE

My great-grandparents on my mother's side owned a bakery in Ukraine and came to America in 1912, before the revolution. I grew up listening to stories about the bakery and about the family samovar, and I fell in love with the late imperial period of Russia—the years of Fabergé and Tchaikovsky and Tolstoy—as well as the old Russian fairy tales. I wondered what life in the late nineteenth century would have been like if tsars had possessed magical powers like the tsars of the old legends. Katerina's story grew out of this wonder.

ACKNOWLEDGMENTS

So many talented people who have helped me and Katerina along the way deserve tons of thanks and chocolate. Two crit partners who have been with me since the earliest drafts, Mandy Morgan and Jill Myles, are more precious than any Fabergé jewels. Ilona Andrews helped with Russian details that I could not find in any of my many research books. German professor Franziska Rogger helped me get Katerina accepted into a nineteenth-century medical school. The amazing people at the Alexander Palace Time Machine shared history and beautiful old photos of the Romanovs. My undying gratitude to everyone at Ethan Ellenberg's agency—Ethan, Evan Gregory, and Denise Little—as well as to my wonderful editor, Françoise Bui, and the rest of the staff at Delacorte Press. Thanks to my family for putting up with a nocturnal mom/wife and for supporting my Diet Coke habit. *Spasibo*, everyone.

ABOUT THE AUTHOR

By day, Robin Bridges is a mild-mannered writer of fantasy and paranormal fiction for young adults. By night, she is a pediatric nurse. Robin lives on the Gulf Coast with her husband, one soon-to-be teenager, and two slobbery mastiffs. She likes playing video games and watching Jane Austen movies. (Alas, if only there were a Jane Austen video game!) *The Gathering Storm* is her first novel. You can visit her at robinbridges.com.